THE DARCY MONOLOGUES

EDITED BY
CHRISTINA BOYD

THE DARCY MONOLOGUES

For more information:
The Quill Ink, P.O. Box 11, Custer WA 98240

Library of Congress Cataloging-in-Publication Data
ISBN: 978-0-9986540-0-3

Cover design by Shari Ryan of MadHat Books
Layout by Shari Ryan of MadHat Books

PRAISE FOR AUTHORS

SUSAN ADRIANI

The Truth About Mr. Darcy, "Adriani is a fantastic story teller." —Austenprose

Darkness Falls Upon Pemberley, "Adriani's word choice is perfect, rich, and exact." —Leatherbound Reviews

SARA ANGELINI

The Trials of the Honorable F. Darcy, "Delicious! It is finger-licking, lip smacking, delicious…definitely my favorite modern re-telling of *Pride and Prejudice* to date." —A Bibliophile's Bookshelf

KAREN M COX

At the Edge of the Sea, "…intoxicating and heartfelt romance … Readers will be entertained and inspired by this winning tale." —Publishers Weekly

Find Wonder in All Things, "…no wonder at all why it was awarded the Gold Medal in the Romance category at the 2012 Independent Publisher Book Awards." —Austenprose

1932, "A sexy and exciting story, *1932* is a truly fresh take on this timeless tale." —Bustle

Undeceived, "Love it when an author can surprise me." —Delighted Reader

J. MARIE CROFT

Love at First Slight, "There was not a single thing I did not like about this novel. … The author's sharp wit could rival that of Jane Austen … a pure delight to read." —Addicted to Austen

A Little Whimsical in His Civilities, "If there's an Austen hero that deserves a good chuckle at himself, I can think of none other more deserving than the proud and staid Mr. Darcy. Ms. Croft helps him loosen up his cravat in a manner that is playful, poetic and utterly romantic."
—Just Jane 1813

JAN HAHN

An Arranged Marriage, "Passionate and sensual but never over the top, you do not want to miss this treasure!" —Sensible Romance

The Journey, "I loved this story! …I couldn't put it down!" —So Little Time

The Secret Betrothal, "…I devoured like manna from above." —Addicted to Jane Austen

A Peculiar Connection, "…beyond daring. Heartrending. And written so painfully well." —Austenprose

JENETTA JAMES

Suddenly Mrs. Darcy, "…a touching, sometimes dark, often playfully sexy interpretation of what might have been…" —Jane Austen's Regency World Magazine

The Elizabeth Papers, "…a novel that will appeal to fans of Jane Austen and romantic mysteries." —Publishers Weekly

LORY LILIAN

Rainy Days, "I smiled a lot while I read and even cried a little… Great story!!!!" —Just Jane 1813

Remembrance of the Past, "The journey couldn't have been more endearing." —From Pemberley to Milton

Perfect Match, "…an understated little gem!" —My Kids Led Me Back to *Pride & Prejudice*

His Uncle's Favorite, "Lory Lilian is a good storyteller." —More Agreeably Engaged

Sketching Mr. Darcy, "Marvelous: one of the best JAFF stories I have read." —Goodreads reviewer

The Rainbow Promise, "…heartfelt and lovingly crafted…" —Just Jane 1813

KARALYNNE MACKRORY

Falling for Mr. Darcy, "With its light-hearted, heartfelt, amusing tone, *Falling for Mr. Darcy* is a perfect piece for an afternoon pick-me up." —Leatherbound Reviews

Bluebells in the Mourning, "…her interpretation of the characters was just about perfect." —Indie Jane

Haunting Mr. Darcy, "Mackrory's lilting prose is pleasantly reminiscent of Austen's, and readers will enjoy the unique twist to the familiar tale." —Publishers Weekly

Yours Forevermore, Darcy, "As far as Regency Adaptations that stay true to the original, this one is my favorite!!" —Margie's Must Reads

BEAU NORTH

Longbourn's Songbird, "North gives a voice to a whole new demographic of characters and expertly navigates the social confines of conservative Southern expectations of the times." —San Francisco Book Review

The Many Lives of Fitzwilliam Darcy, "I absolutely adored this novel from the first page…one of the best books I've read this year, possibly one of my all-time favorites…" —Diary of an Eccentric

RUTH PHILLIPS OAKLAND

My BFF, "… excessively diverted…read with a perpetual smile upon my face." —Austenesque Reviews

NATALIE RICHARDS

Then Comes Winter (A Man Whom I Can Really Love), "…definitely the most adorable of the collection." —Austenprose

SOPHIA ROSE

Sun-kissed: Effusions of Summer (Second Chances), "A truly beautiful and compelling romance!" —Austenesque Reviews

MELANIE STANFORD

Sway, "The characters are vivid and perfectly flawed, and the story is imaginative and wonderful." —Books in Brogan

JOANA STARNES

From This Day Forward, "A beautiful love story…that any Janeite purist should enjoy." —More Agreeably Engaged

The Second Chance, "I was completely swept up by this evocative and gripping variation!" —Austenesque Reviews

The Subsequent Proposal, "I love it when Austen-inspired fiction shakes things up a bit, and Starnes certainly does that!" —Diary of an Eccentric

The Falmouth Connection, "Joana Starnes writes with great verve and affection about the familiar characters — and an intriguing cast of unfamiliar ones." —Jane Austen's Regency World Magazine

The Unthinkable Triangle, "…full of feeling…a book full of soul."
—From Pemberley to Milton

Miss Darcy's Companion, "Beautiful, rather clever and shocking…"
—Obsessed with Mr. Darcy

Mr. Bennet's Dutiful Daughter, "'She did it again,' I told myself as I savored the feelings whirling around inside of me." —Just Jane 1813

CAITLIN WILLIAMS

Ardently, "To say I was swept away into the storyline may be an understatement." —Just Jane 1813

The Coming of Age of Elizabeth Bennet, "This is a story to be completely and emotionally wrapped up in and consumed with!" —Austenesque Reviews

DEDICATION

For the creator of Mr. Fitzwilliam Darcy

TABLE OF CONTENTS

OTHER ERAS

INTRODUCTION

"You must allow me to tell you..."

For over two hundred years, women have loved Jane Austen's brooding and enigmatic hero, Mr. Darcy. Handsome, rich, strong, cerebral. You might find Fitzwilliam Darcy in disguise, including his imperfections, as numerous other literary paragons and film icons such as Gilbert Blythe, John Thornton, Gabriel Emerson, Edward Cullen, Lloyd Dobler, Jake Ryan, Richard Blaine, Mr. Big . . .

"I have faults enough, but they are not, I hope, of understanding. My temper I dare not vouch for. It is, I believe, too little yielding—certainly too little for the convenience of the world. I cannot forget the follies and vices of others so soon as I ought, nor their offenses against myself. My feelings are not puffed about with every attempt to move them. My temper would perhaps be called resentful. My good opinion once lost, is lost forever." —Chapter XI.

Despite the manifold of faults against him, Darcy has other estimable qualities that have stood the test of time: constant, cool-headed, honest, gallant. Although he is flawed, he is willing to change for the love of a worthy woman. And we adore him for it.

"My object then," replied Darcy, "was to show you, by every civility in my power, that I was not so mean as to resent the past; and I hoped to obtain your forgiveness, to lessen your ill opinion, by letting you see that your reproofs had been attended to. How soon any other wishes introduced themselves I can hardly tell, but I believe in about half an hour after I had seen you." —Chapter LVIII.

I have always had a weakness for this powerful and noble man. After having the pleasure of meeting so many other readers who also cherish this classic hero, I have long dreamt of assembling my own team of exceptionally talented authors that I have either had the good fortune of working with on past projects or I have fangirled over for years. In *The Darcy Monologues*, fifteen Austen-inspired authors have sketched Darcy's character through a series of original re-imaginings of *Pride and Prejudice*, set in the Regency through contemporary times—from faithful narratives to the fanciful. Readers will meet the man himself as he reveals his intimate thoughts, his passions, and his own journey to love—all told with a previously concealed wit and enduring charm.

As 2017 finds Janeites from every corner of our world celebrating Miss Austen's life during the bicentennial anniversary of her death, I invite you to fall in love with Darcy all over again as you savor this collection of short stories that aim to captivate readers' imaginations. Rediscover why Mr. Darcy has the timeless distinction of being referred to by millions of readers as the ultimate catch.

"It is your turn to say something now, Mr. Darcy."

—Christina Boyd

N.B. For authenticity, each author has written in the style and spelling pertaining to their story setting and era or proclivity to their prose. In the spirit of the collective and to be consistent throughout, this anthology adheres to US style and punctuation. Additionally, as a work inspired by Jane Austen's masterpiece, *Pride and Prejudice,* her own words and phrases may be found herein.

SUSAN ADRIANI
J. MARIE CROFT
JAN HAHN
LORY LILIAN
KARALYNNE MACKRORY
MELANIE STANFORD
JOANA STARNES
CAITLIN WILLIAMS

THE REGENCY

"I admire all my three sons-in-law highly," said he, "Wickham, perhaps, is my favourite; but I think I shall like your husband quite as well as Jane's."
—Mr. Bennet to Elizabeth, Chapter LIX.

DEATH OF A BACHELOR

CAITLIN WILLIAMS

In four days' time, I will be a married man. Though not particularly profound, the thought stopped Fitzwilliam Darcy mid-stride on the path to Longbourn. What did it mean to be a husband? He had once considered it a state to be feared and avoided and retreated quickly away from the sort of romantic entanglements which might ensnare him into matrimony. Oh, he had lived in the world, known women, but never properly courted one with the serious intention of making her his wife. He was a man already burdened with many obligations, heavy responsibilities and now he was about to assume more. The words, the promises, the vows he would take were much on his mind, swirling constantly through his consciousness.

"forsaking all others, keep thee only unto her, so long as ye both shall live?"

He ought to press on. It was cold enough for him to see each breath he exhaled, and though his boots were thick and expensive, he could no longer feel his toes. He thought he wiggled them now but could not say for certain whether they moved or not. It was late November and the temperature was dropping rapidly. The skies were a brilliant white; it would surely snow soon. Yet he had chosen to walk from Netherfield to Longbourn. He might have ridden or used the carriage but walking would take much longer, and time to be alone—time to think—had become a rare commodity. Peace was now a thing to be treasured. Since he had proposed for the second time to Elizabeth Bennet—on this very lane thirty-two days previously—time had accelerated. Minutes, hours, and days had rushed by, eaten up in a swirl of preparations, tedious visits, dull parties, and never-ending fittings for gowns. Having imagined a courtship full of long country walks and stolen moments in the shrubbery, he was frustrated at having been largely confined to over-heated, noisy parlours—too many small rooms filled with too many chairs on which garrulous matrons placed their full derrières. Mrs. Bennet's friends and relations seemed blessed, one and all, with the ability to talk endlessly, loudly, and about a great many nothings. Even worse, they brought with them their daughters! Simpering, stupid girls who stared at him while whispering and giggling behind their hands.

The only relief from this torture had been five days in London when Mrs. Bennet had taken her two eldest daughters to London to shop for wedding clothes. There they had managed to escape, he and Elizabeth, and strolled happily through Kensington Gardens, pretending it existed only for them—the trees and paths and the sunken Dutch garden. The burnt orange, wintry sun, which tried but failed to warm them, had sat so low in the sky it seemed to balance on the surface of the Serpentine, making the water sparkle. As they had strolled over it, the grey stones of the bridge had been bathed in the reflected light of the brilliant orb, making them turn golden and glow—as did Elizabeth's face, as did his heart. He had thought to risk a kiss while she admired the view and he admired her, but Bingley had interrupted them. His untimely friend had turned back and shouted for them to *"Hurry on,"* as *"dear Jane is half-frozen. I will not have her catch a cold, Darcy."*

He had also escorted his betrothed with much pride to the theatre, where she looked fine in her new silk, tailored by a French modiste who was fashionable amongst the *ton*. His first sight of her in the daringly, low-cut gown had left him breathless and giddy. Though his pleasure had been curtailed when he had realised he was not the only gentleman on Drury Lane playing worship to the beauty of her décolletage. The rest of the evening was thus spent in a battle of hands and wits, whereby he repeatedly placed her shawl about her shoulders and she repeatedly complained and took it off again.

"Sir, this gown, which my mother insisted upon, has cost my papa a great deal of money. I fear it would be unfilial of me to keep covering it up."

"Then, the sooner I am allowed to bear the cost of clothing you, the better."

"Why? Shall you be buying me many shawls under which to hide myself?"

He had sulked until she had leaned over, whispering—her lips tantalisingly close to his ear, her breath ruffling his neckcloth.

"I am yours. I shall never love another." There she had avowed herself to him as reverently as if they were already stood before the altar.

An invitation to take tea with his uncle and aunt had marred her last day in London but had been issued in a manner that brooked no refusal. The earl and countess looked Elizabeth over and talked at her with some contempt. However, her polite detachment and her refusal to be ruffled or cowed seemed to impress them, and a gradual softening towards her followed. The countess had even promised at the end of the conference to hold a dinner for them when they next returned to London, in a manner which suggested she was bestowing a great favour and demanding their fervent thanks.

Darcy had left Mayfair cross, offended, and all at odds with the world and his family. Yet, there was a shameful sense of relief too, for the approval of the countess, a doyenne in high society, would make Elizabeth's entry into it far easier than first imagined. When they had retaken the carriage, Elizabeth had sensed his tension and laid her elegant, slim hand on his arm. *"Am I not very fortunate to have secured her patronage? Now I might be disapproved of regularly in all the great drawing rooms of England."*

"I cannot laugh at it. I cannot laugh at them because I was once the same."

"No, you were not. You were far more pompous. Now do not think of them. I demand all of your attention. Between here and Gracechurch Street, you must think only of me."

That journey had lasted fourteen minutes—perhaps the most delicious fourteen minutes he had ever spent in a carriage. He would not be treated to anything near fourteen minutes alone with Elizabeth again before they were married. Longbourn grew busier, and noisier, as their wedding drew near, and Darcy grew ever more reluctant to go near the place. Yet it was expected. He must.

On entering, he was greeted first by Mr. Bennet, who was directing a servant in the movement of some trunks. "Ah, Mr. Darcy, leave your sanity on the table there—along with your coat and hat—everyone else has. You will have no need of it again until you leave."

The trunks were Elizabeth's and had been stationed in the hallway since her return from London. They were frequently moved from one corner to another under Mr. Bennet's instructions, and their presence seemed to bother him unduly. He would fuss about them frequently and tut often.

"I have arranged for their removal tomorrow, sir, and am sorry for the inconvenience," Darcy said. "I am remiss and ought to have attended to it sooner." They both looked at the brown wooden boxes, bound by thick leather straps. Some were old and simply bore her current initials, "E.B." Others were newer, smarter—purchased by Darcy—and were embossed with what was to be her new title in elegant, gold script, "Mrs. Fitzwilliam Darcy." They were all labelled with directions, winter clothes bound for London and summer ones for Pemberley.

Mr. Bennet waved his apology away but frowned, particularly at the newer trunks. "No matter, my boy, no matter. Ladies require so much." His wit might have been as sharp as ever but recent events seemed to have taken a toll upon Mr Bennet, and he had aged rapidly since the year before. He stooped a little now and had lost his vitality, looked weary.

Darcy realised it was perhaps not the placement of the trunks that bothered his future father-in-law. Though they cluttered his entrance way, it was their very existence that brought him pain. Elizabeth was not just his favourite child, she was his friend too, and the only one of his daughters who could offer him a conversation of some intellectual value: his reading partner, his confidant.

"Yes, ladies do come with a great deal of luggage. As my wife, your daughter will always travel thus with every frippery and luxury I can provide. I will take great pleasure in spoiling her, and do my utmost to ensure her continuing happiness. In this, you have my word."

"Thank you, Mr. Darcy," Mr. Bennet replied, emotion making his voice tremor.

"No sir, it falls upon me to thank you. I know you are not overly fond of Town and would not expect to see you when we are there, but I hope you will visit us often at Pemberley. Elizabeth, I think, will miss you and your wise counsel."

"I think, young man, that it is I who will miss Elizabeth's excellent, perspicacious advice, rather than the other way around." He laughed. "And how are you bearing up, now that you cling to your bachelorhood by only the slimmest of edges? Will you mourn for it at all?"

Darcy was considering his answer when they were interrupted by excited shouts, loud counting, and a thundering noise made by many small feet as they descended the stairs, and she was with them—his wise beyond her years betrothed, his normally sensible and calm, future wife. The Gardiner children scattered in every direction. Mr. Bennet was surprisingly faster across the hall than any of them, shutting himself in his study and slamming the door shut with an alacrity that belied his years.

Darcy's hand was caught, and he followed Elizabeth, not unwillingly, into an under-stairs cupboard. "We must hide," she said, before shutting them in. His eyes were slow to adjust to the dark, but his other senses came alive. She smelt wonderful, of soap and flowers. Her fingers curled around his. He tightened his grip upon them.

"Must we hide?"

"I am sorry. Is it beneath your dignity?"

"I find my dignity bears it well. 'Tis no bad thing to be confined to a small space with you."

"Is all your business done?" she whispered, after a few moments of silence.

"Yes. I am sorry I was not here sooner."

"No matter. I am glad you are here now."

She understood, bless her dear heart, that there was only so much of Longbourn a sensible man could take.

"You know, you might kiss me now," she said, a tad breathless. "I should not wait for another opportunity today. It might not come."

"I fear if I were to start kissing you now, I might not stop."

"I might not want you to stop," she said quickly.

"I meant that I might not stop—at just kissing."

"Oh, well…" was all he heard before the door was flung open by a young Gardiner—a handsome, grinning boy of perhaps ten who pointed an accusing finger at them.

"Found you, Cousin Lizzy and Mr. Darcy. You are not very good at hiding."

There was nothing to be done but leave the closet. Darcy did so reluctantly while behind him he heard Elizabeth sigh. She reached up to pluck a cobweb from his hair before they were parted by a shrill call of "Lizzy" from her mother that could not be ignored.

Dinner passed off with great cacophony—everybody spoke at once, talking over one another. There were so many courses and dishes flowing by and over him, children running around, and aunts and uncles everywhere that Darcy was not sure what he had eaten nor how much. Elizabeth was very talkative—maybe too ebullient—perhaps in an effort to compensate for his reticence.

There was a brief separation of the sexes. The gentlemen had drunk, smoked, and talked a great deal the previous evening when the Gardiners had first arrived, leaving the ladies alone too long—and had been told off for it by their hostess—so tonight they went in earlier. He was the last to leave the dining room and dallied in the hall until Elizabeth came to find him. She led him firmly by the hand—half proudly, half shyly—into the drawing room, ignoring the raised eyebrows of Mr. Bennet. Darcy said nothing but felt much as he took a seat beside her.

Charles Bingley, across the room, sat beside his own future wife. Jane flipped through the pages of a fashion plate and spoke of lace and fabrics. Bingley nodded and feigned interest. Darcy could picture them in twenty years' time. Jane Bingley, her figure already Grecian, would have grown even more fulsome from numerous lying-ins. Yet she would never lose her classical features, her innate beauty. Charles would grow thin on top and spend years trying to cover it over while sucking in his stomach. He would shoot; his wife would sew. It would be a happy match, both blessed with the ability to be still and content.

And what of him and his little nymph? Elizabeth, as different to her sister as day was to night. Such a curious creature: dark, lithe, and never still. Whatever else may happen, he would certainly never be bored. Occasionally, he would hear his mother speaking to him from beyond the grave. *"She has nothing, Fitzwilliam. No name, no dowry, no connections, nothing to recommend her. What are you thinking? She is entirely wrong."* And he would sit and ponder his choice but never for very long and only while he was away from her. When she was near, the pull was too strong, his desire too great.

"You are very quiet tonight," she said.

He answered only with a brief smile and found he had nothing to say. Elizabeth fidgeted, took up work and then put it down again. She spoke to those close to her but seemed unable to focus on any one conversation for long. Tea and coffee were brought in and she almost ran to offer assistance but upon taking hold of the coffee pot, jumped back immediately, having scalded her palm where it had touched the hot metal.

Mr. Bennet was already halfway out of his chair with concern, but it was to Darcy she came for comfort, holding out her small hand for his inspection, her lips pursed into a pout so deep Darcy was tempted to laugh at it. Her father, with a look of defeat, sank quickly down again. Darcy wetted his handkerchief from the water jug on the table, folded it into a neat square, and pressed it against her hand. It was a minor injury, one that would be forgotten with the sunrise, but she blinked quickly and her lip quivered, as if she were fighting back tears. Understanding dawned, regarding the oddness of her mood. While it was Darcy's nature to grow quiet when nervous, her anxiousness took on a different form, made her energetic and excitable. She was soon to leave her home, her family, all that was familiar, and place herself entirely under his care. Of course she was worried. *This is what it means to be a married man: to offer her assurances, to lend her my strength when hers temporarily fails her.*

"It is not too late to change your mind about London," he said quietly. "Would you prefer to stay at Netherfield for a few days after we are wed? With Jane?"

She shook her head, making her curls bob and bounce delightfully about her neck.

"Or you might bring Catherine or Mary with you to London?"

"You are very kind, but no."

"It is not too late for me to send word to Pemberley, even, if you would like to go there instead. I think there is a great deal of snow on the way, but I would be willing to risk the trip if you so desired it. There are a great many closets to hide in."

She laughed. "I am pleased to hear it. You know, Fitzwilliam, I would not be hiding from you, I would be hiding with you."

"But we are braver than that, I think. Shall we remain steady to our original plans?"

At her nod and more confident expression, he took his handkerchief away to examine her injury, and there, in the drawing room, with not a care as to who might be looking on, he raised her palm to his lips and kissed it better.

"I shall not call tomorrow."

"I do not blame you. You have been very forbearing thus far."

"Nonsense, I am becoming accustomed to Longbourn. Fond of it even—and not just because it has sheltered you all these years. I thought to stay away so you might spend some time with your father. He has a very few days left with you now. He deserves a little of your attention."

"Which I have been remiss in not giving him. How am I to thank you for correcting my error?"

"I can think of a hundred different ways but only one that would truly please me," he said, fixing his gaze on her lips.

She arched a brow at him. "Can you wait for your thanks then?"

"I do not wish to but as you have pointed out, I have become forbearing of late."

The fire crackled and spat next to them, but its heat seemed insignificant compared to the warmth of her gaze, the sparkle in her eyes.

In four days' time, I will be a married man, he thought again but with far less trepidation than he had earlier. Now all that remained was a deep longing, a wish for the days to pass quicker.

"love her, comfort her, honour, and keep her, in sickness and in health"

As of five hours ago, I am a married man. He ought to be merry and blithe. In the quiet of his stately, comfortable carriage, his legs should be stretched out and crossed at the ankles. A hand ought to be firmly clasping the waist of his newly acquired wife. They ought to be sharing a bench seat, embracing, kissing, giddy with relief that the fuss and ceremony was over, and they no longer required permission to be alone together. Instead, he sat rigidly, his shoulder muscles knotted so tightly together that the collar of his shirt brushed his earlobes. His jaw twitched and his hands were tightly gripped around the pewter handle of his stick.

And what of the aforementioned newly-acquired wife? She looked no happier than he felt. Elizabeth sat opposite him, absentmindedly turning her newly-acquired ring around the third finger of her left hand in slow circles, while gazing out of the window at the falling snow.

"I hope Georgiana and the colonel have made it to London safely," she said, at last breaking the tense silence.

"They left quite some time before us. I am sure they are there already. The weather will not be so bad in Town as it is here," he said, trying not to sound sharp.

"My goodbyes should not have been so lengthy. We should not have stayed so long at the wedding breakfast. It snows so hard now."

"It is only right you said your goodbyes properly. It is only right you should enjoy your day with your family and friends. You were not to know the weather would turn so foul so quickly." He forced a smile.

They had come out of the church laughing, their feet slipping and sliding over the frosty ground, and Elizabeth wiping away the occasional flakes of snow which fell upon his lapels. It had felt perfect, as if they were in a painting. She, the beautiful bride, in front of the country church, surrounded by well-wishers, and everything about them covered in a white, wintry blanket, masking anything unpleasant.

Yes, he had taken great pleasure in the scene and felt fit to burst with happiness, but upon their arrival back at Longbourn, his mood had quickly deteriorated. He had found himself trapped *twice* in a corner. On the first occasion by Sir William Lucas, who regaled him with tales of his adventures at St. James's Court—most of which Darcy had heard already. Then by William Collins, who had the temerity to lecture him—felt fit to explain that Lady Catherine's displeasure at his marriage to Elizabeth was only right and natural and advised him that he ought to offer his apologies for marrying so far beneath him! Furthermore, the parson had opined that perhaps if he were to visit Rosings without his wife—because Her Ladyship could not yet be expected to receive her—to show his contriteness, it might go some way towards healing the current breach in their relationship.

"Desist, sir," he had said. *"I am a gentleman, but that would not prevent me from taking you by the seat of your cheap pantaloons and throwing you through the nearest window if you persist in speaking of Mrs. Darcy in that manner. Desist immediately. In fact, I bid you never to address me again unless there be an urgent matter of life or death."*

"Sir—"

"No, not a word more."

"But—"

"I shall say it again very plainly, and then you will be quiet. Go away and do not speak to me again. Another word and I shall not be responsible for my own actions."

Mr. Collins had opened his mouth again but then thought better of it and slithered away through the crowds, as might a snake through the grass.

Even the remembrance of it caused Darcy to grip the handle of his stick tighter, imagining how very satisfying it would be to crack the pewter handle over the nasty little man's head.

However, Mr. Collins had not been the only source of vexation. There had been Kitty giving Georgiana flirting advice; Mr. Bennet, more sardonic than usual, struggling to be pleasant to anyone; Mary sulking, and with a face so solemn she looked more as if she were at a funeral than a wedding. And there was not one person in the room who was left in any doubt as to his worth, thanks to his new mother, who was heard frequently proclaiming that Lizzy had done "extremely well"—as if he had been won in a competition.

He had grown used to them, liked them enough not to mind their eccentricities, for they all had good hearts. Yet seeing them anew through Georgiana's and his cousin's eyes was a different matter. The colonel had waggled his eyebrows and smirked. *"Interesting lot, aren't they, Darcy?"*

"What are you thinking of?" Elizabeth asked him, leaning across the carriage to brush a small hand over his.

"I am thinking that I hope your father lives to be a hundred and one, in order that he might continue to frustrate Mr. Collins' hopes of inheriting Longbourn for the next fifty years. My dislike is profound."

"I have not yet met with anyone who does truly like him. In that, I include his wife."

"Why in heaven's name did she accept him?"

Elizabeth shrugged. "What were her other options? To be the spinster of the parish? Pitied, ignored, living off the charity of her father and then her brothers, or more shamefully, her younger married sisters? Why not instead be mistress of Hunsford, and maybe later Longbourn, where she might run her own home, be of use to her tenants, perhaps raise a family? To be a gentlewoman is considered a position of privilege, but it comes with few frank choices."

"You are extraordinary. I hope you know that."

She raised a brow at him and he crossed the carriage to sit beside her. "You refused me. And yet, you see the world exactly as it is. You chose poverty or charity over marriage to a man you disliked. I am the richest man in Derbyshire, but I did not meet your moral standards. You would have preferred spinsterhood."

"Ah, but you see I am vain enough to think I might have had other offers after yours. Who is to say the second richest man in Derbyshire might not want me?"

"I daresay he would."

The carriage now moved at a crawling pace, driven back by the thick snow and howling winds. They were in the middle of a blizzard. Darcy sighed heavily.

"Fitzwilliam, will you please never say that in front of my mother? About you being the richest man in Derbyshire. I fear it would surpass *'ten thousand a year'* as her favourite phrase."

He laughed and moved to kiss her forehead, but then everything slid sideways. There was much noise from outside as his coachman shouted and the horses protested. His arms went protectively around Elizabeth and he threw up silent prayers to the heavens—which were thankfully answered. Though they tilted and moved at a perilously odd angle for a few moments, they did not tip over completely and the slide was halted with a firm, but soft, thud. Darcy looked at the window to their left which was now covered completely with snow. Instead, he flung open the door on the right and jumped down to see John the coachman perched at a peculiar angle, clinging to the rails of the carriage which had tipped sideways, ever so gently, into a snowdrift.

Darcy checked on the postilion and his manservant who had been riding next to the coachman. Thankfully, no one was hurt, but they were well stuck. Darcy offered his assistance in digging the carriage out, but the blizzard raged on and his men would have none of it, insisting he should walk Mrs. Darcy to the nearest inn, a third of a mile down the road. He nodded his gratitude and looked back up into the carriage. Elizabeth was calmly putting her gloves on. He held out his arms and she fell eagerly into them.

He carried her a few paces before she protested.

"For heaven's sake, put me down."

"No, I mean to carry you. I will not have you soaking and cold."

"For a third of a mile! I shall be a widow before I have had a chance to be a wife. I may have no dowry, sir, but I do have two strong legs."

Which I would very much like to have wrapped around me before the night is out, he mused, then chided himself. What a time for such thoughts! He set her on her feet as requested but feared for her safety as a sudden gust of wind-whipped snow attacked them, nearly blowing them off their feet and covering them in white flakes.

She swiped at her eyes, threw back her head, and laughed at it. "Will anything ever be easy for us, do you think?"

Darcy shook his head and tucked her under his arm, throwing his greatcoat over the pair of them as they set forth. For every four steps they managed forwards, they were blown back one, but eventually the light of the inn came into view. Lanterns glowed gently in the windows and a smart-looking sign creaked as it swung on a pole outside. It did not look too bad, respectable even. Darcy's spirits rose as they went through the door, stamping the snow off their boots and grateful for the immediate warmth its four walls provided.

The landlord was quickly found and told Darcy he was in luck. There was still one room unoccupied which he might rent. He nodded quickly when told the price. He would have paid anything. They would be going no further. The snow continued to fall and even if his carriage was quickly rescued it would be foolhardy to try and reach London now. He would not risk it.

He quickly apprised the landlord about his servants and gave instructions for them to receive food and shelter as soon as they arrived. He turned back to Elizabeth, relieved and triumphant. Though far from being the evening he had planned for them, they would have some privacy, a fire, some wine. It was not so very terrible. Or, at least it would not have been, but the door opened again, admitting a young man and his lady, she very heavy with child and looking dreadfully weary. They had arrived in a battered cart. Darcy guessed him to be a shopkeeper or clerk of some sort and knew—before the man even spoke—what would happen. There would be a request for a room; the landlord would shake his head regretfully and explain that they were full. Elizabeth's large, exquisite eyes would implore him to be kind. And it was exactly so. He sadly handed over the key—which had not been in his hands for more than two minutes—to the man whose wife burst into grateful tears. Kindness was supposed to have its own rewards. Darcy felt he was being punished for his as he watched them disappear up the stairs.

He needed a drink.

"Mrs. Darcy should not have to spend even a moment in a saloon bar. Let alone an entire night sitting up in one." Blinking in disbelief at the situation he found himself in, he took a seat next to Elizabeth on the hard, wooden bench. There had been nowhere else to go but the main room of the inn—a rowdy, noisy place, bursting with people from every station in life. And so, Darcy had found her a seat before securing a tankard of ale for himself. There was no brandy or port to be had, it had all been supped. This news was not a surprise, convinced as he now was, that this was an evening when nothing was destined to go right for him.

"Mmm, yet here I am." Elizabeth peeled off her gloves and took hold of the tankard he had put on the table in front of him. She sipped the beer and set it back down again. "And Mrs. Darcy is very proud to have such a good husband. You are the very best of men."

Her words warmed him and he slid closer to her on the bench.

"I suppose you had very different plans for this evening."

"Yes. There was to be good wine, an elegant, intimate supper, flowers direct from a hothouse, and some very fine confectionery."

"Chocolate?" she asked with a smile.

"Indeed. You see how well I know you already."

"I will be a very spoilt wife." She leaned forward to take another sip of beer. "And what else did you have planned?" she asked, tilting her head up to look at him. She was so enticing, her mouth so full.

"When you have been married some time, Elizabeth, you will realise it is not kind to ask me such a question in a crowded room, while looking at me in that manner."

"Shall we talk of something else then? What think you of books? Tell me what you are reading at the moment."

Reeling from her sudden shift of mind, and his body taut with desire for her to the point of snapping, he shrugged and replied gruffly, "Some nonsense I picked up from the scant library at Netherfield. I have a novel, but the plot is implausible."

"All novels are implausible," she said decidedly and took another sip of his beer. "We would not wish to read them if they were not. Can you imagine how dull a tale would be if it were completely founded in reality? I do not read a novel to hear how Mary or Anne went to the shops to buy ribbons or that they sat at home sewing for three days without a single letter or caller. I declare implausibility a must if the reader is not to be bored to tears."

"This is implausible," Darcy said, looking about him. "This should not be happening. We should not be here."

"Sometimes, I find it implausible that you should love me."

"No," he replied. "It would be implausible if I did *not* love you."

When she reached for his beer again, he stilled her hand with his own.

"Would you like your own drink?"

"Good heavens, no. Whatever would Lady Catherine say?"

Darcy could not help himself. He needed to be closer to her and shuffled until his thigh was pressed against the length of hers. Damn propriety, there was no one here to judge them anyway. Nobody they would ever meet again. No Caroline Bingleys or Louisa Hursts. She did not shift away from him but leant her head against his shoulder.

They had been sitting in such a way, in comfortable silence, for a few minutes when the table in front of them was jolted by an elderly man, slightly in his cups and unsteady on his feet. Darcy was about to take considerable objection but was appeased when an apology was quickly forthcoming.

"Dear me, I am sorry. We are all stranded here with nothing to do but drink, and I have taken more than I normally would. I beg your pardon, sir, and the pardon of your lovely wife."

"No matter," Darcy said and nodded, trying to quickly dismiss him.

The man lingered however, and smiled softly at Elizabeth. "Your lady reminds me of my own dear wife. Gone now, taken from me too soon by a bout of influenza."

"I am sorry."

"I thank you. We were only eight years married. I have now been without her longer than I was with her, but I treasure the memories. How long have you been married, sir, if you will excuse the impertinence?"

"All of eight hours," Elizabeth said, favouring the old man with a broad smile.

"Good heavens, 'tis your wedding day!" he exclaimed, just as John burst through the door, seeking his master and bringing the cold air with him.

"No lasting damage done, sir," the coachman said. "Carriage and horses are fine, but the snow shows no sign of stopping."

"Yes, John. We must stop here the night. I had already resigned myself to that."

"What room is it, sir? I'll have the trunks brought up," John offered.

"We have no room. They are all taken. We shall sit here."

"No! How dreadful. You must take my room," the old man insisted. "I haven't been up to it yet but am told it is a tiny room with just a small cot. I daresay it might be the worst in the whole place, but I would not rest easy in it, knowing your lady had no bed. You must take it."

Darcy saw that Elizabeth was about to object. "If you are certain, I would be most grateful," he interjected quickly.

"I am quite certain. I shall sleep very well down here with my feet up by the fire."

"You are a gentleman, sir."

"I am not." He shook his head; his wrinkles deepening with his smile.

"Yet, your generosity makes you one. For I was recently reminded by a young lady of my acquaintance that it is not always a question of birth. A gentleman proves himself by his deeds and behaviour." He glanced down at Elizabeth. "On behalf of my wife, I accept your kind offer."

He could not allow Elizabeth to protest again, if there was a bed available, she must have it. It was his duty to ensure her comfort, and so, he took the man's hand and shook it vigorously.

Within half an hour Elizabeth had been shown upstairs by the landlord's wife. Darcy went to inspect the carriage and horses himself and watched John and the postilion locate a small travelling trunk, which Elizabeth insisted was the only one she needed for the night. The men staggered about the top of the coach, laughing as they were blown about by the wind and kicking snow at one another. Following the advice of his father, Darcy tried his best to be a benevolent, generous master and had been repaid in kind by loyal, happy servants. He thanked them profusely as they found the desired trunk and hauled it indoors. He remained outside for a while, cooling his ardour and adjusting his temper. He had to allow himself a few moments of bitterness before he could accept his fate sanguinely. When he could no longer feel his fingers, he went back inside and sought directions to her room.

She was drying her face when he went in, stood over a small basin of water on a table with a cloth in her hand. As he had been warned, it was a small chamber, meant for a lone traveller of moderate means. There was a chair, a single cot, and no space for anything else. It was clean and there was a fire blazing, but still, for her to have to stay in such a room rankled and jarred his pride.

"I am sorry."

"For what? The weather? Even the richest man in Derbyshire cannot control that." She sighed. "I feel guilty about that poor old man, however."

"He will be well looked after—I shall see to it. And I will post John to sit outside your door, for protection."

"You will do no such thing. He will freeze to death in the corridor. Besides, I have you here."

"I thought to sleep downstairs."

"Did you now? I think not." She moved towards the fire and he noticed her feet were bare. Her boots were set upon the hearth to dry in front of the flames and she had hung her stockings over the back of the chair. With quick hands, she began to remove the pins from her hair. In her dark travelling clothes, with her toes exposed and her curls flowing freely about her shoulders, she looked more gypsy girl than fine lady.

Her smile was shy and gentle as she began to twirl her ring around her finger again.

Darcy stepped closer, until they were both before the hearth. "That is fast becoming a habit of yours … fiddling with this." He caught her hand and brushed his thumb over the gold band before quickly letting go again. "Does it bother you?"

"No." Her eyes widened in surprise. "I did not realise I was fiddling. It does feel odd. Heavy."

"You do not like it? You may choose another when we get to London."

She put her hand on his lapel. "No, I like it very much. It is just a new feeling. Something else to get used to. New name, new clothes, new … sleeping arrangements."

"I will sleep downstairs," he said firmly.

"Do you mean to embarrass me? Am I the bride whose husband would prefer to sit downstairs in a saloon bar all night than be with her?"

"Embarrass you, no. You misunderstand me. Deliberately perhaps. You must see that this is not the place—"

"Stay," she said simply.

"If I stay here, I should want to … to kiss and touch you."

"And do you imagine that I do not want to be kissed and touched? Am I some statue only to be admired from afar?"

"No, you are all too real, but this is not a place fit for … for you."

Elizabeth moved to the chair, threw herself down quickly, making her skirts fly up for a moment. Darcy saw a sweet ankle and a beautifully, sculptured calf before tearing his gaze away.

"Are you angry with me, for staying so long at Longbourn?"

"No, I said as much in the carriage."

"Did I somehow cause us to slide into the snowdrift?"

"Ridiculous. How could I blame you for that?" he said.

"Then tell me my offence."

"I am not angry with you."

"You are."

"I am not, but God damn it, Elizabeth, if you had accepted me in March, we would have been married in the spring. There would be no snow," he snapped, then immediately cursed himself for it.

She sat bolt upright, her mouth dropped open. She came towards him in a fury. Unsure of what she was about to do, he caught hold of her, trapped her within his embrace, and kissed her before she could properly tell him off. She gasped against his mouth, gave in for the briefest of moments, before pulling back as far as his arms would let her.

"And perhaps we would have had April showers so heavy they would have washed the bridges out, and still we might have been trapped here. What do you say to that, sir?"

"What I say, madam, is that you always seem to have an answer for everything. But I love you for it. Forgive me, Elizabeth. I want you to always have the best of everything, every comfort. Not this awful room, not here. It cannot be what you wished for."

She gave a little shake of her head. "Wishes are hopes that drift in the sky. You ought to know your wife has her feet planted firmly on the ground. And this evening, I am warm, safe, healthy, and longing for you. I might be innocent, as yet, about many things, but whatever you feel and need, I am certain I feel and need it also."

Outside in the storm, he had resolved to wait for her—to wait until London—but she was too close and the room warm enough to melt his determination. Any lingering doubts were done away altogether when she put a hand about his neck and brought his mouth down to hers again, a kiss he returned feverishly. And then his lips began to travel everywhere, her eyelids, the tip of her nose, across her smooth cheek, to her ear, and then down to her neck—where every kiss and brush of her skin with his lips produced a breathless gasp from her. He knew only half of what he did. He reminded himself to go slowly, yet his hands moved quickly. There were clothes, and then somehow, there were far less clothes. *Do not rush her into bed*, but then they were headed towards the cot, pulling and tugging at one another, kissing constantly, until he felt drunk with it. They fell onto the tiny bed, laughing at the singing coming from downstairs, where twenty or so drunken men and women had turned the storm to their advantage and were busy making merry.

Afterwards, he would remember the sounds more than anything. Footsteps on the stairs, and how they temporarily stilled her exploring hand on his thigh, until the noise passed by and she continued her experimental caress. A dog barking when he asked her to bare herself to him completely, and how it had howled when she had bravely pulled off her chemise and thrown it aside. The rattle of the glass in the window frame as the storm attacked it while he thrust into her. And when they were done, while he was still on top of her, his back soaked with perspiration, his lungs struggling for air, his heart full, his legs heavy, and his whole body shaking, there was the distant sound of a glass smashing, and a cheer going up as the clumsy individual was mocked.

Then there was only the two of them again as Darcy concentrated on nothing but her comfort. He whispered into her ear and gave reassurances until she laughed, but she was crying too. "They are good tears, I assure you," she told him.

"Good tears," he said incredulously, as he wiped them away. "Whoever heard of such a thing. I think you are too generous. I have hurt you."

"No, you did not. Well, maybe, but only a very little. Women cry for all sorts of reasons and I weep delirious tears of love for you. And I am relieved, I suppose. I always thought of this as something that was to be done *to* me, but it was not so. 'Tis something to be enjoyed together, I think."

Darcy nodded. "You are very beautiful," he said, looking down the length of her, all the way down to her delicate feet. "There is not a part of you I do not adore."

"I have never previously seen more of you than your face and hands, Fitzwilliam. It has been a pleasant shock to see you so."

"I was wrong, Elizabeth. This is a very good room and a very good bed. I have to hold you very close in order for us both to lie within it, and that is no bad thing," he said, thinking of how he had always immediately gotten up before, with other women, when he had been sated and was done; gotten up and washed himself or found a fire to stoke, thought of something he had to attend to, dressed, made his apologies, left. How different this was, he cleaved to her side, wanted to be nowhere else.

"First, It was ordained for the procreation of children, secondly, as a remedy against sin."

I have been a married man for two whole days. Darcy watched his wife sweep her hair into a simple knot and attempt to control its curls with carefully placed pins. The storm had abated, the ice was melting, and the roads were clearing. They would be in London in two or three hours. As much as he was tempted to stay—to say it was not possible to set forth as yet—they could delay no longer. Concern would grow and they would be missed.

How fond had he become of this middling inn, and this small room with its ridiculously small bed. The facilities were bad, the service slow, the food quite terrible, but then, he had no appetite for anything but lying abed with her and watching the snow fall outside the little window. He sighed and Elizabeth's bright eyes met his in the mirror.

"Dissatisfied with married life already, sir?"

"Would it not be very agreeable to forget the world outside existed, for just a while longer?"

"You would grow tired of staring at me. Though you are quite the proficient. Having an audience for my every move is somewhat disconcerting."

"I am sorry. I find it as pleasurable to watch you dress as I do to undress you."

She laughed. "Are you not keen to get to London to spoil me with every luxury? Was not that your original intention? Are you not keen to see your sister?"

"I suppose, and there are matters to be attended to, responsibilities which must be faced before they grow into worries."

Her countenance changed suddenly. She looked down, her forehead creased into a frown. She worried at the ring on her finger. Darcy went to her and put his arms about her waist, pulling her lovely form back against his chest and kissing the hollow behind her ear. "You will be fine. You have such spirit and such a fine, beautiful mind. All will be well, and if you ever do falter, you may always lean on me, like so, and I will hold you up."

There came a knock on the door. It was John, to tell him the carriage was readied. Darcy told him that they would be down shortly.

Elizabeth left his embrace to gather up her coat and bonnet. When she turned back, her smile was bright again. "I believe I am ready. I hope I am ready."

He stood up straighter, tugged his cuffs into place. "As am I. And when we arrive, I may place an announcement in the papers."

"Has that not already been done? Our marriage announcement?"

"Yes, this one would be of a different kind—a death notice. I must happily announce the death of a bachelor—Fitzwilliam Darcy," he said, smiling wryly. How ridiculous his concerns and doubts in the days prior to their marriage seemed now. He would happily dance on the grave of the empty life he had previously led before her. Loneliness was buried. Despair was gone. There was nothing to mourn.

Elizabeth gave him a quizzical look but he simply held out his arm for her to place her hand upon. "Shall we go then?" he said.

"Thirdly, It was ordained for the mutual society, help and comfort that the one ought to have of the other, both in prosperity and adversity."

They descended the narrow steps of the inn and were stood just outside when the coach was brought round. It rumbled slowly to a stop and Elizabeth seemed lost in contemplation for a while. Darcy watched as her eyes examined every detail of it. She bit her lip. "I am afraid my old trunks quite disgrace your livery."

"Nonsense, and it is *our* livery now, Elizabeth."

As John pulled down the step for them, she was looking back up the road, from where they had come two days previously, to her home, towards Meryton, and her countenance was full of melancholy.

"We will come back soon." Darcy lightly touched her elbow, a small caress.

She looked to the trunks again, the old and the new. "But I will not be the same. Elizabeth Bennet is gone, replaced by this mysterious creature, Mrs. Fitzwilliam Darcy. I am no longer Mr. Bennet's daughter but Mr. Darcy's wife."

"On the contrary, with your ability to charm, I suspect that rather than your being known as Mr. Darcy's wife, I will henceforth be referred to as Mrs. Darcy's husband, and I love you, Elizabeth, no matter what your name."

This made her smile. She muttered something into the wind he did not catch, and then they were in the carriage. The horses were encouraged on and away they sped, out of Hertfordshire, towards a new beginning.

CAITLIN WILLIAMS is an award-winning author of two novels, *Ardently* and the bestselling *The Coming of Age of Elizabeth Bennet*, both of which spin the plot of *Pride and Prejudice* around but keep the characters just the same. Originally from South London, Caitlin spent thirteen years as a detective in the Metropolitan Police but is currently on a break from Scotland Yard so she can spend more time at home with her two children and write. She now lives in Kent, where she spends a lot of time daydreaming about Mr. Darcy, playing with dinosaurs, and trying not to look at the laundry pile.

"When I wrote that letter," replied Darcy, "I believed myself perfectly calm and cool; but I am since convinced that it was written in a dreadful bitterness of spirit."

—Mr. Darcy to Elizabeth Bennet, Chapter LVIII.

FROM THE ASHES

J. MARIE CROFT

Hateful, hurtful words rang in my ears as I strode from the parsonage, away from *her* and her unwarranted vitriol.

Across the lane, Rosings loomed before me in all its stately splendour. Faltering, I stopped mid-stride, in no mood for either a banal exchange of niceties or an altercation with my most meddlesome relation.

I made for the stable and therein snapped at a hapless groom. "You there, saddle Boreas. Now!"

Even after spurring the animal at a breakneck gallop through Kent's bucolic verdure, the tumult of my mind remained painfully great. Words like resentment, anger, and humiliation barely scratched the surface of such deeply felt anguish. Yet, despite the havoc she had visited upon me, there remained in my breast a mad, powerful feeling towards that courageous, passionate young woman who had dared to refuse me and taken me to task.

With the moon high in the sky, I turned back, fearing recklessness might cause Boreas an injury. After seeing to the care of my lathered horse, I entered the manor. Managing to dodge Lady Catherine, I hoped to find both refuge and intoxicants in the library but was stopped short at its threshold. "Ruddy hell." Therein sat my second-most meddlesome relation.

"Darcy! Where the devil have you been? To Hell and back? You certainly look like the dickens." Hefting a decanter in one hand and a glass in the other, Richard silently asked another question.

Nodding, I accepted my first brandy of the night.

"You missed dinner." Sprawled on the sofa in a manner inappropriate for either the son of an aristocrat or an officer in His Majesty's service, my cousin eyed me over the rim of his glass.

"If you must know," I replied to his cocked eyebrow, "I had no appetite and opted for a ride."

"And you did not see fit to send a message? Bad form, Cousin, bad form! Our aunt was—and probably still is—exceedingly displeased. According to Lady Chatterin', dear Anne was devastated over your desertion. I, however, could detect no such expression on the poor girl's face as she tucked into her calf's foot jelly. 'Twas unlike you, though, to be so inconsiderate. Deuce take it, man, I became rather concerned myself."

Thus began the army officer's intense interrogation concerning my earlier whereabouts.

When I had had enough of Richard's cajoling and of fending off his probing inquiries, I announced my intention to retire early. The drinks downed on an empty stomach only enhanced my indignant temper. Exhausted, preoccupied, and a wee bit inebriated, I forgot to duck on the way out, whacking my forehead on the library's ludicrously low lintel, thereby improving my humour not one whit. Behind me, however, Richard laughed uproariously.

Cupping the lump on my forehead with my left hand and gripping the bannister with my right, I climbed the stairs to the baroque bedchamber assigned to me in the family wing. Contributing to my vexation, the pompous architecture at Rosings spoke of what an impertinent person might deem arrogance and conceit. If nothing else, it shrieked selfish disdain of my throbbing head.

Having never been given the go-by before, I hardly knew how to comport myself once reaching the sanctuary of my room—the room I had hoped to share with *her* during future Eastertide visits. *Dash it all!*

Baddeley arrived, offering assistance, but was dismissed with a snarl.

I sat, then stood. Choking up at the window overlooking Hunsford, violent efforts were undertaken to free myself from an intricately-tied cravat, and I regretted sending away my valet. Finally flinging off the constricting neckcloth, I peered through the glazing into darkness that perfectly matched my own desolateness. Then I paced, and ruminated, and paced some more.

Within moments of one another, and with differing degrees of force, both Anne and Richard banged on those walls separating their bedchambers from mine. "What," I grumbled, "do they mean by that confounded thumping?"

Providing an answer, the longcase clock in the passage quietly chimed once. Apparently, I had been pounding the parquet with my Hessians for several hours. Dumbfounded by the unnoticed passing of time, I rang for my valet.

"You rang, sir?" Obviously miffed over my earlier surliness, Baddeley stiffly stood to attention, eyes averted.

"Of course I rang! 'Tis high time you came and helped me remove these blasted boots." Flumping onto a chair and bracing myself, I raised my leg and waited for my gentleman's gentleman to lower himself and relieve me of my footwear. "Pack my belongings, Baddeley. We depart tomorrow . . . erm, later this morning." Gesturing in the general direction of the four-poster's canopy, I sheepishly added, "Also, my good man, please see about retrieving my accursed cravat from up there before we go, would you?"

"A bit hot under the collar tonight were we, sir?" Whilst enduring my glower, Baddeley helped prepare me for sleep that would not come.

My astonishment, as I thrashed about reflecting on what had passed at Hunsford, was increased by every review of it. That I had lowered myself to make an offer of marriage to *her*! That *she* would not have *me* was almost—but not quite—laughable. The humiliation suffered at her hand was a carking blow to my pride and certainly no laughing matter. Fists clenched, I pounded the mattress. *Fool! Why, why, why did I expose myself to such contempt and ridicule?*

For nearly three weeks the woman had willingly accepted my courtship. Then, without any warning, the confounding creature brutally rejected my generously proffered, ardent affections. *Is she mad?*

Eventually I dozed off, landing in a nightmarish landscape in which appeared a bizarre bluish-green dragon of puny proportion. We circled one another in various venues until, suddenly, we became entrapped in a nondescript, smallish parlour. In a show of true colours, the creature turned a reddish hue and increased in size, flapping its wings, until it towered above me. The Elizard's fine eyes shot sparks while its mouth spewed flaming criticism, all directed at my head. I raised my shield in defence against the hail of fiery particles and—I awoke. Upon sitting up, the dream proved ephemeral. The reality of her rejection, I feared, would be long lived.

Pondering such stupidity—hers for refusing a lucrative offer and mine for making an ill-advised one—I eased back onto the pillows. I had, until her refusal, admired the woman's intellect and wit, amongst other things. However, it had just become evident that Miss Elizabeth Bennet was not so clever after all.

Witlessness, I thought, *probably runs in her family. Collins is certainly as barmy as they come—as thick and unpalatable as the ghastly gruel, calf's foot jelly, and other restoratives served to Cousin Anne at her mother's insistence.*

My stomach rumbled. I had eaten little since breakfast.

And I had slept fitfully the previous night—too busy dithering about either making an offer of marriage to *her* or making a hasty retreat to London. Decision made, I had then fretted over the wording of my proposal. Along with the honour I was to bestow upon her, I thought she should be made aware of my struggles regarding such a mésalliance. *All those sleepless hours and all that deep consideration . . . totally wasted on an ingrate!*

She was to blame, once more, as wakefulness resumed. Somewhat spiteful, I hoped the spitfire was similarly suffering insomnia, regretting her rebuff, thrashing about in bed at the same time as me, and—*Oh, God!* A vision of a breathlessly satiated Elizabeth in my bed—her tussled tresses, flushed skin—invaded my brain.

Sitting up again, I pounded the pillow into submission. Flumping back down, I stared at the canopy—upon which her impassioned visage had appeared. "You!" I grumbled at the image. "You have done all this, involving me in misery of the acutest kind. And you, madam, deserve to have that malapert mouth of yours silenced by a blistering kiss . . . with tongue!" Groaning, I rolled onto my side, resisting the urge to curl up into a ball. All I had ever received from her was a tongue-lashing. *Quit thinking of tongues, wretch!*

Continuing in agitated reflection, I tossed and turned—ruminating on all I wanted to say to her, if given the chance. Having been rendered nearly dumbstruck by her rebuff and attack, I had not spoken articulately at the parsonage. Of course, being tongue-tied in her presence was nothing new to me. *Tongues again.*

The bed linens had become an impossible jumble, so I disentangled myself and arose with purpose. Having long dismissed poor Baddeley for the night, I rooted around by the fire's dim light for my banyan as well as a fresh candle, writing supplies . . . and more brandy. My stomach, after all, demanded sustenance.

My rummaging about—plus the utterance of "Bejabbers!" upon the stubbing of my toe on the trunk I had demanded be packed—must have awakened Richard.

Barefoot, wild-eyed, and dishevelled, the cretin barged, unbidden, into my bedchamber and marched up to where I stood in shock and confusion. After giving my head a good and totally unexpected clout, my cousin stormed off without a word . . . although he might have muttered "Nocturnal numbskull!" on his way out.

Shaking my head at Richard's peculiarities, I settled at an ornate desk to sharpen my pen and make my point. Harsh accusations levelled at me could not go uncontested. Mistaken presumptions could not go uncorrected. And I could not go to sleep until giving a certain someone a piece of my mind. My stance would be explained with adherence to every detail—to the letter, as they say.

It was either that or drink until I cast up my accounts into the ghastly, gold-rimmed chamber pot depicting a clash between cherubs and gorgons who, in my opinion, all bore a striking resemblance to one Miss Elizabeth Bennet.

The comparison was unmerited. Even in anger, Elizabeth was utterly lovely.

Like some sort of avenging angel, she had passed judgment upon me for perceived wrongs. Misguided though she was, I admired the girl's staunch defence of her family and of the supposed downtrodden. Of course, I *had* hoped to win such fierce allegiance for myself. But alas! Her trust had been placed with a lecherous lickpenny instead of an honourable man. "By George," I muttered, "the harridan will soon learn to regret casting Fitzwilliam Darcy aside like fireplace ashes spread upon Pemberley's peony patch."

As I had discussed with her at Netherfield, wrongs against me were not soon forgotten. Once my good opinion was lost, it was lost forever. Be that as it may, although resentful, I was never a vengeful man. Had I been the vindictive sort, her charges would go unchallenged, but I cared too much about her welfare to be callous. She needed to beware of Wickham. *See, Miss Elizabeth Bennet? No selfish disdain to be found here!*

Believing myself perfectly calm and cool, I dipped pen to ink and struggled with an opening. Having written countless letters of business, "To Whom It May Concern" flowed with precision from my pen. That, however, appeared a tad impersonal for a recipient not *entirely* unknown. As it turned out, the Elizabeth Bennet last visited at the parsonage *was* almost a complete stranger to me. Nevertheless, that aloof salutation was summarily scratched. *Expressions which might make her hate me*, I decided, *must be avoided*. I snorted. *Hah! 'Tis a little too late for that.*

I bristled at beginning the letter with "dear" because, at that moment, she was anything *but.*

A little voice—a niggling, treacherous one—whispered that Elizabeth *was* still tremendously dear to me. However, I squelched that inner scream whilst gripping the quill so tightly that it snapped in two and nicked my middle finger. "Rot!"

Moving about quietly so as to not reawaken the beast next door, I searched for another pen as well as a sticking plaster for my wound. Adding insult to injury, ink from the broken goose quill had seeped onto my hand and was transferred to whatever I touched. *Splendid! Now I can look forward to Lady Catherine's gartering her hose with my guts . . . which is just what I need after being flayed alive by another harpy, attacked by a lintel, cuffed by my cretin of a cousin, and cut to the quick.*

Flickering wildly from my floundering about, the candle guttered, spilling a blob of hot beeswax onto the page. "Oh, for the love of . . .!" One would not think writing a letter at half past three in the morning would prove so taxing; but, apparently, nothing was easy where Elizabeth Bennet was concerned.

I crumpled the waxy paper and tossed it at the fireplace.

The matter of a salutation was then readdressed. "Greetings and Felicitations, Termagant" was deemed uncharitable—one of those aforementioned "expressions which might make her hate me."

A simple "Miss Bennet" was contemplated. My mind, however, wandered to tributes I *had* anticipated addressing her with . . . My dearest, loveliest Elizabeth. My darling Lizzy. My beloved Mrs. Darcy. My precious lover . . .

Alarmed by such lapses, I snatched a pristine sheet of paper from the ink-stained drawer and quickly wrote: **Be not alarmed, madam, on receiving this letter** . . .

Having experienced a prolonged spell of success, I paused to admire my penmanship and evenness of lines. Reading through the initial paragraph, I gasped and leaned forward. Near the end of the section, I had written: **You must, therefore, pardon the freedom with which I demand your affection . . .**

What? Affection? Noooo, not affection . . . attention! Egad. Stupid, unfulfilled, and unattainable desire! Perhaps I should just march over there, barge into her room, drag the woman from her bed, and insist upon compliance. "Miss Bennet, I demand that you love me!" Yes, yes, numbskull, that would go over well.

Instead, I resolved to defend myself on paper with all the eloquence at my command.

The page containing the offensive erratum was crumpled and flung in the general direction of the hearth. In doing so, my elbow knocked into the rummer. Brandy spilled across the desk and sweat broke across my brow. Forgetting about the egg-shaped lump thereon, I swiped at my forehead with a handkerchief and howled in pain. Clamping one hand over my mouth while mopping up brandy with the handkerchief in the other, I eyed the door, praying Morpheus held the cranky creature next door in thrall.

Thrall. I certainly knew how it felt to be in someone else's power. I had been in Elizabeth's thrall just as surely as my friend had been in her sister's. *What,* I wondered, *is it about those two eldest Bennet sisters? Pish! I should be thankful Bingley and I were saved from those sirens and their seductive powers.*

The desk drawer held at least a quire of hot-pressed paper, so I plucked out a handful of sheets and, contriving to write evenly despite exhaustion and umbrage, began anew. **Be not alarmed, madam, on receiving this letter . . .**

Minutes later—another section achieved and spleen vented—I mended the quill point with my penknife. Then, having allowed brandy and animosity to dictate my words, I went back and scratched out all traces of acrimony and inappropriateness in that second paragraph and replaced them with a bit more civility.

Two offences of a very different nature, and by no means of equal magnitude, you ~~in a rather unladylike manner and with an evident design of offending and insulting me~~ **last night laid to my charge. The first mentioned was that, regardless of the** ~~questionable~~ **sentiments of either, I had detached** ~~my wet behind the ears friend~~ **Mr. Bingley from your** ~~unfeeling, mercenary~~ **sister**~~'s clutches~~**; and the other, that I had, in defiance of various claims, in defiance of honour and humanity, ruined the immediate prosperity, and blasted the prospects of** ~~a posturing pustule~~ **Mr. Wickham.**

Glancing at the clock, and knowing I wrote rather slowly—and, as Bingley would say, not with ease—and that my letters tended to be lengthy ones (riddled as they were with words of four or more syllables), I decided the expensive paper would not be tossed at the fire but employed as a preliminary version of my elucidation. A cooler head would prevail, and a final copy would be neatly written out, with neither errata nor enmity to spoil its perfection.

Satisfied with my subsequent sentence which contained a vehement comparison of her two accusations, I then wrote: **But from the** ~~ferocity~~ **severity of that** ~~condemnation~~ **blame which was last night so** ~~seathingly~~ **liberally** ~~hurled at me~~ **bestowed, respecting each circumstance, I shall hope to be in future secured, when the following account of my actions and their motives has been read. If, in the explanation of them which is due to myself, I am under the necessity of relating feelings which may be offensive to yours, I can only say that** ~~the truth sometimes hurts~~ **I am sorry. The necessity must be obeyed—and further apology would be** ~~beneath me~~ **absurd.**

Hostility and heartbreak pressed hard. The nib splintered into sharp fragments not unlike those she had thrust into my breast, and I wanted to weep. Insomnia had created an emotional, ungentlemanly mess.

Gritting my teeth and blinking away tears, I gathered myself. Calmly, quietly, I prepared another pen and, somehow, managed to elucidate my observations regarding Bingley and Jane Bennet without resorting to excessive sarcasm or acrimony.

The next section suffered no such restriction. Her family's situation deserved a bit of caustic criticism.

My objections to the marriage were not merely those which I last night acknowledged to have required the utmost force of ~~madness~~ **passion to put aside in my own case; the want of**

connection could not be so great an ~~abomination~~ evil to my friend as to me. But there were other causes of ~~horror~~ repugnance; causes which, though still existing, and existing to an equal degree in both instances, I had myself endeavoured to forget, because they were not immediately ~~as ungovernable as they were last night~~ before me. These ~~atrocities~~ causes must be stated, though briefly. The situation of your mother's family, though ~~noxious~~ objectionable, was nothing in comparison of that total want of propriety so frequently, so almost uniformly, betrayed by herself, by your three younger ~~hoydens~~ sisters, and occasionally even by your father. Pardon me. ~~But it pains me to have offered for you.~~

Lawks! Yes, it pains me! But my exhausted brain and lacerated heart must not take control of my writing hand.

Shaking cramped fingers down by my side, I bent my weary head to the desk and thereon rested my cheek for just a moment . . . and drifted off, only to awaken with a sheet of paper adhering to my face. Peeling away the page and snatching up the candle, I rushed to the cheval glass and tilted it to the light. "Blast!" As feared, wet ink had lifted from the paper onto my cheek. "Gad!" Stumbling to a ghastly pitcher and ewer—matching the previously mentioned chamber pot—I seized and wetted a cloth and scrubbed at the backwards words.

"Lud!" I muttered. "Backwards, indeed!" My writing had progressively deteriorated, and I had yet to address the most serious charge against me. In the meantime, Bingley had to be finished off.

I trudged to the desk and, sighing, picked up the pen and amended the sentence**. It pains me to offend you. But amidst your concern for the defects of your ~~vulgar~~ nearest relations, and your displeasure at this representation of them, let it give you consolation to consider that to have conducted yourselves so as to avoid any share of the like censure is praise no less generally bestowed on you and your eldest sister, than it is honourable to the sense and disposition of both. I will only say further that, from what passed that ~~horrific night~~ evening, my opinion of all parties was confirmed, and every inducement heightened, which could have led me before to preserve my friend from what I esteemed a ~~blighted~~ most unhappy connection. He ~~fled~~ left Netherfield for London, on the day following, as you, I am certain, remember, with the design of ~~over my dead body~~ soon returning.**

The next section explained my coincidence of feeling and complicity with the Bingley sisters concerning Jane Bennet. In retrospect, like trying to detach a leech, I may have rubbed salt into my friend's wound.

It is done, however, and it was done for the best. On this subject I have nothing more to say, no other ~~justification is necessary~~ **apology to offer. If I have wounded your sister's feelings, it was unknowingly done; and though the motives which governed me may to you very naturally appear** ~~unjust and ungenerous~~ **insufficient, I have not yet** ~~condescended to admit I was wrong~~ **learnt to condemn them.**

Satisfied, I set my pen aside. Further fortification was required to tackle the thorny affair of Wickham and Georgiana. My rummer, therefore, was refilled to an indecent level and its contents imbibed in a most ungentlemanly manner. In other words, fine French brandy was guzzled in three greedy gulps.

It sickened me. What I had to say next about Ramsgate, that is—not the brandy, although my stomach was, by then, a tad queasy.

When I had finished ripping from my chest the sordid details of my association with George Wickham, I held up the page to the candlelight, squinting to read whatever I had thereon scribbled. The brandy burned in my gut, raging ire burned in my breast . . . and the paper burned in my hand, flames licking along the left margin. Overtired, overwrought, and without proper consideration of the consequences, I shouted, "Aargh! Fire! Fire!"

The charred remains were already resting in the grate, and I was sitting calmly at the desk again—rewriting the accursed page—by the time Richard, Anne, Baddeley, and a footman all barged into my room. I apologised, and I thanked them en masse for their concern. All but the footman gave me a withering look as they, respectively, swore, tut-tutted, snickered, or bowed before exiting.

Completely enervated, I had yet to compose a closing, and previous pages still had to be rewritten. *By God, if this is what ensues, I shall never propose to a woman again!* I *had* expected to be betrothed to Elizabeth by then. I *had* hoped to steal a kiss or two from her, and I *had* looked forward to the expectation of much, much more to come. I *had* hoped to have sweet dreams not shattered ones and nightmares. The letter had already taken three hours and a great deal of blood, sweat, and tears to draft, and I was afraid my well had run dry.

My fingers shook as I picked up the pen and dipped it into the inkwell. When lifted out, the nib was deucedly dry. "Confound it!" I had barely enough faculty to rein back a paroxysm of temper and rummage for another pot of Japan ink rather than fling the writing implement clear across the room. It was close, but in my lassitude the exertion of trying to hurl a quill feather any distance hardly seemed worth the bother.

Slumped over the desk, pen poised above the page, I began an ending.

This, ~~my darling Elizabeth~~ **madam, is a faithful narrative of every event in which we have been concerned together; and if you do not absolutely reject it as** ~~resentful rubbish~~ **false, you will, I hope, acquit me henceforth of cruelty towards** ~~that concupiscent carbuncle~~ **Mr. Wickham. I know not in what manner, under what form of falsehood,** ~~the debauched ne'er-do-well~~ **he has imposed on you; but his success is not, perhaps, to be wondered at.** ~~Blind~~ **Ignorant as you previously were of every thing concerning either, detection could not be in your power, and suspicion certainly not in your inclination** ~~except where I am concerned~~.

My hand cramped again, and my heart likewise suffered a painful contraction. It was time. Time to close the letter and, somehow, bid Elizabeth Bennet farewell forever.

I walked away from the desk to compose myself.

Although nothing remained in the grate but cinders, I bent down in front of the hearth staring at the ashes and wishing my heart could be as cold as that dying fire. Poker in hand, I stirred and prodded a few embers, but they refused to rekindle. There was no warmth, no comfort, only a stale, acrid smell.

Drawing myself up, I let the metal rod fall from my grasp and clang on the parquet. Holding my breath, I turned worried eyes to the far wall, the one separating my room from Richard's. I waited a few moments before exhaling and striding away from the fireplace. In want of fresh air, I flung open a curtain and raised the double sash, forgetting that particular window was the one with noisy pulleys and weights. "Pish and a pox on it!"

My cousin, it seemed, was still safe and sound in the arms of either Morpheus or Dawson. The latter was Lady Catherine's personal maid, with whom Richard maintained a liaison since Eastertide of whichever year she came to work at Rosings.

Jumping out of my skin, I whirled around as my door banged open. There was, clearly, no privacy at all to be had in that house.

Apparently awakened by all my thoughtless clatter, Cousin Anne had burst into the room. Barefoot, with hair done up in curling papers, and frilly nightclothes fluttering about her frail form, my petite relation flounced up to me, barely reaching my shoulder.

"Do you *know* what time it is, Witsfailhim?" She, at least, had enough sense to convey anger at a whisper and not call forth the bugbear next door.

"Erm. Do you not have a clock in your room?" My smile was weak and my attempt at humour ill-timed.

Standing on tiptoes and with hands planted on her slim hips, she hissed, "'Tis a quarter to six! Mother says I must have at *least* ten hours of uninterrupted sleep in order to keep my appearance young and beautiful."

Biting my tongue, I resisted any mention of hibernation. "My apologies." Tugging on the sash of my banyan, I added, "Truly, I *am* sorry"—*Lord, am I ever*—"to have disturbed your sleep."

"Oh, you did not awaken me," said she, smiling sweetly. "I was already wide awake, reading." She swept across the room and curled up on an ugly chair. Tucking her feet beneath her, she sniffled and studied me as I fidgeted. "I know why *your* sleep has been disturbed."

"I should imagine not."

She sat there, gloating, nodding her head.

Gesturing at the desk, I explained there had been an urgent matter requiring my attention. "And, as you see, I am still involved in the beastly business."

"Beastly? Oh! Are you writing her a love letter? One full of instinctual need and—"

"Dear God, no!" Horrified, I, nevertheless, nonchalantly strode to the mantle. "I mean, who?"

Anne scoffed. "Do you think I am ignorant of the fact you went to the parsonage last evening and made an off—"

"You know nothing, madam!" Turning, I glared but could not quite meet her eyes.

"I know that you went to the parsonage last evening and made an offer to Miss Bennet." Dragging a handkerchief from her sleeve, she dabbed at her nose and snuffled, looking suddenly quite watery-eyed and miserable.

I crossed the room to crouch in front of her. "I thought we agreed to never marry one another, Anne." I then gently asked, "Are you upset over me?"

She laughed in my face. "Lawks, you are a conceited man! No. I sniff because of your overpowering perfume or pomade or—"

"I do *not* use pomade," I protested, raking fingers through my hair.

"Well, whatever it is, that musky, mossy, minty smell makes me sneeze. It is, by the bye, one of the myriad reasons why you are the last man in England whom I could ever marry."

Rising and towering over her, I snapped, "What?"

"You heard me. The point, however, is moot. I assume congratulations are in order and that you are impatient and restless to see your betrothed and for the intimacy of—"

"I say again, Anne, you know *nothing*!"

"Oh, lud! I *have* read *those* sorts of novels, you know." Suddenly sheepish, she added, "Keep that under your hat, will you? Mother would have hysterics."

"Anne—"

"Have no fear, Fitzwilliam. I like Miss Bennet and support your choice. Pray, do send her my best regards for fulfilment in . . ." She giggled, covering her mouth. "That might be a bit gauche in a love letter, I suppose."

"Anne!"

"I am off," she said, springing to her feet, "and impatient to finish my naughty novel. Do get some rest, Cousin. You will need strength to deal with Mother. She *will* have hysterics, you know, when you announce your engagement to anyone other than me."

With that, she flounced out of the room, leaving me shaking my head at her presumptuousness and wondering how she knew my business at the parsonage.

Sighing, I settled at the desk to close the letter and bid my love goodbye.

You may possibly wonder why all this was not told you last night. But I was ~~out of my mind~~ ~~heartbroken~~ ~~enraged~~ not then master enough of myself to know what could or ought to be revealed. For the truth of every thing here related, I can appeal more particularly to the testimony of Colonel Fitzwilliam, who from our near relationship and constant intimacy, and still more as one of the executors of my father's will, has been unavoidably acquainted with every particular of these transactions. If your abhorrence of me should make my assertions ~~not worth the paper they are written upon~~ valueless, you cannot be prevented by the same cause from confiding in my cousin ~~with whom you seemed quite intimate~~ ~~rather cosy~~ ~~entirely too comfortable~~; and that there may be the possibility of consulting him, I shall endeavour to find some opportunity of putting this ~~accursed~~ letter in your hands in the course of the morning. I will only add, ~~I love you still~~ God bless you.

Fitzwilliam Darcy ~~(the last man in the world whom y~~

Under the circumstances, I thought my adieu was naught but kindness itself. Whether she, in her small-mindedness, might appreciate such charity, I gave not a fig.

Henceforth, her pert opinions must mean naught to me. But the thought of casting off Elizabeth sent *me* adrift. Obviously, I—akin to a certain bridge spanning the Thames—was falling to pieces.

The blighted pages on the desk before me looked as though they had been penned in the most carelessness of execution by either Bingley or a crazed, drunken wretch. "Hah!" I mumbled, "They *were* written by a crazed, drunken wretch!"

Half of my words were scratched out, and the rest blotted with ink, brandy, wax . . . or a clear, unidentified liquid which might have tasted salty had one sampled it.

Bleary-eyed, I stared in disbelief as light filtered through cracks in the draperies. *Good God, 'tis cockcrow already.* Birdsong and the sounds of servants beginning their labours spurred my stiff fingers to the tedious task of transcription.

With daybreak, however, came another dawning. Somehow, I would have to walk away and forsake the one woman I desired above all others. Pemberley needed an heir, and I would be compelled to take another woman as my wife while Elizabeth . . . *Aargh, no!* The thought of *her* as another man's lover was too painful. Expunging that awareness, I applied myself to completion of my occupation.

Following forty hours with little or no sleep, my concentration had become hazy, movement sluggish. My head not only ached but buzzed.

Baddeley, bless his soul, had come with a steaming pot of tea and a plate of toast and muffins with black butter. The breakfast was most gratefully golloped in an inelegant thrice. Then, at seven o'clock, just as I took a last sip and was swiping crumbs from the desk, there came a rap on my door.

"Enter."

In her typical, dignified attitude, Lady Catherine sailed in, eyes narrowed, searching for something with which to find fault.

The shortcoming became immediately evident to both of us as I scrambled to my feet and bowed. My blasted burgundy banyan gaped open, and its silky sash—despite my blindly groping about for it—was nowhere to be found. Reaching only to my knees, my linen nightshirt did nothing to conceal long, strong, hairy calves from the woman's bulging eyes.

"Nephew, I am exceedingly displeased!"

Gathering both sides of the banyan around me, I mumbled, "Well, erm, I would ordinarily be fully dressed by now, but I was not expecting you, and—"

"And I was not expecting *you*, Fitzwilliam Alfred Darcy, to desert my dear daughter during dinner last evening. Where *were* you?"

"Oh, *that*. Well, there was a pressing matter requiring my attention. As you see, I am still involved in the odious business. Um, will you not sit?"

I gestured towards the ugly chair. *If she would just sit, I could too, and conceal my lower limbs beneath the desk.*

Adding to my vexation, she declined, pacing in a manner immediately recognisable as similar to my own. My mother's sister was a tall, large woman, who might once have been handsome. A certain physical resemblance between Georgiana and Lady Catherine might be discerned, but two females could hardly be more dissimilar in temperament.

"Poor Anne was devastated by your unfeeling abandonment last night and could scarcely finish her third calf's foot jelly." Bulging eyes darted down again to my own calves and bare feet.

Shuffling said feet in awkwardness, I apologised for missing dinner and all its scintillating conversation.

"Humph! And well you *should* apologise . . . to Anne! When you marry my daughter—"

Pigs will fly. "Madam, I pray you desist! As dear as Anne is to me, I have no intention of marrying her, or *anyone*, anytime soon."

"Nonsense! You most certainly *will* marry! Since your infancy . . ." Etcetera, etcetera, etcetera.

I had either dozed off on my feet or turned a deaf ear to her authoritative tone repeating the same unlikely story I had been subjected to since coming of age. The pounding of her cane on the parquet jolted me awake and alerted me to her purposeful advance towards the desk, under which I espied the slippery sash from my banyan.

"Nephew! What is *that*?"

Oh, blast! The ink stain! Bolting ahead of her, I sidled in front of the drawer while, with my foot, I rooted around under the desk, hooking the strip of burgundy silk with my toes. Bringing my foot up behind me, I snatched the blasted belt and properly cinched my dressing gown.

"Are you using blotting paper instead of sand? 'Tis unthinkably wasteful to use blotting paper when there is a pounce pot of the finest cuttlefish bone right there in front of you! When you marry my Anne, you must not be so profligate . . ." Etcetera, etcetera, etcetera.

At least she has not gartered her hose with my guts, I thought, as I guided her from the room.

I often wondered if bullying came in handy in Richard's soldiering occupation. The trait obviously ran in the family, as Fitzwilliam blood flowed through both Lady Catherine's and my own veins.

I may have been a bit intimidating last evening at Hunsford—insensitive and cruel to the woman I love. I would not be such a brute, if given a second chance . . . Alas, too late!

Glancing at the clock, I muttered, "Oh, blast! It *is* late! Elizabeth, no doubt, will be in the grove by now."

At half past seven, thinking me gone for either a walk or a ride (as was my wont at that hour in the hopes of meeting a certain young woman on her rambles), a chambermaid slipped into the room to gather ashes from the fireplace. Scaring the poor girl out of her wits as she bent to pick up the crumpled papers strewn across the hearth, I growled at her to leave them be. *Selfish disdain of the feelings of others* echoed in my head, and I apologized to the wide-eyed servant, who bobbed a curtsey and fled.

I picked up those discarded pages myself, placed them in the grate, and set them afire using the candle stub. Flame licked along the papers' edges, devouring my mistakes, turning them to ash.

Back at the desk, I made short work of rewriting the remainder of the page.

Finally, I held an envelope containing two sheets of letter paper, written quite through in close, neat penmanship. At least the first sheet was meticulously done; the second was less well formed. The envelope itself, likewise full, was naught but slapdash. There was, however, nothing to be done for it. I was drained.

At my summons, Baddeley returned and was badgered to hastily prepare me—without our usual fuss and fastidiousness—for another day.

I found myself at the plantation without any memory of having walked thither. Elizabeth, in answer to my prayers, was descried wandering the grove edging the park.

Having had my heart pierced by the woman's refusal and wounded by her sharp, hurtful words, it was somehow fitting that our last encounter be amongst a stand of ash—a tree whose name means spear—and that our parting be amidst plants whose resilient wood was used in bow making. *Over time, my heart may recover, but it certainly shall not spring back as easily as ash wood would.*

Wood would. Splendid, you arse. I determined that, considering my condition, it would be best—should she spare me a moment—that I not speak overmuch.

At my heavy tread, Elizabeth turned away, but I stepped purposefully forward and pronounced her name. Turning, she came hesitantly towards me, hems dampened by the morning dew and cheeks glowing rosily. *By God, she is a handsome woman!* We met at the gate and holding out the letter dated from Rosings at eight o'clock that day, I, with affected tranquillity, passed the correspondence into her gloved hand. Beneath knitted brows, her fine eyes looked to mine for explanation.

With all expectations for a happy future together turned to ashes in my mouth, I had difficulty speaking. "I have been walking in the grove some time in the hope of meeting you. Will you do me the honour of reading that letter?" I bowed and, after one last, lingering look, turned my back on her. Squaring my shoulders, I walked away—and reminded myself to breathe.

The deed was done. All association between us was at an end.

It proved impossible—although I tried—to banish all memory of her, of my proposal, and of its aftermath. How could I forget when my mind continually wandered back there? How could I possibly forsake the one woman who—despite everything—I still loved?

During those early weeks in London, while wholly unmoved by any feeling of wrongdoing, I thought I might run mad as her torturous words rang over and over in my ears.

I was a good man, an honourable man. Why had she, the insolent slip of a girl, not seen that? I doubted the blasted letter would ever make Elizabeth think better of me; but I wondered if she, at least, had read it and, if so, gave any credit to its contents.

Quite some time passed before I was reasonable enough to allow her criticisms the justice they deserved. Then my anger began to take a proper direction.

And I was suitably humbled.

A fortuitous encounter at Pemberley kindled a fire that later blazed into life during a warm autumn day in Hertfordshire and gave me the longed-for second chance.

My darling Lizzy and I have been married these many years now, and the words upon the pages of that letter are but water under the bridge. Having been fed to the flames ages ago by my saucy little minx of a wife, they are naught but powdery residue spread upon Pemberley's peony patch. Long before their incineration, though, those words gradually removed all my dearest Elizabeth's former prejudices against me. The feelings of the letter's composer and of its recipient are now so opposite from what they were back then, that all unkindnesses have been long forgiven and forgotten.

Coincidentally, the flowers rooted in the letter's ash still bloom as strong and as beautiful as our marriage. It might be said that our love rose from those very ashes, but our love is built on a more durable foundation than mere cinders and cleansing ash.

Our union has not always been peaceable. Sparks sometimes fly, but our differences have certainly made our life together interesting.

We are both imperfect creatures, but we see through one another's flaws to the good person within, the person we love. We are each other's strength and refuge. My world is built around her. I live and breathe for Elizabeth and the offspring she has given me—girls all, so far. There is, however, another child in progress.

Given good principles, our daughters are, despite their Grandmama and Grandpapa Bennet's efforts, unspoilt and unselfish. There is no *improper* pride and no prejudice against those beyond our family circle.

One day, God willing, I hope to give Pemberley's heir better guidance than my own parents gave me. As with our daughters, a son would not only be taught what is right but taught to correct his temper.

No son of mine shall *ever* need hand to the woman he loves an epistle such as the contemptible one his father handed his mother.

I am eternally grateful that atrocious missive, written in a dreadful bitterness of spirit, was read by only my beloved's fine eyes. Lawks! Imagine my mortification had the ghastly thing been made available to the world at large.

Pshaw! Unthinkable.

However, as Samuel Johnson penned in *Life of Sir Thomas Browne*, "Of every great and eminent character, part breaks forth into public view, and part lies hid in domestic privacy."

The resentful retort I composed and handed to Miss Elizabeth Bennet on the morn of 10 April, 18__, lies buried deep down in Derbyshire dirt, supplanted by domestic felicity.

Fitzwilliam Alfred Darcy's most confidential and infelicitous thoughts remain, mercifully, untold.

J. MARIE CROFT is a self-proclaimed word nerd and adherent of Jane Austen's quote "Let other pens dwell on guilt and misery." Bearing witness to her fondness for *Pride and Prejudice*, wordplay, and laughter are Joanne's light-hearted novel, *Love at First Slight,* a Babblings of a Bookworm's Favourite Read of 2014; her humorous short story, "Spyglasses and Sunburns," in the anthology *Sun-Kissed: Effusions of Summer*; and a playful novella, *A Little Whimsical in His Civilities,* Just Jane 1813's Favourite JAFF Novella of 2016.

"Lady Catherine has been of infinite use, which ought to make her happy, for she loves to be of use."
—Miss Elizabeth to Mr. Darcy, Chapter LX.

IF ONLY A DREAM

JOANA STARNES

"Good morning, sir. Might I take your coat and—?"

An impatient gesture cut the man off; he bowed then reached to close the door. Even before it was shut, Darcy was already bounding up the stairs. He had barely registered the civil query yet peremptorily dismissed it, along with the softly spoken footman. To his mounting ire, his mind's ear returned to other words, dragging them out from poisonous recesses, as it had for too many hours. Seventeen and a half, to be precise. Harsh words that cut with all the sharpness of a scalpel. *Immovable dislike. The last man in the world. Selfish disdain for the feelings of others.*

A loud snort left Darcy's lips. She was a fine one to speak of the latter, having dismissed his avowal of ardent admiration and regard with contemptuous remarks and an assortment of ill-founded reproaches. *Ungentlemanlike manner*, she had called it! *This* from a woman so lost to every notion of propriety as to champion a smooth rogue in the midst of his proposal and take him to task over ruining Wickham's prospects. Wickham's! He gripped the banister as he gave another snort. Well, now she had the truth of the matter. She must know what vermin she had championed, and nurture no more illusions, once she read his letter. *If* she read it!

Darcy had no time to explore the sense of acute panic that suddenly gripped him, easily dispelling his dark satisfaction at the thought of Elizabeth bitterly regretting her refusal. Imperious tones rang below, breaking his stride and further bedevilling his humour.

"Nephew! What is the meaning of all this?"

He stopped in his tracks, his features twisting into something between a wince and a scowl. Without pausing to wonder why he should even give himself the trouble any more, he instinctively worked to smooth his countenance into impassive blandness as he turned to face his aunt and see her hastening up the stairs after him, her habitual air of haughty dignity entirely lost as she resumed her remonstrations.

"I have just learnt—from the *servants*, I might add—that you have given orders for immediate departure."

Darcy took a deep breath and worked to subdue his temper.

"I have. It is long overdue. I was of course intending to do you the courtesy of informing you in person and—"

Lady Catherine impatiently cut him off.

"Pray tell me, Nephew, when exactly were you intending to do me *and* your cousin the courtesy of addressing other matters that are long overdue? Such as doing your duty?"

Despite every effort at rigid control, the scowl returned and Darcy's lips tightened. He sternly delivered a few words of warning.

"This is not the best of times to remind me of my duties."

Unsurprisingly, the sternness had no effect whatsoever on his aunt.

"If not now, then when? This has gone too far and I will not tolerate further procrastination!"

Darcy's eyes flashed dangerously at his relation.

"Lady Catherine, pray heed me when I say I will not be worked upon today. I beg you would not force me to say something you would not wish to hear!" he shot back, too incensed at his aunt's tone and her untimely interference in his affairs to consider he might well come to indulge her, now that he could no longer hope to marry for love. That thought would come later, when despondency settled, along with the bland acknowledgement that he would have to marry someone after all—and why not Anne?

For now, they glared at each other—Darcy at the top of the grand staircase, his aunt paused on the landing; one fiercely unbending nature pitted against the other and neither in the habit of brooking disappointment.

The drop of a pin could have easily been heard in the ensuing silence; the retreating footsteps of the very discreet footman had died out a full minute ago. As headstrong as the other, the two opponents refused to look away or step back from the confrontation, until all of a sudden Lady Catherine seemed to remember that she had other, more feminine, weapons in her not insubstantial arsenal.

"You would speak thus? To me? Your departed mother's sister and indeed the nearest to a mother that you have?" she fervently exclaimed in accents of injured dismay and, despite the too broad hint, for the briefest moment Darcy's severity softened.

She was advanced in age. Well into her sixties. Overbearing and infuriating, aye, but still…she *was* his mother's sister. And with so few relations left, for Georgiana's sake, if not his own, he would be well-advised to choose his words better. It would not do to cause an irreparable rupture with his aunt simply because a slip of a girl from Hertfordshire had brought him to the limits of his endurance.

His rigid posture lost some of its stiffness and he released his hold on the banister to descend one step and then another, as he brought himself to offer in a conciliatory manner.

"Lady Catherine, you are in the right. I have not dealt fairly with either you or Anne and a frank discussion is in order. Long overdue, even. But this is not the place," he added, briefly gesturing around him, "and pray believe me, this is not the time. I must leave Kent at once."

Lady Catherine gasped.

"What brought this about? You had me thinking your attachment to Rosings was steadily increasing. You have extended your stay with us se'nnight after se'nnight, showing that at long last you have become amenable to reason, yet now you are about to leave with so little warning? You cannot! I will not allow it!"

Darcy's brow shot up. And, as he fought the urge to forcefully remind his aunt how many years had gone by since anyone had had the right to govern his actions, Lady Catherine must have seen for herself that she had overstepped the mark. She offered no apology—it was not her way. Instead, she gasped again and suddenly clutched at the lace and satin covering her bosom as her forbidding visage contorted into agony. Her nephew might have been greatly alarmed, but to the lady's disadvantage he had not missed the swift, calculating glance she cast his way before launching into the consummate performance.

Thus, far from concerned, for all the dark misery of his circumstances, Darcy had the strangest urge to throw his head back and burst into laughter. That calculating glance—he had seen it oftentimes before. In the eyes of the Town's matrons and their marriage-minded charges. In Miss Bingley's. And most frequently in Mrs. Bennet's. His lips twitched as his diverted eye caught further similarities with the latter. The shallow breaths. The eye roll. One hand still clutching at the fabric on her bosom, the other brought theatrically to her temple. All that was missing was the flapping kerchief and the feeble request for smelling salts, mingled with complaints of flutterings in her chest and assurances that she would feel better once she had been allowed a moment's rest.

Lady Catherine's performance was ludicrously close to Mrs. Bennet's attempt to delay her family's departure from Netherfield by every means possible at the end of a most unsuccessful dinner. How did his aunt know the precise ways to re-enact it? Had Mr. Collins given her such a detailed description?

Nay, he could not have. He was not there. It must be in their nature then. Artfulness. Deception. Darcy gave a quiet snort. They were all the same. Lowborn or highborn, young or old, Eve's daughters were all endowed with innate aptitudes for dissimulation. Well, at least Lady Catherine, Mrs. Bennet, Miss Bingley, and the Town's misses and matrons had a valid and acknowledged purpose in employing theirs. What had *she* sought to gain by deceiving him with playful banter, saucy repartee, and sparkling eyes? Another conquest to parade before her friends? Paltry amusement? His humiliation?

Very well. She had her wish. He had been thoroughly humiliated. Let that be her only satisfaction when she aged into a bitter spinster or as a tradesman's wife!

The fresh burst of anger swiftly dispelled the vaguely better humour he owed Lady Catherine, so much so that the performance no longer had the power to divert him; not even when it was skilfully enhanced with a wince and a faltering request:

"Nephew… Your hand… Pray attend me, I am suddenly unwell…"

"Flutterings to your chest, perchance?" Darcy inquired curtly, and Lady Catherine's eyes widened by a fraction.

"I… Yes. How did you know?"

"A common enough affliction, I was given to discover," he replied with so little sympathy that the wilful performer must have determined it was time to become far more convincing.

She swayed—and it was masterfully done. The perfect impression of an aged frame suddenly weakened by illness and ill-usage. Whether she would have stooped to feigning a swoon—there, on the landing—Darcy would never know. Lady Catherine had neglected to take two crucial points into account: one, that her hapless servants had been too often drilled to polish every surface to perfection; and two, that she was too close to the edge. Both points conspired to work against her. The feigned loss of balance turned hideously real. She reached to grab the banister in the utmost panic but found it slipping from her grasp. She fell, rolling all the way from the landing to the bottom of the stairs. She probably cried out, as he might have. Darcy could not tell. Remorseful and anxious, he ran down to assist her. Several servants rushed in too, their shocked glances darting between him and their groaning mistress.

"Send for the physician!" Darcy called out as he crouched beside her where she still lay, face down. He tentatively touched her shoulder. "Aunt? Can you hear me?"

To his relief, she stirred and turned, then reassured him further with a sharp retort, much more in keeping with her nature than the show of dainty weakness on the landing.

"Yes, yes! I have lost my balance, not my hearing. Come now, do not dally. Help me to my feet!" Her Ladyship commanded.

"Are you quite certain you can stand? You took a severe fall," Darcy cautiously remarked only to receive a grim scowl for his efforts.

Lady Catherine sneered.

"Why, thank you for informing me. It quite escaped my notice. Of course I can stand," she snapped. "Help me up!"

Darcy did as bid, but to everybody's shock—herself included—Lady Catherine was once more proven wrong that day. No sooner had she been restored to the dignity of standing on her own two feet than she relinquished it and fell back with a roar of pain, loud enough to be heard from the end of the drive, if not the church and parsonage.

No! It could not be real—this nightmare, this complete disaster.

Yet for all his disjointed inward protestations, Darcy had to concede that the nightmare was real enough. He could not leave Rosings! He was marooned there by his aunt's fall—her own blasted fault and nobody else's—and her deuced broken ankle. The physician harboured no doubts on the matter. The stark reality was plain once Lady Catherine had been installed upon one of the sofas in the drawing room and the injury was examined. By the time the old physician had arrived, her left ankle had swollen more than twice in size and had turned an ugly shade of purple.

"No, 'tis not a sprain." Old Mr. Henshaw despondently confirmed the worst expectations, shaking his head in solemn sympathy. "I could feel the broken bone under the skin—begging Your Ladyship's pardon once again for causing you more pain with the examination. Laudanum will help, if taken in substantial quantity. I will send instructions to the apothecary for a draught. But firstly, you must be taken above stairs and made comfortable in your bedchamber, then the fracture must be immobilised. Thank goodness, only the thinner bone was broken—the fibula, as we call it—and not the stronger tibia. Still, with every pull of the muscles the two ends are drawn further apart and this must be stopped, or the fracture will heal poorly—"

"How long will it take?" Darcy interrupted before Lady Catherine could speak.

"Six weeks at the very least, and that in a young person where the body still has all its healing powers—" the physician tactlessly replied, only to provoke his incensed patient.

"I trust you are not suggesting I am too old to heal," Lady Catherine enunciated, making the other quail under her glare.

"Heavens, no, my lady! Merely that it might take a vast deal longer…"

But Darcy was no longer paying any heed to the man's frantic attempts to mitigate Her Ladyship's displeasure. Six weeks! Lord above! Surely, he was not expected to remain there until she made a full recovery. But he was doubtlessly duty-bound to remain for at least another se'nnight … the exact duration of *her* remaining stay at Hunsford! He had expected that by nightfall he would have put as many miles as possible between them!

His frantic pacing brought him to the wall and Darcy did an about-turn to pace in the opposite direction, his heels hitting the floor in rhythmic and precise succession, with the very sound that an exacting sergeant would expect from his recruits. Colonel Fitzwilliam looked up to assess his cousin's progress with no small amount of interest. Lady Catherine glanced his way as well, her eyes shooting daggers.

"Will you not cease that infernal pacing, Darcy? I suppose I should thank you for your concern, but you are driving me to distraction!" she cast over her shoulder and groaned again.

From his post at the other end of the sofa, Mr. Collins cringed and wrung his hands as he bowed, seemingly to his patroness's injured ankle propped up on two cushions.

To Darcy's growing irritation, the parson had escorted Fitzwilliam back to Rosings on his cousin's return from the, now woefully premature, leave-taking visit, and had bemoaned Her Ladyship's predicament in the most profuse and aggravating manner.

"Pray allow me to hurry to the apothecary and bring you relief for the pain. I will consider myself fortunate if I could spare you a moment's suffering! Sadly, it would not be at all proper for me to attend you but, same as myself, Mrs. Collins will deem it a privilege to serve you. She is gone into the village now with Miss Maria, but I will send her to you directly she returns. Until then I will fetch my cousin Elizabeth. She will do well enough for—"

"No! She has no business here! I will not have it!"

The overpowering silence that followed his instinctive outburst brought Darcy to his senses. To his dismay, he found four pairs of eyes fixed upon him with sentiments ranging from surprise to outrage.

"*You* will not have it?" Lady Catherine was the only one to question his shockingly poor choice of words. "I daresay this very circumstance would not have arisen had you taken steps to earn the right to command at Rosings," she said with a gesture towards her injury, her voice dripping with resentment. "As it is, you do not possess it, and I will thank you to remember that. As for the young woman, she is tolerable I suppose, although vexingly outspoken—"

Darcy valiantly suppressed a wince at hearing his own dismissive words voiced in an uncanny echo of his old *faux pas* and, although disguise of every sort was his abhorrence, he latched upon the opportunity Lady

Catherine had presented for him to cover his unfortunate slip of the tongue.

"Indeed. And at the moment, you do not require further provocation."

Fitzwilliam's brow arched at his disingenuous pronouncement, but its purpose was served, for Lady Catherine appeared slightly mollified.

"I daresay there may be truth in that—" she sniffed "—your thoughtfulness does you credit, Nephew, belated as it might be. Very well. Send your wife to Rosings, Mr. Collins, when she returns from Hunsford, and Miss Lucas too. I imagine Anne will appreciate some company. Speaking of Anne, Darcy, I trust I can rely upon you to extend her your thoughtfulness as well at this trying time," she pointedly instructed, settling a level look upon her nephew.

Darcy bowed, and his reply was no less pointed.

"We can at least be thankful that your injured ankle has not worsened your heart condition," he tersely remarked.

If he imagined she would show signs of discomposure, she was supremely unwilling to oblige him. A lady of her quality was above betraying so plebeian an emotion as mortification. She did not even blush. It was Mr. Collins whose colour and agitation heightened.

"Your Ladyship!" he cried. "A heart condition?"

"I was not aware of it either. My lady, perhaps a more detailed examination is in order," the physician also hastened to suggest.

But Lady Catherine dismissed their concern with a regal gesture.

"See to my ankle now, Mr. Henshaw," she loftily retorted. "I am a firm believer in tackling each difficulty in its own time."

Darcy might have claimed the same once. After all, he had been brought up to uphold the same principles and rules of conduct as his relations. That Lady Catherine chose to follow them in a deceitful manner was something he had deplored and inwardly censured. Yet now that difficulties—nay, disasters—were coming all at once leaving no hope for them to be addressed composedly one at a time, he found himself following in his aunt's footsteps and stooping to deceit as well!

He scowled. What else could he resort to in this pitiful debacle but deceit?

So, there he was, spinning one falsehood after another.

He had told Richard that the sole reason for his foul temper was the unforeseen mishap that tethered him to Rosings when he had more than enough reasons to be elsewhere—and no, they did not pertain to Miss Elizabeth Bennet, for whom he had not offered and had no intention to. The truth would have to be revealed eventually, but not now and not there.

Over and above everything else, he would be damned if he would also endure Richard's pity!

He had told Anne that of course it was no hardship to extend his stay at Rosings—he could not very well leave her to face this trying time alone.

He had told Lady Catherine, when the topic could no longer be avoided, that he would be pleased to address the issue of his manifold duties before the year was out. That was not a falsehood in essentials—only insofar as claiming to be pleased about it. No matter. It had to be done. At least one thing was certain: Lady Catherine would be pleased enough for all parties.

He had told Mr. and Mrs. Collins that he was in their debt for their dutiful attendance. This was not entirely a falsehood either, little as he could bear to spend time with the deeply vexing man. As for the lady, she was of great assistance in providing Lady Catherine with company and occupation—or rather giving her an audience for her rants and complaints. More to the point, Mrs. Collins's regular attendance ensured that the same was not requested of her friend.

He had not laid eyes on *her* since handing her the letter. He had avoided the Hunsford parsonage as though it were riddled with all the plagues of Egypt; likewise, all the woodland paths where there was the slightest risk of an encounter. He had spent the last couple of days doing a few hours' penance in Lady Catherine's sickroom, then riding as far away from Rosings as man and beast could handle, to return with barely enough time to dress for dinner. He would then sit with his cousins, toy with his food upon the plate, and repeatedly assure them that apart from Lady Catherine's condition there was *nothing whatsoever* troubling him.

Yet now the grimmest trial was upon him. This morning he would have to see her again. It could not be avoided. He could not very well absent himself from Sunday service, not when Lady Catherine was incapacitated, and he and Fitzwilliam had a duty to stand beside Anne as she undertook her mother's role. Nothing to be done about it. An appearance in the family pew was mandatory.

Darcy clenched his jaw as the church came into view, the rectangular tower low and squat, barely visible above the yews—a most unprepossessing building for a parish church under Rosings' patronage. It will be done. It must be. A word of greeting, a brief exchange of dull civilities, an hour under the same roof. Surely, he could withstand that after the hell he had endured already! And then he grimaced. No, not an hour. Two, most likely. The verbose parson had already demonstrated he was incapable of composing a short sermon. Two hours! His jaw clenched again and his back stiffened. At his right, Anne gave a quiet chuckle.

"Goodness, Darcy! One would think you were going to the gallows."

With some effort, Darcy brought himself out of dark ruminations. "Pardon?"

"Your grimace," Anne elaborated. "Are you well?"

"As well as anyone can be in expectation of that man's sermonising," Darcy said, dissembling with a practised shrug.

"Oh, you can set that fear aside. And that uncomfortable look as well, if the sole cause is Mr. Collins's sermon."

"Of course it is! What else?"

"Indeed. Well, take heart. I believe he will be more concise today."

"What makes you say that?"

Anne gave a light shrug of her own.

"My mother was in no fit state to advise him, and without her prompting, I doubt Mr. Collins can find quite so many topics on which the congregation needs instruction."

On Anne's other side, Fitzwilliam stifled a guffaw and Darcy could only roll his eyes at his cousin's manner. Both his cousins', come to think of it. Anne's light quip at her mother's expense was novel, yet however undutiful under the circumstances, it was not entirely unwelcome. At least he could find some reassurance in seeing this side of her. It would be easier to live with, more companionable than the bland nothingness she exhibited in Lady Catherine's presence. Companionship for him and Georgiana … what a bland notion that was too, when viewed against what he had dreamt of…

The sharp sense of loss found him unprepared, as did the assault of vividly bright scenes flashing through his overwrought imagination. A life full of joy and laughter. The wince turned into a scowl as he fought against the unwarranted intrusion. If Anne noticed it, this time she did not say a word.

By God, *she* will not have the upper hand! She will not know how much her ill-judged refusal cost him. She *will not* see his pain!

If there was anything he had ever learnt in eight and twenty years, it was self-control and the paramount importance of doing his duty. He would present her with the finest show of cold indifference and she would go forth to whatever life awaited her, while he would return to his. And he *would* do his duty! By Georgiana, by Anne, and by his heritage.

Upon reflection, dwelling on his duty to the latter was unwise just now, seeing as it was so intrinsically linked to begetting an heir with Anne. Not a prospect he could contemplate with anything but dutiful reluctance and the surest way, moreover, of bringing the worst thoughts to the fore. There could not be a starker contrast to the bliss he had longingly envisaged for his marriage bed—and if the previous assault of unwelcome visions had brought a sharp pang to his chest, the violent new onslaught took him to the brink of overwhelming anger. With *her*, naturally, and with himself in equal measure. He *would* conquer this. He *would* exorcise her, one way or another! She would *not* be permitted to wreak this hellish havoc in his life!

Of all the events and people that provoked his ire, for once Mr. Collins ranked so very low, to the point of barely qualifying for that list. Nevertheless, it was the hapless parson who received the full brunt of Darcy's darkest look of anger when he hastened from the porch to welcome the exalted party. Mr. Collins quaked and seemed compelled to bow again.

Darcy did not wait for the obsequious vicar to resume the closest he could come to a vertical position. One hand on Anne's elbow and the other coming up to remove his hat, he muttered through clenched teeth, "Let us go in and get this over with!"

As soon as the words escaped him, Darcy wished he had chosen them better. This was not the sentiment anyone should voice entering the house of the Lord, and for once, Collins's look of dismay showed that their thoughts were in agreement. But the man merely sighed and the dismay seemed to melt into resignation. For all his limited mental powers, he must have had sufficient common sense—or rather enough sense of self-preservation—to forgo putting his censure into words.

The little church was full. Not in recognition of Mr. Collins's abilities as a parson, Darcy inwardly scoffed, but simply because it was the only one in an eight-mile radius. He had barely made his way into the de Bourgh pew behind Fitzwilliam and Anne when profound relief washed over him at noting that Mrs. Collins and her sister were the only occupants of the lesser one reserved for the vicar's relations. *She* was not in attendance. He refused to wonder why. His whole frame lost its tension, and Darcy bowed silently to the two ladies, only to be shocked into further anger when his relief was followed by the most unwarranted sense of disappointment. Lips tight and the dark scowl back in place, he took his seat, willing Collins to get on with the service. Eventually, the foolish man saw fit to oblige, and Darcy steeled himself for the bland offering and began to count his blessings. It did not take him long. The current tally only went as high as *"one"* for, despite the ludicrous flash of disappointment at her absence, he would not see it as anything other than a blessing.

Up in the pulpit, the man began to drone. Listening to his words was as unprofitable an exercise as ever and certainly not likely to soothe anyone's spirits. For all his show of piety, Mr. Collins was far more apt to worship his patroness than his Maker, which must have been the reason he was preferred to the Hunsford living in the first place. There he was, pontificating on the subject that must now be closest to his heart: the benefits of a healthy spirit in a healthy body and the Lord's mercy, which might finally restore the afflicted to their former flourishing state.

Darcy pursed his lips in grim displeasure at the man's propensity to fawn over his patroness even in her absence, and his glance drifted well above the parson's head, towards the vast stained-glass window. Light filtered in, fanning away from Mr. Collins—golden light, mellowed by the multicoloured patchwork into a glow that was almost surreally serene.

With a sigh, Darcy closed his eyes and closed his ears to the officiant as well. Mr. Collins was no mediator between man and his Maker and, rejecting the first, Darcy bowed his head to the latter and silently prayed in his own words for the only blessings he could hope for now: strength and peace. For an end to the severest trial. For the anguished chaos that had become his life to cease swirling into unrelenting misery. For the jagged pieces to lose their painfully sharp edges and, since they could not possibly be mended, to at least fall into some sort of ordered pattern.

The sound of many shuffling feet reawakened him to his surroundings and Darcy opened his eyes to find the congregation standing for the first hymn. He followed, took the book that Anne thrust into his hand, and thanked her with a nod for the kindness of opening it to the right page for him.

Yet he had barely begun to add his baritone to the off-key chorus when he was struck afresh by mankind's arrogance in general—and his in particular—in expecting the supreme power to pay heed to human woes and pitiful conundrums. For, at his left, the door quietly opened for a late arrival who might have hoped to come in unobserved, under the cover of rustle and singing. It was a fruitless hope. From his vantage point, Mr. Collins had already taken note, and taken offence too, judging by the scowl he aimed in that direction. For his part, Darcy knew precisely who the late arrival was without even looking. What subtle sense was responsible for it, he could not tell; yet there was no way of ignoring the staggering jolt that had forced his every known and unknown sense into almost unbearable alertness.

He did not raise his eyes from the book. Pointless diligence, for he could not read a word, nor sing another note, acutely aware that her own diligence had been for naught. Presumably as keen as he to avoid a direct encounter, she had delayed her entrance so that she would not have to sit with Mrs. Collins and Miss Lucas near the Rosings party—near him. Yet this had served no one. The only vacant seat was in front of his, at the end of the wooden bench beneath the de Bourgh pew, less than a yard from where he was standing, gripping the hymn book till the pages were creased.

The grim determination to keep his eyes down served no one either. More to the point, it did not serve him. The empty seat was far too close. Impossible to train his peripheral vision into failing to register the slender form that came to occupy it, for all her haste to lower herself in it as soon as the hymn had come to an end. Just as impossible to miss the slightest move of a straw bonnet trimmed with honey-coloured satin. The book might be raised by a fraction so that it blocked the line of sight towards the bonnet and its owner, but it had the most appalling way of sliding down, almost of its own volition. It was likewise impossible not to stay attuned to every modulation of her voice when the next hymns were sung, even if it was quieter than ever. And through the musty odour of damp fabric and old wood, the scent of lily-of-the-valley unerringly came to find him and drive him to distraction. It could not be rising from chestnut curls, they were firmly tucked under the honey-coloured bonnet. To his insurmountable vexation, Darcy found himself puzzling over its source … her dress … her kerchief … her skin … until he came to spot the small bouquet when she picked it up to either toy with it or seek some comfort in its refreshing scent.

From his pulpit, Mr. Collins cast his cousin a withering stare. An hour and forty-three minutes from the tedious beginning, he was still droning, thus proving Anne woefully wrong. Even without Lady Catherine's assistance, he was perfectly able to put together a long sermon.

Gritting his teeth, Darcy shifted on his bed of nails. Across from him, Collins raised his eyes to the Gothic arch above the pulpit and spread his arms wide.

"At this trying time for our parish, let us invoke the good Lord's blessing upon the one whom we must thank for all our earthly comforts. Our generous benefactress is herself in need of the Lord's beneficence. For her restoration to good health, dearly beloved, let us pray. I have chosen a most fitting prayer for the sick and—Hmm! Hmm! For the sick! If you would repeat after me…"

The church filled with low murmurs interspersed with Collins's pompously declamatory tones. A sigh escaped him, and it was only then that Darcy noted he was intently listening to pick out hers. He scowled once more at his shocking folly and belatedly added the rumble of his own voice to the general chorus—only to see her suddenly start at the distinct addition. His chest tightened. There was no way of knowing why the sound of his voice had made her jump, but now that his eyes had come to be fixed on the back of her neck, he could not force himself to look away. Head bowed in prayer as instructed, she was perfectly still—and the entire world seemed to grow still around them as he sat staring like the most pitifully besotted mooncalf. At least that was what reason claimed—the last shreds of reason growing quieter by the minute; drowned out, along with the real voices all around him. He could not even hear hers any longer. It might have been subsumed into the rushing sound faintly ringing in his ears, much like the so-called murmur of the ocean they had once told him as a boy that he could hear in a conch shell. Or perhaps she had ceased praying to puzzle over his reasons to grow silent. A very different sort of prayer—most certainly not for the sick and dying—rose within him as his gaze remained fixed on the delicate wisp of hair curling at her nape, just underneath her ear. Chestnut brown with auburn tints, in the sharpest contrast to the creamy skin around it. Silky-soft skin, no doubt, warm to the touch. Warm under searching lips dropping light kisses in a caressing trail to the delicate lobe of that perfectly shaped ear … along her jaw line to her chin, to find her full mouth and lose himself into her intoxicating sweetness. The perfect loveliness of her.

His chest ached and his senses reeled. And before he could resume some tenuous control over the latter and ask himself what on earth he was doing, allowing himself to sink into this insanity—in a *church*, moreover!—her hand shot up to brush over the square inch of creamy skin and the enticing little curl. It was as if she could feel his burning gaze, as if it had already left a tangible mark there. She made an instinctive move to turn but instantly suppressed it, and sense finally gained the upper hand enough to make him tear his eyes away. Darcy leaned back, releasing a long breath into an incautiously loud rush; far too loud, upon reflection. To his renewed mortification, her shoulders tensed at the sudden sound, and so he was compelled to suppress the heavy sigh of exasperation at all the ways he seemed to find to make himself conspicuous.

For the remaining minutes of the too-long service, he grew so taut with the strain of governing himself and his reactions that he verily jumped when Anne's hand was laid upon his arm.

"Yes?" he whispered, heartily tired of it all.

"Peace be with you, Cousin." She then cast him an odd look, as if she could guess his thoughts and know he scoffed *"not likely,"* even as he gave the habitual response: "And also with you."

From behind Anne, Fitzwilliam eyed him just as strangely, his left brow arched in a most vexing manner, but Darcy was in no humour to speculate on his cousin's thoughts. It took every strength he still possessed to not look towards *her* bench, but could not help noticing out of the corner of his eye that she was extending the customary offer of peace to the elderly woman in modest garb who sat beside her. She did not turn to him with the same. The elevated situation of the de Bourgh pew made it well-nigh impossible even if she wished to, as it showed quite clearly that the occupants of the exalted spot were not meant to shake hands with those seated on the benches destined for the lesser sort. A stark reminder of his prejudices, but so be it. The touch of her hand would not have brought him peace in any case.

Their eyes met at last when he stood to escort Anne out of the pew, and she to wait for her turn to leave. A bow and a restrained curtsy made the full extent of their exchanges, and Darcy stepped out of the small and very crowded building with Anne on his arm and a reaffirmed conviction there was no peace to be had.

It was marginally better in the open air but not much. No matter. Not long now. A brief adieu and the Rosings party would be on its way. Anne had just released his arm to shake hands with the parson and his wife. Only a few more minutes of enduring Collins's unctuous civilities and they would be off.

But, to Darcy's unmitigated horror, he was to discover that Anne was of a vastly different mind. He could only hope he had not started in shock when he heard her say:

"Mr. Collins, I trust you and your family will join us at Rosings for tea as usual. And allow me to say it was an enlightening service, of which my mother would have certainly approved."

The vicar preened himself on what he took for praise but then was promptly overrun by conflicting emotions:

"It is indeed an honour and deeply felt, but if I might be permitted to disagree with anyone from the great house of de Bourgh … that is, to observe that in the most unfortunate circumstance of Her Ladyship's injury … Hmm! I thought I should say—"

"Mr. Collins would like to ask if you would do us the honour of having tea at the parsonage instead." Mrs. Collins smoothly intervened to curtail an effusion of civilities that threatened to keep them at the church's door till dinnertime.

At that, her husband beamed.

"Indeed, I was. I thank you, my dear, for expressing more succinctly what I was hoping to convey—"

Anne's patience was as short as everybody's, but to Darcy's renewed shock, she beamed almost as readily as Mr. Collins.

"What a splendid notion! I thank you for the thoughtful offer, sir, Mrs. Collins. We should be delighted," she spoke up to accept for the whole of her party.

Without taking the slightest trouble to ascertain their wishes, Darcy thought with an admixture of vexation and panic. No! He would *not* subject himself to more time in her company. Having tea at the parsonage, of all the cursed things—no doubt in the same wretched parlour where she had refused him! Beyond his control, his glance flashed towards her and their eyes met in a split second of shared dismay—no, not dismay but acute mortification—before she looked away, blushing to the hairline.

Darcy's jaw tightened to the point that it was a wonder how his teeth did not splinter. Across the path from him, Fitzwilliam's teeth were faring a vast deal better. In fact, they were on full display in a wide grin as he offered an arm to Miss Lucas and the other to Elizabeth. Darcy failed to notice Anne turning her head to join him in glaring at the sight. Nor did he stop to ponder on how shockingly like her mother she sounded when she spoke to him.

"Come, let us not dawdle. Your arm, if you please," Anne enunciated in response to his blank stare, and he was finally jolted into speech and motion.

"You will forgive me. I must return to Rosings," he declared—and despised himself for the pitiful subterfuge when he felt compelled to add, "Someone ought to check on Lady Catherine."

Further up the path, Fitzwilliam glanced at him over his shoulder and rolled his eyes. *She* did not turn. Not when Anne observed that a brief delay would make no difference, and that her mother was very well looked after. Not even when Collins spoke at length to beg the privilege of attending Lady Catherine in his stead. She stopped and turned only when the ludicrous display made Darcy repeat tersely:

"You will forgive me. I must leave you now."

He gave them a clipped bow, his glance hastily sweeping over everybody. It met Elizabeth's for no longer than a second. Not long enough to tell what her eyes held. Relief, no doubt. He could vouch for that without taking the time to scrutinise her closely. Darcy gave an ill-tempered shrug. Of course, she was relieved he did not join them. So was he—to have avoided the continuation of the nightmare.

Yet the mental picture he carried with him all the way to Rosings, as he covered the distance in long strides, was of Elizabeth looking upon his hasty retreat, not with relief, but ill-concealed regret and disappointment.

The stone that found itself in his path was kicked right off the road into the grass as Darcy cursed under his breath, encompassing all wishful thinking in the oath, along with all the dunces who indulged it.

Mercifully Lady Catherine was asleep—the laudanum still performed its office—so he was not obliged to keep her company. Nor was he prepared to tolerate the others on their return from the parsonage. He had changed into riding clothes as soon as he had learnt he was not needed in Lady Catherine's sickroom. In deference to her and truthful to his words earlier that morning, he remained at Rosings until Anne and Fitzwilliam could be seen approaching up the pebbled walk. He left the house then and headed to the stables before they could take him to task for his desertion or drive him to distraction by mentioning—or not mentioning—*her*.

This time he did not return for dinner to be served lavish fare he could barely touch, along with a side dish of cousinly probing. He could not bear it. Not after this morning. Not tonight. Darcy returned from his ride at dusk, sent word he would not be joining them either in the dining room or the drawing room, and took himself for a long walk, safe in the knowledge that at such an hour *she* would not go rambling through the woods.

Another sleepless night in his bedchamber was as unpalatable as could be. He had endured two such nights already. So, instead of making his way above stairs, Darcy bent his steps towards his aunt's library. He scoffed as he walked in and made a beeline for the decanters to pour himself a brandy. Reading was not an option but, if nothing else, this would afford him substantially more room for pacing.

As he was considering a refill, Darcy came to discover there were marked disadvantages to choosing the library: Richard's company, to be precise. His cousin eventually wandered in to quietly remark, "Ah. So, you are not hiding above stairs for a change."

"Why should I be hiding?" Darcy snorted in what he thought was a convincing show of unconcern.

Whether fooled or not, Fitzwilliam retorted pleasantly as he filled both glasses, "Shall we say, from my prodding?"

Darcy took his and walked off to the fireplace.

"I was rather hoping you would refrain from it," he replied, in truth with little expectation of a respite.

He was not mistaken; they knew each other far too well for that.

"Might I ask why you have taken to surveying all the roads of Kent?" Fitzwilliam asked, settling into a nearby armchair.

Darcy shrugged.

"I thought it was fairly obvious. I cannot bear inaction."

"And people asking what is troubling you," Fitzwilliam mildly supplied.

"That too. I told you both, time and again—"

"That you are fine and dandy," his cousin interjected. "Yes, I heard. But why do I find it so deuced hard to believe you?"

"Because you are an interfering busybody," Darcy snapped, draining his glass. "There must be something in the air at Rosings."

"Oh, that I do not doubt! There *is* something in the air, I will give you that. Now, since you are well on the way to being foxed, would you be so kind as to clear a certain point that has me flummoxed?"

"I imagine there are countless points that have you flummoxed. And in any case, I am not foxed."

"That is a matter of opinion. Now, that point I was speaking of—"

"What would that be?"

"Why have you not proposed? Anne cannot understand it either. We have spoken at great length about it."

"Have you now! Well, let me reassure you both. I shall."

"Praised be!" Fitzwilliam grinned. "So, you have regained your senses. When?"

"When all this settles down," Darcy replied with a vague gesture towards his aunt's bedchamber, or at least in the direction where he assumed it lay. "Before the year is out. I promised Lady Catherine."

Fitzwilliam stared.

"You promised Lady Catherine you will offer for Miss Bennet?" he exclaimed. "And she is still alive? Good Lord, Darcy, have you set out to finish the poor old she-dragon off?"

"Are you a complete blockhead or merely feigning it for effect? Of course, I was speaking of offering for Anne!"

Fitzwilliam frowned.

"So, my rejoicing was for naught. You have not regained your senses."

He ignored his cousin's snort of exasperation and came to refill the glass Darcy had left on the mantelpiece, but forbore from being quite so conspicuous as to hand it to him outright. Instead, he walked back to set the decanter in its place and conversationally observed:

"I hold great hopes that one of these days you will tell me why you would still consider offering for Anne when you love another."

With a tired sigh, Darcy spread a hand over his brow and rubbed his temples.

"More fool me for hoping for a modicum of peace and quiet. Must I hide in my bedchamber to escape you after all?"

Fitzwilliam picked up his glass but did not drink. Instead he leaned against the sideboard and gave a careless wave.

"Rest easy, I know full well it will not be tonight. Pulling teeth is a vast deal easier than getting a full confession out of you. But speaking of fools and blockheads, you *are* a greater fool than you imagine if you have not seen she has no wish to marry you."

Darcy's eyes shot up in shock bordering on horror.

"You *knew!*" he burst out before he could help himself—not a question but an accusation. He reached for his refilled glass and downed a sizeable portion. "You might have said. Then why the devil are you goading me now?"

"Oh, smooth your ruffled feathers." The other chuckled. "You will have me thinking you are so conceited as to be offended at the mere thought of anyone refusing you."

"Offended!" Darcy glared. He was that, and injured by his cousin's callous manner, so much so that he could not hold back the same reproach. "You might have warned me."

The bitterness grew worse when Fitzwilliam merely shrugged.

"I am warning you now," he carelessly said at last. "Anne has not the slightest wish to marry you, so you might as well save yourself the trouble of proposing."

Anne! Darcy stopped himself at the last moment from saying the name aloud and withheld the relieved breath as well. It was Anne that Richard had in mind. He sipped his drink and turned away, grateful for small mercies.

"How do you know?" he asked, not really caring—just words, to distract the other from the near-loss of his composure.

"We talked about it. How else? That is what people do. You should try it now and then. It has its uses in ascertaining another person's thoughts. When one is so patently unable to read between the lines, that is. I wonder at you, Coz. Anne has made it plain as day for years that she has no intention of following in your mother's footsteps. Or Lady Catherine's, for that matter."

Darcy sipped his drink again, silently acknowledging the relief for what it was. Not only at the fact that his most painful secret was still safe and he was not forced into stark revelations yet but also at the intelligence Fitzwilliam had supplied. Anne did not wish for them to become united any more than he. Just as well. She was a good enough sort and fairly pleasant company, at least in Lady Catherine's absence, and it was far easier to imagine accepting her society, enjoying it even, now that he no longer had to contemplate the unpalatable prospect of marrying her—bedding her.

"Nevertheless, you should do her the courtesy of a frank discussion on the subject," Fitzwilliam said, and Darcy nodded. There was truth in that. "Between the pair of you"—his cousin resumed—"you should be able to determine how to best play your hands and break the news to Lady Catherine."

"How was she today?"

"Not well. She slept for rather too long due to the laudanum, but then she grew dreadfully restive. As you would imagine, she is not taking well to house arrest," he affectionately quipped. "Thank goodness for the company from the parsonage. By the bye, as to Miss Bennet's, I would call it stimulating rather than provoking. And not just for our aunt."

"You are not willing to let it rest, are you?" Darcy scowled over his shoulder.

The other grinned with disarming candour. "Of course not. When have you known me to?"

"Very well," Darcy replied through gritted teeth and abruptly set his glass down, making the amber liquid slosh and spill over the rim. Sadly, neither cared enough for Lady Catherine's sideboard to wipe the spillage—least of all Darcy, who turned to retrieve his discarded coat before striding to the door. He did not get there. Fitzwilliam stopped him with a hand on his arm. Every trace of teasing was gone from his eyes and countenance, leaving nothing but unmistakable affection.

There was deep affection in his voice as well, when he quietly observed:

"You can hide from me in your bedchamber if you wish, but where are you hoping to hide from yourself? Or from your feelings?"

"Lord Almighty, Richard!" Darcy groaned, the full burden of the hideous secret unbearable under his cousin unknowingly cruel jabs. He *could* speak out. And have Richard's pity to contend with. Surely it could not be worse than this!

Fitzwilliam let his hand drop.

"Never mind. I'll go. You can have the library and your so-called peace and quiet. But I beg you, Cousin, do yourself a favour and cease stumbling over difficulties of your own making. So, she has unremarkable connections and no fortune. But you must have seen she has everything else a man could wish for. See sense and secure her, and I daresay she will be the making of you yet."

She—will—not—have—me!

The anguished truth was battering to come out into the open—and, had they been safely away from Kent and the accursed Hunsford, Darcy would have given in and let it. But not here. Not now. Not when Richard would very likely see her on the morrow—and only Bingley was less poker-faced then he.

She had taxed him for his prideful manner. Very well. He had nothing left now but his pride. And he would rot in Hell before giving her the satisfaction of knowing she had reduced him to a pitiful wretch with her refusal!

The words that could not be allowed to leave his lips must have put such fire in his eyes that Fitzwilliam finally released his arm, took a step back and raised a hand as if to forestall an onslaught.

"Fine. I'll go," he muttered.

His breath laboured as though after a long run, Darcy stood watching his cousin walking to the door. But, hand on the handle, Fitzwilliam turned to face him.

"She asked about you," he quietly supplied.

"Did she?" Darcy bolted to attention.

"She did."

Darcy's lips tightened. Yet they still released the burning question:

"What did she wish to know?"

"How you were keeping."

"And what did you tell her?"

"Precisely what you have maintained for two days together: that you are concerned for Lady Catherine, but otherwise fine. What else?"

Darcy loosened his unconscious grip on his crumpled coat and dropped it on a chair.

"Thank you." Then his head snapped up. How the deuce had he neglected for two whole days to address that crucial matter? "Did she mention Wi— Georgiana?"

"No. Why should she? They are not acquainted, are they?"

"No." But as his cousin made to leave the library, Darcy stopped him yet again, little as he had imagined wishing to, only a minute earlier. "Richard, wait!"

"Yes?"

Darcy swallowed.

"If she— If Miss Bennet happens to ask you about … Ramsgate—tell her."

"What?" Fitzwilliam gaped.

"You heard me. Tell her. All of it."

A new warmth crept into his cousin's gaze.

"You would trust her with that?"

The reply came—crisp, brief, and without equivocation.

"I would."

Fitzwilliam's lips curled into an unexpected smile. But all he said was, "Very well." Then he quietly walked out.

There were only so many hours one could spend pacing—drinking—twisting an anguish that was already too old on every facet—before exhaustion of body and spirit claimed its dues. Darcy gave up pacing at long last to drop onto one of the sofas and eventually stretch across it, his head propped against the armrest.

The careful examination of his anguish engrossed him for a fair while longer as he lay there, in the oppressive quiet of the vast and pretentiously ornamented library, designed to impress rather than offer sanctuary or comfort. While he had often sought sanctuary in like manner in his own library at Pemberley or in Town, it had never crossed his mind to do so in his aunt's, least of all lie down—and not just because the surrounding show of opulence was as far from his notions of comfort as could be.

Yet now that the cat was bedridden with a broken ankle, the mouse would play. Or rather stare at a heavily ornate ceiling as unwelcome recollections of past encounters and sparkling exchanges perversely played before his eyes, over and over. Even before closed eyes. Even when the fire died out and the three candles in the candelabrum on the sideboard burned very low and came to be extinguished, one by one. Yet the darkness, the brandy, the punishing rides, and the previous restless nights finally worked together to bring merciful blankness. Without notice, Darcy drifted into dreamless sleep.

The dreamless state came to an abrupt end with a sound which in different circumstances he might have identified as the muted thud of a dropped book, followed by a softly-spoken "bother!" But the apparition was effortlessly recognised as she rose from the floor to stand before him, ethereal in the glow of a single candle. That she should still visit him was a surprise, but his unruly heart gave the same old twist. Consolation, was it to be, or eternal punishment? No matter. The visitation was achingly welcomed, either way.

"So, you are back," he could not help remarking, and the apparition started, turned, and gasped.

"Mr. Darcy!"

"Mr. Darcy, is it? Whatever happened to 'Fitzwilliam'?"

"I beg your pardon?"

"You used to call me by my given name."

"I never—"

"Oh, I beg to differ. You did, in all my dreams of you. Right from the beginning."

The vision froze then faltered.

"You…dream of me?"

"Every night. With excruciating clarity. Ever since Sir William's soiree. Or earlier. I cannot say. Nor does it matter."

"I am…distraught to hear it…"

"Are you?" Darcy sighed, or at least he thought he did, and ruefully resumed the surreal conversation. "I daresay it cannot be helped, this distress you speak of, and the return to 'Mr. Darcy.' Ever since *she* has made it crystal-clear she is violently against me, I suppose so must you be. A pity."

"She?"

"Your earthly form, safely asleep at the parsonage as we speak, I imagine, and knowing nothing of your exploits. It would be too much to hope that your visits mean she dreams of me while I dream of her."

"It would" —the vision quietly agreed.

"Oh, well … So, you have come to chastise me too?"

"No. I … I suppose this is as good a time as any to say that I … that she read your letter."

"Ah. And did she believe me?"

"Yes."

"Thank goodness for small mercies. I know she has not asked my cousin for confirmation. Just as well. It would only add fresh grist to his blasted mill. Hmm. I suppose I should beg your pardon for the language—"

"No need. It would be odd to apologise to the figment of one's imagination."

"Not necessarily. Speaking of which, pardon me for not doing you the courtesy of standing. But it would defy the object."

"Oh?"

"I would wake up and you would vanish."

"By all means, stay as you are. But…of what mill and grist were you speaking?"

"Richard's. And he needs no encouragement. He has made himself deuced unbearable already."

"How?"

"He pesters. All the time. Well-meaning but a nuisance with it. Cannot help it, the poor wretch, such is his way."

"Pesters?"

"Keeps telling me I cannot hide forever. That I should overcome my scruples and offer marriage. I had to hear it several times tonight."

"Oh. So, your cousin does not know…?"

"Lord, no! I could not tell him. Perhaps I should. Then at least he would stop reminding me you are the very best a man could hope for, and that you would be the making of me yet. As if I needed to be told. As if I have not known that for almost as long as I have known you—her … Forgive me. This is…confusing."

"Yes. It is."

"Knowing him, once he hears the rest of the sorry tale, he will have a vast deal more to say. That silent stares make for an odd courtship. That man was given words to speak his mind and open his heart. That I was the greatest fool in Christendom to denigrate my ladylove's relations in the same breath as offering for her. And he would not be wholly in the wrong there."

"That is as may be. But you still despise them and would have nothing to do with them if you could help it."

"I would have little to do with mine, given half the chance. Except Georgiana and Richard. Anne too, perhaps. As for the rest, heaven help us."

"Heaven help us indeed. Their opposition to the marriage would have brought you to your senses soon enough."

"Pardon?"

"Cured you of your infatuation."

"No change there, then." Darcy smiled. "Still contrary for your own amusement. You know full well it is not mere infatuation and that chance would be a fine thing to find myself cured, as you call it, anytime soon. Just as you know I could not forsake you. My family's opposition, your relations' improprieties. Small prices to pay for a lifetime with one's perfect match."

"Your perfect match?" —came the astounded whisper.

"You know you are, in everything that matters. Were … Would have been … Might be safe to say … Oh, confound it!"

"Shh … Never mind. Rest now" —the vision urged with something like the softness of old, and it could not fail to soothe him enough to make his lips curl up again. But this time, the smile was rueful rather than diverted.

"Oh, not that. Could not give a damn about finding the right words. I just thought it might be safe to say you will always be."

"I wish you would not say that!"

"Why not? Little as you care for it, we *are* perfectly matched. But disbelieve it, by all means, it might serve you better. For my part, I cannot. I have not felt thus, nor found your equal in all the years I have been old enough to wed. Longer, I imagine. Not since I began to notice dimpled smiles and pretty faces. What chance is there of it happening again? Of finding someone else just as bewitching? And challenging, downright infuriating, desirable, adorable, and everything that is honourable and good? If you come across another such paragon of grace, artlessness, and spirit in your night-time rambles, pray point me in her direction. But for now, it seems there is no escape. I love you, Elizabeth, and I am very much afraid I always will."

"With the utmost force of passion" —the apparition breathed.

"Just so. Have I already told you that?"

"You wrote it in your letter."

"Oh. I should have told you sooner."

"Yes…"

"Don't go. Not yet," he pleadingly whispered some time later, when the glow of her presence seemed to fade.

"I must. 'Tis very late."

"True. Too late," he agreed.

Lost in the gathering gloom, the apparition gasped. Or sobbed. He could not tell. Nor could it make the slightest difference to the agonising sense of loss that settled in his wasted heart.

"How's the head, Coz?"

Which one? Darcy felt vaguely inclined to quip but could not be bothered to follow through with it. He felt as if two more had sprouted on his shoulders overnight, and all three were now pounding. The grim rewards for unmitigated folly. As if the heartache was not bad enough. That dream, that impossibly perfect dream! As vivid as all the others, even in his befuddled state. And, just like all the others, leaving him bereft. As always, the details were hard to grasp as they flitted in and out of his memory. Despite every effort, as was the case with dreams, they were forgettable. The agony they left behind was anything but.

He supposed he should thank his cousin for turning up in the hours before dawn to coax him above stairs into his bedchamber, so that Lady Catherine's servants would not discover him slumbering in the library. He would thank him. Eventually. When he could face stringing the necessary words together.

"I take it that you will not go riding this morning."

Heavens above! Riding? With three pounding heads?

"No."

"Good. Stay put. Who knows what might happen to bring you to your senses."

Darcy gritted his teeth.

"I beg you would not start again. Not now. I have not the stomach for it."

"That, I do not doubt. Not on a weakened stomach, and an empty one, I'd wager. Muffin?"

Darcy's weakened stomach heaved.

"I thank you, no. Coffee will do."

"Fine." Fitzwilliam set the plate of toasted muffins back on the table. "Nevertheless, you might wish to know that—"

But Darcy was of the firm opinion that he did *not* wish to hear anything that Fitzwilliam saw the need to preface with "nevertheless."

"Is Anne coming down?" he swiftly asked.

"No. She chose to break her fast above stairs with Lady Catherine and Miss Bennet."

The little coffee Darcy had drunk threatened to make its way back up his gullet.

"She is here?"

"She is. Spent the night, in fact. Reading to Lady Catherine."

"What?"

No—no—no … No! She did not … Was not … Good Lord in Heaven! Did she?

The utter shock and the flurry of mindless speculations muffled Fitzwilliam's quiet words and Darcy caught precious little of his cousin's explanation. Still, whatever he did register served to sufficiently clarify the matter. Lady Catherine could not sleep. Had dozed off for most of the day in a haze of laudanum, and at night, she had been wide awake. Asked for Mrs. Collins to come and read to her. Miss Bennet came instead so that her friend could rest. She came. Spent the night reading to Lady Catherine. And very likely went to fetch a fresh stock from the library. Not a figment of his imagination. Real. There. *No!*

"Darcy? Are you unwell? Here, leave that coffee and have a glass of water."

He could not spare either words or thoughts for his cousin plying him with water and goodness knows what else, as though he were a damsel about to swoon. Laughable under normal circumstances.

There was nothing normal about his current ones. And nothing remotely diverting either.

Mist swirled around Lady Catherine's topiary, turning it into a hazy and nightmarish landscape. Fitting. Uncannily so. As hazy as his numb brain felt, and as nightmarish as his day had become ever since he had learnt the mortifying truth from Richard. She had been there in flesh. Heard everything—whatever he had seen fit to carelessly disclose. Why she had stooped to perpetrating the deception … he had not the strength to contemplate as yet. Not now, when he could only look upon his miserable state over the last few days with longing and nothing short of envy. He still had his pride then. Until last night when, having blabbed so uncontrollably, he had denied himself even that refuge. She knew everything now. Good Lord above!

It was not cowardice to skulk in the gardens rather than seek her out—*was it?* They could not speak in Lady Catherine's bedchamber, for goodness' sake! And even if she left her post and he found the means for private conversation, what on earth was there to say that he had not blurted out already?

He still had no answers—not even when, patently braver by far, half an hour later Elizabeth came to find him.

Darcy sifted through the oppressive fog of convoluted thoughts for any words that might suit the purpose as he watched her picking her way towards him through Lady Catherine's misty garden. A slender form wrapped in a dark cloak that billowed behind her—very much like another apparition, the impression enhanced by their eerie surroundings.

All manner of sentiments warred in his breast as he sought to conquer the crippling mix of yearning and mortification brought by the hazy memory of last night's visitation. All the words he might have selected—inadequate as they were—fled at her approach, just like the small flock of easily-frightened sparrows disturbed from their hideout in the topiary. He chased after them nevertheless—the words, not the sparrows—with as little success in catching the first as he might have had with the latter. And before he could do else but bow and say her name, the civil and socially acceptable "Miss Bennet" this time, she shocked him further with her unexpected expressions of contrition.

"Mr. Darcy, I came to apologise for my conduct yesterday—"

"There is no—" But she would have none of it.

"There is every need. I took advantage of the situation in an unpardonable manner. I should have instantly corrected your misapprehension."

"Pray do not trouble yourself over it," Darcy interjected, more forcefully than he had intended. It was beyond him to take his own advice, but as he fought to suppress a grimace, he also sought to lose some of the sternness, lest his tone be construed as resentful or reproachful. He was vaguely successful in his efforts when he added, "Sadly, there is nothing either of us could say or do to erase the wretched episode, much as I would wish to."

"You would?" she tentatively asked, her voice very subdued.

"At this point in time, more than anything," Darcy retorted hotly. "You already think so very ill of me and you certainly did not need another reason." He saw her open her lips to speak, but he would not be dissuaded from firmly adding, "For all that it is worth, pray let me assure you, I do not make a habit of intemperance to the point of losing my senses."

"Oh, I know that!" she hastily replied, then grew hesitant again. "I am distraught you were driven to it yesterday. But you have not lost your senses. Just … your reserve."

"That is very nearly as bad!"

"You think so?"

"Do you not?"

She shook her head, once; then her eyes flashed up at him and she put her negation into words.

"No. I think reserve serves very ill sometimes, and this is one of the occasions. I should not wish to let reserve prevent me from saying what *must* be said."

"And that is?" Darcy cautiously inquired.

"That I am heartily ashamed of how abominably I have acted," she replied with energy, her troubled eyes not veering from his. "I have allowed vanity to lure me into grievous misjudgement. I cannot apologise enough for abusing you in defence of an infamous villain."

The look in her eyes and the warmth of her declaration made his chest tighten. His breath caught and his heart lurched insanely into joy, before he checked the misguided emotion and spoke up to absolve her from unmerited self-reproach.

"You could not have known any of the particulars and suspicion is not in your nature. I suppose ..." He sighed and reluctantly resumed. "I suppose I should have told you sooner. Put you on your guard against him. Yet—"

"You had your sister's reputation to consider. I understand, and I thank you for your trust in revealing this to me. You may be assured, I will not breathe a word of it to another soul."

Darcy nodded in quiet gratitude, and all that he could say was:

"Yes. I know."

Her glance drifted to the mound of verdure to her left—to her joined hands—her feet. A deep shadow was settled in her eyes when she finally looked up again. "Your sister ... Is she…recovered?"

Darcy's eyes narrowed into an involuntary wince.

"No," he replied curtly as he looked away. Somehow, the respite from trying to ascertain her thoughts in every play of emotion on her features moved him into elaborating. "She is not. She seeks to put up a brave front and go on as she always had, but the pain is there still; the insecurity, the injured feelings. She cannot hide any of this, much as she tries."

"Yes. I know your meaning. I have seen it—"

She broke off, and this time it was Darcy's turn to voice her thoughts for her.

"In your own sister," he said, only to see her bite her lip, her countenance a picture of the deepest sadness.

The last time she had spoken to him of Miss Bennet's disappointed hopes and broken heart, it had been with bitterness and barely restrained anger. The pained look she cast him now was a thousand times worse. Her distress—his—Bingley's—Miss Bennet's—who was served by the never-ending misery? He knew the answer now. No one. Except perhaps Bingley's sisters. Just as he knew that his was the greatest share of the blame. Bingley would have ignored his sisters' ambitious request that he attach himself to a lady of greater consequence and fortune. It had been his own belief in Miss Bennet's indifference that had carried the most weight.

"You wish I had not interfered," Darcy said, and he could see her nod.

"I do."

"So do I." It was the truth, God help him, and she might as well know it. "Ever since you told me of your sister's true sentiments for Bingley, I cannot think without abhorrence of the pain I have unwittingly caused them both—of having played the villain's part there. It is not a welcome thought."

"I should imagine not." She sighed. "But you still wrote that you have not yet learnt to condemn your motives."

Old mannerisms from the days when he was a nervous schoolboy summoned by the headmaster resurfaced unbidden, yet Darcy was in no frame of mind to recognise them as such as he tugged unnecessarily at his waistcoat, his gaze fixed on the ribbon tied under her chin, until he raised it to her eyes with a determined effort.

"That letter" —he valiantly began— "was written in a dreadful bitterness of spirit. I believed myself perfectly calm and cool, but I was severely mistaken. I hope you have destroyed it. There are parts of it which I dread your having the power of reading again."

"I have not burnt it, but I will do so if you wish," she whispered softly.

There was a new softness in her eyes as well—was there not? And warmth followed, gradually seeping in. He could almost see it. They used to sparkle with mischief. On that wretched day, they had burned with contempt and anger. This was…

His chest filled with much-needed air, and his senses with the dizzying proximity of the most beautiful eyes he had ever seen. Never so close, in the whole course of their acquaintance. Never so warm either. And never this—a long, unbroken gaze that drew him in and thoroughly robbed him of his caution. The words were out, unfiltered, before he could check them.

"I do. The facts are unchanged, and I will not have you question their veracity. Only the sentiments that went with them. You spoke of my claim that I have not learnt to condemn my motives. In truth, I have learnt a vast deal since the morning when I wrote that letter. Among other things, that I must be lacking in imagination. Even as I saw Bingley pining for your sister after our return to Town, I had not grasped how he must feel. I have lately discovered I should neither wish nor work to inflict that sort of pain on anyone. Least of all, one of my closest friends."

"Mr. Darcy, I—"

Her quiet gasp and truncated exclamation belatedly returned him to his senses. What the devil was he doing—saying? A short while ago he had watched her approach through the mist-shrouded garden feeling backed in a corner and mortified in the extreme by last night's debacle. Yet there he was now blurting out words which might seem calculated to elicit pity—the last sentiment he had ever wished to inspire in her! Before he could sink further into a mire of his own making, Darcy added swiftly:

"Pray, set your heart at rest in that regard. I … I sought to make amends. By now Bingley must have received my letter informing him I was utterly in the wrong about your sister's sentiments. Knowing him, he will be at Longbourn in no time at all."

"You wrote to him? Already?" Elizabeth asked with a beatific smile that took his breath away. And then she chuckled lightly. "Poor Mr. Bingley. I fear he will have a wasted journey. I hope he can bear the disappointment."

Darcy stared, nonplussed. Clearly, he never had a hope of understanding her, for all his prideful confidence to the contrary. There was no rational connection between her light-hearted, almost blissful manner, and the dispiriting picture her words had just conjured.

"I fail to understand your meaning," he frankly owned. "I thought you implied your sister would welcome his addresses."

"She would, with all her heart. But she is not at Longbourn. She is still visiting my uncle and aunt in Town. That is to say in … Cheapside."

She eyed him squarely as she concluded, her countenance suddenly closed and guarded. He silently cursed the cloud that had dimmed the precious brightness of a few moments ago, along with what he had done to put it there—the abysmal choice of words at the time of his ill-starred proposal. His features tightened into a grimace of profound discomfort as he spoke up to give her her due.

"When your sister was taken ill at Netherfield and you came to care for her, my friend most astutely pointed out that having relations to fill all of Cheapside would not make either of you one jot less agreeable," Darcy quietly offered, then bit his lip. Not so much at the recollection of his reply to Bingley's warm avowal, little as he appreciated the irony of Fate and the perverse ways it chose to deliver punishment by humbling the prideful. Rather, it belatedly occurred to him he might well have made yet another *faux pas* and instead of taking it as the compliment it was meant to be, Elizabeth might find his remark vexingly condescending.

He fully expected her to purse her lips and mordantly deliver something along the lines of "How very generous of him—and you—to say so!"

She did purse her lips as she searched his troubled eyes. And before she could tax him yet again for prideful conceit, Darcy hastened to forestall her:

"I should have worded it better. Forgive me. It was … intended as a compliment," he added, narrowing his eyes and nervously running his fingers through his hair, only to instantly wish that he had not. His headache had only marginally abated.

The little smile that curled her lips and crinkled the corners of her eyes could not do much against the headache, but was vastly more effective on the dull ache in his chest, as was the mildness of her brief reply—when she finally made one.

"I know," she whispered.

More than anything, it was the mellow glance and the hint of gentle laughter in her voice that emboldened him to continue with a tentative attempt at a self-conscious smile.

"It seems I have a vast deal to learn about passable compliments and avowals from my best friend and my cousin. Fitzwilliam will doubtlessly say that only the greatest fool in Christendom would abuse a lady's relations in the midst of his proposal."

"Yes, you mentioned that."

"Did I? When?"

"Last night."

"Oh."

Darcy cleared his voice. This was unsound, wildly hazardous and beyond mortifying, but he *had* to know.

"Might I ask what else I said?"

"You do not remember…?"

Was there wistfulness in her voice? Or condemnation? Either way, the heat of a profuse blush spread up from behind his collar.

"To my discredit, I must own I cannot tell the difference between reality and fantasy."

She dropped her gaze and a severe blush crept into her cheeks as well, giving such a glow to her beloved countenance that yearning swelled to take over his heart and easily prevail over the mortification.

"That bad, was it?" he found himself asking with a rueful little twitch of his lips that masqueraded as a smile.

She did not return it, but her eyes shot back towards his, and they glowed too.

"You said you dreamt of me. Every night since November. With excruciating clarity."

"That was badly put, and far from the truth," Darcy replied with fervour, deciding he might as well be hanged for the whole hog now that they were so far beyond equivocation. "The clarity is not excruciating. In truth, it brings a measure of comfort. As last night did. And I should thank you for your kindness."

Lord above! There he was again! What had come over him and taken command of his wretched tongue? Darcy sighed in profound exasperation as he ran his fingers through his hair once more, forgetting he had already deemed it patently unwise. But the giddiness that overcame him had little to do with the nervous gesture. Rather, it was promptly ascribed to the rightful cause: the small hand that came to rest on his sleeve and press his arm in an unexpected offer of reassurance and comfort.

Instinctively, Darcy reached to cover it with his. Thin fingers, delicate and very cold. His hand curled around them as he desperately sought to rally whatever was left of his scattered senses before he said the wrong thing at the wrong time—again!

Her soft reply put paid to all his efforts:

"I would not wholeheartedly agree with your cousin's censure. My ill-judged defence of Mr. Wickham must have been more than sufficient provocation for some of your remarks."

Had Darcy been able to spare his nemesis more than a moment's thought, he might have found it quite extraordinary that for the first time since their early days at Cambridge the mention of his name brought pure and unadulterated pleasure. She was willing to excuse his ungentlemanly outburst on account of her defence of a loathed, suspected rival?

Yet the dizzying heights of hope were not heady enough to render him less than truthful.

"You are too generous. But that cannot justify my speaking of our … of the envisaged union as a degradation in the same breath as professions of ardent love and admiration. That was sheer ineptitude and, as you have rightly pointed out, selfish disdain for the feelings of others. I aimed to assure you of the strength of my regard, that it was not the work of a moment, nor passing inclination but deep devotion conquering any and all difficulties. Had I thought more of your feelings and less of mine, I would have seen it was the worst possible manner of offering marriage."

Her hand was no longer on his sleeve. He had gathered it to cradle it in his as, once more, he found himself drawn deeper and irremediably lost in dark eyes specked with golden amber.

The amber suddenly began to shimmer under a film of tears, and when she blinked, a glistening droplet escaped to run over her cheek. His free hand came up, and Darcy brushed the single tear with his thumb. Her skin was very soft and very cool, the earlier blush gone without a trace. Pale cheeks, impossibly wide eyes, a puff of air—the beginnings of a sigh—escaping from trembling lips.

His hand froze with the desperate effort of not reaching to cup her chin and tilt it up, nor winding into her auburn tresses to draw her close and claim those trembling lips with his. His breath caught and Darcy drew his hand back by a fraction, lest he succumb to the achingly sweet temptation, but could not quite bring himself to drop it yet. Rational thought governing words and actions was slipping further and further from his grasp—and Darcy lost the battle altogether when his poised hand was covered with hers and pressed against her cheek.

A sharp intake of breath—his?—hers?—filled the air between them, and every hope of sanity and guarded conduct vanished with it. His lips crushed on hers with all the accumulated hunger of the many months of longing for the exquisite indulgence, with all the despair of the agonising days since he had lost her.

If this was madness, then so be it. Sense had nothing to recommend it anyway, not when measured against this sweet insanity that spiralled into absolute perfection when her hands came up to clasp his shoulders, then tangled into his hair, and when her lips matched the wild fervour of his as they responded to his kisses. He clasped her closer—could not even tell how he had come to take her in his arms—and still devoured her lips, past caring and well beyond the reach of reason.

Of all the powers under Heaven, there was only one that could make him stop; and that was the compulsion to plead, "Elizabeth, let me start again. Do it right. Court you. Make you love me. Persuade you I cannot live without you and I cannot even bring myself to try. I—"

She stopped him with a kiss—with several—and between them she eagerly whispered, "Yes!" And then again— "Oh, yes. I will."

Barely daring to believe his ears and allow awed delight into his already brimming heart, Darcy drew back to search her eyes and seek the desperately needed confirmation:

"You will allow me to court you?"

Her eyes were very bright and still shimmering with unshed tears, and their glow took his breath away. But it was her words that brought him reeling onto the brink of a brand-new world:

"I will marry you," she fervently replied. "Let it be said it was a whirlwind courtship. Let it also be called unwise. But in mere hours, I saw deeper into your heart than in several months of my slow and misguided wisdom."

His hungry lips found hers again—a blissful, tangible reality in a world that had become almost too perfect to be true. It was some time until he could bring himself to draw away again, but no further than to rest his brow on hers. He was a fool to ask, now that he had everything he had ever dreamt of, he knew as much. Yet he also knew he had to.

"My love, are you absolutely certain? Three days ago, I was the last man in the world whom you could be prevailed upon to marry. If you need more time, Elizabeth, I could… I *would* wait"—he amended, if only to be truthful.

Her hand came up to stroke his face.

"I think I have already learnt everything I needed to." Then she glanced up and laughed through her tears. "Besides, it seems we have little choice in the matter, and a lengthy and decorous courtship is no longer an option."

"Oh?"

Puzzled, he followed her gaze and they stood cheek to cheek to look up together in the direction she had indicated. Laughter rumbled in his chest. Despite the swirls of mist shrouding the house, he could easily spot Fitzwilliam watching them from what must have been the drawing room windows. Two frames to the left, in the music room most likely, there was Anne watching them as well. Fitzwilliam gave him a mock salute, then had a cheerful bow for his future cousin. Anne was grinning widely—unheard-of for her—and, when spotted, she gave them an impudent little wave, then vanished from her post. Fitzwilliam was more laggard in showing the same courtesy, but at long last he did. Darcy chuckled and was about to seal his most public betrothal with another kiss when movement at one of the windows above the *piano nobile* chanced to catch his eye. He squinted for a better look, only to discover Mrs. Jenkinson, her impassive countenance altered beyond recognition into wicked, positively vicious glee. She did not school her features into a different sentiment, nor showed any remorse at being found there, but merely walked away—and, throwing his head back, Darcy burst into unholy laughter.

"What amuses you so, my love?" Elizabeth asked, and the breathtakingly exquisite novelty of the appellation made this completely the wrong time for Darcy to explain how he had suddenly learnt that the quiet Mrs. Jenkinson was in Anne's full confidence about her matrimonial intentions, or rather lack thereof, and also that she heartily detested Lady Catherine.

So, he only said, "Come," and taking her hand, he led his future wife away from the house and from prying eyes.

"Where are we going?" he heard her ask as they were losing themselves deeper and deeper into the misty garden.

He turned to her and squeezed her hand.

"Do you trust me?"

"Implicitly," Elizabeth replied with an impish little smile and a look of such warmth that he was filled anew with love for her, and a boundless joy his heart could scarce encompass.

She did trust him. She had just entrusted him with her heart and her future. Thus, out of character as it might have been for the solemn young master of Pemberley, particularly in the manicured gardens of Rosings, Darcy lifted his future bride to twirl her in a playful circle, before leading her into an alcove so abundant in greenery as to ensure they had all the privacy a newly-engaged couple might have ever hoped for.

He did not dwell on entertaining thoughts, such as how little he had imagined in his boyhood, when he had first discovered this alcove's uses in hiding him from Lady Catherine and her minions, that twenty years later it would shelter him and the woman he adored. Or what Lady Catherine might say if she ever heard of the practical uses he had just found for her pretentious topiary. He would amuse Elizabeth with those notions later. For now, the warmth of her embrace and the intoxicating thrill of her kisses was sufficient inducement to forget a vast deal more than Lady Catherine and her mist-shrouded garden.

By the time they felt compelled to return to the house lest Fitzwilliam and Anne no longer be able to prevent Her Ladyship from sending out a search party led by Mr. Collins, spears of cheerful sunlight were already piercing the suffocating mist that had been hanging for too long over Rosings.

JOANA STARNES lives in the south of England with her family. Over the years, she has swapped several hats—physician, lecturer, clinical data analyst—but feels most comfortable in a bonnet. She has been living in Georgian England for decades in her imagination and plans to continue in that vein till she lays hands on a time machine. She is the author of seven Austen-inspired novels: *From This Day Forward—The Darcys of Pemberley*, *The Subsequent Proposal*, *The Second Chance*, *The Falmouth Connection*, *The Unthinkable Triangle*, *Miss Darcy's Companion*, and *Mr Bennet's Dutiful Daughter*. You can connect with Joana through her website joanastarnes.co.uk and on Facebook via her timeline and her author page, *All Roads Lead to Pemberley*.

Their eyes instantly met, and the cheeks of each were overspread with the deepest blush. He absolutely started, and for a moment seemed immoveable from surprise.
—Chapter XLIII.

CLANDESTINY

KARALYNNE MACKRORY

"Are you consulting your own feelings in the present case, or do you imagine that you are gratifying mine?"

It took quite an estimable degree of effort but I managed to keep my expression to a raised brow. *What was Miss Elizabeth about?* Though her own admixture of pertness and challenge was, as always, entirely bewitching, I had begun to suspect tonight's performance contained a bit more of an edge. Her sharp tongue, delightful as it was, was aimed with precision at myself. The dance afforded me a moment's reflection after my riposte, as the ladies performed a fleuret, allowing me the pleasure of seeing Elizabeth truly glide through the movement, the ribbons hanging down from her bodice the length of the gown accenting her trim waist, before she again placed her delicate hand upon my own gloved one.

I kept my gaze forward, as was proper for the dance, but could not help noticing the twitch of her lips as she then answered my question.

"Both," replied Elizabeth archly, "for I have always seen a great similarity in the turn of our minds. We are each of an unsocial, taciturn disposition; unwilling to speak, unless we expect to say something that will amaze the whole room, and be handed down to posterity with all the éclat of a proverb."

Clever girl. Clever, teasing girl. It was all that I could do not to tug on the four fingers within my own and prompt her to stumble into my own *unsocial* arms, the amazement of the whole room be damned. She was like a heady drink I could not seem to refuse. Even now as she smugly arched her brow at me, her neck curving up to my inspection as she anticipated my reply—God in Heaven, but she was temptation personified!

What was she about though, to be flirting so, in full view of the room? I began to suspect the warmth climbing up my neck to be less from the exertions of the dance and more from the ministrations of a certain lady's carefully, though publicly, performed allurements. I experienced a moment's pang for this most certain evidence of her raised expectations—

ones I absolutely could not fulfill—before I stamped them from my consciousness. This was to be a onetime indulgence. One dance—before adding the healing balm of many miles between this siren and myself as I left Netherfield on the morrow.

"This is no very striking resemblance of your own character, I am sure," said I. "How near it may be to *mine*, I cannot pretend to say." I paused, pleased with the stirring of something in her regard at my words. "*You* think it a faithful portrait undoubtedly."

She made her reply, though it was, to my disappointment, a conciliating statement to end the debate. We resumed our attention upon the dance, though it was not long before I soon began to crave her attention again. I was like a jealous animal finding her consideration not upon myself but on the dance. I watched her from the edge of my vision, begging her in my thoughts to speak again. This need to engage with her had built since her stay at Netherfield to nurse Miss Bennet, and I had not got the better of it, as evidenced by the building pressure in my chest. It felt similar to when my cousin Richard and I would go diving at Black Moss Pot in the Lake District. My lungs felt apt to burst, the pressure building as I kicked off the rock at the bottom and raised my head to watch the water's surface come closer. Up and up I rose, with each foot's ascent bringing more pressure upon my lungs for air until, with a burst of energy, I expelled my breath as the water broke across my face.

I had to speak then if she would not. I had to have that breath of air that her attention gave me. I could no longer countenance her studied attentiveness on the backs of the dancers ahead of us.

With a rush of words that sounded to my ears like a burst through the surface, I called forth her eyes to mine with, "Do you often walk to Meryton?"

She considered me for a moment before answering, and her eyes upon mine were like great gulps of air to my hypoxemic soul. I trampled down that voice in my mind that registered the suffocation I would feel when I left.

She spoke then and I was very nearly too caught up in the pleasure of the sound to register its meaning. Something about a new acquaintance. I forced my mind to shift from the pleasure of memorizing her countenance to reflect upon our last meeting in Meryton.

Chest constricting again, this time having nothing to do with Elizabeth's allure, the heat rising up my neck now spoke not of her tempting presence but of the dawning realization of her allusion to *him*. I shuddered as anger rippled through my frame, my manifold effort to disguise my reaction to her words barely succeeding. *God, do not let me hear his name pass her lips*, I pled in a silent prayer. To have *him* in Meryton, of all places, was a cruel twist of fate, and I had once again an admixture of pain, anger, and betrayal swirling in my gut at the remembrance of seeing *him* beside her on the streets of this insignificant town. Of seeing *him* smiling cavalierly at me as he tipped his hat, as if he had not attempted to shatter my world some months back.

I happened to glance at Elizabeth then; the question in her eyes was not enough to pull me from the black anger within. However, the slightest of a pinch about her eyes settled me enough to prepare a controlled response. She glanced briefly to our clasped hands, and it was then that I realized my grip had become quite firm. Immediately, I lessened the pressure upon her small fingers, remorse flowing into the arterial pathways wherein the anger and hate had traversed. It was enough for me to reply with tolerable control.

"Mr. Wickham is blessed with such happy manners as may ensure his *making* friends—whether he may be equally capable of *retaining* them, is less certain."

I was pleased with my response. It spoke the truth without betraying the agitated state of my mind. Elizabeth seemed to digest it with some measure of incredulity. What poison could the scoundrel have administered to her in such a short acquaintance?

"He has been so unlucky as to lose *your* friendship," Elizabeth replied with emphasis, and I felt my jaw clench painfully. "And in a manner which he is likely to suffer from all his life."

Though I wished most of all to change the topic, at once regretting and condemning this addiction I have for her attention that prompted me to speak at all, I could not allow such a statement to go unanswered. Wickham, how even his name upon my thoughts was vile, did not deserve her sympathy. I could not stand the thought of it. Drawing a deep breath, I prepared to warn her when we were interrupted by that circus master of a man, Sir William.

Our dance being interrupted to hear him speak nonsense was at once a distasteful reminder of the backward manners of this little hamlet—a welcome reminder. A quick assessment of Elizabeth revealed she too was displeased by the interruption. The side of my mouth quirked up slightly into a smile as I saw that, despite our previous topic, she did not wish to be kept from her dance with me. It was attuned exactly to be the antidote I needed to eradicate the toxin Wickham was to my sensibilities. I took pleasure in watching as her cheeks, pinked already from our exertions, warmed further at something Sir William said, her eyes dropping to the tips of her dancing slippers. My eyes followed to her toes only briefly before my ears, curious as to what could prompt Elizabeth's blush, attuned to Sir William's droning again.

Much to my surprise he was alluding, quite astoundingly, to the possibility of a marriage. Surely not! I could not have been so transparent as that. But no, he was speaking of Bingley and Miss Bennet. The relief that coursed through me then was great, even if it brought with it a stain of disappointment. My eyes followed to the subjects in question. I saw my friend standing nearby the fair Miss Bennet in what was clearly a proprietary manner. My eyes narrowed at the impression that, if Sir William was bold enough to voice, was surely on the minds of every attendant at this ball.

I felt her eyes upon me then, and I hoped that my concerns on the match did not show. It would not do to be so public about them. I did not wish to embarrass my friend nor the lady by being so blatant. I turned slowly to meet her scrutiny, confused by the darkened look in her eyes.

Sir William left us and we haltingly resumed what was left of our dance. Elizabeth was no longer the spritely, engaging partner of before the interruption, nor was she the impassioned defender of Wi—*him*, thank God in Heaven.

It should have troubled me to have been prevented from warning her regarding my former friend, but I could not find it in me to feel anything but relief to have had the topic dropped so ceremoniously. I could not like giving *him* anymore of my time with her. But, though we attempted further discourse, it was for naught. I was not so entirely master of myself to propose new topics for conversation, and she did not seem inclined to offer either.

I half-heartedly suggested books, to which she archly replied it to be preposterous. I felt a tinge of affection for her further weave itself into my heart at her attempt at playfulness and at her avowal that a discussion of books was impossible in a ballroom. The only remaining pleasure I took in our dance was then to have her claim a wish to understand my character.

The moment came when the orchestra rested and she boldly faced me full on. Her shoulders were square and pressed back, giving her figure the full benefit of a woman's beauty. Desire slinked up from my feet, consuming me as it burned a path through my whole body. It was torture. It was pleasure. But alas, reason surfaced and I could acknowledge: it was not for me. I hardly remember my reply, though it contained something of a warning to not sketch my character yet, plus a vague implication of future opportunities providing better results—although I knew it to be a lie. There was no future for us, no chance for better understanding. Though it felt like a pervasive ache in my chest to accept, this was my last evening with her.

Of a sudden, I could take no more and felt the urgent need for solitude and distance. I bowed to her deeply, for I could not do otherwise to her—to the Elizabeth of my heart. I left her with her relations and began to stalk around the outside of the room, hoping that this agitation and unrest of my heart would slack with the distance, with the familiar.

I had only accepted that I could not regain my equilibrium in company and needed the refuge of my private study, a small room encapsulated at the end of the corridor that Bingley had granted for my personal use, when I was accosted again. This time by a stout clergyman I had never seen before.

He began, much to my surprise, to introduce *himself.* It was the most disgraceful display of manners I had ever been so unfortunate to witness in all my seven and twenty years. My shock became my ally for it kept me from displaying equally distasteful manners in the form of a severe cut to this presumptuous oaf.

I registered that he spoke of my aunt Catherine, his benefactress it seemed. That explained, perhaps, his wish to speak to me but did not account for his lack of proper introduction. I regained enough of my countenance to attempt to excuse myself *twice* but to no avail. So great was my agitation now that I could scarcely have held back the sharp retort and set down that was at once on the edge of my tongue when the little man again stunned me by uttering *her* name.

" . . . your dance with Miss Elizabeth, my fair cousin . . . " He buzzed on; his words once again lost to my thoughts.

Mr. Collins. His name. A cousin of Miss Elizabeth? My eyes instinctively searched the room for her. My heart stumbled a few beats as they connected with the steady gaze of Elizabeth, looking directly at me. Our eyes seemed locked for a moment and I could see within hers mortification and a building fire. The mortification I could understand—for her relations were truly awful. But the fire—the anger—I could not. My legs, of their own accord, stepped towards her when she broke eye contact and, with a dip of her head, she began towards the ballroom's exit.

"You'll excuse me, sir." I tossed back at the parson as I began my circulatory pursuit of Elizabeth. What madness had consumed me, I know not, but I was compelled to go after her. My heart racing, I was nearly upon her. Alas, the last I saw was her long, lavender ribbon slip through the door before it closed behind her.

When I reached the doors, some impulse stopped me. My hand was raised and pressed against the grain of the wood, though my legs would not go further. My heart began to beat fiercely at the manner in which I had nearly lost myself. Coolly, I turned around, and it was confirmed that at least the boorish parson had registered my single-minded pursuit of

Elizabeth, for his eyes were upon me. I could not go to her now, not just for her reputation—it censured every logical thought my poor, addlepated mind could throw out in the fight against my heart.

Instead, though the desire to escape to my study once again gripped me so fiercely I could hardly think of anything else, I backed against the wall near the exit for a few minutes. I would make my own exit soon enough, though not so close to Elizabeth's as to cause suspicion.

When enough time had elapsed, I slipped out of the ballroom; the coolness of the hallway compared to the hot press of bodies within was a sudden surprise. To my surprise, Elizabeth had not gone far, or I had not waited as long as I had suspected, because I witnessed that same fluttering ribbon following her again around the right side of the large staircase, down the corridor that led to the ladies' retirement room.

Though temptation once again flared inside me, reason had enough of my mind to allow me to choose wisely—and take the corridor to the left of the staircase instead and all the way back to the dark wooden door to my refuge.

I closed the door behind me and turned the key to lock it, though I knew it was not necessary. Not even Bingley had sought me out in this sanctuary. The stillness of the room was at once exactly suited to calm my agitated state. Never in my life had I experienced so many fluctuations in my feelings as I had in that last hour.

The room was cool, though a fire was in the grate. I again compared it to the heat of the ballroom and was refreshed. Despite the welcome change in temperature, I stirred the coals and added a few pieces of wood. The light that the newly fed fire gave to the room was sufficient to reach even the furthest recesses.

I pulled at the restrictions of my tailcoat and managed to remove it without difficulty. The chill kissed the slightly dampened and wrinkled arms of my shirtsleeves as I draped the garment across a chair by the fire.

The distant sound of girlish laughter echoed, ghost-like, through the wall behind me. Turning, I studied the plain paneling of the blank wall there. The other side of that must be near enough to the ladies' retirement room to have allowed some of the occupants' pleasure to sound through.

I wondered at once if one of the ladies whose laughter came weakly through the wall was Elizabeth. While she looked to have been upset upon her hasty retreat from the ballroom, perhaps I had been mistaken and she simply needed a break from the heat. Slowly, I walked to a nearby decanter of spirits and poured myself a small measure in a crystal glass. As I brought the dark liquid to my lips, I allowed myself the pleasure of thinking of Elizabeth, laughing with her companions, her eyes lit with sparkling, good humor as her natural joie de vivre shone through her countenance.

Abruptly, I forced my thoughts in another direction. I did not like this feeling inside me. This out-of-control madness that had taken over my carefully cultivated reserve. Never in my life had a woman so disturbed me. With her, I could not think, act, or feel in a reasonable manner. It was as if she had weaseled her way into my organized world and thrown it into chaos—complete and utter chaos.

I rested an arm heavily on the mantel as the other came up to attempt to dislodge the lump in my throat with a hefty gulp from my glass; the burn from the liquor entirely ineffective at its job.

"Elizabeth," I whispered to the room.

I did not want to admit it, but I believed that I had gone far from admiring the lady. My affections had spiraled out of control, growing into a living, breathing thing—growing into love.

I felt the blood drain from my face, despite the heat from the fire pressing me.

"I cannot. It is not possible."

But I knew it to be true.

With shuddering breath, I raised the glass to my lips again, only to find it empty. When had I finished it? No matter, its contents had made me numb, or was that the recent revelation?

My other hand placed the glass upon the mantel and provided balance as the surge of realization made me feel weak. There I stayed, gripping the marble as if on the edge of a cliff, unable or unwilling to let go to the inevitable. So jumbled were the rushing thoughts in my mind that I barely registered the creak of wood and whine of long unused hinges.

But the feminine gasp behind me most certainly caught my attention.

I whirled around towards the blank wall, the very one I had studied moments before as I wondered if Elizabeth was the source of laughter behind it. Only this time, it was not empty paneling but an alarmed and white-faced Elizabeth!

Her hands were splayed wide against the wall, arms and body pressed against it. Her chest was heaving, the rapid breaths doing nothing to bring back the color of her startled and disbelieving face.

Mine, I could venture to say, would not have looked much different, though I dared not turn to the looking glass above the mantel behind me to confirm. Seeing Elizabeth before me, in my own study, was much too much a shock to risk looking away. Together we stood staring for what could only have been a moment but felt like a strange, never-ending dream.

I dared a quick glance to the door, the key still turned in the lock. Even as the thought registered through my mind that she had followed me and slipped in the door, I dismissed it. Impossible! I had locked the door myself and could now see with my own eyes that it remained so.

"How?"

She whimpered, nearly just a squeak of her own in response, and stupidly I looked again at the door.

"Pardon me," I blurted, and bowed—ingrained rules of propriety falling into place in the absence of anything rational. "Excuse me, but . . . how?"

Elizabeth—I saw—parted her lips to speak and my eyes were drawn unwaveringly toward them. They were pale like her face, and absurdly, I felt the wish to kiss them into color. What a desire to have when the impossible had just happened! Totally inappropriate, and nonetheless, I could not shake it. I felt as if I had conjured her into existence and yet I knew her to be real, despite the dim light touching some of her features and casting the rest into shadow.

She seemed to come to her senses better than I did, for I was still suffering from the most acute freeze of thought as I stared at her beautiful countenance, when she spoke.

"I hardly know. I was . . . and now I am . . . "

She looked around, and I knew the moment she went from the bewilderment of her changed location to the realization that we were alone. *Ahhh, there is the color to her cheeks.* The warmth that now flooded her ivory skin was intoxicating, especially through the lens of soft light from the fire. I took an involuntary step toward her. She stiffened and pressed herself further against the wall.

I stopped immediately and placed my hands up in gentle supplication. "I do not mean to frighten you, Miss Elizabeth."

"How did I get here, sir?"

I did not like the waver in her voice, and compassion filled my breast and softened my tone. "I do not know. I am trying to figure that out myself. Perhaps, if you explain what happened just prior to your . . . your arrival?"

I spoke as if to a startled animal, wishing to make her feel comfortable. The reason in my voice calmed her and she transformed a little right before my eyes. Her panicked press against the wall relaxed slightly as the search for logic seemed to settle her mind and propelled her to answer.

"I was on my way to . . . refresh myself. But the room was quite clearly full of others. Their laughter was . . . I was not . . . I did not feel myself inclined towards company so I found an alcove."

She looked around her as if expecting to be still in the alcove.

"I know it." The alcove would have been directly behind her, if his memory served.

"I hid myself in the shadow created by the space to regain my composure, when my shoe slipped on the molding behind me." She looked down at the base of the wall behind her. "Something clicked, and the rest I do not understand, for when the air swirled around me, I shut my eyes."

I raised my brow at this, a reasonable explanation now coming to me.

"When next I opened my eyes, I was no longer in the alcove but here, sir. With you."

I could not prevent the half smile that tugged at my lips when she once again colored with a beautiful blush. So Netherfield had secret passageways and doors! Pemberley had a few I had loved to explore as a child. This one had clearly not been used for some time for I recalled the groan of the hinge. I nodded to Elizabeth, now noticing an unlit sconce above her head that had not been on this side of the wall before.

When my eyes finished categorizing of the wall, I once again looked at Elizabeth. Though her eyes were on me, they did not meet mine. They seemed to harbor a mixture of embarrassment and interest. Her eyes roamed over my person, and I looked down to see what drew her inspection with such silent interest. I remembered at once my state of undress. Hastily, I withdrew a few steps, clumsily stumbling into the very chair I wished to reach in pursuit of my tailcoat.

"Forgive me, Elizabeth. I had not expected to be in company," I said with evident agitation. I stood and immediately tried to don my tailcoat with as much speed as was possible for the restrictive garment, only to halt my effort in horror. With no little hesitance, I turned to look at Elizabeth, confirming to my mind that I had indeed addressed her by her Christian name.

Her face registered astonishment but no condemnation. Before the latter could manifest itself, I spoke. "I must beg your forgiveness, Miss Elizabeth. I had no right . . . I should not have addressed you so informally . . . "

Laughter bubbled up out of her, bringing with it a stop to my bumbling speech and effectively stunning me with the added brilliance that magical sound brought to her smile. Her smile! I was so relieved to see a smile, instead of her face turned in disgust at my presumption, that I too began to laugh.

Pressure and tension from the entire evening began to release at the sudden hilarity, and I found it entirely wonderful to feel it go. My deeper tenor of laughter mixed headily with her higher pitched tones for a moment before I noticed I was the only one laughing. Elizabeth had stopped and was staring at me. I did not understand her fascination, for everyone laughs. I smiled at her, my grin broadening to see her smile tremulously back again and her cheeks reddening charmingly once more.

After a moment of unrestrained admiration, I stood tall and resumed a more formal air. I walked towards her tentatively, so as not to startle her as before. "It seems as if you have discovered a secret door. If you would step aside, I might find the lever again and you can be on your way, no one the wiser for our secret little meeting."

She nodded her assent as I was but a few steps away. She ducked her head and stepped further into the room to allow me access to the wall. The next wonderful moment I found her in my arms, having stumbled forward into them. I know it could only have been a moment before my hands left her slim waist to travel to her arms and help her to stand assured again, but it was a wonderfully, long moment.

Between the next series of apologies, blushing murmurs, and half-whispered explanations, we discovered the point at which the secret door fit against the room's wall, for several of her naughty trailing ribbons had become caught in it during the swift turn of the hinge at her entrance. Thus, her stumble into my arms.

With a bit of a smile, I said, "I am afraid, Miss Elizabeth, that you are quite trapped."

"Oh!" Her hesitant laughter, clearly meant to hide her uneasiness but not quite effectively doing so, charmed me further. Boldly, I availed myself the touch of her arms as I placed my own hands on them again.

"Step back again to the wall, Eliz—" my eyes caught hers again at the near mistake "—*Miss* Elizabeth, lest you tear your gown. Perhaps you might repeat what your slipper did to bring you here."

Nodding, she said, "Yes, I . . . good idea, Mr. Darcy."

The bottom of her skirt rustled as beneath the folds her foot repeatedly pressed against the wall. After a time, it was clear she could not detect the lever which brought her to my sanctuary.

"Shall I . . . ?" The words died in my throat as I indicated the wall behind her.

She nodded, and I threw her a glance of apology as I crouched down near her feet to run my fingers along the molding at the base of the wall. I felt along from the point at which the ribbons had been pinched between the wall and the secret door until my hands reached where her gown hung. My heart beat fiercely in my chest, though my breath was held. My hands stilled.

I cleared my throat, and with a good measure of embarrassment to be so obviously affected by our position, I attempted to speak steadily.

"I need to feel behind you. May I have permission to move your skirts aside?"

I kept my gaze down, for I could clearly feel the heat in my cheeks and did not trust that my desire for her would not register in my eyes. When I heard no reply, I forced myself to look up. Her face peering down at me only drove my madness further, making me wish to stand, take her in my arms and press her against this very wall with a kiss that would break the tension that swirled between us, between our locked gazes—secret door be damned!

Instead, I waited and soon Elizabeth nodded slightly. I thought it best to look down again quickly, lest I lose whatever tenuous control I had to the formidable strength of my feelings for her. I noted her hands clenched in fists within the folds of her gown. A part of me hoped that at least a small measure of her discomfort was due to matching emotions. The flood of temptation this thought caused again forced me keep my head down.

Carefully, I pushed aside her gown with one hand as the other slid along the molding, looking for some lever or indentation to reveal the means to engage the door. Her perfume wafted in the air around me. As I pushed the gown aside, it was all I could do to concentrate on the texture of the wall—and *not* the soft silk falling through my fingers like water nor the glimpse of slender ankle revealed along with her delicate slipper. I cleared my throat again and shifted to inspect the molding on the other side of her.

With disconcertion at being unable to detect even the smallest irregularity, I stood to voice my confusion when my complaint evaporated in my head. I was much closer to her upon standing then I intended, and we were close enough for the near embrace of a waltz. I could not have helped what happened next, for I found myself stepping even closer, my attention locked first on her fine eyes and then dropped to her full lips. I swear upon my father's grave, I did not imagine myself the type of gentleman to importune a woman but my head bent of its own accord.

Elizabeth gasped at the realization of my intent, pressing herself against the wall just as my hand rested gently on the curve of her hip. Her feet shuffled and her hands pressed the wall behind us, and with a whoosh of air and the same creak of the hinge, suddenly we were *both* in the alcove.

The echo of footsteps, the tinkling of laughter coming closer was as effective a means for sobriety as ever I had experienced before. I was now fully aware of my proximity to Elizabeth, of the compromising position, and most acutely of our impending discovery. My head snapped towards her and caught her frightened eyes. Had they been so before the movement of the door? I had no time to chastise myself for my rakish behavior, though.

"Quickly, press the lever again. For otherwise we will be discovered!" I whispered.

"I do not know what I did any more than before, sir!" She was understandably flustered, perhaps even angry. Had I time enough, I too would have been justifiably angry, for I had put her in this position.

The voices drew closer and my heart, already quite radically beating, picked up into a feverish pace. I looked behind me, knowing we were out of time, as the voices nearing us were only steps away. Turning back to Elizabeth, I whispered fervently, "Forgive me this. I must hide your identity."

And then I pressed myself up against her again, covering her entirely with my larger, broader frame. I intended merely to shield her. But she gasped and began to object, and in an attempt to prevent notice, I captured her mouth with my own.

On my word as a gentleman, I swear I had not planned to do it. You might say it was a crazed impulse of the moment. I meant to only silence her. I could not have anticipated that the feel of her warm lips upon my own would effectively silence all my other worries regarding discovery and propel me well beyond simply shielding her. It felt a lot like destiny as I was thrown into a world of pure joy. My instincts took over as I gently pressed another soft kiss on her stunned lips, caressing them with my own. At first, she stood stiffly between me and the wall, but finally she melted. When my mind registered the ecstasy of feeling her arms come about my neck, her fingers diving into my dark hair, I knew pure bliss. I slowed our kiss and allowed my lips to brush past her cheek to speak in her ear.

"Be still, my love. We are almost safe."

I was pleased I could muster enough coherency to utter that much. My words were meant to ensure she did not speak. I meant to keep her from drawing any more attention to our small alcove then necessary. I had hopes that the space would be dark enough not to bring anyone's attention at all, but at least she would be hidden. Nobody would know her identity.

The headiness of our kiss evaporated at my words, and I did not relish the return to her stiffness, as her hands slipped back to her side. Still, I was pleased to note she remained silent as the sound of ladies walked past our hidden spot without so much as a pause in their chatter.

For some moments we remained thus, in our close positioning. Then the alcove was again empty but for us. The depressing blanket of reality began to suffocate the fire of emotion within me, causing me to step back a little.

Neither of us spoke. We just looked at each other. When her pink tongue slipped out to taste her swollen bottom lip, I nearly cried out with sudden want again. Desperation and self-preservation forced me to look away, which is when I discovered Elizabeth's hand upon the dado rail behind her—the molding there having a slight irregularity.

Without thought, I reached for it, covering her hand with mine, causing her to step back against the wall in surprise. That proved the solution, for with a whoosh of air I should have expected, and she should have become accustomed to, we were once again in the privacy of my study.

I stepped away from her then and motioned to where her hand was pressed against the wall—at the level of the dado rail.

"There is the lever."

Elizabeth stepped away from the wall to look; this time her ribbons had not caught in the hinge.

"It must have only appeared to be your foot, for when you first slipped, you must have caught yourself on this molding here."

Elizabeth agreed with me, her happiness at discovering such a mystery easily seen upon her features. My own delight quieted upon seeing her pink lips.

I could no longer live in this alternate world of delightful Elizabeth, carefree of consequences. Those consequences of my actions now came upon me with full force.

Motioning to the wall, "I . . . forgive me for my presumption."

Elizabeth took my meaning immediately, for she was a clever girl. Her cheeks pinked again, at the memory, I supposed. But then her chin lifted and when I caught her gaze, they were not darkened with desire as I expected, but with anger. It stunned me, for had I not all but declared myself in our previous interactions? I had expressed my interest in my singling her out on more than one occasion. She could not be surprised by my desire, certainly not.

"Lucky for you, the encounter was brief."

I could not take her meaning. Her words drew my brows together in confusion.

"But I would appreciate it if you did not repeat it."

My face relaxed; she was merely concerned with proprieties. I could assure her on this point. While it had been my intent to leave Netherfield on the morrow—I knew I must revise my plan. No, it would be impossible to forsake her now.

"You are correct, for until I speak with your father, it would not be proper—"

"My father? There is no need for that, sir."

"I did not think you were of age? Besides, you would wish for his blessing."

She sputtered, and her reaction once again drew my brows together. I had known she was Mr. Bennet's favorite. Even if she were of age, she could not have wished to marry without his approval.

Elizabeth seemed to regain a measure of composure, for her expression cleared and she stood taller. "You can hardly think that I am expecting you to marry me."

So stunned by her words was I that I stepped back into the armchair near the fire. For most certainly I was expecting we should marry. If not because of our recent intimacies, for the fact that I loved her!

"Elizabeth, be reasonable. You must know marriage is—"

"Please do not make free with my name, sir. I would not require marriage of you, sir. I do not believe we were seen, nobody would require it of your honor, and I certainly would not wish to force you into a marriage with me."

"Force me?" By all that was holy, I could not understand what was prompting such a speech from Elizabeth. I acknowledged I should not have used her name without permission—but surely by now we were beyond those formalities.

She crossed her arms and stared defiantly at me. "I am not tolerable enough to tempt you to make me your wife, sir."

I scoffed at this and stalked towards her, secretly smug about the way she drew in sudden breath and backed against the companion chair to mine. I stopped only when she was trapped there between myself and the chair.

"I should think you would know you are more than tolerable and quite enough to tempt me, madam." I pointedly looked to the wall with the secret door—the very wall where moments ago we were pressed against each other in a kiss most passionate.

Elizabeth met my eyes again, and all the fight had left her. Instead what brought me up short was the softness and defeat in her voice.

"But you do not even like me, sir." I opened my mouth to protest immediately when her next words stopped me. "And I do not like you."

I suppose the clock kept ticking. If pressed, I might have even been able to hear it where it sat upon the mantel only a short distance from us. But when Elizabeth uttered those words, I could not have been more lost to time. The words kept playing across the backs of my unseeing eyes, a jumble in my mind, echoing in a frequency I could not register. Soon the six words transformed themselves into recollection after recollection of our past interludes. Her time at Netherfield, the dinner at Lucas Lodge, our dance not an hour ago. It all looked so different under the lamp of those six words. So lost was I to my internal struggle that I did not realize that I was still in the same attitude as I was before her lips—her lips—ones whose joy I just discovered—uttered those six words. *And I do not like you.* Deliberately, I came to myself and withdrew from my position that had trapped Elizabeth to the chair.

What a beastly man I was! I looked about for some excuse, wishing there was some easy reason for the madness, to help explain and acquit myself of the brutality of my past assumption. Here I was profoundly overjoyed to spend this time with Elizabeth, readily expressing my love and desire for her, and all the while, it was not received with *pleasure*—but with . . .

I met Elizabeth's eyes again and could see upon her expression that my own disturbance of mind was not as well hidden as I would have hoped. In fact, I detected a measure of pity and regret at her words. My stomach churned, and the taste in my mouth turned bitter. I neither wanted, nor needed, her pity. Fool man that I am.

I knew I should say something. And yet, what was there to say? I told her I loved her, and she had said she did not even like me.

But then I realized . . .

I had *not* told her I loved her. And I most certainly could not now. I could at least protect myself of *that* embarrassment. Instead, I turned around and walked to the hearth. My head bent to the fire now burning lower. Oddly enough, I thought that I ought to put another log on the fire.

A rustle of skirts behind me reminded me that I was not alone. I turned as Elizabeth approached me with the evident wish to say something. I straightened, prepared to allow her whatever justice she wished to mete out upon my head, for it was rightly deserved.

But then she must have changed her mind for her eyes could not reach mine, and instead said, "Good evening, sir."

She turned toward the secret door and aligned herself back with it once again, her gaze meeting mine then. Though my mind protested mightily, self-preservation at the front, my heart beat so fiercely that I felt again as if I was coming up out of the water—needing the air that Elizabeth alone could give me.

"Wait! Please, just a moment more of your time." My words broke into a whisper. My chest constricted as I held my breath waiting for her reply.

It was nearly too quiet to hear when it did come a moment later.

"I will be missed."

Acknowledging this truth, still I pled. "Just a moment more, if you will."

She barely nodded and stepped away from the door but hesitated. I hated that hesitation—hated that I had given her reason to pause.

"I promise you will be safe with me." I did not wish to kiss her again, not if it meant the kiss would be repugnant to her. How I wished our kisses before were not stained with such. My eyes blinked for in my mind—the ever logical being that it was, until this point—so unwelcome a voice—

reminded me that for a moment during our kiss in the alcove . . . my kiss was not repugnant. Warmth and hope spread through me as I allowed the memory of her reaction to fill me completely. She had responded to me—with passion! Elizabeth was not totally inclined to dislike me.

I indicated she seat herself, and I took the companion seat with careful composure. I did not want my sudden hope to register in my mannerisms and frighten her away. For a moment, I contemplated my next words. When I had asked her to stay a moment, it was an impulse—a desperate plea—of the moment, and I knew that this was all I could afford to ask of her. A moment. With that I knew now was not the time to hedge around. It was time to be plain.

"You have made your opinion of me clear, but I begin to realize I had not the same opportunity. Please allow me to do so now." Elizabeth simply raised her brow by way of answer. "From almost the beginning of our acquaintance, I have found myself in the possession of a most ardent admiration for you. You say you do not like me but I can assure you, Miss Elizabeth, that you have been most dear to me. I have admired you from afar, though. I—"

"Sir—"

"Please, a moment more." When my eyes met hers, she must have seen something of my profound feelings, for her expression softened and she nodded her assent.

"In truth, I came to love you. You see, I have never wooed a woman before. It is clear now to me that I do not know how to please a woman worthy of being pleased." I held her eyes as I said this and would not allow my uncertainty to look away. "I have not wooed you well enough, it seems, and I would very much wish to. Could you . . . would it be too much to ask you to tell me where I have erred?"

Clearly, I had embarrassed Elizabeth but I could not care. I needed to know what it was she held against me—for I could not make her love me if I did not know what offenses I had given her.

After a few silent moments, wherein I began to despair I would hear anything at all from her, she smiled somewhat kindly at me, her lips perking up in that delightfully pert manner I adored. My heart soared.

"Shall I list them in alphabetical order, or would you prefer chronological, sir?"

I could not help it; I laughed quietly at her playful manner, and a welcome release of tension in my shoulders slipped away. It was one of the reasons I loved her: her wonderful way of easing my way conversationally. Without thought, I shifted forward on my chair and availed myself of her hand. It was only after I felt her soft skin against mine that I realized I had once again acted so unguardedly and in a bold manner. I kept my eyes down, not wishing to see her playful smile turn to a frown.

But she did not pull her hand away. Instead she began to speak in hushed tones—almost apologetic in expression—of the offenses I had caused her. She spoke of the Meryton assembly, and I knew mortification and misery at the sound of my own words upon her lips—at once realizing her allusion to them earlier. She spoke of my general disdain for the feelings of others; she spoke of conceit and pride and judgment of her neighbors and of her family. Though I knew every word she spoke was the unvarnished truth, and I felt the weight of each offense upon my heart—I marveled at the kindness in the way she expressed them. She did not speak them to lash out or rebuke me. Her gentleness worked much better and proved to me all the more of her worth. I knew it must not be at all comfortable for her to sit with me in the near darkness of an empty room, her hand in mine, and speak of my manifold disgraces.

When she finished, there was a poignant silence. My shame was profound, and I brought her hand up to my face and kissed it gently. Whispering into the suppleness of her skin, I implored, "Is there anything that can atone? I know nothing can . . . I am grieved."

She made some noise to protest but I could not let her absolve me so easily. Looking up into her eyes, I was surprised to note they glistened slightly.

"I am everything you said and more. Pride has been my friend and prejudice my means. It is no wonder you do not like me."

My head bobbed in acceptance as I reverently placed her hand once again upon her knee. Rubbing my own hands on my legs, I stood and turned my back to her as I once again stared unseeingly at the dying fire.

A rustle of skirts again prompted me to speak, though this time I did not turn around to witness her escape. "Thank you for your time, Eliz . . . Miss Elizabeth." I anticipated another spell of disgust at my inability to properly address her even then.

"Considering our recent encounter, sir, perhaps *Elizabeth* would not be too forward."

Her words were spoken again with such a playful voice that I could hardly believe my ears. She was not granting me permission to address her so, was she? I spun around in my disbelief and saw that she had not retreated to the secret door as I expected. Instead she had stepped closer to me.

My heart did not even dare to beat when she reached for my hand and held it of her own accord.

"You have been kind enough to hear me and have granted me the trust of the honest feelings of your heart, sir."

"Fitzwilliam," I whispered unthinkingly. If I were dreaming this pardoning angel before me, I might as well have the pleasure of my name upon her lips.

"Fitzwilliam," she said with a smile. "In return, I ought to be more honest with mine."

What she could mean I dared not try to guess. She looked down then at my signet ring on my finger. Her dark auburn curls blocked my view of her face as she ran her finger along the Darcy crest engraved there. The feeling was too much, and yet her words pulled me from drowning in emotions. A good thing too, for I might have once again presumed upon her in a like manner as I did in the alcove.

"I said, I did not like you. And I cannot take back those words. You have not been the easiest person to admire—but we have addressed this. Please, no apologies. I have my own to speak."

"Elizabeth?"

Still she kept her expression from me. I waited, though I could not fathom for what she had to apologize.

"The truth is that I *do* admire you. I have struggled with my admiration though. I liked you against my will, against my reason, and even against my character at times."

Here she kissed my hand, and the shock sent such a thrill of joy through me that I could not be offended by the scruples that had long prevented her forming any serious design on me. It was not as if I had not had my own.

"I fought my admiration for your intellect, and for my attraction to your person, for I knew I was beneath you. Your inability to hide your knowledge of this disparity in our stations helped me to dislike you. For it only confirmed my own thoughts on the matter. You might say it comforted my wounded pride."

I could not allow her to go on. "Let us speak no further of our past. Neither of us can be truly proud of our actions with regards to the other. I do not deserve any admiration from you, Elizabeth . . . but I hope you will allow me to try to be worthy of it from this day forward."

Finally, she raised her eyes to mine. The last of my shattered heart began to piece itself back. She nodded and said to me the most beautiful words. "I should like to start anew."

My hand lifted and pushed aside a curl. I marveled that it was as silky as her dress. My eyes were drawn to her face as she closed her eyes at my caress and leaned her cheek into my hand.

That madness inside me, that I knew was no madness at all but the sanest of all feelings—a love and desire for Elizabeth most profound—surged in me again and I could not breathe.

"I promised not to kiss you again," I whispered. It was a plea to her. Despite all that she had confessed, that I had confessed, I could not dare assume that I had any right to kiss her. I needed her to step away, for I knew I did not possess the will to remove myself. I hoped she would understand my plea, for I was not so noble as to clarify if there was a chance she would remain otherwise.

She did not open her eyes, but a smile touched her lips. I swallowed, for the temptation was great and I was only a man.

"That was quite foolish of you," she whispered, her eyes still closed. "Yet, I fear I must correct you. You promised I would be safe with you. You made no direct promise not to—"

I did not let her finish—for another word would have been too much. With relish, I bent my head to her lips and claimed them with my own. Whatever magic had wound its ways around us then, I did not care to disturb. Elizabeth was with me, in my arms again—willingly—and I was determined not to lose this again. It was because of this that I slowed my kiss once more, reluctantly breaking our connection. I could not bear it if I frightened her with too ardent an expression of my love.

"Will you permit me to court you, Elizabeth? Properly, as you deserve."

"Yes."

My joy was such that I could not help a wide smile breaking forth on my face as I bent to place a quick kiss upon her lips again. With a sigh, I knew I ought to let her go. Taking her hand in mine, I thought to walk her back to the secret door.

"I ought to let you leave now, though I do not wish it."

Elizabeth did not respond. Her countenance was downcast. It should not have brought me happiness to see her saddened too, but it did. Her next words could not have surprised me more though.

"Fitzwilliam, I have seen a new side of you this evening, and I begin to fear that I owe you another apology."

I lifted her face to mine with a finger, knowing nothing she could ever do would dispel the joy I felt at that moment.

"I believed a man, a man of a very short acquaintance, over a man of far greater consequence and goodness—not to mention of a longer standing acquaintance, because one flattered me and one did not."

Her reference was clear. But I did not wish to think about Wickham, and I certainly did not wish to have him spoil our moment. It gratified me that she thought me the better man—my pride still a long-time friend.

"He is not to be trusted, Elizabeth. That is all I will say now, for you really will be missed if you do not go. But if it pleases you, I would like to call upon you tomorrow. I should like to ask your father for his blessing on our courtship, and I should like to share with you my history with that man. For now, hear this. Think no more on your previous judgment of either of us. Let us begin again, as you said."

Elizabeth nodded and smiled at me, and I thought then that I would do anything for the rest of my life if I could see that smile every day.

She stepped up against the wall, and I moved in front of her. I allowed my finger to run gently down the length of her cheek before bowing low to her for the second time that evening.

"Until tomorrow, my love."

"Until tomorrow."

With a push of her hand upon the lever, a familiar whoosh and whine of the hinge, she was gone. I stood looking at the wall for a full minute, a smile upon my face. I had but dragged my eyes away when the door sprang around again and Elizabeth's arms were around me, her face buried in my neck. My arms did not stay stunned at my side for long—they came up quickly to hold her to me. If there was a better feeling in the world than this, I had not known it.

She giggled, the warmth of her breath upon my neck sending a jolt straight to my heart.

She slowly released her arms and slid them down me, my arms still about her.

"I only wanted to say goodbye again."

Her blush was endearing, and any words I had stuck in my throat. Instead, I bent to kiss her chastely on the lips once more and rest our heads together.

"Go, you beautiful girl. Go before I cannot let you leave. I will see you tomorrow."

Elizabeth stepped away from me again, and I regretted the distance immediately. With a smile and a little wave, she pressed the lever and once again was swept around to the other side. I bit my lip, a smile threatening to split my face in half. Stepping forward, I leant my head against the wall, somehow knowing she was still there.

"Elizabeth." I spoke just loud enough I thought she might hear.

Her laughter sounded back, and then faded away as she left the alcove. I imagined her skipping away, and that smile that had threatened before broke out in full force upon my face.

KARALYNNE MACKRORY is no newbie to the writing world. She made her debut as an author at the tender age of thirteen when she wrote her first set of bad poetry. As a young adult, she steered clear of bad prose and achieved a degree in social work. Years later, she has published four Austen-inspired novels so full of romantic sensibilities as to give you a swoon and hopefully a few laughs. Her books turned out better than her poetry and are: *Falling for Mr. Darcy*, *Bluebells in the Mourning*, the IPPY award-winning *Haunting Mr. Darcy*, and *Yours Forevermore, Darcy*.

"There is stubbornness about me that never can bear to be frightened at the will of others. My courage always rises with every attempt to intimidate me."
—Miss Elizabeth to Mr. Darcy, Chapter XXXI.

THE BEAST OF PEMBERLEY

MELANIE STANFORD

It is a truth universally acknowledged, that a hideous face will cause a single woman to run the other way.

This truth I had come to know intimately. In consequence, I stopped going out into society, withdrawing inside my home where no one could startle or grimace, reminding me of my ugliness.

It was not always thus. As a boy, I was loved and spoiled by my parents. I was given good principles, but left to follow them in pride and conceit. After my parents died, leaving me the estate at Pemberley, I hid my grief under a raised chin and haughty glare to anyone in the village who dared show an ounce of pity. I did not want their pity; I had no need. I was a man on my own, rich and handsome, the world mine for the taking.

But I had not taken the world; it had taken me.

"It should be a warm day today, Mr. Darcy," my valet Cogsworth said, holding out a freshly pressed coat for me. "A walk might—"

"No." I yanked the coat from his grasp and shrugged it on. No matter how many times I had told him I did not need his help, Cogsworth still insisted on dressing me. I no longer cared how I looked—why bother, with such a face? At least my loose linen shirt and trousers covered the rest of the scars that etched my skin all the way to my ankles.

I tugged on my worn leather boots and stalked from the bedchamber, my valet on my heels despite his limp, keeping up a steady stream of inspired ideas for my day. Would the man never tire of his relentless pursuit of the past? Life would not turn back to the way it was, before the wizard Wickham entered my life.

In my study, I slumped into my favorite chair . . . breakfast and a steaming mug of hot cider set before me on a platter. Mrs. Reynolds hovered nearby, her right hand shaking from the pain of her scar.

"Leave me!" She was one of the few remaining servants at Pemberley. Most had fled after Wickham's dark spell, believing if they ran far enough away from Pemberley—from me—they might escape it. The rest remained, though I was not sure why. Perhaps they thought I could somehow end their constant suffering. It surely was not because of my black moods, my temper always boiling at the surface, covering despair.

When Wickham cast his spell, I had been on my way to meet him, not wanting the wizard to step one toe inside Pemberley's gates. I took the brunt of the hex, the magic rolling over me like waves of fire, the pain excruciating. Inside the house, the servants were not spared. The dark magic pierced them in different locations on their bodies, leaving each with a single wound which never healed or ceased to cause agony. Cogsworth limped because his wound was on his left foot. For Mrs. Reynolds, easily the best cook in the land, her scar circled her right hand. Lumiere's, across his neck. Plumette's marred her cheek. No one was exempt. Lumiere had left Pemberley not long after, but he returned months later, missing home, the wound still fresh on his skin. That was how we knew that leaving did not erase the scars.

Though the torture never ceased, we had all become accustomed to it.

The scent of cinnamon and pastry was tempting, but instead of reaching for breakfast, I picked up my mirror. The silver frame wrought with vines and roses was what I cherished most of my mother's.

As a child, I had spent hours staring into the mirror, asking it to show me far off places that my parents spoke of or I had read about in books. After Wickham's dark curse, I found no satisfaction from seeing lands I would never visit, so I put the mirror away. There was nothing else to see. No family. No friends. No one who cared what happened to me. And I certainly had no desire to watch the local villagers go about their easy and happy lives.

But I became weary of the nothingness. Lonely. I was no longer a youth with passing fancies but a man who longed for more.

In consequence, I had started watching through the mirror. "Show me the village square"—I would say, watching it endlessly, never expecting to come across someone like Elizabeth Bennet.

"Show me Elizabeth."

The mirror flashed, and she appeared. Dark hair, curling down her back but pulled from her face, tendrils escaping in the wind. Her eyes were bright, full of intelligence and verve. She smiled, and I found my own lips itching to match her expression, until I remembered she was not smiling at me.

Stunning. She was immensely beautiful, but not in the classical style like her sister Jane, who strolled beside her. Every few moments I caught sight of Jane's blonde hair or the shoulder of her cloak. She was long thought the loveliest of the daughters, but she lacked the sparking light which made Elizabeth glow. At least, she glowed to me.

"You must let me buy this for you, Jane"—Elizabeth was saying. I stared intently at the mirror, wishing I was beside her, in front of her, wishing she was speaking with me.

"You mustn't, Lizzy," Jane replied, though I could not see her face. "I do not need it."

"Of course you do. Every woman needs a new hat to celebrate her forthcoming marriage."

Jane laughed. "Is that a rule, then?"

"It should be." Elizabeth's gaze was drawn down to the table of wares. "How about a new pin for your cloak? Or this beautiful wooden box? You could hide things from your new husband within."

"I would never hide anything from Charles!"

A secret smile stole over Elizabeth's face. I could see it; Jane could not. "I suppose you would not. And how much less fun for you."

Elizabeth linked arms with her sister as they walked away. I flipped the mirror over, pushing it into my thigh, my scars, ignoring the discomfort.

The anguish of wanting Elizabeth was worse. Wanting—and knowing I could never have her.

"Elizabeth, your father wishes to speak with you"—her mother was demanding now.

Elizabeth's creamy cheeks flushed a rosy pink. Her eyes flashed. "Yes, Mama." Her mouth tightened with words unspoken. She walked through the Bennet house, a small stone cottage that lay on the outskirts of the village.

I put my feet on the ottoman and relaxed into my chair, wondering what would come next, what could be vexing this young lady so greatly.

"Yes, Papa?"

"Sit down, my child," a graying man in spectacles answered.

The mirror followed the motion as she perched on the edge of a chair. Her hands clasped tightly in her lap. I had learned that the scene in the mirror would move with my thoughts. Though I had to voice what I sought, once my desire was in view, the scene would widen or magnify at my unspoken wish. I took much pleasure in admiring the entirety of Elizabeth's person, the arch of her graceful neck, the roundness of her curves . . .

"Your mother has insisted I speak with you"—Mr. Bennet was saying.

Elizabeth's hands twisted in her lap.

"You know what this is about."

It was not a question, but Elizabeth answered, "I do, Father."

"Mrs. Bennet insists that you marry Mr. Collins."

My body jerked upright. *Marry?* No, not my Elizabeth. And not to someone as odious as Mr. Collins.

Elizabeth lifted her chin. "I cannot marry him. I will not."

Though I could not see Mr. Bennet, I heard him sigh. "Very well then."

A clatter echoed from the mirror. "You must! You must marry him, Lizzy."

"I will not, Mama."

"He inherits Longbourn when your father is gone, and he will throw us all out of the house. You must marry him!" Her mother's voice sounded like a bird screeching through the forest.

Elizabeth remained firm. "No."

"Think of the money, Lizzy. We need the money that he will bring to the family. Jane's marriage is one of love. You may not get such an offer yourself. Marry him so that we might be solvent again."

There was a pause. I gripped the handle of the mirror.

"I am sorry, but I cannot. Mr. Collins is an odious toad of a man." Elizabeth's voice started to rise with her passion. "He never listens when I speak. He cares nothing for my thoughts or opinions. He thinks me, nay—all women—beneath him. I will never marry such a man!"

Elizabeth fled the room. Mrs. Bennet's voice followed her, shrieking of duty and money and how they would all end up in the hedgerows.

Thoughts whirling, I set the mirror down, Mrs. Bennet's voice dying away.

While it was obvious the Bennets were not rich, I had not known they were in such financial difficulty that they feared losing their home.

Thank heavens she had not agreed to marry Collins. He was everything she said and worse. Though he was a prominent member of the village, he would never make Elizabeth happy.

But I could try. And I could make their family solvent.

Elizabeth had no other suitors.

My hands began to shake. I could do it. I could be the one. I loved her. I would value her. Was not that enough?

If the family needed money, Elizabeth would need to make a good match, and with the village sorely lacking in financially independent gentlemen . . .

I rubbed at my face; the friction caused my scars to burn. I looked at my hands, the angry red lines snaking into my sleeves. She would not have me. A woman's prejudice against such an unsightly beast would never consider me.

Unless . . .

Cogsworth had delivered my letters. I had informed the servants. Pemberley was spotless from top to bottom. Even the grounds had been trimmed and the recent fallen snow brushed from the paths.

I toyed with the mirror, my confidence in my plan waning. Elizabeth would not want this. How could she? She did not know me. The letter I sent to her parents would be enough to convince them, of that I was sure. But no matter how hard I tried to make my case in my letter to her . . . despite my eloquence, I feared she would not come. Yet, I knew her parents could force her, which would bring her wrath.

I loved her, and I would make her love Pemberley.

"Show me Elizabeth."

The mirror flashed and she was there. Crying.

Regret filled my heart, the kind that could not be ignored.

"Please, Papa," she said between sobs. "You know what the townsfolk say about Mr. Darcy. About Pemberley. Don't make me do this." An arm was around her shoulders, and as the mirror drew back, Jane came into view. My letter was crumpled on her lap.

"Please, Elizabeth." Her father's voice cracked. "Mr. Collins was angry at your refusal. He assumed some of my debts, and now they are being called in. I have no way to pay them. He will turn us out for certain."

Her watery eyes rose to meet her sister's. "Jane?"

"Mr. Darcy spoke well," she replied, and hope surged within me. "There was nothing improper in his proposal. Indeed, his letter shows a tenderness of feeling. It is a great compliment to you, not to mention the relief it would bring for Mama and Papa." Bless her! "But I know you, Lizzy. You will be sacrificing your happiness for that of your family."

"How can I do this?"

"I cannot force you."

"Unlike my parents," she said bitterly.

"We are not—" Her father started, but Elizabeth would not allow him to finish.

"Don't, Papa." She rose from the chair. "I will marry him because I must. Let us not pretend I have a choice in the matter."

My heart both lifted and fell at the same time. She did not want to come. Of course, she would not *want* to come.

But she was coming.

I stood at the altar, stiff and upright. Tense. Anxious. Nervous. Excitement overpowering the throbbing from my scars. The clergyman in front of me avoided my face. I had a mask on, but still he would not look at me. The elaborately knotted cravat that Cogsworth insisted upon for my wedding day felt tight, and I tugged at it.

The chapel on Pemberley's estate had been unused since my mother died but had been aired and thoroughly cleaned. Cogsworth had helped me into my wedding coat, and I fitted the mask over my face myself, the stiff black leather covering everything but my eyes and mouth. I only glanced in the mirror to make sure it was straight, but that was enough for the flash of anger and self-loathing to tumble through me. Handsome no longer. But better the mask than the scars.

The doors opened, and a sharp wind blew in, piercing the stillness. I turned . . . and there she was.

Enchanting.

Alone—because I made it so. And brave. I did not want anyone else gawking at the man in the mask with scars snaking from his coat sleeves.

Her gown was white lace adorned with flowers. The bodice was tight, enhancing the swell of her breasts, a golden cross resting on her neck. The skirt fanned out, lightly brushing the floor as she walked. Her hair was arranged with baby's breath and coiled into a floral crown. She carried a bouquet of borage and dahlias in her hands. For courage and dignity?

Her slippered feet barely made a sound as she made her way down the short aisle—leaving silence in its wake. The only guests in the pews were my servants. She would not look at me.

I could not take my eyes off her. The parson spoke, but I heard nothing. She stared blankly ahead when she recited the words betrothing herself to me. I wondered how she could say the words she so evidently could not mean. Even when she was forced to face me as the marriage ribbon was tied around our hands, she would not meet my eyes. Her hand was warm in mine, soft against my scars. Yet, she did not flinch at the sight, and I adored her even more for that.

The ceremony ended. My servants rose with a smattering of applause. Elizabeth yanked her hand from mine, the ribbon stinging against my wrist, and she fled the chapel.

"Attend her," I murmured to Mrs. Reynolds.

The servants left, and I was alone.

Married.

There would be no wedding night, not that I had been expecting such things. I knew it would take time for her to come to me. I would not force anything more of her today.

"This way, madam," Mrs. Reynolds said to Elizabeth.

"Are you sure?" she asked.

"Of course. Mr. Darcy would not want you to starve."

Staying in the shadows, I followed Elizabeth and Mrs. Reynolds. Torches lit the corridor, but there were plenty of shadows for me to disappear into.

"We are so happy to have you here, madam," Mrs. Reynolds said.

Elizabeth's shoulders were up near her ears, but at the words, she relaxed. A little. "Please, call me Elizabeth."

"Yes, madam."

"Or Lizzy . . ." She stopped. I pressed against the wall, peering from beneath my hooded cloak. "No . . . I cannot . . ."

Mrs. Reynolds turned to her. "Madam?" She reached out, her hand shaking. "Mrs. Darcy?"

"I am sorry, I meant . . . I cannot imagine . . . This cannot be my life now."

Mrs. Reynolds patted her on the shoulder—awkwardly—as if she had not touched another soul in a long time. "It will get better. You'll see."

Elizabeth made a very unladylike sound. I smiled.

They continued down the hall. I waited a moment and then followed.

"How long have you been in the household?" Elizabeth asked.

"Since I was but a girl. The late Mr. and Mrs. Darcy were the very best. And Mr. Darcy is just like them. He is the best landlord and the best master that ever lived. Some people call him . . . well, I think it only because he must keep himself shuttered up here at Pemberley now—"

"Things change," Elizabeth said bitterly. It was like an icicle to the heart.

"Do not judge him too harshly, madam. He's been touched by . . . overwhelming sadness . . . and too many changes."

I stiffened at her words.

"How did his parents die?" Elizabeth asked, trailing one hand along the wall as she walked.

"An illness took the elder Mr. Darcy first. Mrs. Darcy was a great sorceress, and she spent months searching for a cure among the magical arts, but eventually she fell ill as well. There was no hope for either of them."

Elizabeth whipped her head to look at Mrs. Reynolds. "She was a sorceress?"

"Yes. Many students came to Pemberley to learn from her. One . . ."

"Yes?"

Mrs. Reynolds waved her hand. "Never mind. I am surprised you did not know."

"There are rumors of course," Elizabeth said, her voice lowering. I moved closer. "Many of them so fanciful, I dare not . . . Does my new master have power? Is that why he hides himself? But then, why would he seek me for a wife?"

Mrs. Reynolds shook her head quickly.

"Does he want me for . . . some spell? Is that why I'm here? A virgin bride. I have read books, you know. Is he evil?"

"Oh, tosh, he's not evil. Hunger has you speaking nonsense. Let's get you to the family dining room."

They disappeared down the staircase, Elizabeth continuing to pepper Mrs. Reynolds with questions about me, but I stayed above.

Despite my letter to her, despite explaining how I would care for her, she thought I only wanted to use her ill. That I was evil. Little did she know, I had no powers, nothing special except a grand, lonely estate and a curse I knew not how to rid.

She needed to know me, know that I was not evil, but that could not happen if I stayed in the shadows.

I would breakfast with her.

I hesitated outside the door. Anxious and frightened in a way I had not been for some time. Or ever, perhaps.

Her voice echoed from the dining room, thanking the servants. Her laugh rang out, and it was a boon on my aching scars. She had been kind to the servants thus far when she could have been angry or demanding. But I knew Elizabeth to always be kind.

She would be kind to me.

I stepped inside.

Her knife clattered onto the table.

"Good morning," I said, my voice harsher than I intended. I cleared my throat. "I have come to breakfast with you."

Elizabeth flinched.

Taking my chair, I peered under my hood at her. My fingers tapped on the wood table.

Her eyes narrowed and she pushed her breakfast away.

"Is the food not to your liking?" I asked.

"Mr. Darcy." Mrs. Reynolds had appeared. "Mrs. Darcy, I have brought you more preserves."

She shook her head. "I am no longer hungry."

I pinched the bridge of my nose. Elizabeth's eyes followed the motion, resting on my hand. My scars.

"It is rude to stare," I snapped.

Her mouth tightened. She pushed away from the table.

"Wait," I said, regretting my anger. "I apologize. I only wish to dine with you."

"Take off your hood."

I froze.

She moved around the table toward me. I was so surprised, I backed away.

"Show me your face. Take off the cloak." She reached for me.

"No." Panic edged my voice, and I recoiled from her.

She stopped and placed her hands on her hips, her chest heaving.

I straightened. And found my own courage. This time, I stepped toward her. "You are my wife. You will not make demands of me."

Her face flushed. "I feel like your prisoner."

Before I could stop myself, I grabbed the table, pushing everything from it with a roar. Dishes, candles, Elizabeth's half-eaten breakfast—all fell to the floor with a loud crash.

I panted for breath. My hands clenched, the scars tightening painfully. My whole body was on fire, made worse because of my outburst. I slowly turned to Elizabeth.

She trembled against the wall and summoned the most unlikely words:

"My courage always rises with every attempt to intimidate me."

All my anger and frustration evaporated. I opened my mouth to apologize.

"You will never be my husband."

Her words cut into me, more agonizing than any scar, any spell.

She turned smartly on her heel and left me alone.

I destroyed the dining room. Nothing was left standing. Nothing intact. Nothing whole. Including me.

When I calmed, I went in search of Elizabeth.

I found her in her room. My senses enflamed at the sight of her sprawled on the bed, a book in hand, and her fingers absently twirling the curls at her neck.

She looked up when I entered, my face still concealed under my hood. Her face colored at the sight of me. I pushed away the longing that threatened to derail my purpose.

"Get out!"

I bristled. Desire turned to anger. "No."

"I do not give you permission to enter my room." She clambered off the bed.

"I do not need your permission!"

She lifted her chin. Her hands gripped her dress. "So, this is how it will be? You have come to . . . to . . ." Tears sprang to her eyes and quivering, she looked away.

Understanding dawned. Such a wretched beginning. I took a breath, willing my anger to evaporate. "No! I came to apologize."

Her trembling slowed, but still she would not look at me.

"I lost my temper before, and for that, I am sorry."

She crossed her arms over her chest.

"Elizabeth, you must know . . ." I swallowed. Women had never made me nervous before. But I had never declared myself either. "You must allow me to tell you how ardently I admire and love you."

She blinked.

"Despite your circumstances, I think you the handsomest, most intelligent woman I have ever . . . encountered. This connection can only benefit your family. I paid your father's debts."

Her eyes flashed.

"You will have everything you desire. Clothes, food, a large estate—all to call your own. You will never want for anything nor will your family."

"Nothing except free will," she said quietly.

Her words stung. "Would you have preferred Mr. Collins?"

Her eyes searched for my face, but she could not find it under the hood of my cloak. "How did you know about that?"

"Collins is a toad of a man," I said. She snorted. "I can give you so much more than him, than any man." I paced before her. "And I will. You are lucky to be married to such a man as I."

"Lucky?"

"You must see the great honor I have bestowed upon you by making you the mistress of this estate. I could have chosen any woman from the village for my wife, but the only woman whose love and good opinion I desired was you."

Her eyes were hard as she said, "In such cases as this, I suppose I should express gratitude, if, in fact, I felt any. But I cannot. I do not." She exhaled a loud breath. "I am sorry if I have caused pain, but it was unconsciously done."

I paced. "Is this all the response I am to expect?"

"What would you have me say?" She shook, with nerves or anger, I knew not. "I do not know you. I do not know how you came to choose me, or love me, as you claim. But I despise you for buying me. I despise my parents, too, for—"

"I did not buy you!"

"You just admitted that you did!"

"I sent you a letter. I made an offer of marriage—"

"Which was only accepted due to the money you imparted. My father never would have parted with me for less than a generous sum."

I moved closer to her, aching to touch her. To feel the warmth of her skin against mine. My fingers reached for her shoulder.

She stepped beyond my reach. "Do *not* touch me."

"Elizabeth," I said, exasperated. "I will not hurt you nor touch you if you do not wish it. Of that I swear."

As she turned to me, her countenance was sharp but her voice softened. "How can I possibly trust your word? A man who will not even show me his face."

"You do not want to see my face," I said gently.

"Why?"

"Trust me."

"Did we not just establish that I do not trust you?"

Obstinate, headstrong girl! My fear rose at the thought of revealing myself to her but how else could we live together without her trust.

"Very well."

She looked up in surprise.

Slowly, reluctantly, I ducked my head and lifted the hood from my face. It fell on my shoulders. I inhaled for courage. Then raised my face to meet her eyes.

She gasped.

It was slight, but I heard it all the same.

She lifted her hand toward me then dropped it. She stared at the hideousness before her.

Flipping my hood back over my head, I turned away in shame. I could not bear her gaze.

Weeks had passed and she still refused to dine with me. Or be in my presence.

After another lonely dinner, I heard a noise from within my study. The door was ajar, and I hovered at it, peering inside.

Elizabeth had her back to me, her head bent, studying something intently.

"No," she said. "No!" Her body shifted, revealing my mirror, my mother's mirror, in her hands.

"What do you think you are doing?" I roared, bursting into the room. "Put that down at once!" How dare she touch my mother's mirror! I had given her everything, filled her room with gowns and jewels and mirrors more beautiful than the one she clutched in her hand.

She spun to face me. "This is how . . . ?" Her words stopped me where I stood. "How you knew about Collins, about my parents' private affairs? About me?" She brandished the mirror as if she would strike me with it. "You have been watching me."

"You have no right to that mirror!" I declared, my anger erupting. "It is mine!"

"*I* have no right?" she spat. "You have no right to spy on me, like some . . . some . . ."

"Give it to me." I grabbed it, but she would not give way. We tussled, and my cloak fell from my face. I yanked the mirror from her grasp, and she tumbled to the floor. Horrified, I reached for her. "Elizabeth, I—"

On her knees, she looked up at me, her face filled with repugnance. "You disgust me."

"Do not—"

"You are vile."

I backed away. "Stop."

"You have invaded my privacy, watching me while I . . . You are not a man but a loathsome creature."

"Be silent!" How could she know I never spied on her like *that*? And yet, she quickly assumed the worst.

She rose to her full height. "You may have forced me into this marriage, but I will never, ever be your partner in it."

My hands gripped the mirror so hard I was afraid it would shatter. Anger, self-pity, and despair threatened to sink me. Without my strict regulation, I would surely turn into the horror she thought me, and she would witness it all.

"Get out."

She stilled.

"Get out!" I bellowed into her face.

She fled from the beast she knew me to be. The monster I had become.

I wished for magic so that I could destroy the study. Pemberley. Myself.

My mother had been gifted with magic, not me. Nor my father. Wickham had it—but my mother refused to guide and teach him any longer once she discovered him meddling in the darker arts. She threw him from the house, barring him from ever returning. But he did return to take his revenge. When he could not take it out on my parents, he unleashed it on me.

He was the monster, yet I was the one to pay. If I could have had a normal existence, perhaps I would have met Elizabeth in the village the proper way. We would have talked, courted, become engaged with her father's permission. She would have loved me.

She would never love me now.

To my surprise, Elizabeth did not run away. I knew because I watched her in the mirror. She explored Pemberley, she was friendly with my servants, she read books. When she threw on a cloak and stirred outside, I tensed, ready to follow—all the while loathing my insecurity and suspicions. But she never left. She meandered through the grounds, brushing snow from the fountain, snapping a stick off the barren hedge and twirling circles in the air. Then I watched her draw shapes into the snow; as the mirror magnified, I inhaled sharply. She had written: Are you watching me?

I turned the mirror over quickly in my shame. I looked out in the gardens in search of Elizabeth. When I could not find her, I continued my search inside. I wandered the halls, wanting to explain. I would tell her my history. And I needed to apologize.

"Where is your mistress?" but none of the servants knew of her whereabouts. She was nowhere to be found.

"Show me Elizabeth," I said to the mirror, chagrined that I was exploiting what she reviled.

Elizabeth appeared. Her face was twisted in fear. Tears had frozen on her cheeks. Her hair flew wildly about her head. As the image in the mirror broadened, I could see trees and snow, a dark sky above. She was running, her breath coming in loud gasps.

The view swung wide, the image blurring. It sharpened on a pack of wolves chasing her through the snow.

Elizabeth screamed.

Flinging the mirror aside and grabbing my sword, I was at the stables in an instant. Forgoing the saddle, I threw myself on my horse, Phillippe, following her tracks in the fresh snow. Ignoring the tree branches that snapped at my scars, I spurred the horse on.

I found Elizabeth circled by the pack, waving a branch at the snarling wolves.

I threw myself from the horse directly into the battle. Thundering my rage, I slashed at them. Despite my attack, they did not retreat.

Spinning, I stabbed my sword into fur and sinew. I lashed out with my feet; I tackled and rolled. Teeth snapped at my face, grazed my chest and legs, tore into my arm. Pain had been a companion of mine since the curse, and I embraced it. It could not stop me. Screams pierced the air; I did not know who they belonged to, but I would not, did not stop until the last. Until Elizabeth was safe.

I had slain them all.

My eyes found Elizabeth, willing her to be unharmed.

Her shocked eyes met mine, tears stained her face, her mouth gasping for breath.

I searched for blood on her but saw none. I stepped toward her trembling form.

I thought to comfort her, to assure her that all was well.

Instead, I collapsed to the ground, and the world faded to black around me.

I woke covered in warmth and thinking of my mother. When my eyes opened, Elizabeth's face was near to mine.

Blinking sleep away, I sat upright in my bed, blankets piled atop me. A bandage wrapped around my arm, and I could feel others on my legs and chest.

"Elizabeth?"

She had moved away from my bed. Her hands were clasped, her face blank.

"The wolves, and you . . ." I pressed a hand to my temple, a headache blossoming at the base of my neck. "Are you alright? Were you hurt?"

"Not much, no," she said, her voice filled with hesitation.

"Thank heavens." I rested my head back on the pillow. "How did I get here?" I could remember nothing but the scene in the woods.

"Your horse is a smart animal." She fidgeted with the folds of her dress. "It knelt in the snow, and I had to heave you . . . We rode back."

She had saved me!

"Thank you."

"Cogsworth and Lumiere carried you to bed," she continued. "Mrs. Reynolds bandaged you." She blushed and looked at the floor. "Cogsworth undressed you."

Had she seen the scars that painted lines over my entire body?

My face was uncovered; I ran my hand down one cheek, the scars pulling painfully. I was shirtless, and the blanket had fallen to my waist when I sat up. I was unused to being so exposed. I tugged the blanket to my neck.

"How long was I asleep?"

"A few hours."

"Have you eaten?" I did not want her to stay out of duty. I did not want her to leave.

"Yes."

I stared at her. Why had she not left my room? Pemberley? She could have fled while I was asleep, and no one would have stopped her.

Silence stretched between us until I could no longer bear it.

"Elizabeth—"

"Thank you," she blurted. Her face flamed again. I glowed seeing the color infuse her cheeks. "For saving my life."

I paused. "I know you would wish it otherwise, but you are my wife. I will always protect you."

She looked at her feet. "Who will protect me from you?"

I winced at the heart rending her words induced.

"Elizabeth, please—" My voice willed her to look at me.

Her body stiffened, but her eyes met mine.

"I know my face is abhorrent to you. I know I am the last man in the world whom you ever wished to marry." She winced. "But I will never, ever hurt you."

"So, you say," she mumbled as she turned back to the door.

I had to prove I was not the beast she imagined. I climbed shakily from the bed, wrapping the bedsheet around my person.

"Wait."

My legs were stiff and my scars burned as usual, yet the injuries dealt by the wolves were but another throbbing ache atop the rest. I went to my dressing table where my mother's mirror lay. Cogsworth must have returned it here—he knew how much it meant to me. I traced the silver engravings in the handle, ignoring my reflection. I kissed the rose carved into the top before turning to Elizabeth.

"Here." I held out the mirror.

She blinked.

"Please, take it. So you will know I do not exploit its power. Perhaps, in time, you will learn to trust me."

She hesitated a moment before closing the distance and taking the mirror from me. She stared down at it.

"You understand how it works?"

She nodded.

"I am sorry I did not welcome your family at the wedding. I did not want them to see me."

"My family."

I failed to discern the emotion in those words, but I said, "I know how important family is. That mirror was my mother's."

She finally looked up at me. "I shall cherish it."

"I know."

Her eyes moved to my chest.

"I should . . . I need to . . ."

"You should rest."

Relief and annoyance crossed her face. "As should you. In fact, I think you need it more than me."

I bowed my head at her. "Yes, madam."

Before she left, did I imagine the wisp of a smile?

Elizabeth remained seated when I came to breakfast. She nodded mutely at me when I offered a "good morning." We breakfasted in silence. But together. At nuncheon, when she joined me again, my heart swelled.

"My family is doing well," she said. "I have been checking on them in the mirror."

Smiling, I stared at her across the table as she toyed with her food on her plate.

"Their situation seems to have improved."

"I am glad of it." I sipped the wine.

She nodded at her plate and lifted the fork to her delicate mouth. I swallowed as she licked at some morsel on her plump lip.

"Are you close with your mother and father?"

Elizabeth laughed softly. "My mother is . . . she suffers from nerves and is often excitable. She only wants the best for her daughters, though. I cannot fault that."

Her description fit perfectly with all I had witnessed in the mirror.

"And your father?"

She pushed the treacle around the plate. "There was a time when my father and I were very close."

I understood. Their estrangement was because of me, because of the marriage arrangement.

"You can be close again."

"Perhaps."

Silence filled the room as we finished the meal. I swallowed my nerves.

"Elizabeth, may I . . ." I cleared my throat. "May I show you something?"

Her eyebrows rose.

"It is here, at Pemberley. A room I think you will like." At her misgiving, I said quickly, "A surprise."

I held my breath. Would she trust me in this small thing?

She pushed her chair back and stood. "Lead the way."

I had forgotten what it felt like to smile, but I could not contain it. I bounded from my chair and was out the door in an instant—certain I had heard a surprised laugh behind me.

She followed me through the corridors of Pemberley until we came to a door. I pushed through, checking to see if she was behind me, wishing I could take her hand. Sunlight from the windows lit the portraits on the walls—my ancestors, staring at me.

"Is that you?" Elizabeth asked.

She had stopped in front of the last portrait. A man—a boy, really—standing tall and haughty, one hand on his hip and a knee cocked as if he owned the world.

"That *was* me."

She glanced at me, no doubt comparing the former Fitzwilliam Darcy to the wounded man before her. She turned back to the painting—staring, unmoving. I shifted my feet.

"Those are my parents." I pointed to a different painting, hoping to distract her.

"And you, as a boy?"

"Yes."

The silence was such that I could hear her swallow. Finally, she drew her eyes away.

"Is that what you wished to show me?" she asked in a small voice.

I shook my head, a smile pulling at my lips. "This way."

At the end of the corridor stood a door painted with the many colors of the rainbow—a decoration I had created as a child and which my mother never changed, despite its garishness.

I swung open the door, then bowed, sweeping my arm out. "After you."

Her eyebrows rose a fraction, but she stepped past me and into the room.

Elizabeth exclaimed, "A library!"

She circled the room as if to see everything at once, her eyes wide in wonder, her hands touching the spines of the books. She tilted her head back to regard the volumes which stretched almost to the ceiling and stilled at the sight. She seemed almost as fascinated by the clouds, sun, and stars painted across the ceiling like the sky moving from day to night. She closed her eyes and inhaled deeply, as if reveling in the scent of dusty books.

When she opened her eyes again, true happiness radiated from her expression for the first time since she had come to Pemberley.

"May I . . .?"

"It's yours," I replied. "All of it."

She threw her head back in laughter, as if in ecstasy, and my heart yearned for hers. I had to turn away lest my own face betray my thoughts.

In time, I told myself. *In time* she would look at me like that. For now, I relished her joy, knowing I had pleased her.

"I shall leave you alone." As much as I wanted to stay, I knew I must give her privacy. At the door, she called out to me.

"Thank you."

Pressing my hand over my heart, I bowed.

The library was as inspired as I had hoped. Elizabeth spent more and more time with me each day. At first, I asked if I could read with her in the library. She assented. We read together in opposite chairs enjoying the crackling warmth of the fireplace and the silent companionship. She began to tell me of the books she enjoyed and would read me passages that leapt out to her. Over time we discussed several different volumes and authors.

When the library became too oppressive, we would walk outdoors, the snow crunching under our boots. Elizabeth delighted in throwing snowballs at me. I *delighted* in tucking her cloak about her or warming her mittened hands in my own. She colored at the contact but never pulled away.

We talked over dinner, and I learned more of her family—her beloved sister Jane and her younger sister Lydia. She spoke of her parents—the things her father had taught her, stories of her mother's whims and fits.

"What happened to Pemberley?" she asked one evening. We had both retired to the library, although neither of us seemed to be reading. I had been watching Elizabeth caress the pages of her book, her mind obviously occupied by other things.

I closed the book I had been ignoring and placed it beside me.

"You were not always . . . as you are now."

"No."

"And the servants?"

There was no reason for me to hide the truth from her. Not anymore. I trusted enough in Elizabeth's constitution that she would not faint for fear.

"It was dark magic," I began. "My mother was learned in the magical arts. Occasionally she took on students. One such was George Wickham."

Elizabeth listened in silence, the intensity in her countenance never wavering.

"He was the same age as me. Very charming and a very quick learner. My mother was proud of her pupil."

Elizabeth leaned forward in her chair. "And then?"

"And then he began to delve into darker spells, darker magic. My mother did not approve. Finally, after a great argument, she asked him to leave without a written character." I had never seen my mother more incensed, a formidable woman full of righteous indignation. "Wickham was livid. He vowed revenge. He returned a year later intent on destroying my mother. But she was already dead.

"The night he returned had been warm, the windows and doors of Pemberley open and inviting the breeze inside. It was Wickham who had come instead. A servant had warned me, and I went out to meet him before he could step inside the house, to tell him of my parents' deaths in the hopes that he would move on.

"When he could not have his revenge on her, he cursed Pemberley. Every person in this manse received a mark, a scar that never heals, the agony relentless."

"Just one?"

My smile was bitter. "Except for me."

Her eyes traveled over my body, at the scars she knew hid beneath my clothes to the ones visible on my face and neck. "You are in constant anguish?"

I looked away. I did not want to see her pity. "We have all become accustomed to pain."

The fireplace popped, causing Elizabeth to jump. "Is there no way to reverse the spell?"

I gave her a sad smile, a wish for forgiveness. "None that I know of."

Elizabeth rose from her chair and sat down next to me. Slowly, as if in hesitation, she took my hand in hers. "I am sorry."

I pressed my lips to her hand and her chest rose with a breath. "It is not your fault. But thank you for your kindness."

A thought flashed across her face but I knew not what. "Kindness is easy to give."

I studied her hand in mine. A red patch of skin showed below her knuckles. "Have you been hurt?"

"No . . ." She glanced at her hand. My thumb lightly brushed over the inflamed skin and, she twitched. I let go.

That was the first of many truths and confidences shared. We also had evenings with the servants, small parties where we could talk and play cards. Plumette and Elizabeth would take turns at the piano. I delighted in watching her laugh and smile unobserved—at the heat that would color her neck and cheeks when she perceived me looking.

One evening, Elizabeth called for dancing. I watched the servants ignore the unrelenting aches from their scars and take their turns about the room, Lumiere leading the dance with Plumette. Elizabeth played the piano, the music and laughter filling the spaces that for so long had been empty and cold. She had brought life back to Pemberley—and happiness.

"Might I have this dance," I asked Elizabeth, proffering my hand, my heart, and hoping she would accept both.

Her eyes met mine, uncertain. Her fingers stilled on the piano keys.

"Only if you wish it," I said.

Resolve lit her expression, and I prepared myself for the sting of rejection, but she said, "I do."

I led Elizabeth to the middle of the room, her hand small and warm in mine. Plumette began a waltz, and I twirled Elizabeth around the room, long-forgotten steps coming easily to my feet. My hand pressed into her back, pulling her closer. She did not pull away.

"I must thank you."

She lowered her lashes. "It is just a dance, Mr. Darcy."

"Please, call me Fitzwilliam." She tilted her head up. "And not for the dance. For this."

"Whatever do you mean . . . ?"

"You must know"—I twirled her away from me and then back into my embrace. She was even closer now, her heat pressing into my body, setting me aflame—"Pemberley has changed since you have come. I have changed."

Her lips parted, and I was desperate to taste them. I swallowed. Her eyes moved to my mouth.

"In essentials, I believe, you are very much as you ever were," she said. "But . . ." She glanced away. "I think you improve on acquaintance."

I arched an eyebrow. "Indeed?"

Defiance flashed across her face. "I still do not approve of the marriage contract. Or the mirror."

I blanched. "I . . . I'm sorry."

Her feet stopped moving and she stepped away from me. "Mr. Darcy." My heart sank as the wonderful moment dissipated. "I appreciate the letter you sent me, and all that you have done for my family. It is likely my father would have arranged some match for me, anyway. I only wish . . ."

My shoulders bowed. She still did not want this marriage. Want me.

"I wish you would have taken the time to court me properly first," she said. "Truly know me. Without the mirror."

"I never used the mirror nefariously."

She studied me. "I believe you," she said. "But it was still a violation of my privacy."

I turned away, shame-faced.

Her hand appeared on my arm, a gentle touch. "I think I understand now why you did not. You are humiliated by your appearance. But it would not have mattered to me."

I looked at her in disbelief. "Do not say such things when you do not know."

"I . . ."

"You would not have spared me one moment." She would have seen nothing more than a wounded man. She never would have given me more than a polite greeting.

Elizabeth shook her head, and I could only wonder if I had courted her first as she had said . . . I took her hand in mine. "Let us not dwell on the past, only on what future lies before us."

Elizabeth stared at our entwined hands, my scars blending with the red blotches still on her skin. "Does this not hurt?" she asked.

She had not let go—how could it possibly hurt?

The day was fine and I thought Elizabeth might join me for a walk. Upon inquiring of her mistress, Mrs. Reynolds told me Elizabeth remained in her room.

I knocked at Elizabeth's door.

"C—c—come in." Emotion clouded her voice.

I pushed my way into her room. Elizabeth sat on the bed, her head bowed.

"What is the matter?" Her tearstained face stopped my heart. I rushed to her side.

Elizabeth sobbed, tears splashing onto the mirror in her lap. I wrapped an arm around her shoulders and pulled her close, wanting to take away her sorrow. She rested her head against my chest.

"I am sorry," she said, sniffling. I handed her my handkerchief, and she dabbed the tears on her cheeks.

When she returned the handkerchief, I noticed the sore on her hand had changed. What had started as an angry patch of skin now looked like . . . a scar. My whole body went cold.

"You have nothing to be sorry for." My hands began to shake, anger threatening to burst forth. I tightened my grip on her. "Does it hurt?"

"What?" She noticed my gaze on her skin. "Yes, but it is not that. Nothing can be done." She looked on the verge of bursting into a fresh wave of tears, but instead she pressed her lips together.

I could not stop staring at Elizabeth's wound. Her *scar*. When I had asked, she had not remembered injuring her hand. How then had she gotten it?

I was certain of the answer, but I did not want to admit the truth.

"It is my sister, Lydia."

I blinked. *Lydia?* "What of her?"

"She ran off." She took a shuddering breath. "With George Wickham."

"The wizard?" I could get no air into my lungs. Elizabeth scarred. Lydia with Wickham. I felt frozen. My disbelief quickly turned to shame.

This was Wickham's fault, not mine, I knew that. And yet . . . Elizabeth would not be scarred if I had not brought her here. And her sister. Why had Wickham taken her? Could he actually love her?

"May I see the mirror?" Wordlessly, she handed it to me. Wickham appeared much the same as he had before, just as handsome and cunning, though exhaustion seemed to draw on his features. He was staring right into the mirror, and at first, I worried he could see me, but when I called his name, he did not so much as blink. The image in the mirror retreated from his face to reveal a small room. A bed lay behind him, a form curled upon it.

"I do not know how this happened," she continued. "There was never talk of him at home. How does Lydia know him?"

I could only shake my head. He must have concealed himself from her family. Again, why? What was his motive?

Unless it was to exact even more revenge on me. Had he not had enough? Was not his vengeance complete?

Elizabeth pressed her scarred palm to her forehead, then winced. "I know not what to do. It appears my father is starting a search party to discover them, but Wickham is a wizard! Even if my father manages to find them, there is nothing he could do against such a man."

I took Elizabeth's hand in mine while my thoughts moved at a lightning pace. Mr. Bennet would never find Wickham, nor should he. It would only result in more misery.

If Lydia had gone willingly, if she truly loved him, was it my place to interfere?

It was more likely he had deceived her, flattered her, perhaps he used his power on her. Even if she did love him, she was in grave danger, for he could never love anyone but himself, of that I was certain.

"What is to be done?" Elizabeth moaned. "My poor mother cannot leave her bed, and there is no one to care for her—Jane has gone on her wedding tour. My father will leave on this fruitless quest, and oh! How did this happen?" The look she gave me implored me to give her answers. To rectify the situation.

Studying the mirror, I took in the room, the bureau, a small table with a washbasin, the four-poster bed. Wickham stood with his arms folded, staring out the window. "Where do you suppose they are?" Elizabeth asked, her fine eyes wild with worry. I hesitated but felt certain I knew where they were. "Wherever that is, I must go there. I must help her! Someone must rescue Lydia!"

It took me but an instant to realize I would do all in my power to rectify this— to stop Wickham and bring Lydia home. I would never allow harm to come to Elizabeth.

After this moment, I might never see her again.

"Elizabeth." I set the mirror down and took her face in my hand, brushed my thumb across her cheek. "My wife."

She did not flinch at the title. A fire in her eyes joined the despair that flooded her features. Her lips parted as my fingers brushed across them.

"You must go to Longbourn."

She stiffened. My eyes flitted to her scarred hand and continued. "I believe Wickham and Lydia are in the village. Return home. Stop your father from forming a search party. Keep your parents at home. Be with them. They need you. Stay inside and keep them safe. Do not search for Lydia. I will take care of this."

"But . . ."

I desperately wanted to hear the rest of her thought. *But* she was frightened for me? *But* she did not want to leave me? *But* she loved me?

Nothing further was said.

"Go home," I said. "I release you from the marriage contract." I swallowed, my throat thick. Escaping the nearness of her, I rose from the bed and turned away. "I will ensure your protection." If I died, Elizabeth would become a rich widow. Even if I survived my encounter with Wickham, she could not come back to Pemberley. I had already scarred her. What if the scarring were to spread? What if she became like me? "You will be Elizabeth Bennet once again. Your family will owe me nothing."

I looked back one last time. I ached for her; the distress near unbearable. "You will be free." Of Pemberley, of me. "Keep the mirror— so you may always remember."

"Mr. Darcy." She stood and took a few hesitant steps toward me, and I turned to meet her again.

I drank in her beauty—her poise, the turn of her mouth, and the brightness of her eyes, the intelligence behind them—and could not help but say, "You have been a balm, a healing power for the scars I carry, both inside and out. You have been a light in my darkness." Her face so close, I could feel the warmth from her sweet breath on my cheek, her breast rising and falling quickly. My heart ached for her. For all that might have been. With something like regret, I took her hand and kissed it, then gently turned it over in my own and kissed her palm, her scar. There was no time for anything more. I bowed goodbye to my wife, my Elizabeth.

Elizabeth did as I bade. From my room, I watched her gallop away from Pemberley.

"She will never return," I whispered to myself.

I turned away to concentrate on my mission. I armed myself with a bow and arrows, a sword, and three daggers which I hid about my person. It had been long since I had trained in such martial arts, but I would not approach Wickham completely helpless. I worried the Fates were against me, but I felt more confident with a sword at my hip.

"Mr. Darcy, wait," Cogsworth called as I headed for the stables. He and Lumiere had followed me outside. "You should not go alone."

I stopped. "This must be done."

"It will mean your death," Lumiere said.

"If I do not return, go to my study. In the top drawer of my desk is a letter. Read it." Elizabeth would receive a large sum of money, but Pemberley would belong to all who lived there. They could remain or sell and divide the earnings, I did not care. It was all I could do for those who had remained loyal to me in my darkest moments.

"But sir—"

"I am sorry about the agonies you have had to endure. Truly sorry."

They continued to call out to me but I ignored them, leaping onto my horse and galloping for the village, ignoring the pain that increased when I rode. The road was dusted with snow but the sky was clear and crisp. My cloak streamed behind me, but I slowed as I neared the village, pulling my hood up to conceal my face.

I headed for the village square. The mirror had shown me enough to indicate Wickham and Lydia were at the inn facing the square. I left my horse at the village mews, and tossing a coin to a young stable lad, I strode towards the inn.

I pressed myself against a shop that lay opposite the inn, and peered across to the windows above for a glimpse of Wickham but saw nothing.

As it was market day, the village was busy.

I could draw Wickham out, but then others might be harmed. If I could discover which room they were in, I might be able to take him by surprise. I could not afford to wait. Stealth was my best option. If I could but sneak past the innkeeper, then I might try every door . . .

"Darcy!"

I flinched.

Wickham stood in the doorway of the inn, a smile on his comely face.

He had gained the attention of some villagers as he slowly crossed the square, his cloak billowing around his legs. My heart beat wildly as I pressed into the wall behind me.

Wickham stopped at the fountain in the center of the square.

"Darcy. I knew you would come."

Trembling, I straightened to my full height. Wickham had taken so much from me; he would not take my pride.

I stepped out of the shadows and into the square.

Wickham smiled. "There you are." He cocked his head. "And yet, is it you? Let us see that face of yours. Let everyone see it."

My cloak flew from my face. People around me gasped; a child screamed.

"Monster!" Wickham hissed. The cry was taken up by the villagers.

Wickham's expression was too knowing, too satisfied. If he wanted more revenge on me, this was it, and he had to do so little to get it.

Fear and self-loathing filled me, but my righteous anger ruled. The monster was not me. Elizabeth had helped me to control my temper. She had seen me beneath the scars.

The true monster stood before me.

I unleashed my bow, cocked an arrow and aimed it at Wickham's heart. A hush fell over the square.

"Give Lydia back to her family."

Wickham threw his head back and laughed. He muttered under his breath and flicked his wrist. My bow and arrow were wrenched from my grasp.

I pulled my sword, gripping it tight. "Give Lydia back to her family."

His lip curled. "Her family can have her. She has satisfied my need."

So, it was as I had surmised. He had taken Lydia to draw me out.

"When will your vengeance be satisfied?"

"When you are dead. When Pemberley and all you hold dear is mine." He cocked his head. "Including Elizabeth."

A scream tore from my throat and I lunged at him.

A force hit me, and I flew backward; my breath knocked from me as I landed on the ground. Shouts rent the air. Villagers were running. Some were hurled to the ground as Wickham tossed them aside to stand before me.

My scars were aflame, but I ignored the sensation. I lashed out with my sword. He grunted as it grazed his shin. My satisfaction was short as he once again threw my body with his power as if I weighed nothing. I smashed into a market cart, crushing fruits and bowls under me. My sword slipped from my grasp.

"Your mother denied me. But now I will finally have it all."

Clenching my teeth, I rolled off the cart to my knees. I struggled to stand, but Wickham placed his foot on my back and pushed me to the ground. He dug his shoe into the scars he knew rested beneath my clothes.

I grunted, pressing my lips together to keep from screaming.

"You cannot win."

"I know." It came out as a gasp.

Wickham bent over me. "What was that? Are you giving up already?" He lightened the pressure on my back slightly.

"I cannot win against your magic."

But I cannot let you have Elizabeth, I thought, and plunged my dagger upward.

It never reached its mark. Wickham knocked the dagger from my hand. I had failed. Wickham's foot disappeared from my back, and I looked up at him. He had turned away from me, laughing.

"You brought reinforcements!"

Arrows started to fly at Wickham, but he knocked them aside. He moved away from me; his laughter turned to words I could not understand.

Someone was there . . . a shaking hand . . . helping me to stand.

"Mrs. Reynolds," I said in surprise. And then I saw them—the servants of Pemberley—shooting arrows or throwing rocks at Wickham. Cogsworth, wielding an axe, had the lead of this ragtag army.

A tiny army that would soon perish, for they were no match for Wickham's power. He knocked them down, bodies crumpling to the ground. But they stood again. They continued to fight, these people who had become intimate with pain. And that's when I knew. They were not only fighting for me, they were fighting for themselves.

"Make sure Elizabeth is safe!" I said to Mrs. Reynolds. I quickly located my sword then ran for the wizard.

He stopped me before I could strike, knocking my sword away. I managed to keep my grip and swung again. Again, he threw me backward.

I struggled to my feet. A body lay crumpled beside me. Lumiere. Blood leaked from his mouth, trickled into the scar on his neck. His eyes were closed. Gritting my teeth, I lunged back into the fray.

We could not beat his dark power. The servants of Pemberley were falling around me. They did not rise again. Soon it would be only me against Wickham once more, and I did not know how to defeat the wizard.

I attacked but Wickham was ready. My sword spun from my grip. I lunged at him, throwing my body against his. He did not expect it, and I tackled him to the ground.

We struggled. I reached for a hidden dagger, the hilt brushing against my palm. His fist punched into my thigh just as I freed the dagger from my boot and brought the blade upward. His mouth opened in surprise. I leaned away to see the blade buried into his side. Wickham's eyes met mine.

"Why the ruse with Lydia?" I implored. "Why not just take Pemberley?"

He coughed, blood forming at his lips. "I cannot touch Pemberley. I cannot even enter the grounds."

"But the dark magic? The servants?"

"Loyalty and love to the Darcy name bound all to you. If it had not been for your mother's protection spell . . ."

My mother. Her magic had protected me all this time, and I had not known. If I had ventured outside Pemberley, I was vulnerable. But my wounded pride had protected me from ever leaving the grounds. Wickham could not get to me. Thus, he had taken Lydia.

And before that even . . . "The wolves." He had sent the wolves to attack Elizabeth. He knew I would come after her. He had probably anticipated the wolves would finish me off.

Wickham began to laugh, a choking sound, drawing my eyes to him.

He still lay on the ground but the blood was gone from his mouth.

I heard a scream from behind me.

"No!"

My heart froze at Elizabeth's voice.

My own dagger plunged into my belly.

"No!"

I fell back, my hands gripping the hilt of the dagger. Wickham rose to his feet and stood over me, grinning.

"I will not be denied," he said. "Everything you have will be mine. Including—"

Elizabeth.

He lifted his hand and muttered a spell, casting a blinding light at Elizabeth. She leapt past me, the mirror in her hand, and she swung it at Wickham.

The reflected spell struck Wickham in the chest. His mouth gaped in a silent scream as the light consumed him, then blinked out.

Wickham fell to the ground.

I felt my own lifeblood draining away.

"Elizabeth."

She stood with her back to me, frozen, the mirror still raised. I wanted her to turn around so I could look at her.

"Is he . . . did I . . .?" Her arm dropped to her side.

Wickham did not breathe.

"He's dead."

She finally turned at my words.

"It was the mirror," I said, then clenched my teeth at the pain. "Not you." Either Wickham's spell had hit the mirror and rebounded on himself, or my mother's magic was still protecting me and those I loved. I wanted to think the latter.

Her eyes moved to the dagger protruding from my belly; tears began to fall. She knelt at my side. "I am so sorry . . . I'm sorry I was too late."

I touched the curls that had escaped down her neck, ran my fingers along her cheek to her lips.

"I never wanted another but you." My thumb grazed her lips; they parted under my touch. "I am sorry for what I did, but I will never regret the time you spent at Pemberley as my wife."

The pain was becoming nothing now, and I knew I was slipping away.

She held my hand to her lips and kissed it. "Please," she cried. "Don't leave me. Not now."

I wanted to do as she asked, but my eyes grew heavy, and it became difficult to draw breath.

Elizabeth leaned over and kissed my forehead. "Mr. Darcy." She kissed my cheek. "Fitzwilliam."

She had never called me that before. I would not regret if my name on her lips was the last I heard.

Her lips touched my chin. "My husband."

I opened my mouth to reply, to call her "wife" and "my Elizabeth", but she captured my last breath in her mouth. She kissed me with lips as soft as a rose petal.

As my eyes slipped closed, I heard her voice once more.

"I love you."

Death was not how I imagined. I had lived in the darkness, and pain had been my friend. I had been proud and conceited, then ashamed, angry, and full of hate.

Death should be cold, but I was warm.

Death should be dark, but I was surrounded by light.

Death should be lonely, but my eyes were open and Elizabeth was before me.

"Fitzwilliam?"

My heart beat beneath my chest; blood flowed through my veins. I breathed, and it was life.

By some miracle, I was alive.

The light around me had faded, the warmth gone with it. I shivered at the sudden cold, my fists clenching, anticipating the pain of my scars.

But there was no pain.

I looked down at my hands. I raised my sleeves, lifted my shirt.

"No scars," I said in wonder. My gaze met Elizabeth's. Her eyes were on my bare chest, and she blushed. I grinned.

"Mr. Darcy!"

Cogsworth was running toward me. Running, with no limp! Behind him came Lumiere—alive—pressing a handkerchief to a wound, but his neck was unscarred. Mrs. Reynolds and Plumette were hugging, Plumette's laugh ringing through the village square. Everywhere I looked, the servants of Pemberley were smiling, free of pain at last.

I rose to my feet. I grabbed Elizabeth's hand, searching, but there was no trace of her scar left. I kissed the unmarred skin. "You did it. You freed us from the dark magic."

She shook her head. Her lip trembled. "I am sorry." She touched my cheek, and I knew it was there. Her fingers traced one jagged scar that cut across my left cheekbone. I smiled and felt nothing. I moved my hand to her hand, drawing her palm to my lips.

"Elizabeth." I wanted to reach for her, to take her in my embrace and kiss her. My lips remembered hers, my ears the words she had spoken. Had it all been a dream? A last wish of a dying man?

"You have given me everything, and I would like nothing more than to spend the rest of my days giving you all that I am in return."

She opened her mouth, but I stopped her from speaking.

"You said once you would never forgive me for the things I did. I will always want you for my wife, but I set you free. If that is your wish? My wishes are unchanged, but one word from you will silence me on this subject forever."

"Mr. Darcy." She placed her hands on her hips. "I am your wife. You are my husband. You cannot be free of me."

"I will not have you stay out of obligation."

Her fingers pressed against my mouth.

"I love you," she said. "I hardly know how, but I know why. And while you spend your days giving me all of you, which I very much look forward to by the way"—she raised an eyebrow and my whole body lit aflame—"I will spend my days telling you why."

I grabbed her hips and pulled her close. She wrapped her arms around my neck.

"I am still scarred."

"Does it hurt?" she asked.

I shook my head.

She pressed her lips to the scar, and I felt like she was sealing us together, more than our marriage vows ever had.

I took her lips in mine. Her mouth was soft and warm, and I wanted to lose myself in her. But she pulled away.

"Take me home," she said. "To Pemberley."

And I obeyed my wife, my Elizabeth. The beauty who had tamed the beast of Pemberley.

MELANIE STANFORD reads too much, plays music too loud, is sometimes dancing, and always daydreaming. She would also like her very own TARDIS but only to travel to the past. She lives in Canada with her husband and four kids. She is the author of *Sway*, a retelling of Jane Austen's *Persuasion*, shortlisted for the Kobo Emerging Writer Prize, and the short story "Becoming Fanny" featured in the anthology *Then Comes Winter*. Her second novel, *Collide*, inspired by Elizabeth Gaskell's *North and South*, is coming soon. You can find her at melaniestanfordbooks.com, on Twitter @MelMStanford, and on Facebook @MelanieStanfordauthor.

"In vain I have struggled. It will not do. My feelings will not be repressed. You must allow me to tell you how ardently I admire and love you."
—Mr. Darcy to Miss Elizabeth, Chapter XXXIV.

A RESENTFUL MAN

LORY LILIAN

The sound of the piano suffused the room, throwing a spell over those listening. My heart filled with love and pride for my sister, who seemed enraptured in her music and oblivious to the twenty pairs of captive eyes.

Georgiana's talent was only equalled by her sensible soul, and together with her diligent practise, had raised her proficiency to the rank of art. She, of course, was not affected by such praise. She loved music and—most of all—I knew that she aspired to please me. Every time our eyes met, I felt my sister's affectionate heart. And I sensed her sadness.

Though I knew myself to be a good, older brother, I often bore the guilt for the time I left her alone. Consigned to the company of our relatives and the amity of Mrs. Annesley, Georgiana was lonely, and her smiles were rarely more than polite.

My chest tightened as I realised I could not remember the last time I had heard her laugh. Other girls of sixteen seemed more playful, lively. An unwelcome vision of the youngest Bennet girls dancing and laughing at Bingley's ball flitted through my mind. Such careless behaviour I have witnessed, even in Town, of other young women of the same age. Why was Georgiana different? Was I at fault that she grew up restrained, so reticent? Had I not offered her enough affection, kindness, attention? She was always modest—and I could not recollect her ever asking for anything for herself.

I knew I must be to blame that she lacked confidence—that she could be so easily deceived by the scoundrel Wickham, that she had believed herself to be in love with him! But it was entirely to her merit that she was strong enough to remember her duty and reveal the mischievous plan soon enough for me to interfere. What if I had not visited her in Ramsgate that day? Too often I had envisioned that ghastly outcome and praised God for His intervention! Had I carried any hope that Wickham was an honourable man, that he possessed deep and genuine affection for Georgiana, would I have opposed him courting my sister and perhaps even marrying her? Surely not! Knowing Wickham as I did though, I could do nothing but break the connection—hopefully forever. . . . My deepest regrets were the heartache and the turmoil that unfortunate happenstance brought upon my dear sister. I would do anything to take her despair upon myself. And I would never forget Wickham's betrayal nor would I ever forgive him. For Georgiana—and many other transgressions.

The music stopped and several guests ventured to congratulate the performer. I knew she was uneasy in company and was tempted to hurry to her side but resisted the urge. Everyone in attendance was a family intimate: the Matlocks, their elder son with his wife, Bingley and his two sisters, Mr. Hurst, and Mrs. Annesley, as well as two young ladies—Lady Matlock's nieces. Georgiana was in no danger.

"This is a lovely party, Nephew," Lady Matlock said, from such a small distance that I startled.

I took her gloved fingers to my lips, feigning composure. Like my mother, she could ascertain my temperament despite my efforts to conceal it. "I thank you, Your Ladyship. I thought Georgiana deserved to celebrate her sixteenth birthday before we depart for Pemberley. We do not intend to return to Town next Season nor to travel during the winter."

"I understand. However, you must take into consideration that she must come out soon. Perhaps not next Season but the next."

"Yes . . . soon . . . She is still very young and not inclined to attend balls and parties."

"She likes nothing that you do not like," Lady Matlock replied with amusement. "I am not certain if it is her disposition or only her desire to please you."

I sensed my face frowning. "I always encourage her to speak freely and to pursue what she pleases. It is not my intention to impose my tastes on my sister."

"Of course not, my dear, do not be so grave. But you must admit that she not only loves you as a sister but also as a daughter might and would do nothing to disappoint you."

"She never disappoints me. One could never hope for a better sister."

Nodding to the companion at Georgiana's side, my aunt said, "Mrs. Annesley seems a very pleasant woman and quite fond of Georgiana."

"We have every reason to be satisfied with her services." A sudden lump lodged in my throat as I was reminded of Georgiana's former companion Mrs. Younge, and her deception . . .

"This is comforting. . . . However . . . I am thinking . . . she might benefit from the company of younger people . . . perhaps a younger companion . . . like a sister. . . "

I frowned again and said nothing to this.

"Miss Bingley and Mrs. Hurst are obviously intent on gaining her favour, although in a most cloying manner. Poor Georgiana shows more distress than pleasure from their company. It is transparent how Miss Bingley hopes to win your attention through friendship with your sister."

"Indeed. Transparent and unrealistic." *And ridiculous.*

"Touché. I was never concerned in this regard." She raised an eyebrow at me. "Mr. Bingley is also very friendly with Georgiana. And she looks quite at ease with him."

"Yes . . ."

"Do you suspect there may be more from this? Would you allow such an unequal union to take place? I know he is your friend, but his father was in trade. We cannot ignore that."

"Aunt, I value Bingley's friendship because he is one of the kindest, most honourable men I have ever known. I have no doubts that he shall make an excellent husband for the woman he chooses as his wife. And I would never oppose a match between Georgiana and a worthy man. However, I see no inclination toward any attachment beyond mutual friendship between Georgiana and Bingley."

"I see . . . well, we often see marriages started from less than a close friendship. . . . It is apparent that you dislike the subject."

"Dear Aunt, I am not averse to discourse with you, but this matter is irrelevant."

"Then I shall not persist. However, have you any news for me? Catherine is writing to us weekly, asking of you, insisting of your increased attachment to Rosings. You cannot keep Anne in such uncertainty for too long."

"I do not keep anyone in uncertainty, Aunt." I congratulated myself on maintaining my equanimity and yet, I continued. "Anne knows she cannot expect any engagement from me. And I repeatedly told Aunt Catherine that I will always keep Anne under my care and protection, but I have no marital aspirations with my cousin. It is only Aunt Catherine who perseveres."

"Just like Miss Bingley." Lady Matlock smiled.

"Quite."

"But . . . you must allow me: Is there any reason why you are against your marriage with Anne? All the circumstances would be in favour of such a union and I know you have great affection for her. And I never noticed you paying particular attention to any young lady. Might your interest and hopes lie elsewhere?"

I frowned again and my patience betrayed me. I could not bear to speak on that subject any longer. "Dear Aunt, I believe we have spent enough time with a conversation that will lead nowhere. Might I offer you another drink?"

She shook her head, and as I stepped to refill my own drink, I felt my aunt's gaze. With glass in hand, I took a chair at the corner of the room, grateful to Lady Matlock for not following me.

The music started again, and I gulped my brandy, attempting to calm myself. "You must allow me," my aunt had said, the words cutting me. *"You must allow me . . ."* I had said those same words three months before. They were the preamble to my surreptitious fall. The storm that started at the parsonage had ravaged everything. I had no marital interest nor hopes. *She* had burned them all and only ashes remained.

London was not far enough from Longbourn and her image still haunted my days and nights. I wished for nothing but to depart for Pemberley and leave behind my memories of her. I was obligated to take the Bingleys and the Hursts as I had invited them long ago, but—dear Lord—how painful the recollections their presence brought back. However, I had little else to do but bear it. My consolation was that Georgiana might benefit from the presence of a few guests. After all, I might retreat unto my own company if my guests entertained one another midst the delights of Pemberley.

"You must allow me to tell you how ardently . . ." That confession—my demand to her—still shamed me. Ardently. How ridiculous that word sounded after all these months. What was I thinking? Had I completely lost my reason? I had never named the word before I met Elizabeth, just as I had never associated the word "love" with anyone beyond Georgiana or my parents. How had I spoken those words to the very woman who wished to hear them least? My affection, my love, my passion, my desire—my hand and my heart—were rejected with such disdain, such anger, such horror that I knew I would never forget. Nor offer them again, to anyone, ever.

From so many faces, eyes of all colours and shapes had looked at me shyly or with pluck, pleading or demanding my attention, but none succeeded in catching my interest or stirring my thoughts or emotions. For many years, I had recognised and admired beauty, as I might a painting—from afar—until I fell under the enchantment of Elizabeth Bennet's eyes. Those fine eyes that sparkled and laughed even before the smile found her lips. She drew me in with a strength I could not defend and discovered myself trapped by a desire stronger than anything I had known before.

This unknown, powerful desire had permeated my senses: to be with her all the time, to hear her voice and her laughter, to speak to her, to touch her hand, to admire her light and pleasing figure. I had been plagued by vivid imaginings: removing her hairpins to allow the heavy locks to fall freely on her shoulders, brushing my fingers over her skin, tasting her lips, kissing her eyelids. . . . To be in her presence, every day, every moment. Forever.

My fascination quickly turned to alarm when I understood I had completely surrendered my desire to her. I could not fight these feelings I barely recognised or admitted. I was powerless. Profoundly aware of the impossibility of any connection between us, I reconciled that all hope was gone. At the Netherfield Ball, even the briefest touch of her hand during our one and only dance was more arousing than any other sensation I experienced with any other woman. Her closeness intoxicated me; her scent made me dizzy. Yet, her family's appalling behaviour and the prospect of Bingley marrying Jane Bennet—putting me in Elizabeth's proximity for a lifetime—panicked me. Thus, the very next day I departed Hertfordshire and cowardly allowed distance to contest my longing and sorrow.

I had thought, by detaching Bingley from Miss Jane Bennet as well, that I had been acting in the service of a friend. Alas, I now knew I had erred and was angry and penitent for my disservice.

I prided myself—and declared even in Elizabeth's presence—that I was a resentful man—that my good opinion once lost, was lost forever. After all my mistakes, after making a fool of myself, I had completely lost my own good opinion and the resentment against my own folly had been relentless.

When I left Netherfield, I was convinced Elizabeth had recognised my feelings and reciprocated them; that she was awaiting and encouraging my attentions. I imagined she was suffering after my departure. From November to April, I blamed myself for the distress I thought I had caused her.

As soon as I had received news from Lady Catherine that Mrs. Collins expected guests from Hertfordshire, including a certain Miss Elizabeth Bennet, a single sleepless night was enough for me to decide to leave for Rosings earlier than in other years. I was aware of the tremendous danger, recognising the trap I was setting for myself—but I could not resist the desire of seeing her again—just once more—under the perfect pretence of visiting my aunt and cousin. *"Disguise of any sort is my abhorrence."* I had pronounced to her once whilst at Netherfield. What a pretentious fool! I had done nothing but dissemble whenever I had crossed swords with Elizabeth Bennet.

Upon arrival in Kent, all my previous resolutions disappeared. I had taken every opportunity to call on the parsonage, enjoy her teasing nature and her inviting looks. I was convinced she purposely informed me of her favourite walks in the park. She played the piano at Rosings and while my cousin Colonel Fitzwilliam turned the pages for her, she used an affected joke to include me in their tête-à-tête. I had no doubts of her contriving little schemes and I was delighted to enjoy them. She referred often to our time in Hertfordshire and in rendering her feelings known to me, my desire for her grew until it conquered any resistance.

I knew I should run away but I could not. My bond to her had become unyielding. I postponed our departure twice to my cousin's puzzlement. At the first opportunity when I was certain she would be alone, I declared my defeat to her. I proclaimed my love, admiration, and passion were stronger even than my pride, duty, and reason. That no flaws of her family were enough to keep us apart. That I was willing to fight all of society for the bliss of being with her for a lifetime.

"You must allow me to tell you how ardently I admire and love you."

I spoke with determination, with fervour—with all my heart. Then the world collapsed around me.

"...you were the last man in the world whom I could ever be prevailed on to marry."

"...had you behaved in a more gentlemanlike manner."

"...your arrogance, your conceit, and your selfish disdain..."

In less than one half hour, the gate opened and threw me into the deepest hole. Even to this day, I cannot credit the words we said. She had held me responsible for interfering between Bingley and her sister and ruining their happiness but also for Wickham's misfortunes! Misfortunes indeed! The sting while witnessing the eager interest she proclaimed on behalf of that rogue was unmistakeable as was the cut of jealousy that only added to my turmoil.

Later that evening, I had made one last gesture of chivalry by writing her a letter, even explaining the sorry business between Wickham and my sister, and hoping to acquit myself of any wrongdoings toward my friend Bingley. Days later, I could not understand what induced me to make such a reckless gesture. I attributed it to my tormented mind and fatigue and that my love was more formidable than my sensibility. When sound judgment finally conquered my resentment, I admitted that I had no motives to doubt Elizabeth's discretion. She *had* disappointed me and betrayed my trust in her intellect by believing the most dishonourable of men, but I knew she would not expose to the censure of the world the error of a young girl.

As the days passed, I have come to accept the justice of Elizabeth Bennet's reproach. Although she had been wrong in some of her accusations, she was justified in others. Her low opinion of me was entirely due to my own poor manners during our acquaintance. Many other women would have eagerly accepted me, placing my situation and wealth above my behaviour. But she had not—and that was a proof of her worthiness; I was finally reasonable enough to accept that. And recognise what I had truly lost.

"Darcy, are you unwell?"

"Pardon?" I shook my head to return from my ruminations and was met by Bingley's furrowed brow. "I should not have had the second glass of brandy, I suppose."

Bingley laughed. "I cannot believe that. I have yet to see you affected by any kind of drink. You must be distracted with business matters."

"Hmm . . . I hope you are enjoying yourself. Georgiana is pleased to see you."

"As are we to see her. And very obliged to you for including us in your family party." Bingley continued. "And for inviting us to Pemberley."

"It was long ago established we would spend the summer at Pemberley together, and I saw no reason to rescind it," I said, and we chuckled over our drinks.

"True . . . long ago . . . since we were at Netherfield even," Bingley added in a lower voice.

My guilt cut fiercely and the recollection spoilt my mood again. Expectedly, Bingley was even more affected. Poor fellow. He knew only that his felicity had been shattered and he still suffered for his unreturned affection. I had long planned to confess the whole truth to him at Pemberley, accepting the risk of jeopardising our friendship.

We spoke nothing more—what could be said on that subject between two gentlemen during a party?

"I need another drink," I said while moving toward the sideboard. "Would you join me?"

"Most certainly."

Close to midnight, silence eventually wrapped Darcy House, and I offered Georgiana my arm as we walked together along the hall towards our apartments.

"Brother, how can I thank you for this lovely evening?"

I gently kissed her hand. "Surely you do not intend to thank me, dearest. Or perhaps you should wait until we arrive at Pemberley. There may be a few more surprises waiting for you and you might thank me for all at once," I quipped. Her clear blue eyes widened in delight.

"More surprises? Oh, you should not have told me, because now I will not be able to sleep. But no surprises are needed, leaving for Pemberley is enough. I am so happy! Mrs. Annesley is all anticipation, and rightfully so. I am sure she has never seen a more beautiful home than Pemberley."

"I only hope you will not grow weary of the retired pace at Pemberley."

"Never. I would be perfectly content to live only at Pemberley for the rest of my life. But how are you feeling, Brother? Are you eager for this journey? I see you smiling so rarely."

"I am pleased to see you happy, dearest. Your joy makes me smile. There is nothing more important to me than you, Georgiana."

"As there is nothing more important to me than you, dear brother. I would do anything to see you smiling more. I saw you quite preoccupied during the party too. Was it because of Miss Bingley? I know her attention to you is tiresome . . . I wonder how will you bear such a long journey in her proximity?"

"You are very perceptive, my dear. It is quite tiresome, but it is surely not enough reason for concern. And I already planned to travel by horse, thus I will not be in anybody's *proximity*."

Georgiana released a small laugh and I continued, "But is Miss Bingley tiresome for you too? Does she trouble you?"

"Oh no . . . perhaps only sometimes . . . when she insists that I am perfectly accomplished and she praises me exceedingly. I know she is only dissembling to draw your attention . . ."

"Well, I cannot fault her in this matter—you are perfectly accomplished and I could not be more proud."

"Oh, you are simply partial to me, as a good brother should be . . . but any accomplishments I might have, I owe entirely to your guidance. I confess, besides my playing, I enjoy improving my mind through extensive reading—as you advised me years ago," my sweet sister replied with good humour.

Instead of smiling, I felt the blood drain from my face as those very words spoken so condescendingly to Elizabeth at Netherfield came flooding back to me. My sister's distress shadowed across her countenance.

"Brother?"

I cleared my throat and kissed her hand again. "I was only considering that it is very late and we must retire for the night."

She did not insist further as we continued toward our apartments, but her curiosity—and her concern were apparent. While climbing the stairs, my thoughts became restless. Before my sister entered her room, I suddenly turned to her. "Dearest, would you mind if I left for Pemberley a day early? I remembered I must arrange several things before you arrive. Would it be acceptable for you to travel with Mrs. Annesley and Bingley? I will make all the arrangements to ensure you a safe and pleasant journey."

Georgiana's surprise was impossible to conceal and her face paled. I have seen her anxiety too often to miss its significance. "Only if this is acceptable to you, my dear."

"It is, Brother, if this is your wish. Anything that gives you peace and comfort is acceptable to me. I only wish to see you smiling more."

In the middle of July, remaining faithful to my precipitate journey, I left London one full day ahead of my party. I was anxious to leave my anguish behind, inducing me to hurry toward Pemberley. I prepared Georgiana's travel as promised and included my valet in the servants' coach. I congratulated myself for the brilliance of travelling alone. Having to bear three days on the road with Miss Bingley and Mrs. Hurst was an ordeal that I happily avoided.

I found contentment to ride alone with nothing to disturb me except my thoughts. During the journey, I stopped at every inn where my party was scheduled and confirmed their arrangements. I rested only as needed, thus, at noon on the third day, I reached the boundary of Pemberley Park.

I hoped, nay, waited to feel the same peace which enveloped me every time I arrived home. The serenity, beauty, comfort, and safety that Pemberley always granted me was what I sought. Perhaps now I would be able to find rest and sleep, then forgive myself, and Elizabeth—and forget. The estate's chestnut trees dancing in the wind were the proper shelter in which to hide from the reminders of the past.

The splendour of Pemberley overwhelmed me and once again I felt proud to call it my home. However, unlike other times, my restlessness only increased with every step.

My trusty steed, Duke, showed signs of impatience, too, as he recognised the surroundings and I gave him free rein to gallop through the pastures. I took off my hat, allowing the breeze to cool my head—and troubled mind. I urged the horse on as if in a competition with my old self—as I struggled to leave behind the past and the agony.

The race ceased only when we arrived at the stables. By then, Duke was lathered from the exertion, but I felt more alive, more spirited than in a long while. I abandoned my beaver and coat to an awaiting footman and ambled toward the garden. I was home. At last.

I took the path by the river, to admire more of the beauties that surrounded me. I breathed deeply, inhaling the serenity of Pemberley and closed my eyes, enjoying the peace. When I opened them, the entire sky collapsed on my shoulders, and I almost knelt under its weight at the vision before me. I remained still, the beating of my heart thrumming through my entire body.

It was not a spectre bursting from my restless dreams. It was as true as it was agonising to see Miss Elizabeth Bennet, the woman who had invaded my mind and soul, walking toward me at Pemberley.

"Mr. Darcy!"

Profound astonishment struck me silent and unmoving. I heard her incredulous voice but was not certain if I answered her. She was within twenty yards of me. I had not missed her intention to turn away and I wondered what she could be doing there. My eyes instantly met hers, and I saw her cheeks colour whilst I felt my own face burn. I noticed a fashionably dressed lady and gentleman approaching her; however, my attention returned to Elizabeth in an instant.

Feeling all the embarrassment for my unseemly attire, I exchanged a quick glance with Elizabeth, and a battle began between my mind and my soul. I wished nothing but to vanish into the house while joy raced my heart and I prayed for the strength to stand still. I gathered my courage, tugged at my waistcoat, and strode towards the party then bowed to Elizabeth.

"Miss Bennet . . . what a surprise. Your family is in good health, I trust." My tone was hardly composed, but I hoped I sounded at least civil.

"I . . . we . . . I am travelling with my uncle and aunt . . . we did not. . . . It is indeed a surprise to see you too, sir. Yes, my family is in excellent health." Her anxiety was apparent in her eyes and the blushing of her cheeks was now replaced by pallor. She seemed breathless. The gleam in her eyes, the smiles, the teasing voice were replaced by civility. "We did not expect to see you here, sir. . . . Your housekeeper told us you were not expected until tomorrow. And we inquired in Lambton and everybody ensured us that you were not here. . . . Otherwise, I would never have dared . . ."

Her incoherent speech was less impressive than the expression on her face and the inflections in her voice. I understood that she struggled to tell me more than the words allowed, but my previous faulty understanding of her feelings forbade me to assume too much. However, the obvious could not be rejected. She was embarrassed, ashamed, and rightfully so. To come to my estate after everything that had happened was—

"My aunt grew up in Lambton and she has spoken highly of Pemberley. She insisted on me seeing it. If not for her I would not have . . . we did not know . . ." Words tumbled from her trembling lips and her hands clasped tightly to her reticule.

She had come to Pemberley at her relatives' insistence. She had been convinced I was away. I *should* have been away, and had I not hurried to leave London earlier I would have never met her. I could not fault her for her appearance. Many day-trippers visited Pemberley this time of year. She had come believing in my absence, not my presence.

"We beg your forgiveness for the intrusion, Mr. Darcy. We shall leave now," Elizabeth murmured, turning hesitantly.

She looked abashed, distressed. Perhaps even regretful. Perhaps only at that moment did she realise what it meant to be the mistress of Pemberley. What did she think when she understood she could have been the mistress of all before her? At that moment, had I felt less, I might have had my revenge; my resentment might have found its gratification.

And yet, as I studied her carefully, as I used to do in Hertfordshire and Kent, I felt all the mortification that troubled her. I wanted only to relieve her anguish. Her shoulders fell under the weight of my scrutiny and her eyes lowered to the ground.

My heart broke. This time not because of her, but for her. I could not permit her to feel humiliation in front of her relatives. I would never forget her present mien and would never forgive myself for causing it. I could not overlook her discomfort an instant longer. "Miss Bennet, would you do me the pleasure of introducing me to your relatives?"

I hoped my voice was welcoming; she turned toward me, her bewilderment and disbelief impossible to miss. "I . . . yes, of course . . . Mr. Darcy, these are Mr. and Mrs. Gardiner. They live in London, near Cheapside," she added and for an instant, I recognised a wisp of Miss Elizabeth Bennet's wry tone. She had not forgotten how Miss Bingley and I had commented about her relatives in trade nor my tirade about the unworthiness of her family during my proposal.

". . . had you behaved more gentlemanlike manner."

I bowed and offered a polite smile. "Mr. Gardiner, Mrs. Gardiner, it is a pleasure to meet you. I am glad you decided to visit Pemberley and I trust you will not be disappointed in it."

"We are honoured to make your acquaintance, Mr. Darcy," Mr. Gardiner answered. "Indeed, we are amazed at the beauty of your estate. I can safely declare it is one of the finest in England."

"The finest," Mrs. Gardiner said with genuine delight on her face. "Sir, I must confess that I grew up in Lambton, and I have always admired Pemberley from afar as a child. Now that I have seen a little bit of the house, I can say my imagination did not do it justice."

It was my turn to be surprised. The Gardiners looked like impeccably fashionable people, and they expressed themselves admirably. Did I also recognise relief on Elizabeth's face as she witnessed our amiable conversation? Did she still believe I would be rude and indifferent? Of course she did. She had shared her opinion of me clearly enough at Hunsford.

I tried to widen my smile. "I am pleased to hear your positive account, Mrs. Gardiner." Smoothing the silk of my waistcoat, crushingly aware of all the dust and sweat from my travels and all the awkwardness at such a meeting, I continued, "I have only just arrived from London. I must beg your forgiveness, but I must leave you now. I hope you will stay to continue your tour of the estate. I would suggest you follow the path near the water and take a stroll in the wood nearby. There are some fine trees and lovely flowers to admire. Soon enough, you will reach the highest place, which will offer you the finest view of the valley, the hills, the stream, and the house itself. I believe it worth your effort."

"Thank you, sir, we will do just that," Mr. Gardiner answered.

I bowed again, and I departed as quickly as possible. My neck prickled as I imagined Elizabeth following me with her eyes, and I needed all my strength not to turn around. What was she thinking of me now? Will they continue the tour? What if they leave? Were they staying in Lambton? What a fool I have been not to inquire.

When I was certain I had disappeared from their sight, I almost ran inside. Mrs. Reynolds greeted me with her usual enthusiasm. I responded briefly and then hurried to my apartment, where a footman was unpacking my bag.

"Wilford, help me change. I do not have a moment to lose."

"Of course, sir."

Indeed, my mind and body had received a dose of energy that made me dizzy. I was nervous but an enormous burden had been removed from my shoulders, and the deep fog that had kept my mind prisoner had vanished. I could think. I could breathe. I could even smile.

I had little patience whilst Wilford searched for proper clothes. Staring through the glazing to the lake, I could not see the visitors and attempted to guess where they might be—hoping they had not left the park.

Astonishing! I had travelled to Pemberley to escape memories of Elizabeth Bennet only to meet her at Pemberley.

Now, all my thoughts were fixed on that one spot of the estate, wherever she might be. I longed to know her mind and what she thought of me. Had her opinion of me changed since last April? Did she give any importance to my letter? Was she still angry with me for the sorrow I had caused her sister? Did she approve of Pemberley?

Surely, she was surprised by my civility. But what did she think of my wild appearance? Dear Lord, how she had seen me dishevelled upon arrival! That was shameful indeed. What had made me take off my coat?

Did she feel more pain or pleasure in seeing me? Did she feel any pleasure at all?

If she loathed my memory, surely, she would not have come to visit my estate. Even if she was certain about my absence, she would not have approached a place that brought her remorse.

By the time I was refreshed and properly attired, my decision was made. I would do everything in my power to make a favourable second impression. I exited the house, looking for the visitors.

My spirit lifted when I observed them on the opposite bank of the river. Their progress was slow, Mrs. Gardiner holding onto her husband's arm. She was certainly not a great walker, I mused. Elizabeth appeared distressed, looking around absently and turning often to her relatives.

When she noticed my approach, surprise held her still again. Would she prefer my absence?

Upon reaching the party, I was content to see their enthusiastic greeting. Of Mr. and Mrs. Gardiner's feelings about my presence, I had no doubts.

"Mr. Darcy, I cannot congratulate you enough on this wonderful property," Mr. Gardiner said. "We are only desolate that we could not see more of it. We intended to take a tour of the entire park, but we were told that it would be a walk of more than ten miles."

"True. It is quite a long walk. Perhaps Miss Bennet would not mind taking it, but for most people it would be too long."

I did not know what caused me to make such a teasing remark. I glanced to her only to witness her countenance blush most becomingly. Although I could not claim any proficiency in reading her thoughts, she did not look displeased.

Mr. Gardiner laughed. "True. Lizzy is a great walker, almost as accomplished as she is a great reader."

I decided that it was safer to turn my attention toward Mr. Gardiner and said, "Yes, I am familiar with Miss Elizabeth Bennet's excellent walking skills and her love for reading." At the guest's puzzled expression, I chanced a look at Elizabeth and this time I caught the amusement in her eyes. "I had the pleasure of Miss Elizabeth's acquaintance at Netherfield when she took care of Miss Bennet. I was quite impressed with her determination to walk three miles to be at the side of her sister, as well as with her obvious passion for books."

"I surely do not deserve such praise," Elizabeth intervened hesitantly. "But I confess I would gladly walk ten miles for the pleasure of admiring all the beauties of your estate."

I felt the beginnings of a smile as her embarrassment seemed to dissipate. A smile hinted at her lips, too, and her eyes brightened.

"Well, I fear, this will be the split within our party. Mrs. Gardiner surely wishes to rest here a moment. Whilst Lizzy rambles amongst the picturesque, I will gladly stay right here and glimpse the trout. If only I had my fishing tackle with me, I would want nothing more."

They laughed together, some more at ease than others. Mr. Gardiner seemed gentleman-like and I would surely enjoy spending more time in his company. My disposition brightened with each passing moment.

"Perhaps we could find a way to ensure equal entertainment for everyone. If you happen to remain longer in the neighbourhood, it would be my pleasure to have you come and fish at Pemberley, sir. I will happily supply you with fishing tackle and will point out those parts of the stream where there is usually more sport. I enjoy fishing myself. As for the ladies, we can offer them a small phaeton and they can spend as much time as they like visiting the park."

At the stunned faces in front of me, I could not help but wonder how low—or frightening—was their opinion of me that they took such an invitation so hesitantly? Had Elizabeth spoken of me poorly to her relatives?

"Mr. Darcy, this is beyond any of our expectations," Mr. Gardiner finally replied. "We could not possibly intrude . . . we understand you expect a large party of friends tomorrow. . . . But we are deeply honoured and flattered by your attention."

"Sir, rest assured that I never issue an invitation to people whose company do not give me pleasure. Miss Bennet can testify to that." At that, I could not help but notice Elizabeth bite her lip as if to stifle her own laughter.

But her uncle's joy was unrestrained. "In this case, sir, I shall gladly accept your invitation. To be honest, I do not intend to disturb anyone but your fish."

I laughed and turned to the ladies, expectantly. Elizabeth averted her eyes, allowing her aunt to answer, although it was Elizabeth's opinion that mattered the most to me.

"I do have fixed engagements with my friends in Lambton, but it will be my greatest pleasure to accept your generous invitation, Mr. Darcy. And you, Lizzy?"

I stole a look at Elizabeth. She still would not meet my eyes.

"Yes, of course. . . . It is a very generous offer, sir."

"Excellent." I motioned for the ladies to take the lead, while Mr. Gardiner and I followed. Mr. Gardiner peppered me with questions about the estate and I struggled to attend his conversation, eager as I was to speak with Elizabeth.

After walking some time in this manner, Mrs. Gardiner declared she was fatigued and found Elizabeth's arm inadequate to her support and consequently preferred her husband's.

With no little eagerness, I took her place by her niece, and we walked on together. My steps turned hesitant and my breathing irregular. She smelled of rose petals and sunshine, and her proximity warmed me more than the summer day. I knew I must speak, but I feared the words would betray my emotions.

"Mr. Darcy, I . . ." Her voice was timid, then stopped as she seemed to gather her courage. "Sir, please allow me to apologise again for our unexpected appearance. Even before we left Bakewell, we understood that you were not immediately expected in the country; and then your housekeeper informed us that you would certainly not be here till tomorrow. Otherwise, I would never have dared to trespass upon your privacy."

"Miss Bennet, I beg you not to distress yourself. It was indeed arranged that we would arrive no sooner than tomorrow but I came a day early. I have some business to complete."

Then, with a will of their own, before my mind had time to caution against such imprudence, words tumbled from my mouth. "I confess I am glad that all these coincidences occurred. Embarrassed at first, troubled still, but pleased."

As soon as I finished, my heart stopped, too. Her answer came after a brief hesitation, her voice still trembling. "I am pleased too. . . . Embarrassed . . . troubled . . . incredulous to receive more attention than I could ever expect. . . . But glad . . ."

My heart must have started beating again as a wave of exultation—such as I did not believe possible to experience—spread through me, and I could feel the truth of her confession.

She was pleased. Happy to be at Pemberley. With me.

We continued to walk in silence, as the short dialogue drained all our remaining bravery. The distance between us slowly diminished and I was exceedingly aware that, if I but stretched my hand, I might have easily touched hers. The marvel was not lost on me that she had continued at my side.

When the silence became too heavy to bear, I gave her news I hoped would please her. "There are a few friends that will join me tomorrow and among them are some who will claim an acquaintance with you."

She nodded.

"Mr. Bingley and his sisters." I sensed her tension and understood her uneasiness, as I remembered the last time Mr. Bingley's name had been mentioned between us. It was my turn—my duty—to say something more.

She deserved at least a hint of my regrets for my past behaviour. "Mr. Bingley and I have not seen each other as often as we used to. . . . He . . . neither of us was in our usual disposition in the last months," I confessed.

"Oh . . . I see . . ."

"Bingley will be very pleased to see you."

"As will I to see him." Her hand brushed along the fragrant lavender, adding to the intoxicating scent of her presence.

"I imagined as much. I know you always held him in esteem and rightfully so. He is one of the best men I know." The conversation glided to a dangerous point and I was aware of the peril, but I wanted her to understand that I took on the entire responsibility for what had happened between my friend and her sister. "He can hardly be held culpable when he has been misinformed."

After an unbearable silence, Elizabeth said, "I do have an excellent opinion of Mr. Bingley, and I value his qualities. However, as you once listed your manifest of ideals in accomplished ladies, I will say that a true gentleman must show determination, strength, and self-confidence and he must fight for what he believes in. A man who is easily distracted from his purpose has, in my opinion, room for improvement."

The answer surprised and puzzled me. I understood that Elizabeth blamed Bingley too for her sister's distress, but did it mean that she changed her mind about placing all the guilt on me as well? Had her resentment towards me diminished? Or was I again misinterpreting her words?

"As I say, I will be delighted to see Mr. Bingley again," she concluded.

A few moments later, Elizabeth turned to admire the lake. I could not see her expression, but her posture was so different from earlier. Her shoulders, her head, the line of her back, the locks of hair escaping the back of her bonnet. . . . She was indeed the Elizabeth Bennet I knew—yet altered in a way that I still feared to hope for.

"This place is wonderful . . . it is like a fairy tale. . . . The house is magnificent too, but the way nature surrounds it enhances its beauty. I wonder that you wish to ever leave it. I would not trade one day here for the entire season in London."

By the end of her statement, her voice turned into a whisper and I easily observed her body tense. I smiled at the nape of her neck, certain that she was troubled by her own sentiment and uncertain of my impression. After all, she was the one who refused my offer to be mistress of Pemberley.

I stepped within inches of her. For a mad moment, I contemplated wrapping my arms around her and pulling her to my chest. My mind was already lost to her—as was my heart.

"I share your feeling, Miss Bennet. I would gladly remain here forever if I did not have business in Town. And Georgiana is at that age that she must come out soon. We are both more anxious than eager for that moment, but it must be done. I must think of my sister's future. Hopefully, the time will come when we will stay at Pemberley for as long as we like."

"Your affection for your sister is admirable, sir. And Miss Darcy has proven—at this tender age—that she possesses extraordinary fortitude and strength of character. Many women much older might not have shown equal wisdom in difficult situations."

Was she showing me that she read the letter and took it to heart? I smiled before I said, "I hope I offer her all the happiness that she deserves. I would do anything to protect her from any suffering and now I better understand how devastating it can be to know that someone had ruined the happiness of a beloved sister." It was my turn to show her that I admitted my faults and was prepared to make amends.

She turned to me and our glances remained locked for a moment. Only the approaching voices of the Gardiners reminded me to master my countenance. We resumed our walk, careful not to touch her hands but close enough for the thrilling possibility.

"Miss Bennet, there is another person in the party who more particularly wishes to be known to you. Will you allow me, or do I ask too much, to introduce my sister to your acquaintance during your stay at Lambton?"

This new surprise seemed to impress Elizabeth and she opened her mouth as if to speak but no words came. My attention was drawn to her full lips and I wondered for the hundredth time what it would feel like to claim them. Will I ever satisfy my dreams? Will I ever satiate my thirst?

"I would like that very much," she whispered. Was it possible that she shivered on such a warm day?

I swallowed and murmured, "Excellent."

We now walked on in silence, deep in thought. My eyes travelled to her every movement, and I noticed her quick looks observing me as well.

I was not comfortable, nor tranquil—that had been impossible since almost the beginning of our acquaintance. But my distress, anxiety, wonder, were all so very different than before—just as I finally recognised that her manner of speaking to me, of looking at me, of smiling at me were completely different than before.

"Is your family in good health?" I inquired, hearing a trace of humour in my voice. "Did I ask that already?"

A small laugh bubbled from her. "Yes, you did, sir. They are all in excellent health, thank you. My sister Lydia is in Brighton, as a companion to Colonel Forster's wife." She paused a moment as I turned to her. "The regiment left for Brighton several weeks ago, much to the peace and comfort of many people. Some of the officers will surely not be missed," she added. I understood her meaning and said nothing more.

We soon outstripped her aunt and uncle, and when we had reached the carriage, Mr. and Mrs. Gardiner were well behind us.

"It seems we are both excellent walkers," Elizabeth commented, and I laughed.

I realised that our meeting would come to an end shortly and it might never be repeated. Panic overwhelmed me and I desperately searched for a way to prolong the time in her company.

"Would you like to come inside for a few minutes? It is quite warm and you must be tired," I asked with some restraint.

Her eyes narrowed in a smile. "I thank you but I am not tired. It is a fine prospect and I would prefer to take the air a little longer."

"As you wish. . . . Indeed, the sight seems even lovelier than usual," I said daringly. Her cheeks, already glowing from the exercise, brightened and she turned away.

The Gardiners were slowly approaching but too hasty for my want. I breathed deeply before I risked voicing my thoughts.

"I have often imagined that I walked with you at Pemberley."

I was as astounded by my statement as she must have been for she stole a look at me before turning her attention to the lake again.

My knees unsteady, I placed my hands on the stone balustrade to support myself. We were standing side by side, admiring the splendour in front of us. My mind, heart, and body were desperately aware that no beauty was greater than hers and no joy was more profound than having Elizabeth near me.

At such a time, much might have been said to fill the awkward silence. But I must admit that I had never imagined awkwardness to be so pleasant. Words were useless—those that were but niceties were not worth the effort, and those that needed to be spoken were yet forbidden. For the moment, silence was enough.

As Elizabeth leaned against the balustrade, a light breeze caught her loose curls escaping her straw bonnet. My heart quickened as she brushed one chestnut tendril aside then rested her gloved hand only a heartbeat from my own. I thought—I feared—that she might withdraw it. Instead, she murmured, "I never dreamt of walking at Pemberley with you. But I will—often. . . ."

Does she hint she will think of this moment often? My heart raced, dreading that I had misunderstood her. Before I could voice my disbelief, blessedly, no words were needed as her hand found mine. My fingers entwined with hers and I wondered if she too felt the stirring at this union.

When the Gardiners joined us, we had stepped apart and were properly discussing the weather and the surroundings. I received their praises, wondering if Elizabeth was flustered as well. I extended the invitation to enter the house for refreshment but was gracefully refused. I could do nothing but permit them—*her*—to leave. My only consolation was the hope, the certainty, that the lure of the fishing would bring her uncle and maybe the ladies to Pemberley—that I would see her again soon.

I handed both ladies to the carriage and my regrets made me prolong my grasp of Elizabeth's hand; it might have been hope but, even in the presence of her relatives, she allowed her fingers to rest a moment longer in my palm and gently linked them with mine before she pulled away. The Gardiners seemed too exhausted and too enchanted with Pemberley to notice. Not that I would have minded. The times when I struggled to conceal my affection for Elizabeth Bennet were long gone.

I saw her turn and gaze back at me as the carriage left Pemberley. From afar, I could not see her eyes, but I hoped—I knew—they were sparkling.

FOUR MONTHS LATER

I glanced at my image in the mirror and I laughed as I observed the large smile on my face. I had not been able to stop smiling since the day I proposed again and Elizabeth accepted me.

It was the fulfilment of my hopes and prayers, after six months of disguising my feelings, a horrible proposal, three months of resentment, sadness, despair, and self-reproach, and three more months of dealings with Wickham and her sister Lydia, making remedies to Bingley's situation, arguing with my aunt Catherine, and more hopes and prayers.

My only compensation was that Mr. Bennet—after his initial reluctance that I did not miss—granted me his friendship and accepted a very short engagement. I made Mr. Bennet, Elizabeth, and Mrs. Bennet very happy by procuring a special license—and saved myself much anguish by avoiding elaborate and extended wedding schemes.

I looked in the mirror again, stroking my hand over the freshly shaved face then brushed my hair; I was nervous as a young boy and the sensation was equally amusing and exhilarating.

"May I help you with anything else, sir?" my valet asked.

"No, thank you. You may retire now. I shall ring for you tomorrow when you are needed."

As my manservant exited, I smiled at my reflection again. I did not expect to need anyone else except Elizabeth—not tomorrow, and not for a long while after. Even my dearest sister understood that; she had decided to remain in London and only travel to Pemberley with the Gardiners and the newly wedded Bingleys before Christmastide. She generously gave us one month of perfect solitude at the beginning of our new life.

I checked my watch again. I promised my wife I would come to her in an hour so she might have time to prepare herself. I never imagined time could pass so slowly.

A week before, Elizabeth confessed to me that she would like to spend our wedding night at Pemberley, despite marrying at Longbourn. She had been teasing me as we walked arm in arm, her fingers entwined with mine. I still can see the sparkle in her eyes and the redness of her lips while she smiled at me. We then stopped and I closed her eyes with kisses and tasted her lips, right there in the field.

She might have spoken in jest, but if that was her want, I would make it possible. Therefore, right after the wedding breakfast, we left Hertfordshire and travelled for three days and two nights to Pemberley.

Of course, at that point I had not imagined the extent of the torture to which I sentenced myself. There were three days and two nights when I held her in my arms, enjoying her intimacy, turning tenderness into passion, teaching her the joy of shared love—but still *waiting* for the wedding night. I had every reason to congratulate myself for my excellent self-control. Very few newly wedded men would have showed such patience and restraint. But also, very few wedded men were as deeply, completely in love with their wives.

I had been pacing the room and checking my watch repeatedly when a knock on my chamber door surprised me, putting an end to my anticipation. Elizabeth entered my bed chamber, her gaze locked with mine, and my heart forgot to beat. A silky night gown skimmed her shapely figure while her loose curls adorned her creamy shoulders. A blush coloured her face and neck while my eyes travelled over her beauty.

Over the last few days, our bodies had delighted in each other's touch, our lips yearned for the taste of the other, and our desires had grown to a fevered pitch. We had learnt much about each other, yet there was still much more to discover and to share.

"Am I too early?" she whispered, placing her hands in mine.

"You are quite late for my impatience."

She laughed nervously while I ceased fighting my enthusiasm and allowed my lips to claim hers. I felt her quivering under my caresses and her soft moans made my blood race.

I carried her to the bed which had once sheltered my torment then rested her against the pillows. Her beauty intoxicated me and the glimmer in her eyes ignited the joy in my soul. I stroked her lovely face, lying atop of her, satiating my thirst with eager lips.

Elizabeth's arms closed around me, and she murmured, her voice trembling from desire, "My beloved husband, how can I bear so much love? How is it possible that I feel I belong more to you than I belong to myself?"

My heart beat powerfully and I was certain she could hear it. My lips brushed against hers, my hands lowering to explore her warmth, then I whispered hoarsely, "I can hardly say, my beloved Elizabeth, since I have long lost myself to you. In vain I have struggled to conceal my feelings—they were more powerful than pride. So, my dearest Mrs. Darcy, you must allow me to *show* you how ardently I admire and love you . . ."

LORY LILIAN fell in love with *Pride and Prejudice* thirty-three years ago and discovered the charm of Jane Austen fanfiction exactly twenty years later. She lives in Bucharest, Romania, is a proud mother of an amazing daughter, and is addicted to anything Austen. After a career in business, she dedicates her time to reading and writing. Lory is the author of six bestselling books: *Rainy Days, Remembrances of the Past, His Uncle's Favorite, The Perfect Match, Sketching Mr. Darcy, The Rainbow Promise,* and *A Man with Faults*. JAFF readers call her the "Queen of Hot Mush"—and she loves it.

"I believe I thought only of you."
—Mr. Darcy to Miss Elizabeth, Chapter LVIII.

IN TERMS OF PERFECT COMPOSURE

SUSAN ADRIANI

Seldom, very seldom, does complete truth belong to any human disclosure; seldom can it happen that something is not a little disguised or a little mistaken.

As a boy, Fitzwilliam Darcy was given good principles, and it was upon these principles of honesty, integrity, and fairness that a sturdy foundation for his character was first laid. That his parents left him to follow such admirable criterion with pride and conceit had never even occurred to him. It was honesty and forthrightness that mattered most, not disposition, and Darcy had learnt by their example.

As a man, there was nothing in the world he abhorred more than disguise, for in disguise there can be no honesty, and without honesty there can be no honour. It was the way Darcy conducted every facet of his life down to the most minute detail, until the day his sister, Georgiana, then but fifteen, confided to him her intended elopement with George Wickham. Not only was Wickham a man more than ten years her senior but her brother's childhood friend.

As it turned out, Darcy found there was little he was unwilling to do to preserve his beloved sister's reputation or that of his own. And so, for the first time in his life, he laid aside the principles he valued so deeply and did everything within his power to conceal Georgiana's indiscretion from the rest of the world. In short, he lied, not by intimation but by omission. From that day forth, he never spoke a single word of his sister's near-elopement to anyone, save for his cousin Colonel Fitzwilliam, with whom he shared guardianship of her; nor did he so much as utter George Wickham's name. Though the matter, as shocking and painful as it was, could never be entirely forgotten by any of them, to Darcy, it was at least considered closed.

Not many months had passed, however, before Darcy's path crossed most unexpectedly with Wickham's once more. His habits little altered and his situation likely dire, the scoundrel had taken a lieutenant's commission in the —shire Militia and was posted in Hertfordshire, where Darcy happened to be visiting his friend Charles Bingley. While Darcy and the Bingleys removed to London for the winter, the regiment did not decamp for Brighton until the following summer. No longer under Darcy's watchful eye, Wickham had been free to carry on as he saw fit; and carry on he did, in the most lascivious manner, for upon his quitting the place it was discovered that countless women, many no more than innocent young girls, had become unwitting victims of his debauchery.

That summer, in addition to a host of compromised tradesmen's daughters and maid servants, a gentleman's daughter who was visiting Brighton was persuaded to leave her friends and go to Scotland: fifteen-year-old Lydia Bennet of Longbourn, Hertfordshire. Attractive, lively, and determined to enjoy herself at every opportunity, she gave no thought to her conduct, manners, or reputation. Unlike his own sister, Georgiana, who had a dowry of thirty thousand pounds, Lydia Bennet had no dowry to speak of, only the possibility of inheriting a thousand pounds upon her mother's death.

While George Wickham was a charming, well-mannered opportunist who enjoyed passing his time with pretty, impressionable girls, securing his future was his main objective. With expensive habits and poor prospects, he always intended to earn his fortune by marrying well, and nothing less than a wealthy heiress would do. It did not take a genius to discern there would be no marriage for the youngest Miss Bennet after she'd deserted her family and friends for Lieutenant Wickham and his dashing red coat, only heartbreak and disgrace; a disgrace she would pass on to her entire family by association, and her four unmarried sisters particularly. As it happened, it was Lydia's sister Elizabeth with whom Fitzwilliam Darcy of Pemberley had fallen ardently in love.

Had he not called upon Elizabeth Bennet at the inn in Lambton that summer, where he found her distraught enough to confide her sister's humiliation minutes after she had received the news from home, Darcy never would have learnt of it. Theirs was a history riddled with avoidance, misunderstandings, and one offensively worded proposal of marriage that had been irrevocably refused April last. In fact, Darcy and Elizabeth, after spending three months apart, he in reflection, and she in Hertfordshire, had only renewed their acquaintance three days prior when they had met by chance at Pemberley.

Darcy was grieved, shocked, angry, and appalled; moreover, he was deeply ashamed. His shame, however, was not for Elizabeth, or even for Lydia and the wretched situation she had brought upon herself and her family. Darcy's shame was for none but himself. It was owing to *his* pride and arrogance; to *his* failure to act and expose George Wickham for the reprobate he was, that Lydia Bennet was permitted to run wild, unchecked, and unprotected in the first place, and Elizabeth, dearest, loveliest Elizabeth, left to suffer the repercussions of her youngest sister's disgrace. The fault was his and his alone, and so must the remedy be.

It had taken Darcy some time, as well as a fair amount of money, but he managed to arrange it all in the end. While Elizabeth and her aunt and uncle quitted Derbyshire for Hertfordshire, Darcy, doubting the lovers were going to Scotland, travelled to London instead, where he eventually discovered them, arranged their marriage, paid Wickham's debts, and purchased a commission for him in the Regulars. Darcy had anticipated his involvement in the business being met with resistance, but persuading Wickham to marry Lydia Bennet had not posed his biggest challenge; it was convincing Elizabeth's uncle to allow Darcy to pay for the inconvenience of it, while he, Edward Gardiner, accepted all the credit.

It was one more untruth; one more concealment, however necessary its purpose, but the taste it left in Darcy's mouth was bitter. It was nothing, though, compared to the feeling of disheartenment that constricted his chest once he realised the Gardiners, after having considered all Darcy had done for their family, might very well be anticipating an understanding between himself and Elizabeth as well.

"Will you take another glass of wine, Darcy? Or would you prefer something else?" Mr. Gardiner enquired after their supper had been cleared away and Mrs. Gardiner had withdrawn to see to the comfort of her children. "I have some lovely scotch upon the sideboard, or perhaps a glass of sherry will do the trick?"

Though it had not been Darcy's intent to call upon Elizabeth's aunt and uncle once he had arrived in London four days prior, in the end, the temptation to renew his acquaintance with them proved too great. After meeting with his solicitor and various other business associates during the day, every evening found him dining with them in Cheapside. He sincerely enjoyed their society, Mrs. Gardiner's intelligence and wit, and Mr. Gardiner's easy, elegant manners. He had liked them well enough when Elizabeth had introduced them at Pemberley, but Darcy had come to know them so much better since, in part, because of Lydia Bennet's patched-up marriage, but also because of his continued preference for her second-eldest sister.

With an inclination of his head, he extended his glass to his host. "I thank you, yes. This wine is excellent, Gardiner. A Muscat, I believe.

Wherever did you happen to acquire it? I would not mind adding a few bottles of this one to my own cellar."

"Thank you very much, sir," said Mr. Gardiner with a gratified smile. "It is one of my wife's favourites, and a gift from a very great friend of mine who is just returned from the Continent. His business took him to Italy, though I am to understand he may have ventured a little farther afield. The Alsace region, to be precise."

Darcy grinned knowingly. He had his suspicions as the wine did not taste the least bit Italian. Alsace made perfect sense. "So, this beautiful vintage is French then. I hope my curiosity will not result in any inconvenience for you."

"No. No trouble at all," Mr. Gardiner assured him, "unless you intend to report me to the authorities for being in possession of something that not only ought to have been declared but paid for dearly many times over. Then I am afraid it would be a very great inconvenience indeed, not only for my pocketbook, but for my wife and friend as well."

"Fear not. Your secret, your friend, and your wine are all perfectly safe with me."

Mr. Gardiner chuckled as he proceeded to refill Darcy's glass. "I did not doubt it for a moment. I will let Madeleine know she may rest easy, though, and that her Muscat is safe. May I assume by the smile upon your face that the wine's origin is acceptable, despite your loyalty to the Crown?"

"More than acceptable. Who am I to hold your excellent taste in wine against you?" Darcy swirled the contents of his glass as he admired the clarity. "I have long preferred French wine but confess to being curious. How did your friend manage to bring *this* vintage into England without having it confiscated the moment he set foot on English soil? All things considered, it would be in very high demand."

"Not without difficulty, I assure you. I consider myself extremely fortunate, not only to have such a clever, adventurous friend during a time of war, but to have nearly a dozen bottles of this fine vintage collecting dust in my cellar."

"I would say you are very fortunate indeed," Darcy agreed as he raised his glass to his host. Mr Gardiner returned the gesture, and both men drank to good friends and good fortune.

Conversation continued—news and politics, the economy and trade—until Mr. Gardiner paused and shifted his course. "I have long wanted to ask you a question, Darcy, if you do not mind."

"Of course. What would you like to know?"

After placing his glass upon the table, Mr. Gardiner reclined in his chair, linked his hands over his stomach, and exhaled heavily. "I am afraid there is no delicate way of putting this, so I will simply come out with it."

Darcy's forehead creased with concern. "This sounds serious."

"My question, I fear, is of a personal nature. Understand in the short time we have known you, my wife and I have both come to hold you in high regard."

Unease had settled in his breast. "The feeling is mutual, I assure you. What is on your mind, Gardiner?"

"A great many things but foremost is my niece Elizabeth. I realise I am not her father, but as my brother-in-law has no knowledge of what you have done for Lydia, I feel it is within my right to enquire as to the particulars of your relationship with her."

Though the fire burning in the grate had provided a comfortable, easy atmosphere moments before, Darcy suddenly felt the air in the room grow oppressive and hot. In fact, it was only by sheer force of will that he was able to restrain himself from sliding his finger beneath his shirt collar to loosen his cravat.

The last thing in the world he had expected on this night was to be blindsided by an inquisition. That the inquisition's topic was not only extremely delicate in nature but achingly private as well made everything all the worse. While a fair amount of his interaction with Elizabeth had been pleasant, there were countless other moments that had yielded only mortification and pain, on both their parts. In fact, if Darcy was honest with himself, very few exchanges came to mind that would show the conduct of either to advantage. To bide his time, he raised his glass to his lips and took a slow, measured sip of wine as he considered his answer with utmost care.

As a man of the world, Darcy had not been naïve enough to think Elizabeth's uncle would not be curious about the more intimate details of their relationship, especially as time passed and it eventually became clear that no prior understanding did, in fact, exist between them; but neither had he thought his day of reckoning would come quite so soon.

Since Bingley and Miss Bennet rekindled their courtship, Darcy had hoped perhaps Elizabeth and he would soon renew the connection they had shared at Pemberley. But if her recent, lukewarm reception of him the previous week was any indication of her feelings on the subject, Darcy knew he had been much mistaken. Elizabeth smiled little, said even less, and was barely able to meet his eyes, and though *he* had wanted very much to speak with *her,* Darcy found himself at a loss as to what to say. After several awkward attempts at civility, neither of them seemed capable of anything beyond silence.

What then, remained for them besides more of what had already come to pass? Despite his enduring admiration for Elizabeth, he could not discern that *she* felt any differently than she had last April. Clearly, if that was the case, they had no future to speak of, at least not as husband and wife. Unless both were to make a concerted effort, even friendship seemed unlikely.

Knowing he must eventually say *something* to Mr. Gardiner on the topic, Darcy decided that revealing the more innocuous parts of their history might be his safest bet. Perhaps Elizabeth's uncle would consider that enough for now, and Darcy's honour would remain intact, at least for a while longer.

Setting his wine glass upon the table, he cleared his throat and said, "I first made Miss Elizabeth's acquaintance last year in Hertfordshire, at an assembly in Meryton. It is also where my friend Bingley was introduced to Miss Bennet. Since then we have been in company together on countless occasions dinner parties, card parties, evening parties, and balls. Last April, we happened to meet in Kent, where my aunt, Lady Catherine de Bourgh, owns an estate. Miss Elizabeth was visiting her friend, Mrs. Collins, at the same time I happened to be paying a visit to Her Ladyship. We each of us passed several weeks there until Miss Elizabeth had to return to Longbourn. I did not have the pleasure of her company again until we saw one another in July, at Pemberley."

"I am much aware of *those* details," Mr. Gardiner replied. "Perhaps I ought to rephrase my query, so I will be clearly understood. What interests me most, Darcy, are your *intentions* toward my niece."

Christ. His intentions.

Darcy supposed his intentions were, in effect, exactly what they had always been; yet, at the same time they were entirely different. What he wanted was for Elizabeth to become his wife. Even after all that had happened, their history of consistently misunderstanding one another, her painful refusal of his deplorable proposal, her sister marrying Wickham, and all in between, he wanted her still. In fact, his longing for her was sometimes so powerful he feared it would burn a hole through his chest.

But even more than that, Darcy wanted Elizabeth to be *happy*. He wanted her to be secure, and protected, and well; but most of all, he longed to see her as she was when he *first* knew her: impertinent, teasing, and joyful. He had thought she *seemed* happy when they had met again at Pemberley that summer, but now he was uncertain. At Longbourn, Elizabeth's countenance appeared so far from what it used to be that Darcy found himself wondering if he had not simply imagined her summertime contentment. The possibility of this truth not only disheartened him but confused him as well. Had he acted in *her* best interest by bringing about her sister's marriage to Wickham or his own?

"It is an easy question," Mr. Gardiner remarked when Darcy failed to answer him. His voice was soft, but the warning in his tone was clear. "I trust you have an answer to give me."

Darcy hesitated. "I do, but I am afraid my answer is not so easy for me to give as your question was for you to ask."

Mr. Gardiner pressed the tips of his fingers together and steepled them beneath his chin. "And may I enquire as to why?"

The word "no" was on the tip of Darcy's tongue, but, by some miraculous feat of restraint, he managed to refrain from speaking it aloud. Instead, he expelled a rueful laugh and dragged his fingers through his hair, frustrated beyond words by the turn his evening had taken. With no other options before him, Darcy knew he had little choice in the matter but to divulge the true circumstances of his relationship with Elizabeth to her uncle, no matter how much he preferred to keep them to himself. A voice in the back of his head whispered that *perhaps he had kept his heartache to himself long enough,* but it did not make speaking the truth any easier to bear—rather Darcy found the task infinitely more difficult.

"I am awaiting your explanation, Darcy."

"Honestly—" but the rest of Darcy's words became caught in his throat.

"I believe honesty is best in circumstances such as these," Mr. Gardiner said dryly, tapping his fingertips together.

One look at the elder man's frowning countenance told Darcy his patience had waned. He drew a fortifying breath and, before he lost his nerve, admitted:

"Honestly, I am in love with her." That he found himself able to speak the words aloud nearly shocked him into silence.

As he had expected, Mr. Gardiner appeared unsurprised by his revelation, and so, with a wry turn of his mouth, Darcy persevered. "No doubt you already deduced as much yourself. However, despite my role in Mrs. Wickham's marriage, no understanding exists between Miss Elizabeth and myself, but know that I would ask for the honour of her hand tomorrow if I believed there was any chance she would say yes."

A full ten seconds passed before Mr. Gardiner found his voice. "You mean to tell me," he said slowly and carefully, "not only are you *not* engaged to my niece, as my wife and I anticipated would eventually come to pass once the dust settled from Lydia's union, but you believe Elizabeth would actually *refuse* you?"

"My fears are not the least bit unfounded, I assure you."

Mr. Gardiner gaped at him. "You realise, of course, that you must do a hell of a lot better than that, Mr. Darcy."

Mortification and irritation caused a flush of heat to spread from beneath Darcy's cravat to the tips of his ears. He reminded himself this was Elizabeth's uncle, that he loved her as well, and was therefore entitled to be protective of her. Rather than lash out, Darcy swallowed his pride and admitted in a quiet, clipped tone:

"I have already been once refused."

"By Elizabeth?" Mr. Gardiner cried incredulously.

Pursing his lips into a thin, hard line, Darcy merely inclined his head.

"Good Lord, when? Does her mother know?"

Darcy could well imagine what Mrs. Bennet's reaction would be upon learning her daughter had refused ten thousand a year. There was no doubt in his mind her disapprobation would be heard all the way to Northumberland, never mind so easy a distance as London. "No," he said, confident in his supposition that Elizabeth had not, in fact, shared that news with her mother. "No one knows of it other than Miss Elizabeth, myself, and now you. I proposed to her at Easter, when we were together in Kent. Her reproofs"—and here Darcy could not help closing his eyes against the painfulness of the memory—"her reproofs I shall never forget."

"Let me rightly understand you," said Mr. Gardiner sharply. "You proposed to my niece last April and she refused you, quite spectacularly I gather. No understanding of any kind currently exists between you, nor has it ever; yet, you took it upon yourself, not only to become intimately involved in her family's most wretched affair, but you went so far as to bring about her sister's marriage at your own expense! Do not think me unappreciative, Darcy, but what on God's Earth made you think you had the right?"

"It was not my place, I know, but I felt a responsibility. I told you then that it was owing to my mistaken pride that Miss Elizabeth's youngest sister was preyed upon by Lieutenant Wickham. If I had exposed him before, there would have been no need to arrange their marriage then.

"I want you to understand I am not the same man that I was when I first met Miss Elizabeth more than a year ago in Hertfordshire. Then, I had a different view of the world and everyone in it. I believed myself and my manners above reproach, but Miss Elizabeth taught me otherwise. Any improvements to my character are a credit to none but her.

"I am not proud of myself by any means, especially as I have perpetrated so many wrongs against her over the course of our acquaintance. I believed if I could only find a way to right them. . . . If I could but bring her even a little happiness after all I had done to pain her, then do it I must. I was bound to act. I am bound to act still, for she is deserving of nothing less."

For a long while Mr. Gardiner sat silently in his chair while he traced the rim of his wine glass with his fingertip, a frown upon his face and his forehead creased in contemplation. When at last he spoke, it was composedly, but in his eyes Darcy recognised a flash of irritation and wilfulness that reminded him much of Gardiner's niece.

"You lied to me, Darcy. You may not have spoken the words aloud, but your actions implied you had reached an understanding with Elizabeth when in fact there was no understanding at all, not even a courtship. By allowing my wife and I to believe you had formed an attachment, a line was crossed. You were wrong for allowing such an intimation, and you were wrong for failing to correct it. You were quite wrong indeed!

"But it does not follow that you are the only one who has acted wrongly in the matter, for my wife was certain there was something akin to love between you and Elizabeth. Madeleine and I made our own assumptions based upon your admiration of each other without first confirming every particular. We are to blame as well.

"One fact remains, and it is this: my family and I are indebted to you, sir, and I have always paid my debts."

"No," said Darcy. "You and your family owe me nothing. Much as I respect you and your relations, I thought only of Miss Elizabeth."

"Then you *must* marry." Mr. Gardiner's voice brooked no opposition. "There is nothing else to be done. As I said, my wife and I believed you had reached an understanding with our niece, otherwise I never would have accepted your assistance. If word of your involvement gets out, Elizabeth's good name and those of all her sisters will be ruined. The reputation of the entire family is at risk. Lydia has never been known for her discretion. Lord knows what she is blathering about up there in Newcastle."

Darcy's voice carried evidence of his own agitation. "While I would like nothing more than to oblige you, the situation of which you speak will not be so easily remedied by my simply asking Miss Elizabeth for her hand. Forcing her to agree to a union that is not to her liking would fill her heart with resentment, not only toward myself, but toward you and Mr. Bennet as well, should you choose to inform him of the matter.

"Miss Elizabeth could hardly bring herself to look at me when we were last in company together. We barely even spoke. Her sentiments toward me have not altered, and I refuse to press her to accept an arrangement that will only succeed in bringing her a lifetime of misery and regret."

Mr. Gardiner said nothing as he regarded Darcy with an expression the master of Pemberley could only describe as . . . odd. "How do you know?" the elder man suddenly asked.

"How do I know *what?*" Darcy said, his frustration tested beyond the tediousness, nay, the absolute pointlessness of their conversation.

"That Elizabeth does not care for you as you care for her. How do you know?"

Darcy shook his head with a contemptuous snort. "It is simply not possible. Our entire acquaintance has been riddled with misunderstandings. If I had any idea how Miss Elizabeth honestly felt about me *before* I asked for her hand, I would not have made the request in the first place."

He was surprised when Mr. Gardiner not only covered his face with his hands but began to chuckle. "People change, Darcy," he said, shaking his head. "You, of all people, ought to know that. What makes you so sure my niece has not changed as well? And, since you brought it up, if you were not adept at discerning Elizabeth's preference for you or lack thereof before, why do you suddenly believe yourself so capable of correctly interpreting her feelings now?"

Darcy propped his elbows upon the table and dropped his head into his hands with a groan. Every word Mr. Gardiner uttered made perfect sense, and yet Darcy remained doubtful. If he allowed himself to hope and acted on that hope, pursuing Elizabeth's hand as her suitor, the torturous possibility that she might reject him a second time lingered.

Of course, if he threw caution to the wind and not only pursued Elizabeth, but discovered she *did* return his regard, Darcy's joy as well as her own would likely know no bounds.

But what if he was wrong?

What if he was right?

What if she said no?

What if she said yes?

Darcy's head throbbed from more than the extra glass of Muscat he had consumed over the course of the evening. With an exhalation, he raised his fingers to his temples and closed his eyes. "I have no idea what to do. I cannot afford to make another mistake where your niece is concerned."

"Life is full of mistakes," Mr. Gardiner told him. "Some people take the trouble to learn from their mistakes, and they are often the ones who are rewarded richly for their efforts. We cannot grow as individuals, Darcy, unless we learn. It is up to us whether we put that knowledge to use or set it upon a shelf. I have it on good authority from my wife that my niece may not be quite so immune to your charms as you believe. Do with that intelligence what you will, but know you cannot possibly do anything about it all the way from here. Go back to Hertfordshire at once. Visit my niece, and for the love of heaven, draw her out. I have known Elizabeth all her life, and, in those one-and-twenty years, I have never known her to keep her opinions, or her affections, to herself indefinitely." He slapped his hands upon the table and rose.

Darcy followed suit. "Thank you," he said sincerely as he extended his hand to Elizabeth's uncle.

Mr. Gardiner grasped it between both his own. "You are always welcome, Darcy. Any time, for any reason. My wife and I have grown quite fond of you, and I daresay would like to keep you around."

Too overwhelmed by the elder man's sentiment to trust himself to return it, Darcy merely inclined his head. Instead, he said, "Please be so kind as to pay my respects to Mrs. Gardiner. It seems I am travelling to Hertfordshire tomorrow morning."

As it turned out, Darcy *was* afforded the opportunity to offer his compliments to Mrs. Gardiner that evening, as well as his service, for he was charged with the delivery of a letter. It was by Mr. Gardiner's suggestion that his wife take a half hour to write to her niece, and Darcy found himself incredibly appreciative, not only of the elder man's solicitude in offering Darcy a reason to visit Longbourn and speak with Elizabeth, but of his perceptive understanding of Darcy's reticent nature, especially in so far as the object of his affection was concerned. No one, save for his cousin Colonel Fitzwilliam, had ever gone to such lengths to put Darcy at ease in situations where conversation was required genuine, altruistic ease as the Gardiners. His affection for them grew.

By one o'clock the following day he arrived in Hertfordshire, and though he wanted nothing more than to proceed directly on to Longbourn, Darcy directed his coachman to Netherfield instead. There, he would take some refreshment after his four-hour journey, as well as some much-needed time to better compose his thoughts.

As Darcy ascended the steps to the front entrance, he glanced at the sky. It had been sunny for most of the drive from Town, but here in the country, the heavens were dull with little evidence of the sun in sight; only a few weak rays as could be seen through a sea of light grey clouds. The temperature was cool and crisp, but the day was otherwise fine—fine enough for taking a turn in the garden. Darcy imagined Bingley would be as eager to take advantage of the dry weather as he was to see Miss Bennet, but upon entering the house he discovered his friend much at home.

"Darcy," Bingley exclaimed as he rose from his chair at the breakfast table, wiping crumbs from his waistcoat. "It is good to see you. Come, sit down and have a cup of tea."

"It is good to see you as well," Darcy said as he claimed a seat beside his friend. "I am surprised to find you at home."

"And I am surprised to find you returned before ten days' time, though it does not follow the surprise is unwelcome. In fact, I am glad you have come, for it saves me the trouble of composing a letter. I have some wonderful news to relate."

"Do you?" Darcy enquired as he helped himself to a cup of tea.

"Yes. Since you have been away, I have become engaged to Miss Bennet."

Darcy smiled warmly as he laid aside his teacup and extended his hand to his friend. "Congratulations are in order, then. I am happy for you, Bingley. Sincerely happy."

With a firm grip, Bingley clasped Darcy's hand with his own and shook it vigorously. "Thank you. Miss Bennet is an angel, and I consider myself the most fortunate man in the world to have earned her regard."

"You are indeed most fortunate." Though the moment belonged to his friend, he could not stop himself from wondering whether there would ever come a day when Elizabeth might be able to answer all *his* hopes, much as her sister had answered Bingley's. As there was always a mutual regard and affection between his friend and Miss Bennet, Darcy was doubtful his own resolution would happen so expediently. The most he could do was pray it would happen at all.

"Have you had Cook's boysenberry jam?" Bingley asked. "You must try it, Darcy. I dare say, I have tasted nothing so delightful on my toast."

"Why are you not at Longbourn today?" Darcy asked as he selected some cold meat from a small platter. "I thought you would have set out long before the noon hour. Surely, Miss Bennet has not grown tired of you so soon?"

"Not quite." Bingley chuckled as he scooped a healthy serving of jam from a little crystal bowl on the table and liberally applied it to his toast. "The Misses Bennet are not at home. They are visiting some acquaintance or other, a Mrs. Sutherland and her son, I believe. They own a pretty, little estate near Eastbourne: Willow Crest. I have been by it many times but have yet to make their acquaintance myself."

"You will see Miss Bennet later this afternoon, then?"

"No, not today, for the family is to dine with the Sutherlands and the Philips, and I have been invited to dine with Mr. Jones and his wife." Bingley laid his knife upon his plate with a frown. "Had I known you were coming today I would have arranged to spend the evening at home. Do you mind terribly, Darcy?"

Darcy shook his head. He was disappointed, yes, but his disappointment stemmed from having to put off seeing Elizabeth that day, not having to pass a quiet evening by himself. "It is fine, Bingley. I am quite used to dining alone."

"Good Lord," Bingley muttered with an expression of genuine concern. "That sounds absolutely depressing. No one ought to be *used* to dining alone. Tell me you dined with *someone* while you were in Town. Did you see your cousin, the colonel? Or perhaps his sisters? I dare say, if pressed there is always your staff. From what I have seen, you pay them handsomely. Surely your London housekeeper, Mrs. Sowersby, or her husband, would not refuse you one meal every now and again. I am sure you need only ask and they will happily oblige you. My own housekeeper, old Mrs. Nithercott, is most obliging whenever I do not feel like dining alone, and my butler as well."

The urge to roll his eyes was difficult for Darcy to ignore as he envisioned the shock that would undoubtedly appear upon his rather proper housekeeper's face should he ever instruct her to leave the household to run itself and join him for supper. Only Bingley, who gave little thought to station and ceremony, would ever abandon all appearance of propriety and take his meals with his staff. He could only assume his sisters, Caroline and Louisa, had no idea he did this or else they would have suffered an apoplectic fit.

"I did not eat my evening meals alone," Darcy informed him. "As it so happens, I dined with friends. Their society was excellent, as was their wine."

Bingley appeared placated. "I am relieved to hear it. Do not take this the wrong way, but I often worry about you, Darcy."

Darcy's brow quirked in amusement. It was usually he who worried about Bingley. Rarely was it the other way around. "And why is that, Bingley?"

Bingley shook his head. "It has long been an observation of mine that you seem content to go through life dissatisfied with the world and everyone in it. In my experience, however, the world is not nearly so dark and dreadful a place as you have declared it to be. Whether you believe it or not, there is much good to be found there as well. Someday you will see. Someday someone far more charming and persuasive than I will come along and change your opinion."

He felt his cheek twitch with the beginning of a smile. Though Bingley did not yet know it, someone, a very pretty, impertinent someone, already had. It was now a matter of ascertaining *her* regard for *him* that would either ensure his own felicity in the world or guarantee his disfavour with it.

Dawn broke over Hertfordshire, and with it came the promise of a mild, cloudless day. It was decided between the two gentlemen they would rise early and break their fast at Netherfield, rather than impose themselves upon Mrs. Bennet's hospitality. While Bingley had a standing invitation to dine at Longbourn often arriving before breakfast and staying until after the evening meal Darcy enjoyed no such intimacy with the family; and though he *did* long to see Elizabeth as soon as possible, he *did not* wish to cause any inconvenience to her mother, who would only be expecting to feed Bingley and not himself.

It was still early—just past ten o'clock in the morning—by the time they set out, but Darcy set a quick, steady pace and the three miles between the two estates were covered in good time. The gentlemen had no sooner turned onto the gravel drive that led to the manor house when Bingley remarked upon a stately looking carriage with two matched pairs parked at the front entrance. As they drew closer, Darcy recognised the livery, the crest, and Dawson, the acquiescent waiting-woman seated within, as belonging to none other than his aunt Lady Catherine de Bourgh of Rosings Park.

That the hour was far too early for anyone but Bingley to politely call upon the family mystified him nearly as much as Her Ladyship's presence. Darcy simply could not account for her being there. It was not in Lady Catherine's nature to visit anyone beyond her neighbours in Kent, or Hunsford Village, where she presided over the day to day affairs of the inhabitants as though they were her own. The only explanation he could think of was that she carrying a letter from Mrs. Collins, much as Darcy was from Mrs. Gardiner. It made perfect sense, until Darcy recalled this was Her Ladyship, whose benevolence rarely extended beyond what was convenient to her—and frowned. Traveling all the way to Hertfordshire from Kent, was anything but a convenience.

Before Bingley had even dismounted, Darcy had consigned his own horse to a stable boy and was on his way to the house. "Darcy," his friend called. "Wherever are you going in such a hurry? I will only be a moment."

With an exhalation, Darcy slowed his pace but not without some effort. He was anxious to enter the house for several reasons, but whether his anxiety was most owed to the prospect of seeing Elizabeth again or his impatience to ascertain the purpose of Lady Catherine's visit, he could not say.

Bingley joined him and they went inside, where they were escorted to the morning room and their arrival announced to Mrs. Bennet. Her daughters, save for the one Darcy most wished to see, were all present. Though he had expected the imposing figure of his aunt to be amongst them, a quick scan of his surroundings informed Darcy she was not, in fact, in the room. His unease increased.

After the usual formalities were exchanged, Bingley claimed a seat beside Miss Bennet with an easy smile, while Darcy laid his hand upon the back of a vacant chair and shifted his weight from his left foot to his right. The prospect of being reunited with Elizabeth had made him feel excited and restless, but her absence, in concert with that of his aunt, rendered him far too fidgety to sit down for more than a few minutes together. He therefore chose to remain standing.

After several polite inquiries from all parties, Mrs. Bennet said to him, "How surprised we were to see your aunt this morning, Mr. Darcy! She is a fine-looking woman, and her calling here is prodigiously civil! She is on her road somewhere, I dare say, and so passing through Meryton thought she might call on Elizabeth."

"Yes. I was surprised to see her carriage myself. It is most unusual. Her Ladyship is not in the habit of leaving Kent, especially this time of year."

"Perhaps she has business in Town?" Mrs. Bennet said.

"Perhaps." He thought it wise to keep his aunt's distaste for the place to himself. Soon, however, his impatience got the best of him and he said, "Where might I find Her Ladyship, madam? As her nephew, I ought to greet her properly. She is excessively attentive to such things, and I do not wish to incur her displeasure."

"Oh! Certainly not," Mrs. Bennet readily agreed. "Her Ladyship expressed a desire to walk out earlier, and I suggested Elizabeth show her the hermitage." With a wave of her handkerchief, she indicated a window on the western side of the room. "Ours is much finer than the Lucas's, you know. Everybody says it is so. You must tell me your opinion when you are come back." She turned to Bingley, who had been speaking with Miss Bennet and her sisters, and said cheerfully, "And what do you think of my hermitage, Mr. Bingley?"

As Bingley muddled through his answer, Darcy walked to the window and peered outside, where he noticed two figures emerging from a small copse of trees just across the lawn. Elizabeth was in front and Lady Catherine, just behind, waving her cane about in an agitated manner. It was clear they were headed toward the house and, as they got closer, Darcy could better see their countenances: Elizabeth's, flushed with agitation, and his aunt's, pale with anger.

He expelled a quiet oath. The scene playing out before him did not bode well for their return to the house. Turning away from the window, he quickly made his way to the door and quitted the room. That Lady Catherine was angry, and that her anger was directed at Elizabeth, he was in little doubt, but as to *why* remained to be discovered.

In half-a-minute's time, he had reached the front door. He grasped the handle, fully intent upon throwing it open and making his presence known, but the sound of Elizabeth's voice stopped him.

"How far your nephew might approve your interference in *his* affairs I cannot tell; but you have certainly no right to concern yourself in mine. I must beg, therefore, to be importuned no further on the subject."

Darcy remained frozen behind the closed door, his brows furrowed in bewilderment. He must have misheard her. That *he* could very well be the topic of their discord seemed as unlikely to him as it was incredible. Surely, his aunt had not travelled all the way to Hertfordshire from Kent because of *him*. Darcy could hardly believe such unsolicited involvement in his affairs was even possible, never mind actual, and felt at once mortified and indignant. Before he could decide how he ought to proceed, Lady Catherine addressed Elizabeth, and Darcy, though he knew it was wrong, pressed closer to the door so that he might hear her better.

"Not so hasty, if you please," said Her Ladyship to Elizabeth. "I have by no means done. To all the other objections I have still another to add. I am no stranger to the particulars of your youngest sister's infamous elopement. I know it all; that the young man's marrying her was a patched-up business, at the expense of your father and uncles. And is *such* a girl to be my nephew's sister? Is *her* husband to be his brother? Heaven and Earth! Of what are you thinking? Are the shades of Pemberley to be thus polluted?"

If Darcy had expected his aunt to say anything, it certainly wasn't this. Lydia Bennet's elopement aside, it sounded as though Her Ladyship expected a marriage to occur between himself and Elizabeth! Where she had received such a convoluted impression eluded him, until he recalled that his friend had recently become engaged to Elizabeth's sister, and that the Lucases, in keeping contact with Mr. and Mrs. Collins, must have spread their own assumptions to Hunsford.

"You can now have nothing further to say," Elizabeth resentfully answered. "You have insulted me by every possible method."

"You have no regard, then, for my nephew! Unfeeling, selfish girl! Do you not consider that a connection with you must disgrace him in the eyes of everybody?"

"Lady Catherine," Elizabeth said, and here Darcy could hear more than agitation in her voice; he could hear pain. "I have nothing further to say. You know my sentiments."

"You are then resolved to have him?" his aunt asked.

Darcy's breath caught in his throat. If there was ever a question he wished to hear an answer to, it would be this one, at this moment; but he seemed destined for disappointment, for Elizabeth's reply was not so much an answer as it was an evasion.

"I have said no such thing. I am only resolved to act in that manner which will, in my own opinion, constitute my happiness, without reference to *you,* or to any person so wholly unconnected with me."

Elizabeth sounded as though she had reached the end of her composure, and Darcy decided he had heard enough. Before any more could be said on the subject by either lady, he yanked the door open and stepped outside, making sure to close it firmly behind him lest they draw any attention from those within the house.

As he had anticipated, his sudden appearance was enough to startle his unsuspecting aunt into silence, a rare occurrence in his experience, and he took the opportunity to say to her:

"Lady Catherine. I was not expecting to see you in Hertfordshire. I trust your journey was a pleasant one."

Without waiting for her reply, Darcy turned to Elizabeth, who stared at him with an expression he could only describe as a combination of mortification and horror. It was apparent she was as shocked to see him as he had been to find her engaged in an argument with his aunt. "Miss Bennet," he said, softening his tone considerably, "I hope I have found you well."

Lady Catherine gave a disdainful snort. "Oh, she is well, I dare say. Well enough to refuse the claims of duty, honour, and gratitude."

Elizabeth's complexion, already heightened, flushed deeper still. "Neither duty, nor honour, nor gratitude, have any possible claim on me in the present instance. I bid you a good journey, Lady Catherine." And with that, she stepped forward and made to lay her hand upon the door handle so she could go into the house. Darcy saw that she was shaking.

"You are determined to ruin him in the opinion of all his friends, and make him the contempt of the world," Her Ladyship cried, pointing an accusing finger first at Elizabeth and then at her nephew.

Elizabeth stiffened, but said nothing in reply, and Darcy was appalled to see she looked as though she was about to weep. Without so much as a second thought, he turned his back to his indignant aunt and gently slid his hand beneath Elizabeth's on the door handle, determined to provide for her what small amount of relief was within his power.

"Allow me, Miss Bennet," he said, and with a quiet click, opened the door for her. His skin, where her gloved hand touched his own, tingled with a warmth that spread like fire throughout his body. The sensation was heavenly, and Darcy, though he had always prided himself on his self-restraint, had no idea how he refrained from closing his eyes and losing himself in the exquisite novelty of her touch.

"Thank you," she whispered unevenly, and before he could reply that she was welcome, Elizabeth disappeared into the house.

Doubtful his aunt was done having her say, Darcy had the good sense to close the door behind her.

Sure enough, it had no sooner been done when Her Ladyship began her castigation. "Obstinate, headstrong girl!" she exclaimed, pacing upon the front step. "I am ashamed of her! Is this her gratitude for my attentions to her last spring? Is nothing due to me on that score?"

"Pray, calm yourself, Lady Catherine," Darcy cautioned lowly. "You have upset Miss Bennet. I doubt you wish to draw the attention of her family."

"Her family," Her Ladyship scoffed. "Tell me, who was her mother? Who are her uncles and aunts? Do not imagine me ignorant of their condition."

"We are in full view of the house and within earshot of servants, both yours and Longbourn's. If Your Ladyship cannot adopt a civil tone, I will take my leave and return to my friends. I have no desire to argue with you, either here or anywhere else."

Lady Catherine glanced sharply at him, but did, in fact, follow his counsel. Gradually, her expression lost some of its harshness and she said to him, "Let us sit down and speak sensibly for ten minutes together. No doubt *you* will see reason where some *other* persons have not." Without waiting for his response, she turned and marched to her carriage where a footman assisted her as she climbed inside. "Leave us," she told her waiting-woman, and Dawson did as she was bid.

No sooner had Darcy settled upon the rear-facing seat than his aunt declared, "I came here with the determined resolution of carrying my purpose and I will not be dissuaded from it. I have not been used to submitting to any person's whims. I have not been in the habit of brooking disappointment."

To this, Darcy merely inclined his head, for he could not argue that his aunt *was* very used to having her own way, however much he disagreed with her methods.

"Tell me, once and for all, are you engaged to that girl?"

"To Miss Bennet?" Though appearing ignorant would only further incite his aunt's ire, Darcy could hardly say he cared; not after the way she had behaved on the Bennet's doorstep, and certainly not after she had upset Elizabeth.

"Of course, to Miss Bennet. Do not try my patience, Darcy, for I know well you heard us through the door. Are you engaged to her?"

After a moment's deliberation, he answered, "I am not."

Lady Catherine seemed pleased. "And will you promise me never to enter into such an engagement?"

"I will make no promise of the kind."

Her Ladyship's eyes narrowed with displeasure. "I am shocked and astonished. I expected to find you more reasonable, or have you so soon forgotten your responsibility to your family? To what is owed to your mother? For it was her dearest wish, as well as mine, that you marry Anne." She struck her cane upon the carriage floor, as though to drive home her point. "I shall not leave you alone, Darcy; I shall not go away until you have given me the assurance I require."

"I am sorry to disappoint, Your Ladyship," he said with a mild, even-tempered manner that belied his irritation and anger, "but I certainly *never* shall give it, nor am I to be intimidated into anything so wholly unreasonable."

"Unreasonable!" Her Ladyship exclaimed. "It is you who are being unreasonable! You are already engaged to *my* daughter. Your union was planned while you were in your cradles; and now, at the moment when the wishes of both your mother and myself would be accomplished, to have Anne's happiness prevented by a young woman of inferior birth, of no importance in the world, and wholly unallied to the family! Do you have no regard for the wishes of your friends? To your tacit engagement with your cousin? Are you lost to every feeling of propriety and delicacy? Have you not heard me say that from the earliest hours you were destined for your cousin and she for you?"

Though Darcy had made every effort to present himself as the epitome of calm, he was, in fact, much in danger of losing his temper. He had long known his aunt to be prejudiced and intolerant, but her behaviour on this day was beyond the pale. What most enraged him, however, was not the offensive language with which she had abused Elizabeth, but that *he* was in part responsible for it. Had Darcy not made the decision to ignore Lady Catherine's desire for a union between himself and Anne all these years and addressed the issue head on, perhaps she would not have verbally assaulted the woman he *did* want to marry. If he had only told Her Ladyship, in no uncertain terms, that he had no wish, no desire, and no intent whatsoever to marry her daughter, perhaps she would have left him in peace to forge his own path to the altar.

After sitting in silence for a moment, Darcy felt master enough of himself to say, "You have said quite enough. Once again, I am sorry to occasion Your Ladyship disappointment of any kind, but let me be rightly understood. The union to which Your Ladyship aspires can never take place. My admiration lies, not with my cousin Anne, but with Miss Bennet.

My affections and wishes in this matter are of long standing and shall not change."

"Because she has drawn you in! She, with her upstart pretentions! She, a young woman without family, connections, or fortune! Is this to be endured? But it must not, shall not be! If you were sensible of your own good, Nephew, you would not wish to pluck this unfortunate girl from the sphere in which she has been brought up. By marrying her, you will be disgraced in the eyes of everybody."

Thoroughly disgusted by their entire conversation, Darcy rolled his eyes at the ridiculousness of her uttering such a statement. Surely, the rest of the world would have too much sense to join in any scorn. "Lady Catherine," he said, "I have nothing further to say on the subject." And with that, he opened the carriage door and alighted from it. "I bid you good day, Your Ladyship." And with that, he offered her a polite bow of recognition and returned to the house, where Mrs. Bennet met him in the hall as soon as he had shut the door.

"Why did Her Ladyship not come inside again and rest herself?" she asked the moment Lady Catherine's carriage could be heard in the drive.

"She did not wish it," Darcy said. "She would go."

"Oh." Mrs. Bennet pursed her lips. "Then you must stay for supper, Mr. Darcy. Mr. Bingley will be joining us, and so we cannot possibly leave you to dine alone at Netherfield."

The pleased smile that appeared upon Darcy's face was genuine. "I thank you, madam. I am honoured to dine with your family."

Though Elizabeth had clearly been upset when she had left him with Lady Catherine on Longbourn's front steps, Darcy had not thought she would disappear for the rest of the day. That she was not in the morning room when he returned with her mother came as no surprise; but several hours later, when her family sat down to their midday meal, he learned Elizabeth was to remain in her room, nursing a headache. Neither did she take her tea with them at four o'clock or claim her usual seat at the dining table when the evening meal was served. When she failed to appear downstairs once the gentlemen reconvened in the drawing room for dessert, Darcy's initial concern for her well-being had become much more.

Knowing the truth of what transpired between Elizabeth and his aunt, he could not help worrying about her state of mind. Was she truly indisposed with a headache as her mother and Miss Bennet claimed, or was she simply avoiding *him?* Darcy was determined to find out, and when he saw Miss Bennet pouring the coffee, he formed his plan.

"I hope your sister is feeling better," he said, extending his empty cup to her.

"I am afraid I cannot tell you, sir. When I last checked on her she was asleep. I did not wish to disturb her rest."

Darcy felt his tension ease, if only slightly. Perhaps his fears were unfounded. Perhaps Elizabeth did, in fact, only have a headache. "Of course. A night of rest often does one a world of good. Hopefully Miss Elizabeth will be well tomorrow."

"I am sure she will," Miss Bennet replied with a serene smile as she refilled his cup. "My sister has a hearty constitution and is rarely indisposed for long, especially when the weather is fine. No doubt she will be herself again by morning."

"Thank you," he said, accepting the cup of coffee and raising it to his lips. He was about to return to his friend, who was speaking with Mr. Bennet on the other side of the room, when he suddenly recalled Mrs. Gardiner's letter. Perhaps, having it to read tomorrow morning when she awakens would help buoy Elizabeth's spirits, should she still feel unwell. Though he had hoped to present it to her himself, Darcy knew he need not hand it to her directly. Surely, he reasoned, her aunt's letter would provide the same amount of pleasure whether it was delivered by his hand or Miss Bennet's.

"Miss Bennet," he said, reaching into the breast pocket of his waistcoat. "I happen to have a letter in my possession from your aunt, Mrs. Gardiner. I was charged to deliver it to Miss Elizabeth, but I fear it might be more expedient to entrust it to you instead. I do not wish to delay her delight in receiving it."

The surprise upon Miss Bennet's face could not be denied. "Oh! That is most kind of you, Mr. Darcy. I will be sure to give it to her. No doubt she will be very glad to have it. I did not realise you and my aunt were at all acquainted."

"Yes," he said, thinking fondly of the afternoons they passed together at Pemberley, or more particularly, of the time he passed there with her niece. "We met in Derbyshire during the summer, and Miss Elizabeth was so kind as to perform an introduction. Our acquaintance was recently renewed in London. They are delightful people, your aunt and uncle. I like them very much."

"I will be sure to let Elizabeth know when I give her my aunt's letter."

"Thank you," he said. "Please tell your sister I hope she is better. I am sorry—very sorry—to have missed the pleasure of her company this afternoon." And with that, he returned to his friend.

The evening ended with Bingley inviting the Bennets to dine at Netherfield the following day, and so it was at four o'clock in the afternoon that their carriage was heard pulling up to the house. As the family alighted, Darcy stood with Bingley in the entrance hall, ready to receive the guests as they were announced.

"Mr. and Mrs. Bennet, Miss Bennet, Miss Mary Bennet, and Miss Katherine Bennet, sir," said Bingley's butler as they filed into the house.

Once again, it appeared Elizabeth was absent, and Darcy felt nothing short of devastated. As Bingley escorted his future mother-in-law into the drawing room, Darcy ignored his disappointment and offered Miss Bennet his arm. "It is nice to see you again, Miss Bennet. You look lovely this evening."

And indeed, she did, wearing a beautifully embroidered gown edged with Belgian lace. Her smile was warm as she placed her gloved hand upon his arm, giving him leave to escort her. "Thank you, Mr. Darcy. It is nice to see you as well."

As they began walking, he tilted his head toward her own and said, "I cannot help but notice Miss Elizabeth did not accompany you. I hope she is not worse."

"Oh, no, sir," she assured him. "My sister is much better today. She chose to remain at home this evening and rest, that is all."

"I am relieved to hear that she is better," was all he could think to say.

They entered the drawing room and Darcy handed Miss Bennet to Bingley. He may have been at Netherfield, but his thoughts were three miles away at Longbourn, where Elizabeth was at that moment alone. He could not deny the prospect was tempting. Would she be pleased to see him? Or would she be put out by his presence? Darcy was damned if he knew.

Across the room, Mrs. Bennet's voice rang out, calling his attention back to the present. "And, so I told Lady Lucas there was nothing so comforting as knowing I will soon have *two* daughters married. I always knew Jane was not so beautiful for nothing, and I daresay Lydia is just as handsome. It is no wonder they were able to attract such fine husbands."

Darcy rolled his eyes as he claimed a seat near the pianoforte. Fine husbands, indeed. While he was confident Bingley would do everything within his power to please Miss Bennet and be a good husband to her, he doubted Wickham would bother doing the same for her sister.

"What about me, Mama?" Kitty asked, sounding slightly put out. Beside her, Mary made no comment at all.

"Oh, you are pretty too, Kitty, but I daresay no one is as lovely as your sister, Jane."

Kitty huffed. No doubt, Darcy thought, because her mother's thoughtless comment injured her. He felt like huffing as well. While Jane was certainly beautiful with her blonde hair, blue eyes, and handsome figure, in Darcy's opinion Elizabeth was as lovely. Her countenance was darker, and her build slighter, but there was something in her manner of speaking, in the way she moved, and laughed that captivated him. Her complexion had a certain brilliancy, her lips were pink and full, and her eyes, which he had always considered fine, revealed her intelligence every bit as much as her discourse and her decorum. To Darcy, she was the perfect woman. Mrs. Bennet could say all she wished of her favourite; Darcy had his own.

In this way, they passed the next hour, until it was time to go into the dining room. Mrs. Bennet's conversation revolved around Jane and her upcoming wedding to Bingley, while Darcy's head was full of nothing but Elizabeth. With a rueful turn of his mouth, he finally acknowledged the one thing he refused to admit before: that he had no wish to be at Netherfield when she was at Longbourn. He had too much to say to her, too much to ask her, to concentrate on anything else.

Catching Bingley's arm, Darcy quietly made his excuses: he had developed a headache and lost his appetite. He would withdraw for the rest of the night.

Bingley expressed his concern, but Darcy urged him to see to his guests instead. Convincing him was the work of a moment, and when his friend offered his arm to Miss Bennet with a congenial smile and escorted her to dinner, Darcy discreetly made his way to the door, where he ordered his horse to be saddled at once.

The distance between the two estates passed quickly, as Darcy urged his horse along the lane at a faster pace than he would have done had the sun not been so low in the western sky. Before long he reached the pale that marked Longbourn's drive and turned. As the gravel crunched beneath his horse's hooves, one thought, one rhythm repeated itself: *Make her mine. Make her mine. Make her mine.*

At the door, he dismounted, surrendered his horse to the stable boy's care, and ascended the steps, where he paused to run his hands through his hair. What in God's name was he doing, intentionally calling upon Elizabeth while her family was out? The only other time he had orchestrated such a breach of propriety was in Kent, and he well remembered how horribly *that* evening had turned out.

It was too late to turn back, however, and after drawing a fortifying breath, Darcy raised his hand and knocked upon the door. Rather than the housekeeper, a young maid admitted him and led him to a tiny sitting room toward the back of the house, where she announced his arrival and promptly shut the door.

The only source of light was from a low-burning fire in the grate, which cast the entire room in an intricate tapestry of long, dancing shadows and warm, burnished light. Upon a chaise, with her feet tucked neatly beneath her gown, sat Elizabeth. That she was taken aback by his presence was apparent by the way she regarded him: with parted lips and wide, incredulous eyes. Darcy fervently hoped her astonishment would not soon turn to indignation.

"I hope you are better," he said to her, and grimaced, for he had said very much the same thing last April before he had proposed. He cleared his throat and began again. "You were not at dinner, Miss Bennet."

It took a moment for Elizabeth to find her voice. "Nor are you, Mr. Darcy."

"No," he replied, slightly chagrined. "Your sister informed me you were unwell."

"Oh."

In that one word, Darcy could hear her surprise as clearly as he could see her sitting before him and felt his heart sink. Was his concern for her well-being still so difficult for her to comprehend? Had the fact that he had taken her reproofs of last April to heart and changed for her completely escaped her notice when they were at Pemberley? Or did Elizabeth simply have so little faith in him as to believe him incapable of sustaining such a profound alteration over time?

Three days ago, Mr. Gardiner gave Darcy cause to hope Elizabeth might very well return his regard. His optimism only increased after his aunt's visit, for he knew enough of Elizabeth's disposition to be certain that, had she been absolutely, irrevocably decided against him, she would have acknowledged it to Lady Catherine, frankly and openly. But now, after witnessing her reaction to his concern for her well-being first hand, Darcy's confidence was waning fast. He feared the Gardiners' assumptions were exactly that: assumptions and nothing more. He had no idea what to do.

After a moment, Elizabeth said to him, "I am much better, thank you. It appears you have missed your supper for nothing, Mr. Darcy. Perhaps there is time yet for you to return for dessert."

His agitation increased and, in an effort to retain his composure, Darcy strode to the fireplace, where he propped his forearm upon the mantle and rubbed his forehead with his hand. "May I speak candidly?" At once, he regretted the severity of his tone.

"Do I have a choice?"

Darcy could not discern whether her response was meant to be sarcastic or whether she was merely making an honest inquiry, and momentarily closed his eyes to better master his frustration.

Lord in Heaven. What I would not give to be able to read this woman with any sort of accuracy! If only I was better able to gauge her mood and correctly interpret her cryptic tongue. But Darcy knew such familiarity—such intimacy—could only come with time.

Though he no longer had much confidence in her uncle's observations, he did have confidence in the elder man's wisdom. "You always have a choice," he told her. "Whether you choose to hear me or whether you choose to wilfully misunderstand me is entirely up to you."

From across the room, Elizabeth emitted a soft huff that Darcy could only describe as being both rueful and diverted. He turned to look at her and saw the faintest hint of a bittersweet smile upon her lips. Her smile vanished almost as soon as it appeared, and Darcy was left questioning whether he had seen Elizabeth smile at all.

"You sound much like my uncle Gardiner," she replied. Her voice was quiet and her tone reflective and warm. "He is a firm believer in the philosophy of learning from our mistakes, rather than sitting upon our laurels and remaining in ignorance, for *misunderstandings and neglect create more confusion in this world than trickery and malice.*" She inclined her head. "Very well, sir. You may say your piece."

That she could so readily quote Goethe to him was impressive but not the least surprising given her dedication to the improvement of her mind by extensive reading. Darcy's admiration for her soared to new heights but at the same time, he felt plaintive. Elizabeth's love of literature, coupled with her desire to know more of the world, would truly be magnificent with Pemberley's library at her disposal. While the idea of Elizabeth in his home thrilled him so would her rejection pain him. Once again, his emotions were at war.

Darcy shook off his encroaching disheartenment and shifted his concentration back to the present. Elizabeth had told him she would hear what he had to say, but he hoped she would do more than simply *listen* to his words. He wanted her to recognise the truth behind them, and his sincerity as well.

But where to begin? After careful consideration, he decided that perhaps the best place to begin would be the last place they *had* been. In other words, the exchange he had witnessed the day before between Elizabeth and Lady Catherine.

Darcy cleared his throat. "I am neither blind nor a simpleton, Miss Bennet. I cannot ignore the fact that your headache coincided with my aunt calling here yesterday; neither can I dismiss it as coincidence. I fear she is to blame."

A deep blush spread from the neckline of her gown to her hairline, and Elizabeth turned aside her head. "If you have come to chastise me for my behaviour, Mr. Darcy, you are too late. You can say nothing to me that I have not already said to myself."

"I have come," he said earnestly, "with the hope of finding you better. As for my aunt, what did you say to her that she did not deserve?"

"A great many things." She rose from the chaise with an abruptness that startled him and walked to the window on the opposite side of the room, where she drew the curtains aside and stared into the darkness beyond. "I ought to have held my tongue. The things I said to her! I have no doubt Her Ladyship has shared with you the details of our conversation. You need say nothing further on the subject. I can well-imagine what you must think of me."

He watched her from across the room, as she raised her hand and angrily swiped at the apple of her cheek. This meeting was not turning out the way he had hoped. Not at all. The last thing he had wanted was to upset her. Now he had made her cry. "Come, Miss Bennet," he said with as much kindness as he could inject into his voice. "Will you not sit back down?"

"I thank you, but no," she replied after drawing an unsteady breath. "I do not wish to sit down, but you may leave if you like, Mr. Darcy. I would never presume to . . . keep you."

Darcy sighed. Clearly, he would have to employ another tactic if he wished to make any headway with this conversation. Rather than throw himself into a chair and beat his head against the back of it, like he wanted to do, he walked slowly to her side until they were nearly touching. If nothing else, he would prove to her that *his* opinion of *her* was not nearly so low as hers appeared to be of him.

"Miss Bennet, a moment ago, you told me you could well-imagine what I must think of you. It is not my intent to argue with you any more than it is to cause you distress, but I must defend myself. Despite whatever my aunt said to you yesterday, it so happens that I think very highly of you. In fact, not a single day has passed in the last eight months that I have not thought of you."

When she did not immediately speak, Darcy worried he had gone too far. He attempted to think of an appropriate apology—some way to right any potential indiscretion—but his brain would not cooperate.

Nothing could describe his shock when Elizabeth drew an unsteady breath and whispered, "I think of you as well."

She was clearly in distress; there were tears in her eyes, and her voice was barely perceptible, but Darcy felt her words in his heart every bit as much as he saw them form upon her lips. As difficult as it was to manage his composure at such a moment, manage it he must. It would do him no good to act the fool when he had no idea in what capacity Elizabeth *did* think of him. For all he knew, it was because he had been arrogant and prideful in the past, and his behaviour toward her, as abhorrent as it was, still occasioned her pain. Or perhaps, she only wished to forget him, but could not because she harboured too much resentment toward him for failing to expose Wickham the moment he had set foot in Hertfordshire.

"I hope," Darcy said, swallowing around the lump that had lodged in his throat, "in addition to thinking of me, that you also think *well* of me. That your opinion of me *now* is better than it was in the past."

"It is," Elizabeth replied with feeling. "I do think highly of you."

Despite her words and the emotion behind them, Darcy was disheartened to see she would not meet his eyes. "Are you in earnest, Miss Bennet?" he asked, meaning to tease her. "Or are you merely seeking to gratify my vanity by professing sentiments you do not feel."

Her response was not what he expected. There was no fire in her tone, and when she looked at him—finally looked at him—her eyes held none of their usual impertinence. Instead, what he saw only served to confuse him further, for in their depths Darcy recognised sorrow, bleakness, and shame.

"Indeed, I am in earnest. Since we met in Derbyshire, not a single day has passed when I have not thought of you, and thought of you in all the best light. However, I doubt you can say the same whenever you think of me."

Darcy shook his head. "I have already told you I think *very* highly of you. You must know I consider you—"

"Please, do not," she said, both her voice and expression pained. "Surely *you* must know, Mr. Darcy, that you should not consider me in any way. I am not as impractical as the rest of the world, nor am I the least bit optimistic. Because of my mother's indulgence and my father's neglect, not only is my youngest sister selfish and spoilt, she is lately married to a man who has wronged you in the most reprehensible way. Lydia's union is a sham, implemented by my uncle to avoid casting my family in the shadow of *total* disgrace. While Mr. Bingley is none the wiser, you, sir, know of our troubles and our humiliation. There is nothing I have not told you; you know it all. The fact remains: Mr. Wickham is now my brother. Much as I loathe him and my connection to him, nothing can be done."

"No," Darcy sombrely agreed. "Nothing can be done in that quarter, and for that I am sorry. But I hope you do not think so little of *me* as to believe I am overly bothered by your connection to him. By now, I would hope you are well enough acquainted with my character to know I am not so fickle as to withdraw my good opinion of *you* because of my poor opinion of *him.*"

Elizabeth averted her eyes. "And I, sir, would not blame you if you did."

Darcy could only stare at her. "Do you truly think so little of me, then?"

She would not answer him and, in a momentary lapse of discretion, he took hold of her shoulders and asked her again. Elizabeth's intake of breath was as immediate as the stiffening of her spine, and Darcy, aghast that he had overstepped the boundary of propriety in such a manner—that he had dared to take such a liberty—released her at once.

"Pray, forgive me," he said, thoroughly shaken as he raked his fingers through his hair and desperately tried to forget the way she had felt to him when he touched her: delicate, soft, and warm through the fine muslin fabric of her gown. "Obviously, Miss Bennet, you are justified in holding such a low opinion of me." His voice was full of self-rebuke, and Darcy found he could not bear to meet her eyes.

In his periphery, he saw Elizabeth raise her hand and slowly extend it toward him before dropping it once more to her side. Her voice was as soft as he imagined her skin must be. "I forgive you, sir. I can only hope you can extend the same courtesy to me."

Darcy glanced sharply at her, his brows furrowed in confusion. Why on earth was she asking him for *his* forgiveness when the fault was quite obviously none but his own? "Miss Bennet, *you* have done nothing wrong."

"I have," she told him, and he could hear the earnestness in her voice as clearly as he could her distress. "My conduct over the past year has been . . . regrettable. In fact, I can think of many instances throughout our acquaintance, and one instance particularly, in which my behaviour toward you has been reproachable. I assure you, I have long been most heartily ashamed of it."

Darcy shook his head in disbelief. "Miss Bennet, let us not quarrel for the greater share of blame annexed to that evening. The conduct of neither will be exemplary; but since then we have both, I hope, improved in civility." He swallowed thickly, knowing he was but a moment away from losing his composure and apt to do something rash, if not lamentable.

And speaking of regrets, there was one particular thing the master of Pemberley wished to say; one particular question he very much wanted to know the answer to, no matter how much that answer might devastate him. The time had come, for if Darcy did not say his piece now, he may never have another opportunity again, never mind the fortitude.

He spoke. "You are too generous to trifle with me. If your feelings are still what they were last April, tell me so at once. My affections and wishes remain unchanged, but one word from you will silence me on this subject forever."

Elizabeth gaped at him. "How?" she all but exclaimed, and Darcy could see her own composure was hanging by a thread. "After my sister's shame; after Mr. Wickham's treachery; after the deplorable things I said to you in Kent . . . How can you still desire a connection with me, never mind want me for your *wife*?"

That she could think for one moment that he would never want anything to do with her was absurd, as absurd as forgetting her. As absurd as going about his life and never, ever seeing her again. His reply was as simple as it was honest. "Because I love you," he told her earnestly. "Because I will *always* love you."

Though he had proposed to her once before, Darcy had never felt so vulnerable as he did in *this* moment. In Kent, he had thought only of the honour he was bestowing upon *her*, for he was arrogant enough to believe she had been wanting, nay, expecting his addresses.

But Darcy was not the same man now as he was those many months ago; nor, he was willing to bet, was Elizabeth the same woman. He was neither arrogant, nor confident enough to think that just because he wanted her, she would automatically surrender to him. In fact, it was *she* who would bestow the honour upon *him* should she answer him favourably. Standing before her now in her mother's parlour, Darcy was not the master of Pemberley. He was simply a man who loved a woman with all his heart, and it was because of his love for her that he was willing to risk his heart in the first place.

He realised his hands were shaking, and to distract himself, attempted to think of something other than gathering Elizabeth in his arms or cupping her cheek in his hand or pressing a lingering kiss upon her lips; but the task was easier said than done. If Darcy had learnt anything in the past year, it was never to make any assumptions about Elizabeth Bennet. He held his breath and awaited her answer.

"My feelings," she replied in wonderment. "You honestly do not know?"

"No," he said at once. "I have misread you so many times in the past that I dare not trust my own judgement."

"Then you must allow me, Mr. Darcy," she softly said, "to tell you my feelings are very different. In fact, they are quite the opposite."

And just like that, Darcy could breathe.

"When? When did you realise you loved me?"

Elizabeth laughed and Darcy felt his chest swell with joy and gratitude, for it had been far too long since he had heard her laughter. "I cannot fix on the hour, or the spot, or the look, or the words which laid the foundation. I was in the middle before I knew I had begun. But I do," she said feelingly as she gazed at him, and in her eyes, he could see her affection for him as clear as day. "I do love you."

Overcome with emotion, Darcy closed the distance between them and extended his hand to her, wishing, hoping she would not deny him this one liberty. He was overjoyed when she not only placed her hand in his own, but boldly stepped into the circle of his arms and laid her cheek against his chest. Though he still wore his greatcoat, Darcy swore he could feel the heat of her blush.

"Dearest, loveliest, Elizabeth," he said, tenderly stroking the tendrils of hair that fell upon her neck. "You have made me so happy. I promise to do all within my power to make you as happy as you have made me tonight. Whatever you wish, I shall do."

"I am afraid, sir, that such compliance will make for a dull marriage indeed. If I desired a tractable husband, Mr. Darcy, do you not think I would be much better off with someone like Mr. Bingley, or perhaps Mr. Collins?"

Darcy was pleased beyond measure that she was teasing him again, and so said, "Then I shall endeavour to engage your mind rather than my purse strings. Perhaps we can attend the theatre, or visit a museum? Hyde Park is delightful in the spring."

"They all sound lovely," she said, lifting her eyes to his with a brilliant smile.

"*You* are lovely," he told her, tracing the tip of his index finger along the curve of her neck. "Beyond lovely. I have always thought so."

"Liar," she said, but the smile she wore belied her accusation. "There was a time when you did not think me quite so handsome as you do now. Admit it."

"I shall admit no such thing. I will take a leaf out of your own book, and remember the past only as it gives me pleasure."

"Then kiss me," Elizabeth told him.

If it was at all possible, the violent blush that coloured her countenance made her all the more lovely, and Darcy sent up a silent prayer of thanks that she was his—really and truly his—at last. He released her, but only so far that he could place his hands upon her shoulders and draw them down her arms at an agonizingly slow pace. The muslin of her gown was soft to his touch, but it was nothing compared to the exquisite suppleness of her skin.

His hand found hers and Darcy found himself spellbound; entirely captivated by the feel of her flesh beneath his fingertips. Pale and warm, as smooth as the finest silk, he was certain he could go on touching her forever. He traced the tip of his forefinger along the delicate veins of her wrist and marvelled at her sheer beauty. How did he ever become so fortunate as to win her love?

Elizabeth's breath hitched and Darcy shut his eyes. He had dreamt of this moment for what seemed an eternity. Now that it had finally come, he wanted to take his time and savour every single second; but he felt Elizabeth sway toward him, closing what little distance remained between them to nothing more than a hairsbreadth. Whether she was aware of her boldness, he had no idea; he was only grateful that she appeared as eager to express her affection for him as he was to express his for her.

Their lips met, the barest press of flesh, but it was as though a fire had been ignited. Darcy felt Elizabeth's gasp as much as he heard it, and took the liberty of deepening their kiss. Nothing could describe the taste of her, and Darcy knew, beyond a doubt, there was no other flavour in the world he would ever crave more than the flavour of her lips.

Before long, the sensation of having her in his arms threatened to become his undoing, and Darcy slowly withdrew from her. His heart was pounding wildly as he endeavoured to calm his breathing and regain his composure. Elizabeth was in a similar state with flushed cheeks and fever-bright eyes.

Their eyes met, and Darcy reached for her hand again. She gave it willingly and he raised it to his lips.

"I stand corrected, sir," she said, still out of breath, "I am beginning to see the advantage of having a compliant husband after all."

Darcy laughed. *Compliant, indeed*—and kissed her again.

SUSAN ADRIANI is the author of *The Truth About Mr. Darcy*, and *Darkness Falls upon Pemberley*. While formally trained as an artist, she discovered her passion for writing nearly a decade later, after the birth of her daughter. She currently lives in rural New England, where she and her husband regularly take rambling walks together in the countryside, much like Elizabeth Bennet and Mr. Darcy. You can connect with Susan through her website, thetruthaboutmrdarcy.weebly.com, and on Facebook.

"In such cases as these, a good memory is unpardonable. This is the last time I shall ever remember it myself."
—Miss Elizabeth to Miss Jane Bennet, Chapter LIX.

WITHOUT AFFECTION

JAN HAHN

Ah, there she is, my Elizabeth.

I gaze out the window of my chamber, watching her tending her garden. She clips the last of the late daisies and places them in the basket on her maid's arm before moving toward the larger chrysanthemums. She stops and tilts her head to the side as though she is not sure the sage blossoms or viburnums meet with her approval, but she is quick to gather some rose hips and wild grasses. I know what she has in mind. She thinks to brighten my study with a bouquet. She has no idea one glimpse of her is all I need to make my day lighter.

Fifty years. I shake my head in disbelief.

For half a century, Elizabeth has kindled a spark in my eye and made my heart skip a beat. The old doctor putters around listening to my chest and muttering dire warnings. He still thinks I have a heart condition, but I know better. I gave my heart away years ago. It belongs to that lass in the garden.

"That lass."

"Beg your pardon, sir?" The doctor jars me from my reverie.

I wave him away with a shake of my head and return to my memories. Where did those years go? The first time I saw her, I confess, I had a rather high opinion of myself. Where did we meet? Surely, I cannot have forgotten something that important. Yes, now I remember. At that blasted assembly ball in Meryton that Bingley insisted I attend. Good old Bingley. I wonder, did I ever thank him for changing my life on that crisp, autumn night? Probably not. Like more than one obligation I have overlooked through the years, most likely I forgot that debt of gratitude I owed my friend, and now it is too late. But I will not think about that. I would rather think of Elizabeth at that assembly ball.

So young and beautiful—she could not have been more than twenty—and when Bingley urged me to dance with her, what did I do? Declared she was not handsome enough to tempt me! Not handsome enough to tempt me? Who was the fool that uttered those words? What a pompous ass I was in those days. From that night until this moment, Elizabeth has tempted me with little more than a turn of her countenance.

I watch her snip the spent blossoms from the rose bushes, all the while instructing the maid. Her lovely hair is no longer dark but now silver. It still gleams in the sunlight, though. Her figure is yet trim, although it is difficult to tell beneath those voluminous skirts that are the fashion today. Most absurd design any dressmaker ever contrived! I prefer the styles of our courting days. I smile and begin to chuckle.

"Mr. Darcy, do you find my instructions humorous?"

I look up to see the doctor handing me a slip of paper covered with unintelligible scratching.

"Perhaps I should leave my directions with Mrs. Darcy?"

"No," I say quickly. "'Tis unnecessary to bother my wife. I am still able to read."

"And you will follow my orders, sir? Do we agree?"

"What? Hmm . . . right."

"I hope you mean that, Mr. Darcy. You are no longer a young man, you know."

I frown. Why point out the obvious? "Neither of us are young, Doctor."

"Yes, well, I must be on my way." With that, the gloomy pest left my room and not a moment too soon.

Now, where was I? Oh, yes, remembering Elizabeth as a young woman. Once again, I begin to smile. If I had to choose, when would I say she was at her loveliest? The day she accepted my proposal? I can still see the pink in her cheeks. Well, not the day of my first proposal. Her cheeks had turned scarlet that day. With what passionate ardour I had declared my feelings for her! And then . . . I turned into an arrogant goat. I still recall how my chest swelled with pride. Not only did I vow to marry her even though my family would condemn the union, but I went so far as to disparage her relations. I wince at the remembrance.

'Tis better not to dwell on that part of my life. Much more pleasurable to recall the second proposal on the lane near old Lucas's house in Hertfordshire. Sir William Lucas—how he delighted in his purchased title. I still can see him strutting about Netherfield at Bingley's ball, but why am I thinking of him? Much better to remember that we were left alone outside his house long enough for me to ask for Elizabeth's hand again. And that time—I can see it like it just happened—she accepted.

I laugh aloud. Suddenly, I recall an occurrence that took place shortly afterward. Elizabeth and I left the path and struck out to climb a small rise from which she promised I would have a splendid prospect. Today, I forget the prospect, but I do remember her promise coming true. The excursion proved to be splendid! It marked the first time I kissed my darling girl. Surely, she was at her most beautiful then. But try as I might, I cannot recall her likeness. What I do remember are the words she whispered as soon as I released her soft, warm lips.

"Again, please."

I am certain I obliged her request but for some reason I cannot capture the image. Curses on the cruelty age inflicts! I can remember, however, the surge of passion that flooded my senses at her shocking entreaty. Without a doubt, I knew that woman would lead me on a delightful chase for the remainder of my days.

I turn back to watch Elizabeth sit down on the bench in the garden, her eyes inclined toward the lake. Even at our advanced ages, she is lovely. Can she feel my eyes upon her? Will she cast her attention up to my window? She does not but rises and disappears from view. A cloud darkens the scene before me. How I love that woman and how I need her. Without her I am like the garden without sunlight.

Now, what was the question I had contemplated only a few moments earlier? I detest growing old. Not only does my body fail me, but my mind as well, which is much worse. About what had I been thinking? I recall the subject as most pleasant, and I long to return to that feeling.

I know.

When was Elizabeth the most beautiful?

One naturally would say our wedding day—never had there been a prettier bride. Or perhaps that night when she first shared my bed. I close my eyes, savouring the memory. I strain to see her, but I cannot.

I consider that first year of our marriage as our halcyon days. We devoted ourselves one to the other, and it was like heaven. I took pleasure in acquainting Elizabeth with the joys of Pemberley, and her enthusiasm delighted me. How often we had roamed the park and woods. Later, I set out to show her the wonders of Derbyshire. Some days we left at first light and did not return until sundown. She was eager to explore, and I was as eager to see my home and the surrounding lands through her eyes. But then, toward the end of that first year, the situation changed.

Jane Bingley gave birth to her first child, a daughter, and Elizabeth became enchanted with her niece. Three months earlier, Charles had purchased an estate within thirty miles of Pemberley. My wife and her sister were overjoyed to be within such an easy distance of each other, and after Charles and Jane became parents, we oft-times found ourselves at Summerlin Park. Babies, and our lack thereof, began to occupy the foremost position in Elizabeth's thoughts.

"I have it!" I speak aloud, causing myself to startle. I talk to myself these days much more than I admit but rarely with such fervour.

I now realise the date Elizabeth's beauty was at its pinnacle. It could be none other than the day she gave birth to our son Will.

"Yes, that is it," I murmur. "She was never more beautiful than when I feared for her life." I feel a frown crease my brow because I remember that it also marked the beginning of a troubled time in our marriage.

Jane had asked me to wait in the hall outside the lying-in chamber until Elizabeth and the babe were made presentable. I remember walking into that room, seeing my love dressed in a clean gown, her long curls brushed and spread out on the pillow behind her like a crown. She smiled down at our child in her arms, her expression serene and yet filled with a joy the likes of which I had never witnessed before. Never had I seen anyone lovelier or anyone I loved more.

"Elizabeth?" I had whispered, rooted at the door, hesitant to enter.

Raising her eyes to meet mine, she beckoned me. Quietly, I advanced toward the bed. I was conscious of movement in the background. It may have been Jane and the midwife, or the maids scurrying about, arms filled with bundles of discarded sheets and towels, for the bed was made fresh and clean, but I could not say for sure. I only had eyes for Elizabeth.

The chamber looked nothing like it had an hour earlier. I know it is not the custom for a husband to be allowed in the room during his wife's lying-in. Jane had declared it so when I pushed open the door before the babe was born. I refused to heed her words, so the midwife repeated the order with such emphatic distinction it could not be misunderstood.

"My wife is in pain. My place is at her side!"

I had barked at the poor woman with such force that she withdrew at once. I was not in the habit of speaking to any woman in an ill-bred manner, but Elizabeth had been in labour for two days and nights. I could no longer tolerate having her progress simply reported to me. I had to see for myself.

At that moment, Elizabeth had screamed as the pains resumed, and I ran across the room to her bedside. I took her hand in mine and kissed it. Jane handed me a damp cloth and I bathed my wife's forehead, all the while kissing her hair and assuring her that I was there. As the pain subsided, she opened her eyes.

"Do not leave me," she whispered.

"Never," I cried.

But I did. Three hours later, Jane bade me join her and the midwife beside a window on the far side of the room. "We think the doctor should be fetched," my sister whispered.

"I've done all I can, sir," the midwife added. "Your wife needs more than my efforts to see her through."

"Why did you not tell me this before?" I demanded. "You let her suffer like this for days on end when all along a doctor's skill was required?"

The midwife backed away, and I realised once again I had been overbearing in my distress.

"Darcy," Jane said softly, "things have grown dire only within the last hour. I fear for Lizzy's endurance. She is far too weak. We need help."

I rushed to the bed and gently took my wife's hand again. "Hold on, my love. I will return with the doctor and all will be well. Do you hear me, dearest? Do not give in. Wait for me!"

With that, I strode from the room, raced down the stairs two at a time, and out into the night. The cool breeze struck me in the face, and I gulped it in, grateful to be able to breathe the fresh air after the stifling chamber where I had left my wife. I did not wait for a groom but ran to the stable, shouting orders to the nearest servant to saddle my fastest horse.

Now that I think back on it, I wonder that I did not send a servant for the doctor. At the time, I could think of nothing but accomplishing the deed with great haste. I did not trust a servant to impress the necessity for swiftness upon the physician as I would. When I reached his house, I refused to allow the poor doctor to even dress properly but hastened him from his bed wearing naught but a pair of breeches and his nightshirt while I carried his boots in my hand. Harnessing his horse to a carriage wasted precious time. I insisted he mount the first horse I saw and ride back with me.

"What about my bag? How can I carry it and guide a horse?" he sputtered. "I much prefer a carriage, Mr. Darcy."

I grabbed the bag and held the reins while he climbed into the saddle. With that, we were off and back to Pemberley before the good doctor could raise further objections. Peculiar expressions crossed the servants' faces when I ushered him up the steps and through the front door with bare feet.

"Mr. Darcy, I must have my boots before entering the sick room. I insist!"

I relented and allowed the man to sit down in the entrance hall and pull on his boots. All the while, I stood over him urging him to make haste. When we entered Elizabeth's chamber, I could see my wife's face was not only pale; it had turned grey. I sensed Jane beside me, attempting to secure my attention, but I could not comprehend her words. I wanted nothing more than to learn that Elizabeth still lived. I called her name, but she did not answer. Kneeling beside her bed, I took her hand in mine, but she took no notice.

"Elizabeth!" I cried louder, and yet she would not answer. Taking her by the shoulders, I lifted her head from the pillow and called her name again.

"Mr. Darcy, you must allow me to treat the patient," the doctor said. I felt Jane tugging at my arm, and the midwife entreating me to leave the bedside. I know not how I left the chamber. I cannot recall. It was as though I staggered through a dark, cold tunnel with no light ahead. Elizabeth could not die. I could not live without her. I had nothing if I lost her, nothing at all.

"Darcy, drink this."

I roused, sitting on a bench in the hallway with Bingley beside me offering a snifter of brandy. Brandy? Why would I drink brandy when my wife—I jumped up and headed back to the chamber, but before I could reach the door, Bingley and my valet, Sheffield, blocked my passage. We came close to blows, but the two of them wrestled me back to the bench. I had but sat down when Elizabeth began to scream anew.

Her cries were much weaker than before I had left Pemberley to fetch the doctor. I could feel her life ebbing away from me. I turned to Bingley, wanting to find some semblance of hope in his eyes, but in its place saw dread. When another scream resounded through the thick walls of her chamber, I jumped up and pushed my way toward the door. Just as I reached for the doorknob, a tiny cry, like that of a kitten, made me stop and listen.

"Is that—" I turned toward Bingley and Sheffield.

A huge grin on Bingley's face confirmed what I wanted to hear. The babe had been delivered!

But what of Elizabeth? Without knocking, I pushed the door open only to see a horrifying sight. I shall not describe it for fear of shocking those who are faint of heart. I can only say that God in His infinite wisdom created woman much stronger than I ever suspected. When viewing the remains of the struggle my wife had undergone, my hands began to shake.

Before I could utter a word, Jane was urging me back through the door out into the hall, assuring me that all was well, and that I could see Elizabeth and the babe once the doctor was finished.

"All is well?" I muttered aloud. How could all be well within the scene I had witnessed? I could have lost her!

Of a sudden, Bingley was shaking my hand and congratulating me on becoming a father. Sheffield held forth the glasses of brandy, and that time, I accepted the offer.

"Do you have a son or daughter?" Bingley asked.

I stared at him before acknowledging I had forgotten to ask. Three words kept echoing in my head. "All is well." I prayed to God that it was true.

We gave our son my name—Elizabeth declared it her heart's desire—and we called him Will. He appeared healthy enough, but all parents know that childhood is fraught with disease, and the fear of death is a common worry. A similar anxiety for Elizabeth's health remained in me for I knew many women died from childbirth. The fear of losing her besieged me. I gave my full attention to the doctor's orders and demanded a roaring fire maintained in my wife's chamber day and night even though it was late August. She was restricted to a diet of teas and warm liquors, and solid foods were strictly forbidden. When I entered her chamber on the third morning after our son was born, I ordered blankets placed on the windowsills to guard against outdoor air creeping through the crevices.

That was the day Elizabeth rebelled.

After sitting up in bed, she began to unpin the curtains drawn around the bedframe.

"Elizabeth!" I cried. "What are you doing? You must not yet sit up. And why do you push the curtains back? There are dangerous draughts about."

"Where? I feel nothing but this oppressive heat. If I do not have some air, I shall be roasted alive," she announced. When I frowned at the foolishness of her actions, she laughed aloud. "Fitzwilliam, it is too hot in here to draw breath! Pray, if you do not open the door and allow fresh air into this room, I shall rise from the bed and do so myself."

My wife refused to be swayed either by Mrs. Reynolds's admonitions or my reading a list of the doctor's orders deftly punctuated by a wagging finger. She declared that the doctor had yet to give birth himself; thus, her knowledge was greater than his.

On the fourth day, Elizabeth rose from the bed and walked to the window and back, much to my dismay. Arranging herself in a chair, she then directed the maid to have the nurse bring her the babe, whereupon she promptly put the child to her breast. The nurse's shocked gasp was echoed by Jane, who had just entered the room.

"Lizzy, have you taken leave of your senses?"

"My milk is coming in, and I am feeding my son," she said quietly.

"But why?" Jane turned to me. "Darcy?"

I stood there staring like a simpleton.

"Jane, calm yourself. Why should one of our tenant's wives nurse my child when I have sufficient milk?"

"But it . . . it is simply not done," Jane murmured. "Especially here at Pemberley." She raised her eyebrows in my direction.

"Fitzwilliam, do you object to my feeding little Will?" Elizabeth asked.

I cleared my throat. Did I object? I hardly knew.

"It may not be the fashion," Elizabeth said, "but I have a great desire to do so."

"If it is your desire, my love, and not harmful to you, then do so."

Unknowingly, I had been backing up toward the door and finding myself there, I turned and fled. I sought refuge in the library and closed the great double doors behind me. It seemed my knowledge of caring for a new mother and babe was highly insufficient. My wife, who had been raised in more humble circumstances than I, had her own opinions of child care, and who was I to disagree? I had never actually seen a woman nurse a child before, but the look of peace that descended over Elizabeth's countenance as she held our son filled me with wonder. I decided so long as my wife and the babe thrived, my place was anywhere but their chamber.

From then on, I spent my days seeing to Pemberley, supervising my tenants, and exercising my horses. Of course, correspondence to my family announcing the new addition occupied my time as well. I found so many tasks to complete during the first month after Will's birth that I had little time to visit the nursery and Elizabeth's chamber until the end of the day.

That is not to say I did not miss my wife. My soul ached for her company and for the life we had experienced before the child, her presence at the table, glimpses of her all about Pemberley when I stole a kiss or two, and the moments we found to sit together and talk. I must confess, however, that for me once a day in the nursery proved sufficient. I had little experience with infants—in truth—none at all. I hardly recalled my sister's birth. It had not been of prime importance to a boy more than ten years her senior. When Georgiana was old enough to speak intelligibly, I found her more interesting and the easier our communication became, the closer we grew.

The brief moments I held my son each day seemed more of a task than a privilege. I suppose he was as suitable as most babies, but to me he appeared like a little, old man—wrinkled and toothless. On most occasions, I returned him to the nurse soon after taking him because, after one look at me, he either began to wail or I found myself holding him aloft to keep his sudden dampness from soiling my clothing.

I watched in amazement as Elizabeth cooed and cuddled him close, her eyes filled with excitement at each tiny movement. I failed to see the fascination. Perhaps when he was old enough to ride, Will and I would form an attachment. That is not to say I did not love my child. I would have given my life for him, and I suppose I felt the usual degree of pride a father has in having a son. I simply was not one for spending great amounts of time around a babe's crib making strange faces and speaking in an incoherent language. I left that to Bingley. He excelled in the art.

At night, alone in my bed, Elizabeth's absence tortured me. I wished I had instructed the maids not to launder her pillowcase. At least, her scent would have remained. I attempted to sleep holding her pillow close, but it was a poor replacement and afforded me little relief. How I longed for her!

The day she had departed the birthing room to settle back in her own chamber, she entered my adjoining room whilst the servants prepared her bed. I hurried to escort her to the sofa, fearing she had been on her feet excessively during the move.

"Do not fuss so," she said with a laugh. "I will not break."

I smiled but by no means shared her certainty.

"Come and sit beside me, Fitzwilliam." She patted the cushion next to her.

"You must not tax your strength," I answered.

"I trust I have sufficient strength to walk the length of the hall."

She leaned over and kissed my cheek. Taking my hand, she tugged at my arm until she had placed it around her shoulders. Nestling close to my side, she laid her head upon my chest. I warmed to her touch and held her close, turning to kiss her forehead. How perfectly she fit in my embrace. And how long it had been since we had enjoyed such an encounter.

"Within a few weeks, I shall make another move, dearest."

"Indeed? And where will this next move take you?"

"Why, back to your bed, of course."

Turning her face upward, her lips were unbearably close, but I did not kiss her. Instead, I released her and rose, hastening to tend the logs in the fireplace before us.

"Why do you leave my side?" I heard the reproach in her voice. "Surely, the thought does not displease you."

"'Tis far too soon to consider such things, Elizabeth." I averted her gaze, pretending sudden intense interest in the arrangement of the logs.

"Perhaps it is premature, but you cannot command my thoughts, dearest. And surely, you have missed our nights together, have you not?"

When I did not answer, she rose from the couch and joined me at the fireplace.

"Fitzwilliam? What is it? Has the fact that I am now a mother lessened your desire for me?"

I placed the fireplace poker against the brick before answering. "Giving birth has but increased your beauty, my dear. Believe me. Now, allow me to escort you to your chamber and to your bed. You have been up far too long."

Similar conversations ensued between us as the weeks passed after Will's birth. I dismissed her suggestions for a return to our former sleeping arrangements with various defences but eventually found myself at a loss as to further excuses. To avoid the question, I began planning a journey away from Pemberley. Lady Catherine had asked me to visit more than once, but since my marriage I had declined. She had finally extended the invitation to Elizabeth, even though she disapproved of my choice of bride. Now that my wife could not travel, it seemed the perfect time to grant my aunt's request.

I tarried at Rosings Park much longer than I wished and from there travelled to the home of my uncle, the Earl of Matlock. Correspondence with my wife occurred in a frequent manner, but I could not overlook her words of loneliness at my absence with which she filled her letters. She missed me, and I was in agony when parted from her. Lest you think I only suffered from the loss of our intimate relations, let me assure you that I also missed Elizabeth's keen mind, her sparkling conversation and clever wit, and the genuine connection between our two souls. She was my comfort and joy in every respect.

Our physical attraction, however, was the reason for my journey. Until I found a way to solve the problem, I would forgo the consolation of her company. My resolve was fierce. Never again would I threaten Elizabeth's life by satisfying my physical desire for her.

While visiting my uncle outside of London, my cousin, Richard, invited me to spend a day in Town with him. We took advantage of the colonel's leave with a morning at the club. After several games at the billiards table, we dined handsomely and then strolled through St. James's Park in the afternoon. While in the park, we chanced to rest a bit on a stone bench situated beneath the overhanging branches of large shady oaks. He, of course, had congratulated me on becoming a father and had inquired after Elizabeth's health.

"Cousin, I sense all is not well with you," Fitzwilliam said. When I failed to answer, he began to examine me in earnest. His questions grew ever more substantial until I found it difficult to reply without revelation.

"You may as well tell me, Darce. I will not give over until I have the truth."

I sighed before disclosing the story: how Elizabeth had almost died giving birth, my vow to never allow her to have another child, and my present quandary—how could I convince her we could no longer be intimate? By the time I finished my account, I felt exhausted and desolate.

"Never again?" Richard looked aghast. "But Darce, how will you live with her? Elizabeth is a beautiful woman, and your feelings run deep. Anyone can see how you love her."

We both knew he spoke the truth. My reply was but a raised eyebrow.

"Surely, there must be a better solution than abstinence!"

"And just what would it be, Fitzwilliam? Tell me that, if you please."

The colonel rose from the bench and began to pace. Couples strolled the path before us, some obviously in love, their heads bent one toward the other as they spoke or laughed. A man accompanied his wife as she pushed their baby carriage, his chest puffed up with indubitable pride. Was the babe their first? Did they look forward to a long life together and a nursery filled with children? Was I the only man in the park that day who could not enjoy his wife for fear of taking her life?

At length, my cousin ceased his pacing and sat down beside me. He cleared his throat as though he hesitated to speak. Removing his hat, he ran his hand through his hair before replacing it.

"What is it?" I said, tired of his fidgeting. "Blazes, Fitz, just say it."

He cleared his throat again. "There are always French Letters."

"French Letters!" I rose, filled with indignation, unaware that I spoke louder than I intended. "Elizabeth is my wife. Do you expect me to insult her with a prostitute's remedy?"

"Sit down, and lower your voice, and no, I would not expect you to treat Elizabeth in such a callous manner. But bollocks, Darcy, I know of no other remedy! What can you do?"

That was just it. What could I do? Contraception was not a subject I had ever imagined would be necessary in my marriage, and I knew not where to find an answer. Upon my return to my uncle's house that evening, a suggestion was made that inspired a glimmer of hope. Richard accompanied me to stay the night with his parents, and without my knowledge or consent, he broached the subject with his father. When told that my cousin had revealed all to my uncle, I was vexed at first, but after a conversation with the earl, I overlooked Richard's betrayal of my confidence.

"Here is my physician's card, Darcy," the earl said. "Weston is as informed on the latest medical discoveries as any doctor I know and more so than most. If anyone can assist you, he is the man."

On the following day, I bade my relations farewell and hastened to Harley Street in London where I found the doctor's offices. Although young, Weston possessed an air of authority and a grave demeanour.

"Little has been done in this area, Mr. Darcy," he said after I had defined the situation. "The fact is deplorable. Most women simply accept their fate upon entrance into marriage."

"But not when their fate is death!" I almost shouted.

"In this modern day, more young women die from childbirth than any disease, and yet they continue to marry."

"Insupportable!"

"I beg your indulgence, but this is a debate for the Bishops. I fear the only accepted practice of contraception remains separate bedchambers."

I rose and prepared to leave, my breathing grown ragged from indignation. Why had I wasted my time?

"I do have suggestions, sir," the doctor said, causing me to hesitate. "Common folk have discovered that breastfeeding delays conception. It may be too late for your wife to start, now that the babe is no longer a newborn, but—"

"Mrs. Darcy insists on feeding our son," I said, amazed at my wife's wisdom. "How . . . how long will it . . ."

"As long as she continues, although it is by no means without risk. Still, it offers some hope. Other means exist such as sponges and a practice on your part that few men find satisfactory. Women of the night often take seeds from Queen Anne's Lace afterwards, but I do not recommend it. Some uncomfortable side effects can occur, and conception is still a risk."

Thus far, other than the benefit of breastfeeding, the doctor had told me of nothing I had not already heard. When attending Cambridge with Wickham, he had delighted in repeating tales from the seedier side of town he frequented. I would not insult Elizabeth with such suggestions, especially since Wickham had laughed at how often those precautions had failed.

With an air of regret, Weston ushered me to the door and said he would write if he learned of new procedures that held promise. I departed London for Derbyshire, my spirits low. My travels had separated me from those I loved most for more than three months. Elizabeth's letters indicated she was unhappy and disturbed by my long absence. And sure enough, upon reaching Pemberley, her welcome at best would be described as detached. My greeting was carefully controlled.

Elizabeth met my carriage, along with the housekeeper and butler. Starved for the sight of her, my eyes wandered over her lovely figure now returned to its former size, and I smiled to see the colour in her cheeks and light in her eyes. However, I restrained my greeting by simply taking her hands in mine and briefly lifting them to my lips. After acknowledging Spencer and Mrs. Reynolds, I asked to see my son.

Little Will, now five months old, was a chubby babe able to smile and squeal upon seeing his mother. My presence produced the opposite effect. Upon taking hold of him, he set up the familiar howl. His lower lip quivered and an expression of fear filled his blue eyes.

"Let me take him," Elizabeth said. Placing him on her shoulder, she patted his back and murmured soothing sounds. He soon ceased his struggles. "Will is alarmed because he thinks you are a stranger. And how could he not since you have stayed away so long?" Cutting her eyes at me, she left no doubt that *her* sentiment matched that of her son.

With but few remarks noting Will's progress in size and health, soon I departed the room, indicating a need to meet with my steward. Thus, I avoided Elizabeth for much of the remainder of the day. Upon the announcement of supper, however, I knew I would be forced to face her across the table. I steeled myself, having spent much of the journey home devising reasons to explain the length of my absence. I knew none of them would impress my wife. They did not.

After dining, I asked Elizabeth to play for me. A curious expression passed over her face. "Would you not rather converse? We have been apart for months. Surely, there is much to discuss."

But I had endured enough of her questions at the table. "And our absence has made me yearn to hear you sing. Will you not indulge me?"

Reluctantly, she approached the pianoforte while I settled myself on the settee with a glass of sherry. Her performance was excellent, her voice grown even lovelier if possible. I drank in her beauty from across the room, thankful that at least I could gaze upon her. After the second song, she refused my pleas to continue, professing her throat felt dry. I poured her a glass of sherry and when she took her place on the settee, I moved to an adjoining chair, hoping she would not take notice. She did.

Slowly, she turned her head and deliberately looked down at the deserted indentation I had left in the cushion beside her. With measured execution, she moved her head from the settee to the place where I sat. Unsmiling, she pursed her lips together and raised her eyes to meet mine, her fixed stare soon causing me to give way.

"I suppose you are ready to retire," I said quickly, rising and looking about the room.

"I am not, but then I have not travelled all day as you have. Shall we go up together?"

"I have need of reviewing some papers in my study first, but do not let me detain you."

She rose and placed her glass on the table beside her. "Will you be long?"

"I . . . am not certain. There is no need for you to wait up."

Deliberately crossing the space between us, she stood before me and smiled slightly. "Is there not?"

Her nearness weakened me. *Do not reach for her*, I cautioned silently. She watched my eyes and when I did not answer, she turned to leave but continued to gaze at me over her shoulder. Her inviting smile did not disappear as she sauntered toward the door. I could not tear my eyes from hers until she left the room and I could see her no more.

Trembling, I collapsed upon the settee. "Lord, how do I do this?" I muttered under my breath. I leaned over and held my head in my hands. How was I to resist her? She was my wife. I loved her with every breath I took, yet I could not show her. It was unnatural. Inhuman.

I sat there in distress for some time, but gradually I gained control over myself. "It is because you love her that you will resist," I said aloud. My mind set, I marched to my study and sat down at the desk. I did not review the papers, however. I rang the bell for my valet instead.

Upon his appearance, I asked him to fetch me a brandy. "And then you may retire, Sheffield. I may be up late and can manage on my own."

Two hours later, I crept up the stairs until I could see whether the light still shone beneath Elizabeth's door. It did. With a sigh, I retraced my steps, this time avoided my study and sought out the library. The fire in the fireplace still burned, and after building it up, I found a favourite book and sat down to read. My mind wandered from the printed word.

Why did the light yet burn in her room? Was she waiting for me in spite of what I had said? I could see her clad in her soft, white nightgown of finest lawn, how it skimmed her shoulders and dipped between her breasts. Shaking my head, I attempted to clear my mind, knowing those images were dangerous. I returned to the book. But a few moments later, thoughts of her long dark curls loosened, untamed, and falling down her back returned to torment me.

With a curse, I slammed the book shut, rose and pursued another. My father had collected various law books during his lifetime. Surely, one of them would occupy my mind and distract my imagination. Eighteenth-century laws against poaching succeeded so well that my lids grew heavy, and I proceeded to lose my balance and fall over on the sofa upon which I sat. I awoke with a start and squinted at the great clock standing against the wall. Two o'clock in the morning!

Hastily, I rose and staggered up the stairs. I no longer feared that Elizabeth awaited me in her room, for I saw that the light was out. The entire house was deep in slumber. Sheffield had failed to leave a candle lit in my room. I stumbled in the darkness, feeling my way to the bed. After untying my neck cloth, I cast it and my jacket aside. As I unbuttoned my weskit, I stilled, realizing I was not alone in the room. I heard sheets rustle as someone turned over in the bed. When the movement caused her scent to wash over me, I knew it was Elizabeth. She *had* waited for me but not in her chamber.

Slowly, I crept toward the door, turned the knob as quietly as possible, and exited the room. Once safely back in the library, I extinguished the candles and lay down on the sofa in front of the fire. 'Twas not comfortable by any means but far safer for Elizabeth.

The scullery maid awakened me early the following morning when she entered the library to lay the fire. Having slept without a blanket, I stood before the fireplace, welcomed the warmth, and tried to work out the pains in my back and neck from sleeping on the hard, narrow sofa. Even though it was earlier than my usual time to summon him, I rang for Sheffield. He appeared sometime later, obviously puzzled to find me still in the library and wearing last night's attire, but like all of my well-trained staff, he made no mention of it. After fetching me a steaming cup of tea, he secured me a jacket and neck cloth from my dressing room and informed me that yes, Mrs. Darcy remained asleep.

After finishing the tea, I ordered my horse saddled. I rode for miles through Pemberley's woods and meadows. The sunrise appeared over the eastern peaks, its golden light bringing the world to life. Curling, grey smoke ascended from the tenants' chimneys. The birds began to sing while hunting for food, and the woodland creatures chattered and scurried through the dense, green foliage to avoid the powerful hooves of my horse clattering down the lane.

I returned to Pemberley but once during the day to eat a quick meal and summon my steward to accompany me on visits to the tenants. I ordered repairs made on several of the cottages. Upon each inquiry concerning the general health of the families, I was told that Mrs. Darcy had already called upon those who were ill and seen to their needs. I beamed in approval of the remarks made regarding her kindness and generosity.

Of course, Elizabeth was kind and generous. That was Elizabeth. And yet there I was treating her with rejection, or so she thought. By the time I returned to the house that evening, I had determined I could no longer simply avoid my wife. I must talk with her, and no matter how the matter displeased her, I must be forthright.

Our discussion would not prove pleasant while sharing a meal; thus, I resolved to delay our conversation until afterwards. My plans were set awry, however, when Elizabeth failed to come down for supper. I was alarmed. What could be wrong?

Tapping at the door of her chamber, I did not wait for an answer but rushed into the room. "Are you ill?" I cried.

She sat at her writing desk, a plate of food before her. "I am perfectly well," she answered.

"Then why have you failed to join me?"

"Why should I? Since your return, it has become more than apparent that you do not desire my company. I asked to dine in my room to spare you the aggravation of my presence at your table."

Frowning, I advanced into the room until I stood before her. "Aggravation? *My* table? Elizabeth, of what are you speaking?

She rose and placed distance between us by crossing to the other side of the room. "My maid informed me that you slept on the sofa in the library last night. I saw your cravat discarded beside your bed when I awakened this morning. I can only suppose that upon finding me asleep in that same bed, you would rather squeeze your long frame onto that ill-fitting couch than share a bed with me. I understand, Fitzwilliam. You need not inconvenience yourself by speaking the actual words. I will perform the odious task for you. You no longer care for me."

"Elizabeth!" *How could she possibly think I did not care?*

I covered the distance between us in three long strides and reached for her hand, but she turned away before I could touch her. She raised her hands as though she might shield herself from my advances and shook her head back and forth. "Please, Fitzwilliam, leave me."

"I cannot . . . I will not . . . until you listen to me."

"Listen to you! I was more than willing to listen to you last night. Did I not beg you to converse with me? But no, you insisted that I play for you, and the moment I finished, you told me to retire."

I leaned my head back and closed my eyes in dismay. "I know I am at fault. I dealt with the situation in an awkward manner."

"Awkward? Your manner is unbelievably straightforward. I have been dull and failed to grasp the truth. Since shortly after Will was born, for some reason I have lost your love. Why, I do not know. I have heard tales of marriages where men lose interest in their wives eventually, but we have scarce been married more than two years. Or did you forget our second anniversary passed while you were away?"

I blinked rapidly. I had forgotten. In my quest for information to protect her life, I had hurt her deeply.

"I did not think your indifference would occur this quickly," she continued. "I hoped it would never happen at all, but as I said, obviously, I am dull."

I shook my head while walking to her side. "No, no, no. Elizabeth, you do not understand."

"Then make me understand," she said, leaving me to sit down on the settee before the fire. Her colour was high, but the light had vanished from her eyes. They were filled with pain, and my heart went out to her. How could I have hurt this woman I loved more than life?

I did not sit beside her. I did not trust myself to do so for I knew I would attempt to take her in my arms. Instead, I sat in the chair on the other side of the settee. Where should I begin? What could I say? I swallowed several times. My eyes roamed about the room, all the time aware that she watched me, wariness guarding her heart. *Perhaps, I should stand.* I rose and moved to the fireplace, resting my arm on the mantel. Her eyes followed me, but when I met her gaze, she began to study the rug on the floor. I placed my hand over my mouth. This scene was as clumsy as the first occasion upon which I proposed to her. No, it was worse! Elizabeth believed I did not love her.

At last, I took a deep breath. "Allow me to begin by assuring you that I ardently love you, Elizabeth, with all my heart, with all my being. I do not know how to not love you."

Her face softened, her lips parted and she drew in a deep breath, but neither did the suspicion in her eyes waver nor the rigid set of her shoulders alter. She needed more than a declaration of love from me.

"You are correct in saying I have avoided you, but not because I no longer love you. If I loved you less, I would have no need to leave you."

Elizabeth's eyebrows rose. "That statement does not make sense."

"You would understand if you had witnessed the scene that I did when you gave birth to Will."

Her mouth gaped. "Fitzwilliam, I was there!"

"But you did not see how you suffered. Elizabeth, you came close to dying!"

"I may not have *seen* the suffering, but believe me when I tell you I was intimately acquainted with the fact."

"And that is why I have avoided you." I turned back to the mantel, confident that she now understood my reasoning.

She rose and moved to stand before me. "I see. You cannot bear to *watch* me suffer through having another child, so you think to solve the problem by never causing me to be with child again. Am I correct?"

With relief, I nodded.

She placed her hands on her hips and turned away, taking a few steps before whirling around to face me, fury evident in her manner and her tone. "Fitzwilliam, there is a much easier solution. I fail to understand why even you cannot see it. When and if I ever give birth again, simply leave Pemberley! Then you will be spared the irritation of *witnessing* this misery on my part that you find intolerable!"

Wait! Why must she resort to sarcasm? Did she fail to understand me? I was doing this for her, not me.

While I stood there, lost in the muddle my emotions had made of my reasoning, Elizabeth crossed the room and evidently left the chamber. I heard the door slam behind her. With haste, I strode out into the hall and looked in both directions but saw not a sign of her. On the landing below, I spied Mrs. Reynolds and asked her of Elizabeth's whereabouts.

"She walked out the front door, Mr. Darcy," she said.

Regulating my hurried manner into one of calmness, I descended the stairs until Mrs. Reynolds disappeared on the floor above. In an abrupt change of pace, I raced down the last four stairs and ran out the main entrance of the house. Looking about, I saw not a trace of my wife. It was dusk, and the sun sat low in the sky ready to fade from sight. I quickly glanced toward the gardens, a favourite retreat of Elizabeth's, but she was not there. Neither did she stroll beside the lake on the opposite side of the house. Hurrying toward the stables, I stopped a groom and asked if he had seen her.

He pointed in the direction of the steps leading toward the walk through the woods. "I saw Mrs. Darcy goin' in that direction a few moments ago, sir."

Once again, I tempered my steps to a dilatory pace until the servant returned to the stables, whereupon I flew up the steps and down the path. The trees darkened my view, but not before I glimpsed the whisper of her skirt as she turned around the bend up ahead. It was all but dark when I caught up with her.

We did not acknowledge each other, but I fell into step beside her, my hands clasped behind my back just as hers were locked together in a similar fashion. I wondered if she did so to ensure that I could not take her hand in mine. We walked for some time until the sun had vanished and the path ahead could no longer be seen.

At last I spoke, hoping her vexation had lessened. "Do you walk with a destination in mind?"

"Away from you."

I closed my eyes in acceptance. Had I not known this woman long enough to understand she did not give over quickly, especially when she felt she had been wronged? Effort on my part would be required to secure a return to her good graces. I stopped walking, but she continued.

"Elizabeth," I called. She halted and turned. I could barely make out her features. "Come back to me." I held out my hand.

"Why should I?"

Oh, but she was stubborn! "Because it is too dark to see the path ahead of you."

She raised her chin.

"And because I did not mean to hurt you, but I have, and I am sorry for it."

She still did not move.

"And because I love you so." My voice broke on those last words.

Slowly—very slowly—she meandered back down the path until she stood beside me. She would not take my outstretched hand, but neither did she resist when I reached for hers and tucked it inside my arm. We began our journey home.

"This discussion is not over, Fitzwilliam," she said softly.

"I am more than aware of that, my love."

After a night spent in separate beds, during which I slept little knowing the woman I loved lay so temptingly near, I rose and ate breakfast alone. It was not unusual for me to dine alone in the mornings. Often, Elizabeth had to feed the babe before dawn and would fall back to sleep afterwards. I went on with my day, enjoying a gainful round of shooting that morning and spending several hours that afternoon answering correspondence, among which I penned a long letter to Georgiana and her new husband in Bath. Perhaps it was better that my wife and I spent the day apart, I considered. It gave me time to prepare my thoughts for the conversation I knew I could not escape that evening.

As expected, at the close of our meal, Elizabeth declined to play for me. Instead, she took a chair beside the fire in the music room, accepted the sherry I poured for her, and gazed up at me with pronounced expectation in her expression. I sat upon the settee, a generous brandy in my hand and dread in my soul, and waited. It did not take long.

"What has persuaded you to believe that I shall die in childbirth?"

I had not expected that question. "Persuaded me? What need have I of persuasion? I paced outside the lying-in chamber for days, praying for your deliverance. I saw your suffering, Elizabeth, and I pushed my horse to exhaustion, fetching the doctor to save you! Do not speak to me of persuasion."

"I am neither insensible of your concern, Fitzwilliam, nor ungrateful for your efforts. I acknowledge that Will's birth was long and difficult."

"Difficult! It was brutal!"

"It was troublesome, but I am fully recovered. No harm has been done."

"I thank God you are recovered, and I intend to see that you remain so."

"By decreeing that I never have another child."

"Absolutely."

At that moment, the door opened, and the nurse entered the drawing room, bringing young Will in for his evening visit. She handed him to me, and I was surprised that immediately he did not begin to wail. I walked about the room, lightly rocking him up and down in the hopes he would remain quiet.

"Talk to him," Elizabeth said.

I raised one eyebrow. "And what do you think he wishes me to say?"

"Whatever comes to mind. He wants to hear his father's voice."

I gave her a look of incredulity, but, squaring my shoulders, I attempted to converse with my son.

"I bagged six birds this morning, Will. When you are older, I will teach you to shoot. And to ride—yes, riding must come first before you handle a gun." I heard Elizabeth's laughter behind me and turned to see her attempting to stifle her amusement.

"You told me to talk to him. What did you expect? I cannot coo like Bingley."

"It does not matter." She joined me and began petting the babe's cheek, her voice taking on that manner it does when speaking to a child, a manner I seemed completely unable to render. "Does not matter one bit, does it sweetheart? You love whatever Papa has to say, do you not, my little man?"

"Papa," I echoed. "It seems strange to think I am anyone's Papa."

"But you are," Elizabeth said with a smile.

We spent half an hour thus engaged with our son. My wife showed me how to tickle him under his chin and how to sit him on my knee so that he could look about the room, all the time taking care to support his back. She continued to urge me to talk to him, and so I told him of the last harvest reports, the two new colts born during my absence, and the plans to plant barley in the far meadow. I failed to see the point when I knew the child could not understand a word I said, but, I admit, the way he looked at me when I spoke made me smile. His gaze was extraordinary, as though he was attempting to define who I was. He studied every shade of my countenance. When I spoke to Elizabeth, the babe turned to watch her answer. He missed not a measure. I reconciled my son had uncommonly intelligent eyes, and my heart filled with fatherly pride. Perchance, Will and I would bond before I taught him to ride.

After the nurse retrieved Will and returned him to the nursery, Elizabeth took my hand and led me to sit beside her on the settee. The simple touch of her hand set my senses afire, and I braced myself not to answer in the manner her nearness provoked in me. Releasing her hand, I shifted so that additional space existed between us.

"Fitzwilliam, how can you declare we must never have another child?" She turned her head to the side and looked up at me with those eyes I adored. "Will is perfect."

"He is," I said, nodding. "Why should we tamper with perfection? Who is to say another child could equal Will's excellence?"

She smiled. "Any child of ours will be perfect in our eyes even if he is born with protruding ears and a wart on his nose. You and I cannot help but think him or her beautiful."

"With those defects, let us hope it would not be a girl."

"See," Elizabeth said, taking my hand in hers. "You do want more children."

"Of course, I do, but not if I lose you in the process. No, my love, you cannot give birth again. I will not chance it." I withdrew my hand.

She sighed. "And so, what are we to do? Shall I take a house in Town or move back to Longbourn and live with my parents?"

"Do not speak foolishness. Pemberley is your home. You will not live anywhere but here."

"I see. So, you will be the one to move away. And in this new arrangement you propose, shall you take a mistress to warm your bed?"

I rose and stared at her. "Have you lost your mind? I would never be inconstant to you."

She stood up and met my gaze. "Fitzwilliam, you are not yet one and thirty, and you propose to live like a monk until one of us dies. What a bleak future stretches before you—forty, perhaps even fifty years of being alone." Crossing the room, she fingered the drapes, pulling them aside to stare out into the night.

I began to fume. I had not contemplated the actual amount of years that lie ahead, or the prospect of what it would entail. But I refused to be swayed by her dreary vision. "Neither of us needs to be alone. We are married and we will live together here or in Town. We will raise Will and find joy in dwelling under the same roof."

"Like brother and sister?" She spoke so softly, I strained to hear her.

"No," I said forcibly, "not brother and sister, but husband and wife. There is more to marriage, Elizabeth, than the bedchamber."

She turned, a faint smile playing about her lips. "But what takes place in the bedchamber makes marriage so much more agreeable."

I released my breath in a huff and began to bluster about to keep my passions in check. She purposefully was flirting with me, and every nerve in my body wished to answer in a similar manner. No, in truth, I wanted to do more than flirt. I wished for nothing more than to sweep her into my arms and carry her up to that bed with which she taunted me! Instead, I busied myself by building up the fire. I doubt those logs had ever been prodded and poked with more force than they received that night. When I finished, I observed that she had returned to the settee.

"This will not do," she said, shaking her head, a serious expression upon her countenance. It was plain to see the flirtation had come to an end.

"What do you mean?"

"I am not content to remain in a marriage without affection. We shall have to part."

My heart began to race. I could not live if she left me! I returned to the settee and sat down, positioning myself where I could face her. "Elizabeth, you cannot leave. I believe we can show some affection without danger. I have held your hand tonight, have I not?"

She nodded. "If I recall correctly, I held your hand, but you snatched it away. Besides, hand-holding is not near enough affection to satisfy me."

"Elizabeth," I began.

"I need to feel loved, Fitzwilliam."

"You know I love you. I shall declare it from daybreak to dusk. Will that do?"

She frowned. "I enjoy hearing the words, but I still need more."

"How much more?"

"I must be kissed daily."

I drew back. "How can you ask me to do that? You know how your kisses affect me." *Now, why must my voice come forth as a whine?*

"Then you must learn to control yourself. I must be kissed or I cannot—I will not—live with you."

I swallowed. "Very well, but it cannot be the type of kiss that leads—"

"Kiss me, Fitzwilliam." She leaned toward me.

I swallowed again, but slowly I leaned toward her, my eyes fixed upon her soft, plump lips, knowing full well how sweet they would taste. *Perhaps, if I do it quickly.* Thus, taking hold of her hands, I swiftly brushed her lips with mine and then pulled back. There, I had done it and lived to tell the tale. I opened my eyes to see her staring at me, obvious displeasure upon her countenance.

"Again, please."

"Again?" For some reason, my voice cracked. *What was I, a boy of thirteen?*

"Again."

I did not simply swallow that time. I gulped. *How could I kiss her the way I longed to, the way I had dreamed of for months? Did she not understand a mere touch between us was fraught with danger?* But once again I moved closer, my heart wavering between fear and desire. My eyes held her gaze until mine strayed downward. I could see her breasts quickening as she grew breathless. I turned my head to place my lips upon hers, drew nearer, and then hesitated, lost in the warmth of her sweet breath on my cheek. My heart began to thunder in my ears like that of a drummer calling his troops to battle. *Perhaps if I closed my eyes.* I did so and at last allowed myself to touch her mouth with mine, only to find her lips parting, her hands rashly upon my face, pulling me down, down, down. Before I knew what had taken place, I felt myself surrendering. I reached for Elizabeth and pulled her into my arms. The sensation of her skin touching mine and the feeling of her body within my hands made me wild. Hungrily, I roamed over her cheeks with my kisses, to her little ears, and finally down to her exquisite neck. I wanted her and no force on Earth could stop my craving! When, at last, we parted slightly, I took no more than a moment to breathe and leaned forward to kiss her again.

Imagine my surprise when my wife disengaged herself from my embrace and rose, her pink cheeks the only sign of provocation. "Now that was a proper kiss. Goodnight, Fitzwilliam." With that, she left me, my senses feverish and my brain a rattle of discomposure.

Before retiring, I needed air. I dreaded the thought of sleep, knowing it would prove futile. Sheffield fetched me a heated whiskey mixed with honey, herbs, and spices, and after whistling for my dogs' company, I stepped outdoors and descended the stone steps. I sipped the warm drink and gazed up at the cold night sky. Numberless stars greeted me, but the new moon only produced a sliver of light. I walked down the measure of lawn to the lake where the hounds satisfied their thirst, provoking subsequent ripples to shimmer outward. I thought of the years ahead circling round and round much like the undulating water. How could I live with Elizabeth the rest of my life and not truly *live* with her?

Fear for her safety had been my sole concern. I had not considered how difficult the years would be—not only for me but for her as well. Could I do it? Did I possess the strength of character? Doubts swirled about me while I stood there searching for solutions. What choice did I have? Better to live in privation than to lose her.

I glanced at the windows on the upper floors and noted that her chamber was dark. It now would be safe to take my repose. The taste of Elizabeth lingered on my lips, and I knew that slumber would not be my friend. I determined to retrieve the tedious lawbook I had found the night before in the library. In truth, I might as well order an entire set placed in my room. Years of endless nights waited like great, hungry vultures.

I had dismissed Sheffield for the night when he delivered my drink, but he had left a single candle burning in my chamber. After discarding my clothes on the floor, I suddenly felt fagged. Perhaps, sleep would descend. I dropped the law book onto the table and pulled back the counterpane. That was when I saw her. How had I failed to notice her lying in my bed when I entered the room? Shadows filled the room, but was I that preoccupied?

"Elizabeth?"

"Yes, dear," she answered.

"Wh—why are you here?"

"Another necessity if I am to remain at Pemberley."

"Elizabeth, I will not—"

"And I have not asked you to do so."

"Then why are you in my bed?"

"I have slept beside you since the first night of our marriage, and I confess I slept very well, indeed. Since we have occupied separate beds, I have failed to sleep soundly. I need my sleep, Fitzwilliam. We shall have to share this bed." Her voice was matter-of-fact in tone, as though she were discussing what to serve for dinner.

"Why must you insist on torturing me?" I pleaded.

"I have no desire to torture you, dearest. I love you," she said, her voice soft and sweet, "but I also love my slumber. Now, lie down and go to sleep."

I turned away. "I shall be on the couch in the library if I am needed."

She sat up and caught my hand, leaning toward me, her loveliness more than apparent in the gown she wore. "I need you, Fitzwilliam. Stay, I beg you. I cannot sleep well without you beside me."

"And I cannot sleep at all with you beside me." My voice had now grown quite deep and husky.

"Please," she said. "I do not want to leave you, but—"

I knew I could not refuse her, but with a great blustery show of impatience, I extinguished the candle and crawled into bed. Before I reclined, however, I would make one thing clear.

"Elizabeth, do not think you can continue to add demands by threatening to leave each time you do not get your way. Enough is enough."

"Yes, dear," she whispered, lying on her side to face me.

I turned over, leaving my back to her. I spent some time wrestling the covers until I had settled, all the while thinking a monk's life would be easier than mine. At least, the good brothers were not required to sleep with temptation!

Elizabeth sighed and moved about on the bed. Each time she did, her scent washed over me. At length, she stilled, and I closed my eyes, praying to be overcome by sleep. Silence ensued for some time. I startled when I felt the touch of her hand on my shoulder.

"Did I surprise you?"

"No," I said in a defiant manner.

"I just have a question: Who told you I would die if I gave birth again? The doctor or the midwife?"

I knit my brows together and turned over on my back. "I did not need to be told, Elizabeth. I could see for myself."

"And so, no one made the pronouncement?"

"Well . . . no . . . but—"

"Because neither the doctor, the midwife, Jane, nor anyone else warned me of the mortal danger giving birth to another child would cause. Could it be that you have assumed more peril than really exists?"

"That is utterly false! You have forgotten how you suffered, how you had to fight to live."

My eyes had adjusted to the dim light, and I could see her smile.

"Not true, my love." Her voice softened. "But the memory fades as I recall the joy I experienced when the pain was over, and Will was placed in my arms."

"You were never more beautiful," I whispered.

"And I never loved you more."

"How could you love me? I did that to you."

"You did not act alone. I remember being quite willing . . . in truth, more than willing."

I sighed. There was no winning an argument with the woman, and we were drifting into conversation that had an unsettling effect upon me. Once again, I turned my back to her. She remained quiet for some time. And then, just as I felt my eyelids growing slightly heavy, I heard her voice again.

"Fitzwilliam, are you awake?"

"Yes," I said grudgingly.

"Did I ever tell you that I learned more about the marriage bed from my mother's housekeeper than I ever did from my mother?"

What the dickens was she talking about? I fumed silently.

"Hill told Jane and I what we needed to know about the wedding night, and she also educated us regarding childbirth. She said most daughters were shaped like their mothers."

I almost snorted aloud. Elizabeth's beautiful figure looked nothing like her mother's!

"She said if a mother has narrow hips, oft-times her daughter will, and each will struggle more in childbirth. Hill said Jane's birth was long and difficult, and my mother declared she would never go through that again. As we know, she gave birth four more times, and Hill said each birth became easier. She said with practice a woman's body seems to perfect the skill."

Could that be possible? I wondered. No, that was simply the unschooled word of an old servant, and she, most likely, told that tale to reassure her young charges. It was not the word of a doctor. I would not encourage Elizabeth by giving credence to her statement. I remained silent.

"Fitzwilliam, are you listening?"

I grunted.

"There is another fact we should consider: we were married over a year before I became with child. Do you recall that I had begun to worry since Jane was ready to give birth on her first anniversary?" When I did not answer, she continued. "Perchance, I am not as fertile as most women."

Oh, how my wife could conjure up arguments! Whether she had a child once a year or once a decade, the danger remained.

"When you place all these facts together—my mother's history, my fertility or lack thereof, the fact that I am feeding Will and plausibly protected against conception, and the actual truth that neither the doctor nor midwife said it was dangerous for me to have another child—its seems that we are denying ourselves comfort and pleasure without need."

I heard her words, but my mind was set on Elizabeth's protection, and I would not countenance arguments against it. I began to breathe evenly, feigning sleep.

"Dearest? Are you awake?"

I could feel her drawing near me, sitting up in the bed to peer over my shoulder. I continued my deception until she sighed and lay back down.

"What a pity you are asleep when I am making such good sense," she fumed softly. I smiled in my false sleep. Oh, but she was adorable! Whether she made sense or not.

And then, I felt her move close beside me. I held my breath when she placed her back up against mine. We had often slept in that manner when she was heavy with child, but now I knew her figure to be more than pleasurable. The very touch of her body against mine made me tremble, and oh, how I wanted to turn and take her in my arms. But I would not. I would allow her to sleep next to me and take comfort from the warmth our bodies created while I lay awake and silently debated her contentions through the night.

What was it St. Paul said? Something about it being better to marry than burn? I wondered what he would say about burning while married.

"There you are!" Elizabeth exclaims, sweeping into the bedchamber. "I have been searching for you, dearest. You must come down and see the bouquet I have placed in your study. The chrysanthemums are simply glorious!" She kisses my cheek and begins retying my neck cloth. "How was your visit with the doctor? Did all go well? Is your heart behaving?"

"Not when you are near." I place my arms around her and draw her close.

"Now, Fitzwilliam, tell me what the doctor said."

"Nothing of importance, just his usual grumping about."

"But are you well enough for our celebration?"

"What celebration?" I give her a quizzical look.

Playfully, she pats my chest. "You know perfectly well what celebration. Our fiftieth-wedding remembrance."

I groan. "I fail to see why we must invite the entire family to revel over a private memory. After all, you and I are the ones who married."

"Yes, but our marriage affected all of our family. Besides, we are too old for revelling. Let us enjoy watching the younger generation dance."

"Elizabeth Darcy, you will never grow too old to dance with me." Stiffly, I bow before her and kiss her hand.

She laughs. "And you will never grow old enough to enjoy dancing."

I nod. "True, but for you I will dance as long as these feet will move."

"Let me reward you for such a gallant offer by assuring you that we must lead only the first dance, and then we may take our place on the side. Will that make you smile?"

"Without a doubt." I reach for my cane and follow my lovely wife down the hall to the stairs, her tinkling laugh calling to me all the way. When she reaches the landing below, she flashes those fine eyes of hers in my direction.

"You seem uncommonly cheerful today, Fitzwilliam. Did the doctor give you a new tonic?"

"If I am pleased, it is not due to some vile tonic. 'Tis because I saw you among the flowers from my window, and it gave me pleasure. Elizabeth, you are still as lovely as a girl."

She pulled a face. "Oh, how you talk foolishness. Either your sight grows dimmer or you have something in your eye."

I shake my head. "You are wrong, my darling. In my eye, you will find naught but love."

But, you say, what about the *problem* between you all those years ago? Did you truly live happily as brother and sister for half a century?

Hardly.

In truth, I confess the *problem* dissolved the very morning after Elizabeth had plied me with her arguments the night before. I awoke to find her asleep in my arms, my face buried in her fragrant hair, our bodies entwined as closely as two people so in love could entwine and remain asleep. I could say nature took its course, but that would reflect poorly on my character. Instead, I shall say that I lay awake for much of that night, poring over the truth of Elizabeth's reasoning and . . . Elizabeth won.

And, you ask, did she give birth again?

Naturally.

Our second son was not born until—let me think, how long was it—at least three or four years later. I am profoundly grateful to say the delivery was unremarkable other than Thomas inherited my wife's fine eyes and, in my opinion, is the handsomest of our four sons.

Now as to the grandchildren and great-grands, you must ask my wife. I cannot begin to recall how many there are, but believe me, when they all come, they fill Pemberley.

Elizabeth says each one of them is perfect. I acknowledge they are handsome and bright. And I can affirm that they all possess an unusually keen intelligence. I begin to chuckle. Elizabeth does not agree with me on this, but I take credit for their intellect. In fact, it is a pet theory of mine, and someday, I may write a book about it. When they were babes, I never cooed at one of them.

Award-winning writer JAN HAHN is the author of four Austen-inspired novels. She studied music at the University of Texas but discovered her true love was a combination of journalism and literature. Her first book, *An Arranged Marriage*, was published in 2011, followed by *The Journey*, *The Secret Betrothal*, and *A Peculiar Connection*. She agrees with Mr. Darcy's words in *Pride and Prejudice*: "A lady's imagination is very rapid; it jumps from admiration to love, from love to matrimony in a moment." She is a member of the Jane Austen Society of North America, lives in Texas, has five children and a gaggle of gorgeous grandchildren.

SARA ANGELINI
KAREN M COX
JENETTA JAMES
BEAU NORTH
RUTH PHILLIPS OAKLAND
NATALIE RICHARDS
SOPHIA ROSE

"She is tolerable: but not handsome enough to tempt me."
—Mr. Darcy to Mr. Bingley, Chapter III.

HOT FOR TEACHER

SARA ANGELINI

BACK IN BLACK

"Christ Almighty, Bingley! Is there any friction at all between your two brain cells?" I could not contain my anger as I paced the narrow path behind my desk. "You hired *George Wickham*?"

"He said he knew you!" Charles Bingley, my earnest vice-principal, exclaimed defensively.

"Why didn't you call me?"

"Because he was qualified and because I distinctly recall that you told me—and I *quote*—'Just hire someone with a pulse before September first or we're in trouble.'" He crossed his arms over his chest, his cheeks ruddy with anger. No doubt he was right. He had an uncanny memory for my less diplomatic moments.

I shook my head, too furious to lay out my personal problems for Bingley's entertainment. Instead I sat at my desk, uncapped a pen, and furiously scribbled on my blotter, avoiding his stare.

"And the art teacher? Ms. Brunhilda?" I growled. "What exemplary talent does she possess—aside from having a pulse—that would qualify her as our art instructor?"

"Elizabeth *Bennet* is a fully credentialed art instructor with a master's degree in fine arts. What more do you need to teach a sixth grader how to draw an orange?"

"And I suppose she must have a degree in hypnosis? How else would she have passed muster with a résumé that lists Play-Doh as an artistic medium?"

"If you think you can do a better job hiring on short notice, then you are welcome to it. Until then . . . kiss my ass." Bingley turned and strode out of my office, the glass window rattling as he slammed the door.

I put my head in my hands and closed my eyes. George Wickham. The very name made me want to spit. I have known George Wickham most of my life, and while I could never put my finger on *why*, he made my skin crawl. He'd never done anything terrible—he'd never murdered anyone, or stolen over a hundred dollars, or slept with his own mother—but something about him was just . . . *off.* Like when you stand at the top of a skyscraper. You can't see that it's swaying in the wind, but your gut tells you that things aren't normal. That's the way I always feel around George.

And I've had plenty experience with George. We have the same father.

Like always, the first day of classes began with an assembly in the auditorium where Bingley gave one of his rousing *rah-rah-let's-go-Dukes!* speeches. I watched as he high-fived the football captain and then low-fived the wheel-chair bound equipment manager in the same, fluid motion. I should give him more credit, for he really is an engaging man, but I had still not forgiven him for his thoughtless staff hires.

My new art teacher was straight out of the politically incorrect stereotypes handbook. She wore horn-rimmed glasses that slid down her nose and her hair was piled in a careless heap on the top of her head, held in place, I suppose, by mesmerism and the paintbrush stabbed through it. Her sweater resembled an oversized potholder, both in texture and cleanliness, and broken fabric loops frayed out in a sort of holistic, handicraft aura.

"Welcome to Pemberley Academy, Miss Bennet." I tried not to stare at a smear of paint on her cheek and instead tried unsuccessfully to remember her first name.

"Thank you, Mr. Darcy. I can't tell you how much I'm looking forward to being a part of the Pemberley Academy team—" I pretended to listen while my eyes scanned the assembly hall. Two sophomores were harassing Mr. Collins as he slid his dust mop across the stage floor.

"Excuse me." I left Ms. Brunhilda without another glance and made a beeline for Collins and the boys. I was stopped in my tracks before I could reach them.

"Hey, Will!"

The voice, annoying in its familiarity, grated on my nerves like a shoe on a blister. He was a bastard, and I loathed him, but I had no reason to fire him . . . yet.

"Welcome to Pemberley Academy, George," I said through gritted teeth.

"Nice gig you've got here." His eyes were already shifting as if assessing the resale value of the stage lights. "Bet you get a lot of hot soccer moms, eh?" He smirked. How I wanted to rub that smirk off his face, preferably with my knuckles.

"We have a staff meeting today at four thirty. Please don't be late," I said by way of dismissal. Wisely taking my hint, he gave me a casual salute and sauntered away. I watched him pass a group of cheerleaders—who giggled when he called a suave, "Hello, ladies"—until he struck up a conversation with the art teacher. She would have to fend for herself.

Mr. Collins implored me, through his Coke-bottle lenses, to rescue him. I crossed the floor to the stage, glared the two sophomores off, and gave Collins a curt nod. That guy also gave me the heebie-jeebies but for an entirely different reason: I could practically hear the voices in his head telling him to set the school on fire.

I didn't see Wickham again until lunchtime, when he chased my appetite away with his cheerful—smarmy, really—grin. He sat down across from me.

"I see FitzCo stock is up," he said. "I guess everyone buys ketchup, even when times are tough." Wickham's leer flourished again as he held up the FitzWilliam's Ketchup bottle, my mother's family name emblazoned across the label. His interest in my monetary situation most likely meant he was once again in financial straits. I waited for him to beg for yet another loan. His status as my father's illegitimate by-blow never deterred him. My mother had been a saint to pay for his education, but she had wisely refused to provide him with any type of legacy or inheritance. And, having no inclination or talent to provide for his own needs, Wickham had a way of skating by on the charity of others. I wasn't about to bite this time.

"My mom is in the hospital again," he said, casting a wistful glance at his tray. By "hospital" I knew he meant "rehab," but semantics never mattered to Wickham.

"I hope she gets well soon." She had been my father's secretary, a kind and pretty woman, as I remember her . . . apparently too kind and too pretty for my father to resist, but that was my mother's burden, not mine. Peg Wickham had never done any harm to me, and I wished none on her. I truly did hope she would get well soon. I made a mental note to send her some flowers and push a little money into the account my father had set up for her before his death—an account that I sincerely hoped remained a secret from her son.

Trying again, he changed tactics. "So, when can I apply for a raise?"

I picked up my tray and left without a response.

School let out with the usual racket of slamming lockers and shouted farewells. I strode down the main hallway, taking in all the familiar sights. There was the poster for the Pemberley Dukes football team; homecoming was barely two months away. Bill Collins was lounging on his favorite bench, mop and bucket keeping him company while he finished his ice cream sandwich. He looked up, his eyes magnified to small moons by his glasses, nodded, and resumed licking the ice cream from the paper wrapper.

I tried to recall if I'd ever actually had a conversation with him and failed. I paused in my step, turned, and said, "Good afternoon, Mr. Collins. How are things going today?"

Collins looked at his mop, confused that it seemed to have spoken to him, then started as he realized it was I who had spoken. He scrambled to his feet and grabbed the mop, eyes cast on the floor. I waited for a reply but none was forthcoming. I watched as he and his companion waltzed away, the mop swirling its dirty, fringed dress and Collins in his blue, coverall tuxedo. *That's a couple that was meant to be*— then I shook my head and continued my walk down the hall.

Passing Wickham's classroom, I heard a muffled giggle. I peered through the glass and saw him perched nonchalantly on the corner of his desk, a wavy forelock of hair dipping over one eye. He had the classic air of the moody, literature teacher, the one from every chick-lit book-turned-movie: sensitive, Shakespeare-reading, slightly hipster teacher uses poetry and understanding to coax a shy diamond-in-the-rough girl out of her . . . rough. Except in Wickham's case, I was sure he'd be aiming to coax some unsuspecting PTA mom out of much more than her shell.

He was flirting with Ms. Brunhilda. She was laughing and toying with the paintbrush in her bun, basking her dowdy form in his beaming smile. The scene was revolting, but at least she wasn't a minor.

I rapped on the glass and opened the door, thrusting my head in.

"Don't forget, staff meeting in ten minutes."

"Of course," Wickham said dismissively, his eyes never leaving Ms. Brunhilda's face. "Well, Lizzy, we must serve the Ketchup King if we hope to get away for that coffee I promised you."

I saw her eyebrows shoot up at the moniker, but I left before any more was said. I'd already stomached enough Wickham for one day, and I had another forty-five minutes to go.

SARA ANGELINI

HOT FOR TEACHER

"Another year, another FitzCo Foundation art function." My cousin, Anne, hooked her arm through mine as we looked over the gala crowd. "It gets harder to select the grant recipients every year."

"And yet some decisions remain reassuringly simple." I nodded my head slightly in the direction of local eccentric artist Frances Gardiner, a ten-time applicant and ten-time rejectee of our annual grant. As usual, she was talking to anyone who would listen, and her lips could be plainly read: *ten thousand a year*. She caught sight of me and waved her drink in greeting, sloshing champagne over the edge of the flute with a giggle.

I turned my back, pretending not to see her, and rolled my eyes.

"I'll admit Frances Gardiner is persistent, but it's a mediocre artist who can't keep her lipstick inside the lines." When my quip was answered with Anne's uncomfortable smile, I turned to find myself face-to-face with Frances Gardiner, who was hastily rubbing a fuchsia stain from her teeth. My cheeks reddened, and I cleared my throat.

"Nice one," Anne murmured, thoroughly enjoying my embarrassment.

Undeterred, Frances smiled at me. "Mr. Darcy, I'd like you to meet my daughter, Elizabeth."

I noticed for the first time her companion and was stunned to recognize her as none other than my new art teacher, Ms. Brunhilda. By her cool greeting, I was assured that she had heard my rude comment. My bowtie began to feel tight.

"Oh! Why, Ms. Bennet, I had no idea that you were related to the famous Frances Gardiner!" I effused, trying to smooth over my last remark.

"Why would you? We have different last names," she said, one sculpted brow arched over a smoky, chocolate-colored eye. "Not unlike you and George. Brothers, he says."

"*Half* brothers," I corrected, unable to stomach even for a moment the idea that he and I were anything closer than a chance testicular emission.

"Yes, he does say you prefer that distinction."

I could tell from her tone that Wickham had been up to his usual tricks. He was as predictable as the dawn: find a sympathetic ear, fill it with woe-is-me stories, gain confidence, and betray. I wondered if he would sleep with her or blackmail her. Maybe both.

"Do you already know Mr. Darcy?" Frances's astounded gaze bounced between Ms. Brunhilda and me. (Who, incidentally, was looking very un-Brunhilda-ish in her svelte little black dress and sleek updo. She had gone from plain to pretty, simply by ditching the potholder sweaters and using a comb. I was impressed.)

"Yes, we're colleagues," I said, only to be cut off by Ms. Brun— er, Ms. Bennet.

"Mr. Darcy is my boss, Mom. Unfortunately, I think your chances of winning the endowment this year are pretty slim. I'm sure it would present a conflict of interest for Mr. Darcy to award it to the family of one of his employees."

"Oh." Frances looked positively downcast.

"Actually, it's not Mr. Darcy's decision. It's a decision made by a committee, and he has just one vote. So please, Ms. Gardiner, don't be discouraged." Anne interjected, a kind smile lighting up her face. I had always had an affection for my cousin. She was superior to me in many ways. She was like the sister I never had. "Come on, Mom. This place is too posh for us anyway. Let's go get a burger." Ms. Bennet gave me another glance, as if to ensure I felt her displeasure, and gently led her mother away. God, things were going to be awkward Monday at school.

I wasn't wrong. Monday did start out awkward, but I think I was able to smooth things over at lunch when I cornered Ms. Bennet by the water fountain and gave her an "I'm sorry about last night" comment. She said it was fine. I think it went really well.

I was so glad to have that unpleasantness over with, since I'd found myself thinking about that arched eyebrow and those deep, dark eyes over the weekend. I even caught her looking at me across the Friday assembly later in the week. Funny how I never noticed her dimple before, but there it was, in her left cheek as she gave me an impish grin before turning her attention to a student.

Yes. I think she's adult enough to understand it was just a stupid comment with no intended malice.

"You're looking especially pretty today, Lizzy!" Wickham's voice oozed to my ears from the teacher's lounge as I was getting a coffee. I looked up. He was right, she was looking quite nice. She had stopped wearing the bulky sweaters in favor of more flattering clothes weeks ago. Today she was in a crisp, white blouse and a slender tweed skirt, a pair of pumps showing off her shapely calves. She looked smart and professional. Which was completely inappropriate for an art teacher.

"Why do you look so nice today?" I asked, my eyes narrowed in suspicion. "The last time my art teacher showed up looking nice, she quit. Turned out she had a job interview. I won't appreciate having to try to fill a position in mid-October." I paused to take a sip of my coffee, and it dawned on me. "Of course, there aren't any other positions open right now, so if you did quit, it would probably be to be a barista." I nodded, reassured that she wouldn't be leaving the relatively cushy position of an arts instructor at a private school for the well-heeled in favor of retail or food services. I smiled over my coffee mug at her in appreciation, glad to have worked out that she wasn't planning to leave me high and dry.

"What…?" Ms. Bennet's face was bewildered at first, then she burst into a laugh. I joined her, enjoying our moment. Wickham joined as well, spoiling it. My laugh died, and I left the lounge to retreat to my office. I could still hear them laughing as I walked away.

Okay, I will admit it. I was beginning to like Elizabeth Bennet. She was popular with the students and staff, I never had an issue with her attendance, and she had already volunteered to chaperone the homecoming dance at the end of October. She was turning out to be a real team player, and I could certainly appreciate that.

There were others on the staff who weren't so reliable. Our phys ed teacher, Richard Simmons (yes, I know, it's ridiculous, but I don't pick their names), was an ex-Navy SEAL who ran his classes like boot camp. Wickham started calling him Major Malfunction, and I can't say I disagreed. I've had Collins clean up gymnasium puke on more than one occasion.

Our geometry teacher, Veronica Crane, was, rather unfortunately, living up to the Wickham-given moniker of Calamity Crane. If it wasn't an unexpected car repair, it was a medical appointment, a broken limb, or a dead pet. We were midway into our first semester, and she had already missed four days. I tried hard to be an understanding and compassionate boss, but if things kept on this way, I might need to give her a warning.

But one could always rely on Ms. Bennet. And of course, on Charles Bingley, or, as Wickham calls him, "Charles in Charge." (I may detest the man, but I have to allow that George Wickham has a knack for clever names. I've been the Ketchup King, the Mustard Monarch, the Pickle Prince, and the Duke of Dijon.)

But back to my point. Ms. Bennet could be relied upon. And, frankly, I was beginning to find her, well . . . *pretty*. I suppose this is related directly to her apparently distancing herself from Wickham, which raises anyone in my estimation. If she can see through his self-aggrandizing and false charm, then she must be a sensible woman. Who also happens to be damned attractive.

What's more, she seemed to return my feelings. While I had not yet asked her to go to coffee, we did often sit across from each other at staff meetings, and I was beginning to feel a real connection with her. She always laughed at my jokes . . . always had a witty retort at the ready. I sometimes felt giddy just being near her. I told myself that I would ask her out to dinner, eventually, but that I was content to let the flirtation flourish in a natural way.

To wit, our exchange just yesterday:

She: "Of course I will be at the homecoming dance. I wouldn't miss it. I never went to my own homecoming."

I: "You won't already be out . . . on a date?"

She, after a pregnant pause: "No, I won't." Another pause. (*I believe she likes to create anticipation.*) "I will be there; no ifs, ands, or buts."

I: "No ifs, ands, or buts? What a pity. I rather appreciate a good butt." (*See what I did there?*)

She: "That doesn't surprise me. You have ass written all over you."

The mild sexual innuendo might be slightly inappropriate, but we are, after all, adults. And I think she likes me. A lot.

DAZED AND CONFUSED

Homecoming night. Unlike Ms. Bennet, I had gone to my dance. I remember it being awkward and uncomfortable, as I dislike dancing as a general rule, but it was nothing like the crude grinding I had seen in the last few years. They say every savage can dance. I say they use the definition loosely.

The festivities had been in swing for over an hour when I finally saw Ms. Bennet—Elizabeth, as she insisted I call her—standing in a corner by herself. She had her hair pulled back in that sleek updo again, and she was probably wearing that same little black dress that she wore to the FitzCo gala, but she looked, in the vernacular of my students —*fiiiiiiine*.

I watched as the president of the chess club approached her and extended his hand, which she accepted with a laugh. Some inelegant foot shuffling and hand flapping followed, although I give her credit—I'd never before seen such a huge grin on Tyler Parson's face. She seemed to have that effect on everyone . . . myself included.

Confession time. I don't know exactly how it happened, but I was a bit more than attracted to Ms. Bennet. It came on so gradually that I was in over my head before I even knew I'd started. I didn't just want to ask her to coffee. I wanted to ask her to dinner, to dance, to a weekend away. I wanted to know her and for her to know me. And God Almighty, did I want to kiss her. I couldn't pass a day without my eyes dropping to that full lower lip. I loved the way it curved into that mischievous smile she had, as if she knew a secret and was just about to spill it.

There were other things that drew me to her: her quick wit, her clear compassion for others, her generosity with her time. But there was no denying that she had a great set of legs, hair that I wanted to curl my fingers in, and eyes that promised a night I'd never forget. She even smelled good, dammit. How is a red-blooded man supposed to resist?

But I digress. The point is, over the course of only two months, I'd turned from labeling her a curiosity to wanting to feel her hands on me. From wondering where on Earth she'd come from, to wondering where in heaven she could take me. There was no way to avoid the truth that she had me utterly hot and bothered.

And, being a man of action my entire life, there was nothing for it but to make my move.

I strolled across the gymnasium and offered her a bottle of water.

"Thanks." She grinned at me and took a deep draw from the bottle. "It's really hot in here."

"Want to step outside for some air?" She nodded, and I led her out the side door. We walked across the side lot in comfortable silence until we reached the sports field. As we reached the bleachers, I saw her shiver. I immediately doffed my jacket and draped it over her shoulders. She shrugged into it and murmured another thanks.

"You know, we've known each other for a couple of months now, and I've been wanting to ask you . . . that is . . ." For probably the first time in my life, I found myself at a loss for words. She looked up at me, the moonlight limning her cheek in silver, thick lashes brushing against her cheeks as she closed her eyes. A sigh slipped from her lips, and I found myself drawn like a compass needle to North. My lips brushed hers and my eyelids fell shut.

A scant second later, the spell was broken by her gasp. Cold air rushed between us as she took a step back.

"What the *hell*!" she exclaimed, her brow furrowed in anger. "What is it with you guys? Is it hereditary for you to prey on women?"

"I don't understand." I stammered, utterly confused.

"First George has all the subtlety of an octopus on speed, then *you* . . ." She ripped off my jacket and balled it up before shoving it furiously into my chest. "Unbelievable!" She stormed off, and I hurried to follow her.

"Wait! Elizabeth!" She held one hand up to me without looking over her shoulder and shook her head, the universal signal for "get lost." I watched, stunned and helpless, as she strode back into the gymnasium.

Well, that went well. I can't wait for the harassment claim to show up on my desk.

To say the next several weeks were uncomfortable would be an understatement. I could not fathom how I had been so wrong. I was sure I had read all the signs—the glances, the giggles, the sly comments. Now, in retrospect, it was obvious. She was making fun of me, laughing at me, insulting me, but I was too dense—too smitten—to see it.

It didn't hurt so much that she didn't have feelings for me. It hurt that she *did* have feelings for me—feelings of disgust. Feelings of disdain. I had no idea what I had done to ignite her dislike. And I was too cowardly to ask.

I searched my memory for any slight I'd dealt her. Yes, there was the insult to her mother, but I thought we'd moved past that. I honestly could not think of anything else I'd done. I was the type of person who always wanted to tackle challenges head on, but what could you do when you didn't even know what the issue was? It gnawed at me. It kept me awake at night.

I needed to get over it. I eagerly welcomed the approaching holiday break to escape those angry brown eyes.

On the last day before break as students rushed out the doors like felons on parole, I lingered long enough to make a final round of the halls before making my own getaway. As I passed through the east wing, I noticed a large water spill on the floor. I was not sure where Mr. Collins was, but I could certainly handle sopping up the mess with a few paper towels. I skirted around the puddle and headed around the corner to the janitor's closet.

It was a small room the size of a walk-in closet, and the rolls of paper towels were located on the back wall. I pulled the chain on the lightbulb overhead and stepped inside, allowing the door to close behind me. I rummaged in the dimness until I found the towels then turned to leave . . . only . . . my hand met thin air when I reached for the door knob. I looked down and saw nothing except a hole where the handle once was. I pushed on the door, but it had locked behind me.

Great.

I looked at my watch. Four thirty. I knew Mr. Collins' shift did not end until five thirty, and he would probably come by, so I was in no danger of being stranded in a closet over the two-week winter break. I pulled out my cell phone to call him, but there was no reception inside the cave. I sighed.

All around me were cleaning supplies and newspapers. In one corner was a folded lawn chair next to a small end table upon which was a stack of magazines. With nothing better to do, I sat in the chair and opened the magazine on the top of the stack. The words were English but made little sense to me. I flipped back to the cover. It read: *Astrophysical Journal.* No wonder.

Intrigued, I riffled through the stack. *Annual Review of Astronomy and Astrophysics. Physics of the Dark Universe.* If I didn't know better, I'd say Bill Collins was brushing up on his wizarding skills in preparation for a position at Hogwarts.

I shifted through the rest of the magazines hoping to find something of interest, but nary a *People* or *Playboy* was to be found. I planted my chin in my palm and settled in to wait.

I must have dozed off in the dim silence, because I jerked awake when the door swung open. I raised my hand to shield my dark-accustomed eyes against the sudden glare.

"Will?" Elizabeth's voice asked in surprise.

"Wait! Don't—" the room went dark again as the door closed behind her "—let the door shut," I uttered weakly.

"What? Why? Oh, hell!" I heard her fumbling for the non-existent door handle. She banged on the door for a moment, then said, "Are we trapped?"

"Yes."

She reached into her jacket pocket for her phone, only to arrive at the same conclusion that I had. "And no cell reception. Fantastic."

"Relax. Bill's shift isn't over until five thirty. He'll let us out." I checked my watch again. "In half an hour."

"I came in for paper towels . . ." She hitched her thumb over her shoulder toward the hallway outside.

"Yes, so did I."

Elizabeth rubbed her arms as if chilled. It looked more like a protective gesture, aimed to put space between us. The tense silence made my ears ring.

"Well, this is awkward."

"Yeah," she said. More silence.

"It's going to be a very long half hour if you give me the cold shoulder the whole time." I crossed my legs nonchalantly. *I could do this all night.*

"I could start by making a comment about how you're trapped in the closet."

"Is it some kind of rule that you have to be rude to me? Or is it just voluntary?"

"Rude? Me? Ha, that's a joke. I wasn't the one slobbering all over you."

"I said I was sorry. It was a mistake. Believe me, I'm regretting it more than you."

"Really? Why is that? Ms. Brunhilda isn't attractive enough for you? In my potholder sweater and Brillo Pad hair?"

My mouth hung open. How did she know about that?

She snorted a bitter laugh. "You must know Charles has the biggest mouth in the school."

I did now. I'll kill him. I tried a defensive posture.

"I've seen you bust Richard's balls to his face. You can't honestly be that sensitive."

"That's just like you to turn it around to my problem." She shook her head derisively. "You are the *worst* principal I've ever had the misfortune to work with."

Well, this was getting personal.

"How so? Because I don't hold everyone's hand in a drum circle? Because I expect everyone to do their job well? Because I have *high standards*?"

Even in the dim light I could see her face had flushed red. I guess I pressed a button. Served her right.

"You know, it wouldn't be so bad if you were just an asshole. But the fact that you're completely clueless to it is astonishing. As is your complete and utter lack of social skills. Do you have any friends? Do you even go home at night? Or do you just camp out in your office, calculating your weekly stats?"

"So, it's fine for you to insult me personally but it's overkill for me to provide constructive criticism? Unbelievable."

"Constructive criticism? That's what you call it when Veronica comes to me in tears, asking me if I can help grade her papers because you've given her a warning?"

"Veronica's performance is none of your concern."

"Apparently, it's none of yours either. Did you know that her husband was in a car crash in August and has been in the hospital since then? That man is learning to walk again, and all you care about is whether at least sixty-five percent of her class passes the next standardized test."

I said nothing. I hadn't known.

"Or that Richard teaches yoga at a homeless shelter every Saturday, and that's why he doesn't come to your stupid 'educational enrichment' classes."

Nope. Hadn't known that either.

"Or that George had to take out a loan to pay for his mother's hospital stay because you cut off her trust fund? Oh, wait, I guess you *would* know that."

Now *that*, I knew, was a bald-faced lie. I was glad she'd brought him up; I was beginning to feel bad, but now I was furious.

"You seem awfully interested in George and his finances. If you knew half the truth about him, you'd know why I detest him."

She shook her head, a self-satisfied smirk on her face.

"And that's just my point. He's not good enough for you. *None* of us are good enough for you. If it had been you instead of Charlie who interviewed me, I'd never have taken this job. Almost from the first day we met, I knew that you were a self-absorbed tool."

"That's enough." I ground my teeth and balled my fists. I was about to unleash a litany of insults that would be sure to reduce her to a quivering blob of tears, when the closet door jerked open.

Bill Collins stood framed in the doorway briefly before he stepped inside. Forgetting our argument, both Elizabeth and I shouted, "No!" Alas, we were too late. The door clicked shut.

"What are you two doing in here?" Bill's soft, bewildered voice hung in the air.

"Now we're locked in here for the next two weeks!!" Elizabeth exclaimed, panic laced in her voice. I suspect she was more disturbed by the fact she'd be stuck with me than by the prospect of possible cannibalism.

"Why?" Bill put his hand into his pocket and pulled out the door handle.

"Why on earth do you have the door handle in your pocket?" I yelled.

"In case I get locked in, of course."

CREEP

I had two long, miserable weeks to consider all Elizabeth had said. Was she right? Did I look down on everyone around me? I had to admit that there were times when it seemed to me that what I thought was clearly superior to what others thought, that I was right and they were wrong. But *better* than them? No.

Yet, if I was honest, I could see her point. Being criticized, even with the best of intentions, is never fun. If there's already a seed of resentment, say, planted by a certain person who has reason to despise me . . .

Of course, her accusations went well beyond my interactions with her, and that's where it really stung. How could I have been so ignorant about my own co-workers' life situations? Was I that unapproachable? Was I that . . . disliked?

I vowed to change that. Not for Elizabeth—no, that was a lost cause. But I could make a better effort to know and show that I care for the people who work for me. I owed it to them.

So, I reached out to Veronica Crane over the holidays and stopped by to visit her husband. I assured her that she could take as much time as she needed, that her job would still be there. I helped her fill out paperwork for family leave and committed to ensuring that she was financially stable, whether through insurance, state benefits, or a personal loan. I went completely Charles Dickens on her and sent a full Christmas dinner to her house, followed by several Amazon deliveries for her two kids. It was nerve wracking at first—I don't have any kids and have no idea what ten-year-old twin boys would want. But I figured an X-Box and a few games couldn't hurt. God bless us, everyone.

When school resumed in January, I sought out Bill Collins and asked him point blank about his reading materials.

"What are you doing with these?" I asked, holding up a fan of astrophysics academic journals.

He shrugged. "Just keeping up."

"With what?" I laughed.

"My old friends at NASA."

My jaw dropped. "You were a janitor at NASA?"

"Of course, not. I was an astrophysicist. I retired fifteen years ago."

"What the *hell* are you doing working as a janitor?"

He shrugged. "My wife doesn't like me staying around the house. I had to find a job, and this is as easy and mindless as it gets. I can think about things while I'm working."

"Things?"

"Oh, yeah. String theory. Subatomic particles and their defiance of physics. The simultaneous expansion and contraction of an infinite universe. *Things*. My friend Neil and I had this theory we were working on before he went all Hollywood and became Mr. Tyson."

"Your friend Neil. Wait. Did you just name-drop Neil deGrasse Tyson?"

"Oh, do you know him too?"

"And that, my friend, is why I chose phys ed." I peered over the mountain of geometry homework at Richard, who stood at my office door. "At six p.m. on a Friday, your bachelor life has clearly gotten out of hand." He grinned and sank into the chair before my desk.

"Somebody had to step up. Veronica's out for the next three weeks, and geometry teachers are hard to come by."

"I'm surprised you remember it well enough to grade papers."

"Never underestimate the power of Google."

He chuckled and fidgeted with his ball cap. "You up for a beer? Or whatever girly drink it is you order. Mai Tai or Sex on the Beach?"

I gave the papers a wry glance and tossed my red pen on the desk. "Sure." I stood and thrust my arms into my jacket. "I'll order you your first Blow Job."

His friendship had sort of snuck up on me. We had nothing in common, with him being a military man and me being a wuss, but I liked him and he seemed to like me, so there it was.

We walked three blocks to an old Irish bar and sat at a table. He spun his chair around and sat on it like a cowboy, folding his arms on the back.

"That one's a real cutie," he said, nodding toward the door. I looked over my shoulder and saw Elizabeth shrugging out of her coat. I looked back at Richard. He had a sort of dreamy smile on his face, made utterly ridiculous by the foam mustache left by his beer. My stomach dropped, and I looked down into my glass.

Suddenly, this was the last place I wanted to be. I'd hid from her like a scared mouse ever since school resumed. It was a matter of self-preservation. I couldn't get over the things she'd said to me. I couldn't be in the same room with her. If she entered the teacher's lounge, I'd leave. I'd patrol the other side of the yard when the students waited for pick-ups. I ate at my desk instead of the cafeteria unless I was on duty, and even then I kept my distance. None of it changed how I felt about her.

I hated that she hated me, and I hated myself for still wanting her.

"Hey there, darlin'!" Richard held up his hand and waved her over.

"Oh, hey, hi guys!" Elizabeth's smile lit up her eyes, crinkling the fine lines around them. I always liked that on a woman; I'd take laugh lines over Botox any day. Her hand dropped on my shoulder and I froze. "This is my sister, Lydia. Lydia, this is Richard and Will."

I looked up and nodded politely at the strawberry blonde standing next to Elizabeth. They were film negative images of each other: chestnut hair and chocolate eyes next to auburn hair and cornflower blue eyes. Both were beautiful in their own way, but I'd always have a preference for the warmth of Elizabeth's peach complexion over the cream of her sister's.

"Can we join you?" Elizabeth glanced at Richard and then at me. I nodded, still unable to speak. Richard pulled out the extra chairs and the ladies sat.

Two beers later, I still had not said a word. Somehow the conversation carried on around me, yet nobody seemed to notice that I was there. I wanted to sink under the table. I wanted to go home.

"I saw you, you know." My head jerked up. Elizabeth had pulled her chair a few inches closer to me and was leaning in, her voice low.

"What?" I think it came out as a squeak.

"I saw you yesterday. You paid for the cookies."

I stared at her blankly.

"The Thin Mints. George stole them from the Girl Scouts' table, and you paid for them."

I nodded.

"It was nice."

I blinked and gave her a smile that probably looked like I was crapping myself.

She leaned in further, her voice barely audible. "And . . . I'm sorry."

I shook my head slightly and cleared my throat. "There's nothing to be sorry for."

She glanced at Richard and Lydia, who were deeply embroiled in a flirtation that assured me he was not likely go home alone.

"Do you think we could talk outside?" she asked, touching my forearm lightly. I nodded once, and after giving Lydia and Richard a brief (and ignored) explanation, we stepped outside into the frigid night air.

She pulled her cream woolen coat tighter around her and looked at the ground. I stayed silent while she gathered her thoughts.

"The thing is, I'm really sorry. I said some pretty rough things to you, and you didn't deserve that. I can see it now. George told me . . ." She looked around uncomfortably, then took a deep breath and started again. "It doesn't matter what he said. The point is, I guess my feelings were hurt, and I was ready to believe him."

"I hurt your feelings?"

She nodded and gave me a crooked smile. "You know, Ms. Brunhilda. Not pretty enough to tempt you. It hurt. Then when I changed the way I looked, you accused me of looking for another job. And let's not forget what you said about my mom."

I cringed. "Elizabeth, I'm the one who should be apologizing. Everything you said that day was true. Everything." I took a step closer to her. "I'm sorry. I really am."

She stuffed her hands into her pockets and looked down.

"Yeah, I am too. I'm sorry for leading you on."

I froze. So I hadn't been wrong; she had been flirting with me. I took a step backwards.

"You knew how I felt?"

She nodded.

"And you led me on so that you could reject me? Like some kind of lesson?"

"It sounds terrible when you put it like that, but yes, I guess that's what I did."

"That's really shitty, Elizabeth."

"Why do you think I'm apologizing? I know it was shitty. I feel bad about it. I want to apologize. I hate how things are. I hate the tension. I want us to be friends. Or at least not enemies."

My emotions were in complete disarray. I had a mix of anger and elation, humiliation and vindication all at once. Mostly I just wanted to punch George. I took a deep breath.

"Ok, I guess I did deserve it; I was an ass. So . . . yeah. Not enemies."

That uneasy truce was the best I could hope for.

"So she confessed that she'd led you on." Anne handed me a glass of wine and curled up next to me on her sofa. Her condo was the first place I'd headed from the bar.

I nodded.

"But in response to something George had told her."

I nodded again.

"Let me ask you something, Will. Do you like her? I mean, if all this hadn't happened, if your pride hadn't been hurt, would you still like her?"

I looked up at the ceiling. "That's the problem, Anne. I do. How pathetic is that? I mean, how can I still have feelings for someone who deliberately set out to hurt me? Isn't that at the core of every abusive relationship? Lack of self-esteem?"

"Will, you have plenty of flaws, but low self-esteem isn't one of them." Anne grinned at me over her merlot.

"*Low self-esteem isn't one of them,*" I mimicked.

"Do you just want to vent, or do you want to know what I really think?"

"Please, enlighten me with your womanly wisdom."

"Okay. She flirted with you when she didn't really mean it. Shitty, yes, but essentially harmless. What's interesting to me is that she confessed it and apologized. Why do that? What's her motivation?" Leave it to Anne the thespian to frame the problem in terms of method acting.

"I told you, she was getting an ulcer."

"For an academic you're remarkably dim-witted."

"Just whose side are you on, Anne?"

"All I'm saying is that it took guts for her to do that when she could have pretended it never happened. Why does she care if you know the truth? People don't act in a vacuum."

"And yet ironically, people still suck."

"Why don't you give it another try?"

"That ship has sailed. Over a waterfall. Where it exploded upon impact, killing everyone aboard. And then it sank."

SHE'S SO HIGH

I wouldn't be fooled again, I promised myself. So even if it seemed like Elizabeth was acting more warmly toward me, I refused to consider it anything other than her efforts to be not-enemies. Making someone a cup of coffee just how they like it is something not-enemies do. Saving a seat at lunch is solid territory for not-enemies. Sharing the administrative drudgery of the annual Read-a-Thon might be veering dangerously into the friend zone but was still pretty far from ICan'tStopThinkingAboutYouVille.

I was still in the center of that town though, and it blew. It blew worse than her hating me, because now that I was on the receiving end of… I reiterate…it blew.

"That's strange." Elizabeth chewed on the end of her pen, looking over the spreadsheet before her.

"Hmm?" All I could think was how I wished I was in that pen's place.

"The tally sheets. There's money missing."

"What?" I focused my attention back on the task at hand—reconciling the Read-a-Thon pledges with the donations received. I wasn't too concerned. People always pledged and then didn't follow through. We were always short by a hundred dollars or so; I usually made it up myself. I told her as much.

"No, I don't think that's it. I've already cross referenced, and these pledges have all been marked as collected. So, where's the money?"

I sat up straighter in my chair. I don't usually jump to conclusions, but it was my first thought. Even without any real evidence pointing to him, my internal gyroscope was swiveling again. Like the swaying at the top of the Empire State Building, something was not right.

"Where's George?" I stood up.

"Yard duty."

"Stay here."

"Like hell."

I strode from the office, Elizabeth in my wake, and made straight for the yard where students waited for their rides home.

I found George and tapped him on the shoulder. "Come with me."

"Uh, I'm a little busy." He couldn't contain his disdain for me any more than I could for him; sarcasm was his cover.

"Do you really want to do this here?" I growled.

"The more witnesses, the better," he retorted with a sneer.

"Where's the money?"

"What money?"

"The money you stole from these kids."

He chortled. "Yeah, these kids worked so hard for that money. Mommy and Daddy paid them to read for an hour a night just to get them out of their hair."

"I'm not pissing around, George."

"Relax, I'll pay it back. I needed rent money."

"No need. I'll take it out of your last check. Come get it tomorrow. For now, you need to leave. Employees only, you know."

"You're an asshole, Darcy." I knew he was angry when he used my last name. It had always been profane to him—an unattainable brass ring, the one prize our father wouldn't give to him.

"Look, George, I don't want to call the cops. I won't press charges if you just clear out." *Of my life.*

I turned my back to him and left, confident that he'd be too passive to make a scene. I was wrong.

The next thing I knew, I'd been tackled at the knees and I plummeted to the ground. I twisted and managed to deflect the fist that was aiming for my face; it glanced off my nose and grazed over my right eye. Adrenaline kicked in and in a burst of fury, I managed to flip him off me, roll on top, and land two punches to his face before I was pulled off.

He lunged at me again, but Richard grappled him into a headlock. I could hear him screaming. "I hate you! I fucking hate you! You've taken everything from me and I hate you!" It was like watching a two-year-old in full meltdown mode. Seeing him in his rage—his tantrum—brought me back to calm. I'd seen this before, and I was sure I'd see it again. It was just George's way. But he usually disappeared for a few months after lashing out, so I had that to look forward to.

I didn't even realize that Elizabeth had led me back to my office until I heard the door slam and the blinds ripple closed.

"Sit." She pushed me back onto my desk. Her stern voice shook. *She must be angry.* It was a stupid scene. I'm sure it upset the younger kids. I'd have to quell concerned parents by email tonight and then make some kind of speech at the next assembly about not fighting. *Now children . . . no matter how justified, you must never punch a dick.* But I had to admit . . . it felt pretty damned good to land those punches in his face. I didn't even mind that I'd have to teach his class now.

"Head back." Elizabeth stood over me like Nurse Ratched, cotton pad and antiseptic in hand. Blood had gushed from my nose onto my shirt, and my knuckles throbbed in a mad victory rhythm. I obediently pressed an ice pack to my eye while she daubed at my nose. She was muttering about stupid men under her breath.

My right eye was already swollen shut, so I closed the other. My nose was stuffy with caked blood and it hurt like a son-of-a-bitch—excuse my language.

The tender sweep of Elizabeth's hand over my cheek started a whole new kind of ache—in my chest. She wiped away a smear of blood, and her palm cupped my stubbly cheek. It was a gesture I had often fantasized about. I imagined her lips pressing softly against mine and mine pressing back against hers.

A second later, I opened my good eye. I had not been imagining anything. Elizabeth Bennet was kissing me, her hands holding my face, her thumbs sweeping over my cheeks. I could feel her hair brushing against my skin, the smell of her lotion breaking through the bloody mess that was my nose. The kiss lingered for a moment, and then she drew back slowly, the tip of her nose lightly touching mine.

I cleared my throat. "I'm, uh . . . really . . . confused right now."

A soft chuckle wafted from her. She nodded. "Me, too."

My hands gripped the edge of the desk. "I honestly don't know what to do."

"Tell me the truth. Are your feelings for me the same that they were in October?" Her question was so tentative, so querulous. I almost wanted to laugh.

"No." I confessed quietly. She began to step back, but I caught her wrist. "No. It's much worse now. I feel . . . deeper, stronger. More." My voice rasped over the words. My throat was tight just admitting it to her; that I'd never stopped feeling for her, that I'd been only . . . existing . . . wanting.

Her lips sought mine again, this time less hesitant. My hands crept to her waist and rested there, pulling her close to me. I couldn't breathe, and my face felt like pulp, but I'd gladly have died right then, having found myself in a place I'd never thought possible.

I don't know how long we kissed. It ended with a rap on the door followed by Richard bumbling in, two policemen in tow. Something about

George being arrested . . . did I want to press charges? I went through the motions, giving my information and a statement, all the while tasting her on my tongue. I licked my lips; she was there, too. Our eyes met.

Everything had changed.

PARADISE

Dinner was gone, the first date done. It didn't feel like a first date—it felt like a victory, passing my dissertation, running a marathon, and baking a cake all at once. There were nervous pauses and genuine moments of laughter. We shared dessert and called it a night.

Only we didn't.

She was here with me now, skin on skin, glowing beneath me while I burned over her. Tentative kisses had given way to urgent ones when I walked her to her door. She asked me to come in for coffee and then asked me to stay the night. *No* was not in my vocabulary.

Clothes came off in fits and starts amid giggles. A button on my shirt did not survive, and I wrenched the zipper on her skirt, then promised to pay her seamstress. Her apricot skin edged with lace left me breathless.

And now, my fingers traced over her shoulder, the smooth curve falling perfectly into my palm. I tested the soft weight of her breast in my hand, and goosebumps rose on my arms when she gasped in my ear. Her thumbs feathered over my nipples and I let out a soft moan, unable—unwilling—to hide my pleasure from her.

I kissed her throat, her pulse thrumming on my lips like a hummingbird taking flight. Our legs caressed, smooth over rough, long against limber. The lines of her waist curved like a cello, warm and smooth, inviting my touch to play a note.

There was nothing about her that I could ignore. Dips and valleys, planes and plateaus, smells, sounds, tastes—I needed to explore it all.

Her hands stroked down my back, fingers digging lightly as she urged me on. She moved sinuously beneath me, her legs squeezing my waist until I pushed deep inside of her.

Time fell away. We breathed together, rose and fell together, moaned and gasped together. Pulse, pause, rhythm, beat. The tempo of our heartbeats became synchronous. The duet went on—melody and harmony, fast and slow— until the crescendo.

I gripped her tight and caught her in a kiss that mingled our exclamations into one. I felt her tense around me, then her wave of release, and I let go, falling down, down, down . . .

Sleepily, she twined her fingers in mine. I curled around her, my nose buried in her hair, and kissed the back of her neck. I felt satisfied but also something more.

I felt…whole.

SARA ANGELINI is a lawyer living in the San Francisco Bay area with her husband, three kids, two dogs, a frog, some fish, and a few hundred stick bugs. She never went to veterinary school but if she had, she would have been a true proficient. She enjoys writing from Darcy's point of view in a way that shows his humor and vulnerability. Her first book, *The Trials of the Honorable F. Darcy*, was published in 2008. She is the co-founder of austenunderground.com, where her other *Pride and Prejudice*-inspired works can be read.

"I have not the pleasure of understanding you"
—Mr. Bennet to Mrs. Bennet, Chapter XX.

YOU DON'T KNOW ME

BEAU NORTH

DECEMBER 1961

Exile.

I tried not to look at the situation in such grim terms, but there was just no getting around the fact that compared to my sleek office in Manhattan or my Park Avenue townhouse, Buffalo looked a lot like exile. But hey, it was only one year. I could handle anything for one year. I'm a Darcy, for crying out loud. Hell, I'm *the* Darcy.

It was one moment, one stupid mistake at the office Christmas party that landed me in Buffalo for a year. My whole life turned upside down in less time than it takes to get off the sofa and turn the dial on the television set. The whole affair has made me forswear mistletoe for life. I'd just as soon burn the damn stuff than stand under it.

My boss, Catherine (who incidentally is also my aunt), felt my banishment was important enough to deliver in person the next morning.

"You're lucky I'm just sending you north for the year while this whole thing blows over," she said, pursing her lips at my hastily tied robe. Maybe it was my unwashed hair or the smudge of lipstick still clinging to the corner of my mouth where a pretty and eager woman had left her undisputed mark. The culprit was the same woman my aunt had come to inform me was not only married but was also the young bride of Rosings Communications' biggest client. "Rosings Communications relies on its advertisers. As Head of Accounts, you know that better than anyone. Crawford is one of our biggest clients and we have to keep him happy, and that means *not* manhandling his wife. He wanted me to fire you, so what you should really be saying right now is 'Thank you, Catherine.'"

"I had no idea that woman was his wife. And she kissed *me!*" Recounting the facts proved useless; Catherine wasn't buying. Truth be told, I *had* been tipsy that night. I believe "blitzed" is the word the kids are using nowadays. Gritting my teeth, I let my eyes settle on the painting that dominated my living room—one of Kandinsky's Compositions—trying all the while to ignore the one-two punch of a splitting head and a queasy stomach. Even I couldn't say what was worse: my hangover or my aunt's continuing lecture.

"Will, dear. Your father was half owner of this company. He and your uncle built an institution that has outlived them both. A legacy. I've spent your adult life grooming you to take over for me, and to do that you're going to need to know how *all* levels of the business operate. So, I'm giving you a station to run. We just acquired"—she looked down at the folder she'd brought with her—"ah, yes . . . WPNP in Buffalo. We got it for a song, but the numbers are wretched. We've hired a full roster of new on-air talent, but I want you to get up there and bring this station up to Rosings Communications' standards. If you do well, I might consider an early reprieve."

The jab about my father rankled. I knew exactly what he'd left me. The company that had been his everything. The true love of his life. I was in no hurry to step into his shoes. I wanted to *enjoy* my life.

If only it weren't for that damn legacy clause in my trust fund: as long as I stay with Rosings Communications, I get to keep my money. So instead of pushing back, I decided to take my licks like a big boy and move to Buffalo. Keep the peace, keep the dough rolling in.

A day later, I was standing on a train platform with a steamer trunk and two suitcases. There are only three words I could use to describe Buffalo in late December: Hell on Earth. There was a tang of metal in the air, air so cold it cut through all my layers of clothing. A smiling man with a shock of russet hair approached me. The first thing I noticed was his comically large earmuffs; the second was that his smile was earnest, not at all forced, despite the chore of picking up the new boss at the train station in sub-zero weather.

"Charles Bingley?" I asked, holding out a hand. He took mine in his own and gave it a good shake, no small feat considering my gloves and his mittens.

"Charlie, please. My ma is the only person who still calls me Charles. Will Darcy, is it? Nice to meet you! You picked a helluva time to get here!"

Charlie was the sales manager for WPNP and had been acting as interim station manager until Aunt Catherine could appoint someone. I soon discovered that he hailed from Brooklyn, spent four years in the Army, and had been working for Rosings Communications since his return from what he called "a bit of a wild stint" in Japan. Ordinarily I would find that sort of loquaciousness tiring, but Charlie had a certain affable charm that made him impossible to dislike.

It was Charlie who had arranged for a New Year's Eve celebration—"Seeing as how everyone at the station is still pretty new, it would be a good way to break the ice."

I smiled and nodded and watched as the ugly, grey city rolled past my window, the dirty snow piled up on either side of the road, a fitting welcome to my new home.

One year and counting.

JANUARY 1962

"The one thing I can't get used to is the *noise.*" I have to yell over the din in the bar in order for Charlie to hear me. You'd think with his big, goofy ears he'd be able to hear a pin drop over all the racket.

"The people are always shouting, the cars are always honking, and here I thought Manhattan was loud! Don't know if I'll ever get used to it!" The irony of my having to shout in order to complain about people shouting was not lost on me, but the people of Buffalo seemed to have one volume without variation. Charlie grinned at me and shook his head.

"It's all part of the charm, don't you think?" Maybe a kid from Brooklyn would feel right at home in Buffalo. What did I know?

"One thing you have to admit," Charlie said, looking around the smoke-filled room. "The ladies here are pretty as a picture." He nodded at two women seated on the other end of the table, who seemed to be carrying on a conversation despite the chatter of the crowd and Frank Sinatra droning away on the jukebox.

The fairer head belonged to my new secretary, Jane, who was prim, polished, and always looked like she'd just stepped out of the pages of a fashion magazine. She was polite and personable but not terribly interesting. The other woman, however, was a little *too* interesting.

Eliza Bennet was a tall young woman with a bony figure and a mass of unkempt dark hair that she kept tied back with a colorful scarf. She dressed head to toe in black, from her slim cigarette pants to her slightly off-the-shoulder blouse. When she spoke, her voice carried as loud as anyone else in the room, but I caught a bit of a lilt in her voice that told me she'd had some vocal training like the girls from finishing school.

My first meeting with her, earlier that day at the station, had not gone well. It was a bit of a surprise to learn my aunt had hired a woman as on-air talent. Despite her own position, Catherine could be old-fashioned and I said as much—maybe not in those exact words—to Eliza Bennet. Her eyes, remarkable eyes really, so dark and expressive, turned diamond hard.

"I was recommended for the job," she said, somehow smiling through a clenched jaw. "Mrs. De Bourgh didn't hire me personally. There's an entire department that handles that. As heir apparent, I'd think you'd already know that."

I felt my face grow hot like I was a grade-schooler that had just been scolded by my teacher in front of the class. "I see."

Her thin smile could have cut glass. "Unless, of course, you're not at all serious about the career that's been handed to you on a silver platter."

I felt like a bowling pin that had just been hit with a fourteen-pound ball, only instead of a ball it was a lanky woman with a sneer that could kill a lesser man. I took an instant and fervent dislike to her, and I'd wager my trust fund she felt the same way.

"Even *you* have to admit," Charlie said, reminding me where we were. He sighed dreamily, his eyes fastened on Jane. "Pretty as a picture."

"Yeah, I heard you the first time," I said, rolling my eyes. "Jane is very pretty, I'll admit. But the other one? An absolute shrew."

"Oh, come on!" Charlie scoffed. "You're not blind, are you? She's like a dark Brigitte Bardot!"

"Ha! Think that all you like. I think it's a good thing she's in radio."

"Well it's almost midnight, and I aim to get a kiss from *someone* tonight. Don't feel too badly if I'd rather it wasn't you," Charlie said with a laugh before getting up to join the ladies at the other end of the table.

I looked around, uncomfortably realizing I was sitting alone just as everyone in the bar started an enthusiastic countdown to the new year.

FEBRUARY

"Thank you for joining our continuing coverage of Astronaut John Glenn's mission to be the first man to orbit the Earth." The voice of Jack Fletcher, the station's morning newsman, piped through every speaker in the office.

Everyone but Jack and his producer were crowded into the reception area of the station, listening to the broadcast as John Glenn made his third orbit of the Earth. I'd been listening in my office, but the occasion felt too momentous—too important—to experience alone. So, I ventured out to join the others. Jane and Bingley seemed happy to see me; the person sitting to Jane's left was not. Eliza had come in early, no doubt to listen to the broadcast with everyone else. My eyes caught the way she perched on the edge of her seat, shoulders tight, hands in fists on her knees. I'd seen her in enough meetings to know that this was not her usual languorous posture; she always seemed to drape herself across her chair like a cast-off quilt.

I watched as her teeth began to worry at her full, lower lip, and I understood she was as nervous as any of us. Jack's newscaster voice piped through the speaker on the wall, reminding us all that Glenn was now operating the module manually, after a malfunction with one of the jets. If the calculations were one decimal off, that bright young man would die with the whole world as witnesses, and the United States would be the clear loser in the Space Race.

"Oh, heavens." Jane swooned a little. "I can't imagine how terrifying that must be for him."

Charlie put an arm around her while Eliza took her hand. Jane was that type; she brought out the protective instincts in others. Aunt Catherine called girls like that "precious."

"He's trained for this," I spoke up, attempting to soothe my nervous secretary. "He'll be fine." Eliza was giving me an inscrutable look, those striking eyes distracting me.

"If you don't mind, Mr. Darcy, I'd like to go down to St. Joseph's," Jane entreated.

"Of course. Just be back in an hour. I have a feeling we'll be busy, and it's going to be a long day for Jack. Charlie, you go with her. Eliza, you can go too, if you need to pray."

All three of them looked up at me in surprise. Jane and Charlie gave Eliza a questioning look, which she answered with a twisted smile before shaking her head.

"No thank you, Mr. Darcy. I'll stay here if you don't mind." Again, that bombshell of a smile; it made me crazy to see it. The woman was too audacious for her own good.

I shrugged, feeling prickly. Jane and Charlie shuffled out quietly, leaving me with Eliza and a few other station employees who were speaking quietly amongst themselves. The station receptionist, Charlotte, handed out cups of coffee and a few stronger drinks to the people still assembled. As Jack announced the beginnings of Glenn's descent, I watched Eliza grow pale, her breath coming in panicked little gasps.

Unable to bear it any longer, I took a seat beside her. She seemed not to notice at first; she just kept chewing at her lip, eyes far away and unfocused. Was it terrible that I was less concerned for the astronaut than I was with the state of that lip? I raised my hand, intending to give her shoulder a light squeeze, but instead placed it palm down on the space between her shoulders. We tensed together in mutual surprise, connected by that touch, until I felt her slowly relax, felt the rise and fall of her breath become steady and calm.

I did wonder why I was even bothering when Eliza Bennet and I had never shown each other anything but mutual disdain. For some reason her distress distressed me. For the first time, I'd seen her as more than a thorn in my side, more than just a sharp smile and a barbed remark. Under my palm was a woman who was more than what she seemed.

It wasn't until the room erupted into shouts and joyous applause that I realized they'd confirmed Glenn's splashdown, and that the astronaut had emerged from the craft, alive and unharmed. So, he'd survived, but what about me? I found myself unable, perhaps unwilling, to remove my hand from the warm terrain of her back, a tantalizingly new territory that I found myself wishing to explore. She felt electric to my touch, evoking a pleasurable awareness of my own vitality. I was a red-blooded American man, and she was, I now admit, a desirable woman.

It was Eliza that broke that contact but my disappointment, while surprising, was brief. In her excitement over the astronaut's success, she seemed to have forgotten who I was and the battle lines previously drawn between us. Happy tears stood in her eyes as she craned her neck up, lips brushing against my cheek before she launched herself off of the couch and into the arms of her jubilant cohorts.

I excused myself quietly, unnoticed by the small crowd of happy people. I ducked into my office, wanting to restore the natural order of things. I touched my face—was I imagining the ghost of her perfume lingering on that hand? She'd kissed me. Eliza Bennet kissed *me.* I shook my head, feeling a smile tug at my lips. I took out the small mirror I kept in my desk. The shape of her kiss was there, branded in red lipstick. My fingers traced the curve of her lips before I took out my handkerchief and wiped it away.

MARCH

"Mr. Darcy, sir. Mrs. de Bourgh for you."

I ground my teeth—a reflex to those words—forgetting about the tooth that had been giving me misery lately. I looked up at the ceiling, calming myself before picking up the receiver.

"Aunt Catherine, how are you?"

"Don't Aunt Catherine me, William," the voice on the other end said testily. "You know why I'm calling. I received *another* call from that awful Bliss woman at the Mother's Morality League. She's done it again!"

I didn't have to ask which "she" my aunt was referring to. I'd been expecting this call. I'd been wondering what I'd done to deserve a curse like Eliza Bennet. Surely, I'd paid for my transgressions just by virtue of being in Buffalo. Did she *have* to make my life a living hell?

"Catherine, if you look at the numbers, you'll see that her show is one of our most popular."

"That's not the point, William! Some of *that music* is fine, but we hold our stations to a certain standard. We can't just allow that woman to play anything she wants."

I wanted to laugh. I didn't want to tell my aunt that Eliza Bennet was the most unmanageable woman I'd ever encountered in my twenty-nine years. My inability to bring her to heel was going to count against me and keep my early reprieve just out of reach. Every time I'd tried to take her to task, she neatly turned the tables on me with nothing more than a lifted brow and a turn of phrase. She was utterly infuriating.

And yet.

And yet during my time in Buffalo, my disdain had slowly become a begrudging admiration. Eliza Bennet was whip-smart, funny, effortlessly hip and, in her own way, alluring. Every day she arrived at the studio like an unexpected storm, arms laden with records, her airy voice carrying through the halls and into my office, disturbing my monotonous peace, always leaving some lingering trace of scent—orange blossoms one day, musky amber the next.

"Darcy, have you heard a word I've said?" Catherine snapped in my ear.

"I'll talk to her, Catherine. I'll get her in line."

"Please do. These women apparently have nothing better to do than bog us down with complaints. Collins over at the FCC is a friend and is directing them all to me . . . for now. But Darcy . . ."

"I know, I know. Standards."

I ended the call, feeling irritable at my lot in life just then. I hated Buffalo, hated this job and the station. I hated having to hear Paul Anka and Dean Martin all day. I hated that the only time of day I looked forward to was when I put on my coat and hat and walked home for the day. Charlie had asked me why I didn't just move out to the suburbs like he had, a thought that horrifies me still. I'm city born and bred. The wide open spaces were for the dreamers. Give me a skyline view and a glass of gin any day.

With a sigh, I pushed away from the desk and wandered out of my office. Jane was typing minutes from the last staff meeting, and the steady click of her fingernails against the typewriter keys made my skin crawl. Not that I'd ever say that to her; she really was a sweet kid.

"Jane, what time does our Eliza come in today?"

Jane blinked and looked up at me like I'd just announced myself King of America. "She's not in today, Mr. Darcy. The weekend jockey is taking her shift."

My irritation grew—and another feeling. Was it . . . disappointment? "Not in? Why was I not informed?"

Jane gulped, her lovely blue eyes wide with worry. "It was in your morning messages, Mr. Darcy."

If I was being honest with myself, I was looking forward to having words with Eliza Bennet. Her verbal sparring was a challenge, at least. She broke the monotony.

"Why is she out again?"

Jane's eyes shifted away. "I believe her father isn't well. She had to take him to the hospital for some tests."

"I see." I considered for a moment before saying, "Make sure you get her on the books for a meeting with me tomorrow, if she's back by then. Tell Luke he'll have to cover an extra twenty minutes. And make me a dentist appointment, if you don't mind, Jane."

"I'll see to it, Mr. Darcy."

I wondered, later, if that visit to the dentist hadn't changed things for good. I sat in my office, mouth sore and jaw aching, holding a letter in my hand. I couldn't seem to make sense of it no matter how hard I looked. The return address was from Oak Park, Illinois. The only person I knew from Oak Park was Fitz, my best friend from Harvard, but the handwriting was distinctly feminine. I stared at the page again, but the letters all seemed to blend together.

It was then that Eliza stormed into my office, wild-eyed and furious.

"You're moving me to *nights?*"

I looked up at her, bewildered. Of course, part of me remembered that she was being informed of the change in rotation today . . . my gesture of friendship towards Regina Bliss and the Mother's Morality League. But now, looking at the paper in my hand, that all seemed so insignificant.

It must have all been in my face—my confusion, my sullen rage—because Eliza immediately cooled, like a lightbulb going dark. She shifted back on one leg, studying me.

"Are you alright?"

I shook the letter. "Can you read this? I can't seem to make heads or tails of it." My mouth was still numb from the dentist, and my words came out slurred.

She sat next to me on the couch. That day she smelled of sandalwood and rose, spicy and sweet. I felt myself becoming calm. She took the letter from my hand, chewing her lip as she scanned.

"Oh!" Her breath hitched in her throat. "It was an accident. Your friend, Richard—"

"Fitz," I corrected. "I call him Fitz."

"This is from his wife. He was in a convoy in the mountains north of Saigon. The jeep threw a rod and the driver got spooked, lost control."

"He's dead, isn't he?"

She looked up at me, eyes wide and full of compassion. I said the first thing that came to my mind. "I didn't even know he'd gotten married."

The next thing I knew her arms were around me, pulling me close. Any other day I would have found it exciting, but today it just felt necessary. I thought of Fitz, always ready with a grin and a cheap joke at my expense. His bawdy humor disguised a ruthless intelligence and an unexpected thoughtfulness. Fitz was, had been I should say, the better man, and I'd always known it. What a cruel joke that I was the one left standing.

"Don't say things like that," Eliza said softly, stroking my back. I hadn't even realized I'd spoken the thought out loud.

My arms wrapped around her, pulling her close. I rested my head on her shoulder, and we sat that way for some time.

APRIL

"I understand your frustration, Mrs. Bliss. For what it's worth, I've had that particular jockey moved to the night shift so as not to subject children to her selections."

Regina Caroline Bliss, Grand Poobah of the Mother's Morality League, sniffed and sipped her tea. She was everything I'd expected her to be, rigidly prim with all the polish that her wealthy, suburban life afforded. No doubt in her youth she'd been a beauty; now she could boast of being "distinguished" and "well put-together." She was also as empty as the plate of meringues sitting on the table between us.

"And, as a show of good faith, the station will happily sponsor your next charity event," I added. How I hated having to appease uptight fussbudgets who wanted nothing more than to spoil everyone's fun on the grounds of *their* morality. If *they* weren't having fun, no one was.

Regina Bliss put her teacup down and smiled at me. She was trying for coquettish but couldn't quite make it work. "Mr. Darcy, you're really *too* generous. The Orchard Park Squash League is in desperate need of a new court and equipment. We've been planning a benefit luncheon for the spring."

I somehow resisted the urge to roll my eyes, a heroic effort on my part. That would be just her idea of charity. Objectively, I knew that my circumstances were not so very different from the woman sitting across from me at Buffalo's finest and only tea room. Like Regina Bliss, I'd been born wealthy, went to the finest prep school and universities that money could buy. But there our paths diverged. Regina Bliss had embraced the lifestyle of a wealthy suburban busybody in a way I never could, denying herself the vibrant possibilities of a less . . . monochrome life. Unlike Regina Bliss, I knew things couldn't be categorized into just black and white—not life, not schools, and certainly not music. I'd been born wealthy, not sheltered.

She put her hand on mine, leaving it there a moment too long. Was she trying to tell me what it would take to get her little band of do-gooders to stop lodging complaints about the station? While I wasn't surprised by her (morals can so often be a shaky bedrock to build one's foundation on), I was surprised by how unseemly it felt. After all, it wasn't the first time an older woman had come on to me. And why not? I'm a tall, good-looking guy with a full head of hair and a great smile when I use it. This isn't me so much bragging as being cognizant of my assets. I bring a lot to the table, just not this *particular* table.

Withdrawing my hand, I cleared my throat and signaled the waiter for the check, insisting that lunch be on the station's dime, avoiding her eyes to cover my own embarrassment. If only Aunt Catherine could have been there to see "Darcy, the Playboy" become flustered by an aging socialite with too much time on her hands. How far the mighty hath fallen.

"How was the meeting?" Jane asked as she took my coat and hat. The smell of Regina Bliss' overbearing, powdery perfume had followed me all the way back to the station.

"Between you and me, Jane, I feel like I need a shower."

A snort of laughter from behind me made my guts freeze. *Perfect. Just perfect.*

I turned around slowly, mouth going dry at the sight of her. Her messy, dark hair had been brushed to a shine and was being held away from her face with a large band of green velvet, showing off her high, clear brow and making her eyes look even larger than I had ever seen them before. Since that day in March, I'd only seen her once or twice in passing, never exchanging more than a polite nod.

The urge to pull her to her feet—and into my arms—was almost overwhelming. I wanted to tell her that I'd gone to Oak Park to meet Fitz's young widow, who would too soon be a single mother. I'd made up some story about Fitz loaning me money in college and had left her with a substantially large check, enough to keep her and the baby quite comfortable until Fitz's VA benefits could come in. I don't think she believed me, but she took the money gratefully enough. It felt good to help, to honor my friend, but in that moment, I wanted more than anything to show her that I could be, on occasion, a decent man.

"Miss Bennet, I thought you were on nights now?"

"You're not wrong, Mr. Darcy. I just came by to pick up my paycheck."

"I'm glad you're here, actually. Could you spare a moment?"

"I don't suppose I can say no, now can I?"

With a small smile for Eliza, I held the door open, trying not to inhale her delicate perfume as she marched past me into the confines of my office. After Regina Bliss she was, quite literally, a breath of fresh air.

"Please, Miss Bennet, have a seat," I said dryly. She'd already claimed a chair and sat with her long legs stretched out in front of her. She looked charmingly at home there; all that was lacking was the Sunday Times on her lap.

"I've met with the head of the Mother's Morality League today," I informed her as I took my seat behind the desk.

Her delicate eyebrows rose. "Oh? So, has our *Miz* Bliss gotten her fondest wish at last?"

I felt my face start to burn. Good lord, was I *blushing?* "Er . . . her fondest wish?"

"My head on the chopping block, of course!" She sighed dramatically, and my heart resumed its usual rhythm. "You'd think with a name like Bliss she wouldn't be such a humorless prig. Shall I expect a lecture now or should we just skip to the pink slip?"

I shook my head. She talked too much for her own good. "I know you think I'm your enemy, but I'm trying to help you here. I'm not firing you, but you could just play along and not antagonize her by playing . . . well, you know."

"I see. I'm assuming by 'you know' you mean specifically *black* music?"

I nodded once in her direction. She appeared thoughtful before speaking again. "Mr. Darcy, it has never been my intention to *play along.*" She held up a hand to stop me from interrupting. Infuriating woman.

"Nor do I intentionally antagonize anyone. Well, with the possible exception of yourself. But I'm not here to bide my time or wait out some sort of banishment. Unlike you, I *want* to be here. And I want to play music. *Good* music."

"Miss Bennet—"

"Have you even *looked* at the numbers?" she asked impatiently. "My show had the biggest listenership before you moved me to nights. People don't want Pat Boone. They want Sam Cooke and Jackie Wilson!"

This was a point I couldn't argue. Since moving her show to a later hour, the station's numbers had slipped noticeably.

"Be that as it may . . ."

She rolled her eyes and threw her hands up, letting them fall back into her lap. "I don't even know why I bother with you. You don't even *like* music. I couldn't imagine anyone more ill-suited for this job than you."

"Now wait just a minute!" It wasn't her remark that stung so much as the truth in it. But she would not be halted; her assault on my character continued.

"And I have never, *never*, seen anyone with so much disdain for all the things that have been handed to them."

My hand slapped down on the desk, making my palm sting. "That is *enough*, Miss Bennet! Good God, have you *no* respect for authority? You couldn't dig your own grave better than if I'd handed you a damned shovel! I should think that a working woman would know to tread a little more carefully!"

"Excuse me?" she said, eyes flashing steel.

"I will *not* excuse you! No more excuses! You are suspended until further notice!"

"Fine!"

"Fine!"

She stood, giving me a look so hard it could have shattered rock before storming out of my office, slamming the door behind her. I rubbed a shaking hand across my face, wondering what had just happened. How did she get under my skin so badly? How could I account for the sensation of my heart pounding away like a timpani drum? Like me it felt trapped, longing for freedom, for escape, for that indefinable thing I saw in her. She was everything I wasn't . . . unburdened by family expectations, exuding a sense of freedom that I, for all my privilege, had never tasted.

Jesus, what kind of mess had I gotten myself into now? I hit the intercom button and asked Jane to bring in Eliza Bennet's personnel file.

In the end, it took me a week before I'd mustered the courage to actually go to where she lived. Her apartment wasn't terribly far from mine, but was on a decidedly shabbier street. I climbed the three flights of stairs before finding number 4B and giving it a firm knock.

The door swung open, and I was greeted by a man with thick glasses and a tuft of silky white hair that was sticking up in a variety of angles.

"Yes? Can I help you?" the man said impatiently, in a heavily accented voice.

"I'm looking for Eliza Bennet. You must be her father?"

"Bennet? Bah." The man stepped away from the door, throwing up his hands in disgust. "Bennet my old *tuchis*. Come in, come in, young man. I am Tomas. Ben*owitz*. I have coffee, you want?" The elderly man turned his back on the door and walked away without a second look. I came in and shut the door behind me, a little unnerved at this unusual greeting. I suppose it shouldn't surprise me, given the way Eliza never entered a room so much as touched down the way a tornado might.

"Take your shoes off at the door, or Lizzy will rake me over the coals for letting you bring in the dirt!" Tomas yelled from the kitchen, accompanied by the sounds of running water and clanking pans.

I took off my shoes and stepped into the living room, feeling awkward and alone. The space itself was charming, the walls painted a vibrant blue-green with numerous framed photographs arranged in unusual patterns. I studied the pictures with interest, noting they were mostly of Eliza and a pretty woman that had to have been her mother. They shared the same shape of face, the same mass of wavy, dark hair. One prominent frame displayed an old poster for the Royal Orchestra of Prague, but it was overwhelmed by the sheer number of family photographs. Over and over again, Eliza and her parents, or just Eliza at all ages and stages of life. It was clear that she was loved, adored even. I felt a stab of envy for what must have been a happy childhood.

There were other emotions at war with my simple delight at seeing her home, like the sense of betrayal I felt that she hadn't even told me she was Jewish. If *Benowitz* didn't give it away, the telltale Menorah—perched haphazardly on the edge of a bookshelf like an interrupted thought—was a dead giveaway.

Charlie and Jane knew, I realized with an unpleasant jolt. That's why they had looked at me so strangely that day back in February, when I had offered to let her leave to go pray.

"That was my Hannah." Tomas informed me as he came back into the room, handing me a cup of steaming coffee. I'd been staring blankly at one of the photos, my mind elsewhere as I digested this new information.

"Wasn't she a beauty? We were married almost thirty years, and every day with her was a gift."

"Yes, she seems lovely. I'm William Darcy, by the way. Eliza's boss at the station."

With a twinkle in his eye, the old man nodded. "I knew who you were the second I opened the door. My Lizzy has been whining about the rich goy who's been making her life hell." Tomas laughed and rolled his eyes. "You kids today. You don't know how good you have it! I know my daughter has a mouth on her, I grant you, so I allowed her little embellishments. She's like her mother, that one, doesn't know when to quit."

"Do you know when she'll be home?"

As if I'd summoned her, the door burst open and Eliza arrived as she always did, like an unexpected squall in once-tranquil waters. Her arms were laden with brown paper sacks; the smell of fresh bread filled the room in her wake.

"Pop! Give me a hand!" she said, struggling with the bags as she toed off her shoes. I put my coffee down and rushed over to her.

"Let me take that for you," I said, enjoying the way her eyes widened when she saw me. Did I detect a bit of a blush before she looked away?

"I did wonder who those canoes by the front door belonged to," she said, letting me take her bags. "Do you walk in those or do they require oars?"

"Lizzy, don't be rude to our guest," Tomas chided gently. He pointed a bony finger at me. "You, sit. Drink your coffee. You want a sweet roll? Lizzy, bring this young man a bun."

Eliza brought me an enormous cinnamon roll on a plate with a fork. It smelled heavenly, freshly baked with a light glaze. I don't think I'd ever eaten a cinnamon roll in late afternoon before but with the strong black coffee, it was perfect.

Eliza kept glancing over at me while I ate, which was disconcerting. She seemed uncomfortable around me, which only piqued my interest. She busied herself getting her father settled with a plate and a refill of coffee before sitting down in the chair across from me, crossing her long legs. I felt the hair on the back of my neck prickle. Why were my palms so sweaty?

"So, what are you doing here, Mr. Darcy?" she asked at last. "Do I get to come back to work yet, or am I still in your naughty books?"

It did surprise me that she would begin such a conversation in front of her father, but Tomas watched with an amused sort of interest, as if he knew something we didn't.

"*You* are a perpetual entry into my naughty books, Eliza, but I did come to apologize for my part in our disagreement."

"Which I'm sure has nothing to do with however much the numbers might be slipping in my absence." She smiled that little half-smile, her go-to-hell, devil-may-care smile. She had me dead to rights and she knew it. I felt myself return her smile with one of my own.

"So, I'll expect to see you back on Monday. In the lunchtime spot, as usual."

She blinked, her face startled. She hadn't been expecting that, which meant I'd managed to get some small victory over her. "What about Regina Bliss? And your aunt?"

"To hell with them. It's my station, isn't it?"

She nodded, silent for a change, but I could tell she was pleased. A warm feeling spread through me. I realized, confoundingly, that I *liked* making her happy. The concept was novel to me.

My mother passed when I was very young, and my father, while giving me all the moral and financial support I'd ever needed, had not been a warm person. My dad passed away when I was only twenty, and we'd parted as polite strangers but little more. Father had been slavishly devoted to the company and that left little room in his life for his only son. From my lonely childhood to my admittedly shallow adulthood, my life had been nothing more than a series of long silences, and now here was this girl, this *woman*, with her music and her laughter and all her words, filling up those blanks. I looked over at Eliza as all the pieces fell into place. Was I falling in love with her? Maybe I'd been falling for her for some time—how long I couldn't say.

"I should go," I said abruptly. She sat up and leaned over, putting a hand on my arm, her large eyes warm and entreating. God, but I could swim in those eyes. I wanted to pull her close and breathe her in, to plunge my hands into the soft wilderness of her hair. My skin sang under her palm. Just this simple touch on my arm was enough to light me up like a Christmas tree.

"No, you should stay," she said, plaintively. "Look, I'm sorry I've given you a hard time at work. Maybe we could start over? Truth be told . . . I think you're actually okay. You're still much too unappreciative for your job, and you're stuffy and bossy and well, a little domineering—"

"Please tell me there's a 'but'."

She colored. "*But* you're fair, and you're kind when you think no one is looking. And I like the way you handle your aunt and our dear *Miz* Bliss."

A warmth spread through me. It was all I could do not to lean over and kiss her right then and there.

"Okay. I'll stay a bit."

Her smile brightened, and I actually *did* lean forward a bit, only stopping when Tomas clapped his hands, reminding us both he was still in the room.

"This is good news! What are we doing drinking coffee? Lizzy, get that young man and this old man a glass of wine! It's almost five o'clock. I say let's drink!"

She rolled her eyes affectionately but did as she was bidden. I looked over at the older man, trying to quantify how I was feeling in that moment. Was it happy? Is this what happiness—real happiness—felt like?

"Have you always called her Lizzy?" I asked.

"Since she was a baby! I wanted to name her Rachel but her mother thought Elizabeth sounded so regal, so glamorous. Then we had this scrappy child who we could not keep out of the mud, so to me she was Lizzy and has always been."

"Eliza is just for work," she said, handing us each a glass of dark red wine. "And Bennet is a name that can be said on air without offending the Miz Blisses of the world."

I suppose it made a certain kind of sense, but it gave me a pang that she had never been fully herself around me.

"What drew you to radio?" I asked, wanting to know more.

She shrugged. "What other job is there for someone who loves music but can't sing or play worth a damn?"

Tomas laughed into his wine. "Not for lack of trying on my part, mind you, Mr. Darcy. We tried every instrument, sent her to voice lessons. Ach"—he waved a hand in dismissal—"I've heard frogs sing better."

Eliza threw her head back and laughed. "You're being generous, Pop." She turned to me, her lips still curved in laughter. "It's not easy being the only child of the star violinist of the Royal Orchestra of Prague," she explained.

I nodded towards the poster on the wall. "*That* was you?"

Tomas nodded, his playful smile becoming more subdued. "Many years ago." The words were leaden with the weight of the last thirty years. Before or after the war, Czechoslovakia was not a good place to be a Jew.

"You should play for our guest, Pop."

With a dramatic sigh, Tomas put his drink aside and left the room. He returned a moment later holding a gleaming violin. Eliza sat up straight and began clapping, anticipation lighting her eyes. Tomas, standing straighter than he had been before, gave a dignified bow before fitting the instrument to him. He paused a moment, bow poised over the strings.

The bow came down and drew out a sweet, elegant note. Tomas' withered fingers flitted about the instrument's neck as the note became movement, a swirling sound that made me feel like a fixed point in a storm. I looked over at Eliza and was surprised to see her gazing back at me. There really was no other word for it. Gazing. Was this really happening? She blushed and looked away, back to her father.

I, however, couldn't look away. My eyes stayed fastened on her, the curve of her jaw, the impossibly long eyelashes, her restless lips, always hovering on the edge of a smile.

"Stop it," she whisper-laughed, making me grin before giving Tomas my attention once more. If Tomas had seen me staring at his daughter, he gave no indication. He played with his eyes unfocused, his face set with determination, legs planted firmly while his torso swayed to and fro with the instrument.

"It's Vitali's 'Chaconne'," Eliza whispered. I nodded, caught up in the music. The sound of it filled the room, transforming it from a colorful Buffalo apartment to an exotic place, a moonlit garden. As Tomas' fingers moved faster and faster, a sense of urgency overtook me, a strange imperative that was written into the very fabric of my own creation. I reached out without thinking, taking Eliza's hand. I was soothed, gratified, to feel her fingers intertwine with mine without pause or hesitation, as though she'd been waiting for that very thing.

Only when the song ended did we release each other, standing to applaud Tomas.

"Bravo, Pop!"

I could only echo her sentiments, adding my own bravos. Tomas smiled—the same devil-may-care smile as Eliza's—and gave us a neat bow.

There was a brief knock on the door before it opened, and a middle-aged woman, rather nice-looking, poked her head inside.

"Lizzy! Do I hear your father playing in here?"

Eliza rushed over and opened the door fully. "Aunt Maddie! Come in, come in. We've got wine and coffee, whatever you like."

The older woman came in followed by a sheepish-looking man about her age. "We heard the music next door and had to come and see for ourselves," the other man said.

Both stopped short when they saw me, craning their necks to give me a thorough once-over.

"I didn't realize you had company, dear," Maddie said, giving Eliza a knowing look. Eliza cleared her throat and blushed. I found her embarrassment to be utterly fetching.

"Will, uh—I mean—Mr. Darcy, this is my aunt and uncle, Madeline and Ezra Goldman. They live next door to us. Aunt Maddie, Uncle Ez, this is my boss, William Darcy. He runs WPNP."

They took turns shaking my hand and spoke politely about Eliza and her work, congratulating me on taking over the station which, according to Ezra, "played the worst kind of pig-kicking music" before RCC had taken over.

More glasses of wine were passed around before the newcomers settled comfortably on the other side of Eliza on the sofa.

"A bit more cheerful than that last one, if you don't mind, Tomas," Maddie said with excitement in her voice.

Tomas' brow rose before he brought his instrument back into position. A moment later, the room filled with the sounds of Paganini, but I was lost in thought, pondering the nature and possibility of love. The real, deep love that had eluded me my whole life. Love like a food that I'd never even realized I was craving until I'd had my first taste.

"What are you thinking on so hard over there?" she whispered. "Is everything alright?"

"You know, I have no idea," I said with complete honesty. One smile from her robbed me of my every thought. She raised her glass to me. I raised mine in return.

Tomas played for what felt like hours, maybe minutes—I don't know what—before claiming exhaustion and going to lie down. I rose and shook his hand, thanking him with all sincerity. The music, the wine, the company had woken a part of myself that had been sleeping—perhaps all my life—part of me that yearned for family and camaraderie. Maddie and Ez departed soon after, leaving me alone with Eliza. We looked at each other awkwardly for a moment before she laughed and said we'd have to finish the bottle of wine now that it was open.

With shaking hands, I refilled our glasses while she put on a record. She settled next to me on the couch, closer than we'd ever been before.

"It won't wake your father?" I asked.

"Pop sleeps like the dead," she said with a laugh.

"Is this . . . let me guess . . . Bobby Boy Blue?"

A smile lit her face. "You've been listening to my show?"

"It's a strong release for Duke records. Two spots on the Hot 100."

She rolled her eyes. "You're all business. Have you ever tried appreciating a song beyond its selling power?"

"I'm not sure I have," I said. It was the truth.

She put a hand on my arm. "Close your eyes. Go on, close 'em." I did as she asked, feeling a little ridiculous.

"Everything starts with a song. Life, love, everything. Songs are like living things, like people. Pull away the layers and listen. First come the horns, like breath. Then the guitar starts—that's going to be the backbone. A simple sound comes in behind it. A drum, tapped with the brush. That's the heartbeat."

I opened my eyes enough to peek at her. She sat with her own eyes closed, her bottom lip caught on her teeth. Was she nervous?

My mouth felt impossibly dry the way it does when I have had too much wine; yet for all that, the words that left me were soft and heavy. "I've never met anyone like you."

She opened her eyes and looked at me. What she was thinking I couldn't tell, her expression gave nothing away. When I looked into her glittering eyes, all I could see was my own searching expression reflecting back at me.

I slid closer to her, waiting for any sign either of invitation or unwelcome. For a moment, she tensed, shoulders set tighter than the strings on her father's violin. I reached out, fingertips grazing along the line of her jaw, turning her face towards my own. A second later, I felt her melt against me, breath catching in her throat, before she exhaled with a shaky laugh.

"I bet you say that to all the girls," she said.

I felt a grin split my face. "Oh, shut up and kiss me."

She was still laughing as her mouth met mine, sending a lightning storm of sensation through me . . . white-hot flashes exploded under my skin everywhere she touched, like fireworks on the Fourth of July. Her lips were soft and pliant, tasting of lipstick and sweet wine. My arm found its way around her waist, my hand splayed across the taut line of her back. I'd been wanting to touch her there again since that day in February. She shivered against me.

"You're so *warm,*" she said breathlessly. "I didn't expect *that.*"

With a growl, I grabbed her by the hips, pulling her onto my lap. "My God, do you *ever* stop talking?"

I felt her laugh as I kissed her throat, making a soft sound rise out her. "Sometimes. Give me a good reason."

I lay back against the cushions, pulling her with me so we lay tangled together on the couch, kisses deepening. I shifted, rolling her under me, marveling at the way we fit together. My lips forged a path from her lips to her neck, trailing lower to linger on the lovely little dip at the base of her throat, my hands eagerly roaming the lean lines of her body. My lips found hers again, taking nothing but giving all—what I was, what I had been, whatever I would become, all of it was hers. We were different, but we were the same. How had I not seen it sooner? The lines drawn between us didn't separate . . . they connected.

"Will," she said my name with breathless urgency. How was it possible I'd never felt this before? My blood boiled in my veins; every sense I possessed was filled with her.

"Lizzy." I moaned her name between kisses.

"Will, stop."

I sat up on one elbow, gazing down at her. Her hair was even more of a mess than usual; her lips, pink and swollen. God, but she was beautiful.

"Sorry, am I too heavy?"

"No, yes . . . no," she said with a shaky laugh. "It's not that. I just need to clear my head for a second."

I sat up, untangling myself from her. She sat up too, putting space between us where only moments ago there was none.

"Is it too fast?"

The record player clicked as the next record dropped into place. I hardly recognized the eloquent despair of Ray Charles singing "You Don't Know Me." Eliza ran a hand through her hair in an ultimately unsuccessful attempt to smooth it. "Considering we started this day off not liking each other? Maybe."

"I've always liked you."

She barked a laugh in response. "*Me*? The . . . what was it? Absolute shrew with a face for radio?"

My heart sank. Damn my careless mouth. "You heard that?"

"You didn't exactly try to lower your voice."

I covered my face with my palm and groaned. "God, I'm so sorry. I'm an ass. I was feeling bitter about being here and well, damn it, I'm sorry. You are beautiful. You know you are. You drive me crazy on a daily basis."

She blushed. "Well . . . thanks. But I don't know how this could work. You're my boss, and I love my job. I want to be taken seriously. Do you know how hard it is to be a woman in this industry? Doors don't just automatically open for you. And, well . . . you're not staying. You've made it clear that as soon as your year is up, you'll be going back to the city and leaving us all in your rearview."

"Do we have to have all the answers now?" I asked plaintively.

"I'm not sure what you're hoping for, but I'm not the kind of girl who'd just jump in the sack with someone who is only—" her eyes narrowed slightly as she appeared to search for the right words "—passing through."

"Elizabeth." I took her hand in mine. It was small but steady, firm, and warm. "I like you. A lot."

"And I like you," she said, pulling her hand away. "But I'm not here to help you pass the time. I respect myself too much to be your distraction."

There was no use arguing with that, and truthfully, I couldn't. I did care for her, I probably even loved her, but was it enough? Would I give up my company, my trust, my life . . . to stay here for love? While momentarily a thrilling notion, just walking away from it all forever, I knew myself well enough to know where that would lead—to bitterness and resentment. She deserved better than that. I stood, straightening my shirt, making myself presentable again.

I turned to look at her, sitting there on the couch with her knees tucked under her, and felt a piece of myself shatter and break.

"I'll see you at work," I managed to say before turning around and heading for the door. I just had to make it to the door. Only a few more steps and I'd be free.

"Wait!" she called out as I reached for the door handle. I stopped and looked over my shoulder, unable to turn and face her. Like a coward.

"Don't forget your shoes," she said in a small voice.

I looked down at the neat line of shoes by the apartment door, mine the largest by far. I leaned down and picked them up without a word, closing the door behind me.

MAY

Garden parties are the 1960's answer to the question, "How can we torture men, legally?" I gulped down another glass of iced tea—my third—and silently cursed the Mother's Morality League for their intolerance towards a lovely thing like gin. What did Tanqueray ever do to these women?

The party was sponsored by the station to fulfill my promise to Regina Bliss. I'd spent a fortune on the country club, the catering, and a good deal of my pride calling and begging the so-called elite of Buffalo to attend. The whole thing had been exhausting, but it had come at last, and all I had to do now was ride out the day.

"You might *try* to look a little less . . . forbidding," Charlie said quietly in my ear. I nodded and plastered on a smile.

"How's this?"

He looked at me and shuddered. "I take it back. Forbidding is better."

"*There* you are." Regina Bliss appeared, silver hair swept up into an impeccable updo, her Chanel two-piece flawlessly tailored around her trim figure. I forced myself to smile, hoping it was not the horror that had just driven Charlie away.

"I hope you're pleased with the turnout," I said, searching for a neutral topic.

"Oh, it's *wonderful*," she said as she looped her arm in mine. I fought the urge to push her away. Her husband, an older man that had struck me as being rather simple, stood within shouting distance. Maybe I should cry for help?

"Though I *am* still concerned about the midday programming, your support of our organization has been above reproach."

"Ah, yes. Well . . . " I trailed off. Nothing I could say would change this woman's mind. Why waste my breath?

"Oh, is that your secretary?" Regina asked, pointing at someone in the crowd. My heart sank. Eliza was there, in a brightly-colored dress that was short enough to be shocking. Her chestnut hair was bigger than ever before, reminding me of a lion's mane. I had no doubt it was intentional. She, like a lioness, would cut down her prey on its own savanna.

"Um, she works in the office, yes. Excuse me for just a moment." I untangled myself from Regina, striding purposefully over to the buffet where Eliza was piling a plate high with sweets.

"What are you doing here?" I whispered. "And why are you wearing *that?"* I nodded towards the silver Star of David that hung around her neck.

She blinked up at me before dropping that atom bomb of a smile on me. "What?" she said. "Jews can't be moral, too?"

I took her by the elbow and guided her away towards the exit. "If I thought you were here for anything but mischief I'd let it slide, but you are going to play along with these women and get them off my back. Otherwise your Miz Bliss will never stop trying to get me *on* my back."

She paled, then turned bright red. I admit, it was momentarily gratifying. "I didn't know . . ."

"Of course, you didn't. You just got out of bed today and thought, 'How can I make Will's life more difficult than it needs to be?'"

"Will, I—"

"Put this on," I said, taking off my own silver cross, which I always wore under my shirt. "And give me yours. I don't trust you not to show it off until this ordeal is over."

She looked at the cross in her hand. "This is a woman's."

"It belonged to my mother," I said shortly. "Come on, come on. We don't have all day."

Wonder of wonders, she complied, hastily handing over the silver star. She hung the crucifix around her neck, looking down at it like it was some curio from a savage tribe. Considering it was a representation of a man literally being tortured to death, maybe that wasn't too far off the mark. I hung her silver star around my neck, tucking it under my shirt. It was still warm from her body, and I had to force myself not to press it closer to my skin.

"Don't worry. You won't burst into flames."

"I think I'm more worried that I might lose it," she said in a small voice. I smiled, heart wringing like an old mop. She looked back up at me, face solemn. "I heard you're leaving soon."

I nodded. "Thanks to you. You helped take our station into the top spot. Catherine was very pleased to say the least."

She looked down again, hiding her eyes. "Don't thank me. Thank Chubby Checker."

You love her, my heart reminded me. Sometimes my heart was a real bastard.

"Come on, Eliza," I said in a gentler voice, leading her back to the party. "Let's go make nice."

JUNE

"Welcome home, Darcy!" Catherine rose from their usual table at the 21 Club to come greet me, giving me a dry kiss on the cheek. Out of habit, I held my breath as I was surrounded in a cloud of Chanel No.5, which my aunt has always used liberally. I forced a smile and took a seat at her invitation.

A waiter appeared, putting an Old Fashioned in front of me. Catherine raised her own.

"A toast to my nephew, for a job well done." She clinked her glass against mine and drank. I put mine down untouched. For the first time in my life, I felt like a fraud. The success I was supposed to be celebrating wasn't an accomplishment I'd worked for or earned. Managing to keep Regina Bliss and the Mother's Morality League happy had been my only *true* accomplishment during my tenure in Buffalo. Charlie Bingley kept the advertising ball rolling; my secretary, Jane, kept the office running smoothly. The hosts watched the charts and kept to their schedules. What had I actually done?

"Now, we should talk about what's next for you," Catherine said, pulling me out of my wandering thoughts.

"I'm not Head of Accounts anymore?"

"Oh, I think we can do better than that," Catherine scoffed. "You must be waiting for me to retire."

The thought hadn't crossed my mind. "I think the place would fall apart without you." She chuckled and raised her glass.

"A good reason for a long transition, then. No, it's time you took the reins, William. We'll begin after you're settled and make it official after the new year."

"That's only half a year! That's not enough time to learn anything."

"I disagree. Just look what you did with a nearly bankrupt station!"

"But that was—"

Catherine held her hand up, silencing me. "No arguments. If you don't want to take over, sell me your shares and I'll find another successor. Otherwise, it's time to accept your responsibilities."

I realized she was right. I'd run from my legacy into a life of indolence, and now the bill was due. I owed it to my father, to Catherine—to do what was required of me. And I owed it to Eliza, to keep the lights on if nothing else.

My heart squeezed in my chest to the point of pain at the thought of her. She'd just be getting into the station right about then, arms loaded with records, her voice carrying through the hallways into the office now occupied by Charlie, who I'd chosen to run the studio in my stead.

"All right then," I said, raising my glass to Catherine. "Six months and you'll be golfing in Boca."

She laughed. "I'll drink to that!"

JULY

Closing my eyes didn't help when the plane took off. There was still the queer feeling of my organs shifting inside of me as my back was pinned against the seat. I hadn't been on a plane since I was a kid, when my father would occasionally take me to business meetings in his private jet—never to see the Yankees play the Cubs like I'd wanted—always business. I took a moment to be glad I'd followed Catherine's advice a few years ago and upgraded to a newer model. "Who knows?" she'd said at the time. "You might really need it one day." I laughed then because I knew Catherine would be the one using it to fly down to Florida every chance she got. Bless her. I wondered what my father would think of my purpose in using the plane today? He'd probably be livid. The thought cheered me somewhat.

The day had started normally enough, with meetings and numbers and Catherine finally approving the company bonuses I'd lobbied for. It had been a good summer for radio, between Kennedy's speeches on the escalating tensions in Vietnam and some hits by Dee Dee Sharp and Little Eva. I'd been signing checks when I'd gotten the call from a tearful Jane. "It's about Eliza," was all she'd needed to say to make me jump to action.

I touched my chest, tracing the outline of the silver star that lay under my shirt. After the garden party, I'd "forgotten" to return it to her. And, perhaps purposefully, she'd forgotten to return my mother's cross. I didn't mind. I liked having this talisman of her so close to me. I often wondered if she felt the same.

The plane touched down a few hours later, much to my relief. A short plane ride was nothing to the nine-hour train journey but still felt too long. Jane had promised to have a car waiting for me, and true to her word, there was. Charlie Bingley was leaning against the side of his bright red Plymouth. When I approached, he let out a low whistle and shook his head.

"I knew you were rich but a private plane?" His earnest face was a welcome sight, even down to those big, goofy ears of his.

"How is she?" I asked, cutting through the pleasantries.

Charlie's face fell. "Not good. Get in. I'll drive you."

I was glad for once that Charlie was such an impatient and reckless driver. We shot like a bolt into the heart of Buffalo. It felt strangely nostalgic. It couldn't be that I missed it there?

"Congratulations, by the way," I said absently. "On your engagement. Jane's a lovely woman. I'm sure you'll both be very happy."

A serene look slipped across Charlie's face. I've never been more envious of another man in all my life. To have the promise of his future in hand. To have an uncomplicated love.

"Thanks, Will. I'm a lucky S-O-B."

I silently agreed, on both the "lucky" and the "S-O-B" remarks.

Thanks to Charlie's appalling driving, we reached our destination in no time. I ran up the stairs, not stopping until I came to a familiar door. Heart pounding, I raised my fist and knocked. The door swung open.

"Hello Jane."

Jane's lovely face was tear-stained, eyes rimmed with red. "Come in, Mr. Darcy."

"You may as well call me Will," I said gently. "I'm not your boss anymore."

Jane smiled weakly. "Come in, Will. Don't forget to take off your shoes."

I walked in, toeing off my shoes as I did. The apartment looked different somehow, darker. I realized it was because the mirrors had been covered, the curtains drawn. Ezra Goldman stood just inside. We exchanged a polite nod before I turned to the couch where Maddie sat next to Eliza, the same couch where we'd once become tangled and fused like tree roots. Eliza's hair was pulled back into a bun, making her face look thin and drawn. She looked up and saw me.

"Oh!" she cried out, her tears renewed.

I sank to my knees in front of her, wrapping my arms around her slender frame and pulling her close. She rested her head against my shoulder, body shaking with sobs as I held her and rocked her. Over her shoulder, I could see the violin resting in the corner, now silent for good, looking like an arcane artifact without its owner.

"I'm so sorry, Elizabeth."

AUGUST

"Would you like to tell me what is going on, William?" Catherine asked, looking over the rims of her glasses at me. It was just after our morning meeting, and I'd become distracted as I so often did those days.

"Well, as of July, we were up in the Northeast markets but trending slightly slower in—"

"That is *not* what I meant. What is going on *with you*?"

"I don't know what you mean," I said. *Come on, Darcy. Stiff upper lip.*

Catherine scoffed. "Who do you think you're fooling? You've been moping around the place for months. You don't seem at all happy to be back. I can't complain about your work because that's all you seem to do anymore."

"And that's a bad thing?"

"You're just not yourself, Darcy. You're acting like . . . well, like your father."

That one stung, I had to admit. But she was right.

"Who is she?" Catherine asked.

"I'm sorry?"

She smiled knowingly. "I'm not so old I don't know lovesick when I see it. You're in love. Who is she?"

For one crazy moment, I thought of telling her everything. But what good would it do? Catherine would never approve, and it was all beside the point. I thought of the stack of messages I'd left Eliza since I'd come back after Tomas's funeral, messages she clearly had no intention of returning. I'd wanted to stay and help her, do what I could for her, but her grief was her own and she'd clung to it fiercely. The last time I'd seen her we'd been standing on the baking-hot sidewalk outside of her apartment building. She'd traded in her sex-kitten cigarette pants for a loose-fitting black dress that made her look so frail. She gave me a watery smile and kissed me while the taxi waited. My arms clasped her waist, pulling her closer.

"I can stay," I'd entreated her. She only shook her head, dislodging herself from my arms and said, "No, you can't."

She felt more lost to me now than ever before. It made me feel adrift, anchorless. I thought of John Glenn orbiting the Earth and wondered if it had been lonely for those hours he'd spent up there—the only living thing in a vast unknowable emptiness.

"It doesn't matter," I said to Catherine. "I think . . . I think it's time I moved on anyway."

Catherine's eyebrows rose. "Just like that? Well, I must say I'm glad to hear it, though I'd prefer it if you didn't go back to helling every night. And I know a fine lady who is just your type. She's the daughter of a gentleman I sit with on the board of the Met. He introduced us at the last gala, and I was very impressed. She's just back from Dartmouth."

I nodded absently. I didn't want a fine young lady with a degree she had no intention of using, a woman whose aspirations went no farther than a house in Connecticut and two babies. It was all too placid, too . . . *expected.* I wanted the woman who would want to stay in the city until we were shriveled and old, the woman who would challenge and vex me, who would drive me crazy and fill our every moment with music and laughter and incessant chatter. I wanted the storm. But the storm didn't want me.

"Fine," I said as I gathered my papers. "Set it up."

SEPTEMBER

Another night out with Anne, the Dartmouth ingénue. She was everything my aunt had promised: lovely, refined, the daughter of a real estate magnate. I found her hopelessly dull. We had box seats at the symphony, and I knew that I should be enjoying myself, but the woman beside me never offered an opinion on the music other than, "I liked it," or "It was nice." I couldn't remember ever being so bored, and then I heard the mournful swell of Vitali's Chaconne, and I was no longer sitting in the plush box seats. I was back in Buffalo, in a colorful apartment surrounded by music and laughter and happiness. I remembered Tomas bending like a tree with the music, and my eyes filled with tears. I blinked them back, heart racing as the music swirled around me. I still wanted to reach out for Eliza, to feel her steady fingers intertwining with mine. Instead, I gripped the arms of my seat, riding out the wave of emotion until the song was over. Anne looked over at me and gave me a mild smile.

"I liked it," she said. Somehow, I didn't howl in frustration.

OCTOBER

The shrill ring of the telephone woke me from my half-sleep . . . one short burst of a ring and then nothing. I picked up the receiver, head still muddled.

"Hello?"

"How may I direct your call?" the operator spoke in my ear. Whoever it was had hung up.

"Sorry," I mumbled. "Sorry." I placed the receiver back on the cradle and rolled onto my back, staring blankly at the ceiling.

For ten days, we'd been holding our breath—waiting for news, for hope—waiting for the end. A sickly feeling had come over me when they'd announced the blockade off the coast of Florida. I'm only afraid of the things I can't control. Why else would I be so afraid of flying? The last ten—now eleven—days had felt like that moment of weightlessness after takeoff. I'd seen the school children doing drills on the news, obediently climbing under their desks, as though a simple bit of wood and metal could protect them from anything as powerful as a nuclear bomb.

As expected, I hadn't slept well. How could I? How could anybody? Even the ever-polished Catherine looked somewhat haggard in our morning meetings. I'd postponed dates with Anne, knowing that I would be ending our fledgling courtship. It seemed silly to worry about such things, with the threat of obliteration hanging over us all. I supposed I could have always descended into indulgent hedonism, but that hadn't appealed to me either.

The phone rang again. I picked it up and answered, knowing who was on the other line.

"Eliza?"

"Hi." The sound of her voice made my breath catch for a moment. "Did I wake you?" Strong, vibrant. Her voice soothed and excited me at the same time.

"Not really. Haven't been sleeping much."

A mirthless laugh from her. "Tell me about it. How are we city folk supposed to deal with this? Though I suppose you've got some fancy doomsday vault to live out the end in style. Probably has a full eighteen-hole golf course and its own subterranean Rockefeller Plaza."

"I do not," I protested, feeling myself smile for the first time in days. "What point is there to life if the Yankees *and* the Giants are gone?"

She laughed, a sultry sound that electrified me. How was it I felt more alive, more *in the world* just hearing her voice?

"Well, I'll have you know that Charlie has built himself a rather impressive fallout shelter in his backyard."

"Will you go there?" I asked.

"Absolutely *not*. He built enough space for Jane and her entire family. Mom, dad, three bratty kid sisters. Seven's a party; eight's a crowd."

I laughed and shook my head. God, but I missed her. "How's the station? Is Regina Bliss still giving you a hard time?"

"Only every week. Luckily, the music is louder than she is. We're still holding on to the number one spot, but I guess you knew that already."

She fell silent before speaking again in a more resolved tone. "I'm sorry I didn't call you back or return your letters. After Pop, I just sort of . . . fell away." There was silence on the line and then—"I don't want to meet my maker with any more regrets."

I sat up. "Elizabeth Rebecca Benowitz. Are you saying goodbye?"

"You never know!"

"We're not going anywhere," I said with a confidence I didn't quite feel. "Haven't you figured it out yet? I wouldn't let anything happen to you."

She sighed. "I knew you'd say that. Look, I gotta go. I'm calling long distance."

"I'll see you again, Eliza. When the world doesn't end."

"Yeah. See you then."

NOVEMBER

A few days after my phone call from Eliza, a fragile peace was declared. There would be no bombs, no death from above. People smiled again, though cautiously and never on the subway. Halloween had come, more jubilant than ever. And autumn took a long study of winter as Thanksgiving approached, while the leaves shivered their last on their branches.

I'd been dropping off some paperwork to the company attorney in Gramercy Park when I noticed all the people out shopping for their Thanksgiving dinners. One couple in particular caught my eye: a tall, well-dressed man and his wife—a long-limbed woman with a cascade of dark hair, pulled up into a half-beehive. He carried a box emblazoned with "Polaski's Meat Market" that no doubt contained the requisite turkey. I thought about what I was doing for Thanksgiving and came up short. I'd ended things with Anne, so that was out. A quiet dinner with Catherine didn't sound like so much fun either. I had wondered what Eliza would do without her father . . . probably eat with her aunt and uncle or Jane and Charlie.

"Don't get too far ahead," the man called to his child, a little boy wearing his Roy Rogers cowboy hat, the kind that tied under the chin. The boy turned and gave his parents a tip of his hat, making the couple giggle. The woman leaned against her husband, and he put his arm around her shoulders, pulling her to him for a quick kiss. I looked away, a lump rising in my throat. I envied them.

It was such a small moment that anyone could have observed without giving it a second thought, but for some reason it shook me down to my bones. I felt as though a crack had opened beneath me and I was falling, weightless, waiting for the ground to catch me. I was John Glenn, falling to Earth.

That does it, my heart, that neglected masochist, spoke up once more. *This has gone on long enough.*

I hailed a taxi to take me to Central Park West. I was at Catherine's door a few minutes later and much to her surprise.

"William! Come in! What on earth is the matter?"

"You're right, Cate." I called her by the name I hadn't used since I was a child. "I am in love . . . with *that woman* . . . Eliza Bennet."

Catherine blinked, stunned. She sank into the closest chair, scowling at the carpet I was currently pacing. I continued talking without waiting for her reaction.

"If the last year has taught me anything, it's that there isn't any time to waste. When you find happiness, you take it. Or you let it take you . . . I don't know. I'm still learning."

Catherine looked up at me, her eyes sharp. "Darcy. Pour me a drink, if you don't mind. And pour yourself one, too."

I did as I was bid despite every part of me being pulled away, towards *her*. I handed Catherine a glass and took a seat opposite her.

She seemed to consider her words carefully. "Are you sure this isn't some infatuation? Are you thinking with your brain or your . . . *other* brain?"

I threw my head back and laughed. "Both, actually. But this isn't some whim. It came on slowly, over months. I thought at first she got under my skin, but now I think . . . I think she might have been there all along."

"Will," Catherine said in a more delicate tone, "you do know that she is a Jewess?"

"I know, Cate. And I don't care. I think Christ might give me a pass on this one, too."

Catherine sighed. "You're sure? What about the company?"

"We'll figure it out," I promised. "I'm not leaving you high and dry, that I promise. But I don't want to end up like Dad, more in love with work than life."

She paled and sat up straight. "Is that what you thought? Well, I suppose it would look that way to you. You don't remember your mother. You couldn't have known . . . how very much he loved her. How very much he loved you both."

She put her drink down carefully. "Wait here," she said, and strode out of the room. I got up and resumed my pacing, thinking of Eliza. What would I say to her? How would she respond? I knew her well enough to know that she might very well turn me out on my ear.

Catherine came back in, holding a box in her hand. She handed it to me.

"Your mother asked me to hold onto that until the day came," she said, picking her drink back up and downing it. I opened it to see that it was full of letters, in my father's familiar handwriting.

"I think she knew, or at least suspected, how he'd be if he lost her. If I'd known . . . well, I'm sorry it took me this long."

"Thank you," I said. I was itching to read them, to know that the man I'd always thought incapable of love had actually been human.

"You can read them on the train," she suggested.

"She may send me packing, you know."

Catherine laughed. "If she's half as pitiful as you are right now, I doubt it."

I stood and gave her a kiss on the cheek. "Thank you." She nodded silently, dismissing me, and I was out the door.

I managed to get on the last train to Buffalo, not even stopping at my townhouse to pack an overnight bag. I read the letters, even the ones I probably shouldn't have. I tried to reconcile this man who burned with love, to the cold stranger I'd buried nine years ago. Maybe it was just wishful thinking on my part, but I thought I did remember a pained, faraway look in his eyes from time to time.

The gentle rocking of the train lulled me into a light sleep plagued with strange dreams of being very small, jumping into a pile of wet leaves, hearing my mother's laugh as my father swept her into his arms. When I woke, I couldn't be sure if these were my real memories or if I only wanted them to be. I looked down at my watch. It would be two hours before Eliza came to the station for her shift, and another three hours before I could get there. A thought occurred to me, an idea of how I might proceed. It would either be my greatest success or my biggest failure, depending on her. Everything depended on her.

Three hours and one taxi ride later, I found myself staring at the familiar facade of WPNP, a tumult of emotions. I took a deep breath and strode in, set on my purpose. The station receptionist, Charlotte, jumped visibly when she saw me.

"Mr. Darcy! Welcome back, sir! Was Mr. Bingley expecting you?"

"No, but I know where to find him." I gave her a careless wave as I strode through the double doors leading back to the offices and studio. Charlie was, as expected, hovering near Jane. *Very* near. It was a wonder the man got any work done.

Charlie caught sight of me and startled, jumping up and straightening his tie. Jane looked embarrassed, shuffling the stack of papers on her desk. On any other day, I would have laughed.

"Darcy!" Charlie said, reddening too. "I wasn't expecting you! Did we have a meeting?"

I shook my head, catching the song piping through the overhead speaker: The Crystals singing "He's a Rebel."

"Well, if there was ever a time for *that*," I muttered to myself. Charlie gave me an odd look.

"I'm here to see Eliza," I said flatly.

Charlie and Jane exchanged a wide-eyed look.

"Right." I didn't give either of them a chance to speak. "I'll just go do that."

I didn't wait around to see Charlie's reaction before turning and barreling towards the studio. The click of heels against the linoleum told me Jane was following. Where Jane went, Charlie was sure to follow.

"Mr. Darcy! You can't go in there; she's on the air!"

"Yes, I can see that for myself, Jane."

The red light over the door told me as much, and there, just beyond the door and the window, was Eliza. She was looking down, absorbed in flipping through a stack of records in her lap. I stood there a few moments, drinking in the sight of her, her slight frame, hair falling in a cascade around her shoulders. *So unfashionable, so beautiful. So heartbreaking and unique.*

Jane put a careful hand on my arm. "Mr. Darcy, surely there's a better time to—"

"There isn't," I said shortly, before swinging the door open and walking into the studio.

Eliza gasped and looked up at me, dark eyes huge in her face. "What are you doing?" she said with a hiss. An excellent question. I pulled the needle off the record. Her hands flew up to her face in horror, the records in her lap sliding to the floor.

"Eliza Bennet, you will listen to me, even if that means all of Buffalo has to listen too."

The look on her face became murderous. *Here goes nothing.*

"I love you," I blurted. "It took me too long to see it for what it was, but there it is. I love you. You're the single most infuriating person on the planet. You talk entirely too much and you have caused me no end of trouble, but I need you like I need air. I couldn't wait to leave this place, and then I got back to the city and all I could think about was the way you laugh or that damn smile of yours, or the way you occupy a chair like a cat in a sunbeam. I don't want it to take another loss, or another world-ending scenario to bring us together again. I told you months ago, that night your father played the violin for us, that I've never met anyone like you, and I haven't, and I don't want to—"

"Good God, William Darcy, *shut up!*" She shouted. "I love you, too!" She turned and spoke into her microphone. "Did you hear that, greater Buffalo area? I love William Darcy, the rudest man in New York! Now, here's that new one from the Four Tops."

She dropped the needle on the other turntable, and the room filled with music. She stood, pushing me out of the studio, teeth bared. My lioness.

"Jane! Get in there and cue up the next song. Just pick anything. It doesn't matter." Jane scurried past her into the studio, leaving them alone in the corridor.

"How could you *do* that, you ass? You've ruined my show. Turned it into a damn soap opera!"

Her eyes blazed at me, color standing high on her cheeks. I felt myself grinning even as her eyes narrowed dangerously.

"You love me," I said.

She sniffed. "I do not."

My grin widened. "Oh, yes you do. You love me."

She rolled her eyes. "Fine, I do, okay? I love you! Happy now?"

I pulled her into my arms, feeling her heart racing against mine. We fit together, just so. "You're damn right I'm happy," I said, making her laugh.

"Oh, shut up and kiss me."

I did as I was told. What else could I do?

DECEMBER

"Are you sure about this?"

Eliza chewed her lip as she watched me placing the menorah on the table. It was the one she'd brought from Buffalo, the one I'd seen the first time I came to her apartment.

"Absolutely, I'm sure," I said. "Besides, I need the practice."

In the end, she'd come to New York with me. I think that Maddie and Ezra had been glad to see her move on, being happy, living her life. The promise of frequent visits was made once I'd informed her she could have use of the private plane. We'd already used it once to attend Jane and Charlie's wedding.

"I'm not going to be your rich goy forever," I told her. "Once I convert, you can't call me that anymore."

She grinned and pushed me down onto the couch, sliding into my lap. She put her arms around my neck and kissed me deeply before saying, "Don't be stupid. You'll always be my goy."

I laughed. "Don't you have a show to do?" My hands took hold of her hips, fingers flexing and kneading. She shivered and moaned. "You could always be late," I suggested, nibbling her earlobe.

"You are terrible for getting me in a state before I have to go to work," she said, pushing away from me. "And don't forget, we have dinner with Cate tonight."

Nobody had been more surprised than me when Catherine and Eliza had taken an instant liking to each other. After giving it some thought, it made a certain kind of sense. They were two women who had made a name for themselves doing a man's job. They understood, to some degree, the others' struggles. Their bond extended into merciless teasing of me at every opportunity, and I loved it. Everything was different, better than I'd ever thought possible. When I'd told Catherine I was converting, she'd nodded calmly and asked what day she should reserve a table for us at the club to celebrate. Times change, I guess, and we have to change with them. Even Catherine.

Eliza was looking at the Christmas tree in the corner of the room and said, "You know, I'd like to keep this part of you. The Christmas stuff . . . well, it's pretty fun."

I smiled and took her hand, pulling her towards the doorway. "Want to know my favorite part?"

"What's that?"

I pointed up at the lintel, where a bunch of greenery hung by a red ribbon. "The mistletoe."

BEAU NORTH is the author of *Longbourn's Songbird, The Many Lives of Fitzwilliam Darcy,* and a contributor to the anthology *Then Comes Winter.* Beau is a native southerner who now calls Portland, Oregon home with her husband and two cats. She attended the University of South Carolina where she began a lifelong obsession with literature. In her spare time, Beau is the co-host of the podcast *Excessively Diverted: Modern Austen Onscreen.*

"That the wish of giving happiness to you might add force to the other inducements which led me on, I shall not attempt to deny."
—Mr. Darcy to Miss Elizabeth, Chapter LVIII.

REASON TO HOPE

JENETTA JAMES

ENCOUNTER. 10 OCTOBER 1943

Darkness had fallen over the base by the time I ventured out and it occurred to me that I had become almost completely nocturnal. I could not fix the time or the place that the transformation had taken place, but it had. My years of living in the light were behind me, and on this particular night, there was barely a sliver of moon to disguise the unalloyed grimness of it. A number of new vehicles were parked in the muddy field like barges and a young flying officer stood outside the mess smoking. He was admiring the Derby, as people always did. Even in the darkness, it managed to gleam. I recalled the sight of my car in other circumstances and then pushed the thought away. As I passed him, we saluted one another in the somnolent manner permitted by darkness and fatigue that only the armed forces knew. My group had been stationed here for forty-eight hours, most of which had been spent making the place serviceable, establishing shortcomings, making do with what was available. The whole of the previous day had been taken up with meetings and a corner of my mind ached to think of the interminable talk, the briefings in cramped rooms, the maps and arrows, the wind biting against the prefabricated wall, the short hours of snatched sleep. Another uncertain turn of the dice and then what might come? I knew not—nor did any man alive.

I gathered pace as the unexpected chill of the evening gnawed my skin, and I wondered how far it was to the town I was told is near. Meryton, it is called, but it could be Timbuktu for all I knew of it. "Meryton, Hertfordshire. Jolly easy for Town!" Air Commodore Arbuthnot had barked at me exactly one week ago, moustache quivering. "Bloody long way from 'ome, sir," Smithers, who was a native of the North, had commented when he brought me my tea earlier in the evening. They were both, in their way, correct.

I kept my path along the perimeter fence and then struck out on an unmade track, lined with shadowy trees, swaying in the wind like phantoms. Into my mind, crept the avenue at Pemberley, sun-drenched and richly green, verdant beyond measure. My sister swinging a tennis racket on a cloudless day in August. My cousin Fitzwilliam leading reels in the ballroom, laughing every step. All of it, belonging to another epoch. Such snatches of the past were, by their nature, brief. They came to me routinely, halfway between dream and punishment. I would recall a moment, a flash of time from a bygone age, a wafer-thin remembrance, and then it would be gone as though it had never existed. Knowing that it would be too soon extinguished, I luxuriated in it for a moment. I had resolved to have a decent walk, even alone and in the pitch of the night in an unknown and frankly uninspiring place. Experience had taught me that the outdoors, any outdoors, was a remedy for the occasional visits of my black dog. With this thought, my feet quickened on the mud-caked autumn leaves and I felt myself making real progress, moving farther and farther from the base, into the bleak empty nothingness of what lay beyond.

All at once, the prism of my solitude was broken. A speck of light appeared before me, wobbling somewhat, a moving blur like a vision on radar. It was accompanied, latterly, by the splatter of wheels on mud and the distinct clicking of metal. No sound of an engine, though. I tensed at the approach of what was plainly a bicycle. As it neared, I began to think the light rather bright and soon enough saw the reason. There was, hanging from the handlebars, a torch on full beam. The speck became a ball and my exasperation grew. What sort of bloody idiot cycles around in the blackout with a torch bobbing about like a yo-yo? The skin of my face tightened and I inhaled sharply. I had encountered his sort before. Unthinking, country nobodies for whom any order was beneath them. If he had seen enemy planes screaming over London like angry birds and street after street cratered into the dust, he may feel differently. I could not be silent.

"Stop! Put out that light. What do you think you're doing?"

Before me, the slow moving, barely visible contraption came to an unsteady halt. I straightened to my full height, knowing it to be unmatched by most men. It had been four years since this sorry business began and every fool knew the rules. Tensing, I anticipated that he would switch the damned thing off as soon as he saw my uniform. The last thing I expected to hear was the female voice that came in reply.

"Minding my own business."

Rude and selfish. To say nothing of stupid. This was the last thing I needed or deserved and I was not going to let it go by. I stepped back slightly in an effort to see her more easily but failed. The dark figure before me, I noted, didn't move an inch.

"The blackout *is* your business. It is everyone's business. Miss."

Behind the glare of the light, I could see nothing of her but the vaguest impression. It was from the tone of her voice, and the reality of the situation that I formed what opinion I had. I imagined her standing, straddling the bicycle, feet flat on the wet ground like the roots of a great tree. An urge to see this woman's face came over me, but the torch was facing away from her. I saw the faintest outline of her fingers as she reached for the offending object and removed it from the handlebars. For the briefest of moments before she turned it off, she shone it in my face. If she had been a man, I would have called her out for it. I refused to close my eyes or squint. I would be damned before she had a reaction out of me. The light clicked off.

"Happy?"

"No. I would be happy if I didn't think you were going to switch it back on again as soon as we have parted. People die of foolishness. And worse, they die of the foolishness of others."

"Foolishness? Let's not be dramatic! No one is going to die because of my torch. It was pointing downwards and this track is covered by trees anyway."

"The trees are losing their leaves. And the blackout is the blackout, as you well know."

I could report her, and she knew it. I could ask to see her papers, use the torch to read them, commit name and whereabouts to memory. She would have the ARP on her doorstep by morning, being their usual dreadful selves. But some undefinable thing stopped me. Was it the weariness? Was it the dark? Was it the last vestiges of human sympathy clinging to me like ivy?

My eyes grew used to the complete blackness that assailed us now the torch was off and I strained to see her. She stood about five feet five and wore a dark coat and hat. A cloud of hair, probably dark, appeared under the brim and the fingers that gripped the handlebars were uncommonly slim and ungloved. I could detect no wedding ring, look as I did. Of her face, the darkness gave me almost nothing, but I could hear in her voice that she was young.

Whatever was a young girl doing cycling on a track like this—at this time of night—alone? Her bicycle was, as had become common, painted white and as my vision adjusted, I focused on her legs. It was just as I had assumed: trousers. I had never grown used to women in trousers and I doubted that I ever would.

I was about to nod when she took me by surprise.

"Who are you, sir? You can't be local or you would never suggest that there should be no torches on the way to Oakham Mount."

"Group Captain Darcy."

The moment I said it, I regretted it. Her general demeanour should have told me that she would not be impressed, where others would, by my rank. In any case, it is for me to ask uninvited questions, not answer them. She had won a victory over me, without even trying. All the time, my eyes were becoming accustomed to the inky night and I came to discern the soft curve of her heart-shaped face.

"Really? You are a long way from the air field. You must have walked two miles. Do you need directions home?"

My sense of direction was excellent, even as a boy. Now, I should say, it was faultless. No meandering country track was about to confuse me, dark or light. And I did not require assistance from silly, young women.

"Certainly not."

"Fine." With one swift movement, she sat on the saddle and clicked back the pedals, readying to depart. "But just so you know, you are on my family's land. We are all four square behind the RAF, Group Captain, but do watch out for poachers, won't you?"

She pushed off with one foot and was gone.

SKIRMISH

"Come along, Darcy. It'll do you good!"

Bingley bounded around the mess like an overexcited puppy and I knew from experience that he would not shut up until he got what he wanted. The weeks had dragged by in the racing adrenalin of operations and the crushing fatigue of the time in between. We had become accustomed to the place, nothing more. My friend turned to me, open palmed in appeal and smiled the smile of a man winning the argument. I turned away from him.

The friendship of Charles Bingley, now Squadron Leader Bingley, had taken root around me when I wasn't looking. He had been a latecomer to school, joining at the age of fifteen when most friendship groups were fixed, my own included. At the time, I had not given any thought to the reason. But now, I suspect that his father only made the money to send him at that stage in his life. He is of the nouveau riche, after all, but he wears it well. We had shared nothing more than a nodding acquaintance but had met again at Cambridge. At length, after a number of unexpected meetings and unplanned events, we had come to regard one another as friends. He had paid me the dubious compliment of introducing me to his sisters, who were his only relations, their parents having died in the thirties. I, in turn, invited him to Pemberley for the vac and later, for weekend parties. Those were the days when there still were weekend parties in country houses. For all that, I cannot say that our friendship was ever as strong as it is now. We signed up on the same morning and trained in the same facility, with the same men, many of them now lost. We have fought together and nearly died together day after day. Presently, he drew on that vast well of shared experience and loyalty to push me, unwilling, into his scheme.

"Alright." I poured us each a glass, drank, and felt the amber liquid permeating my chest with fire and flame. "It can't be any worse than our recent visit to the theatre."

"That's the spirit."

He laughed, and well he might. The previous Saturday night had been memorable. Our posting at Meryton has the questionable merit of being extremely close to the country house Bingley's sisters have taken for the duration of the war. Netherfield Park is a handsome, Palladian creation just a few miles out of the village. It is there that Bingley's sisters, Caroline and Louisa, have been sitting out the war for the last four years, reminiscing about their former life in Mayfair and bemoaning the "servant crisis." Many ladies of their inclinations have long since returned to London, but Louisa suffers an overwhelming fear of the bombs, and in the final analysis, that has kept her in situ, together with her sister. I don't doubt that things have been rather boring for them.

Now that their brother and I are stationed so close, they lose no opportunity to spend time with us. There have been supper parties and badly attended tea dances and cakes and conversation with the local vicar. Last Saturday, we attended the local am-dram performance of *Lady Windermere's Fan*. It was Caroline's scheme, and she had insisted I drive her in the Derby, even though the theatre, such as it was, turned out to be within easy walking distance. She didn't appear to notice the actors missing their lines and crashing into props or the fact that part of the curtain fell to the stage during the interval. "It's so nice to get out and about, isn't it, Darcy? One could almost think it was before the war." She leaned towards me as she said this and under cover of darkness touched her heavily jewelled fingers against my leg. It is not the first time it has happened. In response, I do as I have always done. I remain silent and make no sudden movements. As soon as she moved her hand away, I moved my leg and we said nothing about it.

It was for this reason that I was ambivalent about another evening out on the town with the Bingley ladies. A letter from my sister in New York sat on my desk awaiting a response, and there were always logs to write and matters to attend to. Sleep to catch up on, even. Bingley, however, would have nothing of it. It was *Friday night is music night* in Meryton, and I wasn't being let off the hook.

So, that is how I found myself surrounded by Bingleys and entering the sweaty melee of the modestly appointed town hall that evening. A band stood on a low stage and a balding man knocked out tunes from a shabby upright piano in the corner. During their breaks, a cabal of young people crowded around an old record player. Between the town's collective vinyl selection and the band, all the most popular hits of the day jangled around our heads. To this, revellers danced, skirts spun, and smoke formed towering shapes in the space above. To hear the shrieks of laughter, one would hardly believe there were a war on at all. If my cousin Fitzwilliam were here, his eyes would light a smile on his face. He'd say, "They know how to have a good time," and in he would go. For me, something in my character always holds me back. I cannot say what it is or how it operates. Call it melancholy, call it misanthropy. I know my own shortcomings but have never been uneasy with them.

Shortly after arriving, I bought a round of drinks for our party and distributed them. Caroline was put out that they didn't have vermouth, but I couldn't quite believe her indignation. I fancy that it was for my benefit, to leave me in no doubt of her sophistication. This is a beer and skittles sort of place, and it astonished me that they could produce a gin and tonic. A number of the men were here dancing with local girls and getting tight. They needed that of course but part of me stayed watchful. A local man did a turn singing "Don't Get Around Much Anymore" and after a drink or two, I danced with both Caroline and Louisa. Bingley, I hardly saw, as he did his usual trick of being absorbed into the crowd of pretty girls and laughing fellows.

I was leaning against the bar, listening to Caroline's account of the shortcomings of the local population, when a gaggle of women came into the room and stood near to us. They were a rather chaotic lot to look at. There was an older woman, wearing a stole that looked as though it predated the last war, and five young women. The lady, whom I took to be the mother, undid the top button on the blonde girl's dress and whispered in her ear. That one was rather pretty but she smiled too much. The other girls, all dark haired, were dressed alike. Serviceable dresses, slim bodies, victory rolls curling above made-up faces. They shrieked with laughter and one of them immediately grabbed the hand of a young man standing nearby.

Ever since my encounter with the girl in the dark, I had been imagining her everywhere. No visit to the village or out of the base was complete without her appearing. I had seen her in evening dress, WAAF uniform, married, with child, driving buses, selling food at the market, everywhere. Her face and hair changed each time, because, of course, I had not really seen them. I just knew they were there. I couldn't account for this series of delusions but had begun to question my own sanity. Was the girl even real? Was she the creation of my own mind, addled by war? These were the questions I had asked myself, time and again. But now, there she was, as unmistakable as my own flesh. Pulling curly brown hair out of the collar on her red dress and laughing in the corner of a dance hall. I knew by the way she held herself, the way her feet planted squarely on the sticky floor. I knew by the slim shoulders, exactly the right height, by the tapering body and now, the laugh, ringing out over the hubbub of *Friday night is music night.* That was her, sure as anything.

Caroline, who had drained her gin and tonic, leaned closer to me and her fingers began to snake around my arm. She moved to speak, but I caught her off guard.

"What can you tell me about this family?" I have no idea what moved me to ask this, but ask I did.

"Why do you want to know about them?"

"No reason. Just wondering. I spend so much time in the base and in the air, I never meet any of the locals. Come on Caro, indulge me."

The second the word came out, I regretted it. Too inviting, too suggestive. She moved closer, smiling.

"Not much worth saying really. Those are the ghastly Bennets. Of Longbourn. That's the mother, Fanny. Louisa calls her *Fanny by Gaslight* which I think suits her rather. Mutton dressed as lamb if ever I saw it. No husband in evidence, I notice. Probably enjoying an evening off."

"So, she does have one then?"

The idea amazed me. It wasn't that Fanny Bennet was obviously unattractive. In fact, she was rather pretty for a woman of her age. But she had that look about her of an alley cat sniffing around for fresh food. There was an excess about the way she was dressed, the colours too bright, the fit too tight, the cut too revealing. It wasn't a natural affliction; it was how she chose to present herself. She was a grasping, social-climbing sort of woman, one could see simply by looking at her.

"Hmm. She certainly does. Tom Bennet. Fancies himself the local wit. I'm told he's an Old Harrovian, but I don't quite believe it. They live in a ramshackle, old manor called Longbourn, alarmingly close to Netherfield. Louisa and I have had to sit through tea and gossip in their over-furnished parlour numerous times. Old Fanny offered me a 'serviette' with my tea and I almost choked. Anyway"—she nudged me with her boney elbow and the sickly smell of her expensive scent crept around me—"nothing for you to worry your heroic head about Darcy, just a bit of local colour. The country wouldn't be the same without it, you know."

"And the others? The girls?"

The five young women, who were all approximately the same size, swarmed about one another like friendly bees, unfastening coats and glancing about the room, eyes alert for familiar faces. One of them, let out a particularly raucous laugh and a number of young men approached. The one formerly known to me as "the girl in the dark" was approached by another young woman and then a slightly older man, smoking a pipe and exclaiming loudly about the weather. She smiled easily and everyone appeared to know her. She fit in here like a piece from a jigsaw and the exclusion of it stung me. Caroline, at my side, continued to talk.

"Daughters and assorted hangers-on. The blonde is the eldest, and by far the most presentable, Jane Bennet. Perfectly pleasant. Bit Vera Lynn, if you know what I mean. I think she got all the family virtue. The dark one in the red dress is Elizabeth. Forward, if you ask me, and terribly involved in this Land Army business. In fact, you're lucky she isn't covered in mud this very moment."

Elizabeth. I turned the name around in my mind like a gold coin. It suited her and a light flicked on inside my mind as I said it over and again to myself. Meanwhile, the rasp of Caroline's commentary continued.

"I can never quite remember the other one's name, it might be Mary. Bit of a wallflower. As for those two little hyenas, they don't even have the distinction of being real Bennets! Evacuees. Kitty and Lydia Potter. Sisters. Turned up on a bus from the East End with next to nothing in a pillow case and never looked back. One occasionally sees them catching that ghastly green bus back to London for a visit, but the little blighters are always back a day or so later. Fell on their feet if you ask me, because most families wouldn't put up with it. I'm sure you wouldn't, Darcy."

"Put up with what?"

I knew exactly what she meant. But for a single, thinly sliced iota of a moment, I was unwilling to go along with the narrative. I cannot explain why.

"Well, look at them. All ill-fitting blouses and borrowed skirts, and that straggly hair."

She paused, and I considered them. Their clothing had that look of being much altered but that was now common, even among respectable people. Elizabeth, as she was now named, shivered as she folded her coat and I wondered whether the fine, brown line down the back of her legs was the seam of a stocking or the now familiar line of make-up as replacement. Would it smudge if it were touched?

"There's been talk in the village practically from the day they arrived. Running riot in the school, playing havoc with boys who should know better. The vicar's wife told Louisa that she caught them playing kiss chase after Sunday school, and that was two years ago. They say that one of them is sweet on Edward Lucas, and his father is a *Sir*! He's only a tinpot peer for services to industry or some such, but can you imagine? You only need to look at them to see that they are different."

She spat the word more than said it and her eyes turned down to the watery ice in the bottom of her glass. Somewhere in her diatribe, the tone had changed to bitter. The lighting in the theatre of her conversation had moved, and for the first time, I was seeing evidence of the unvarnished Caroline Bingley. It was no more attractive than the usual, more considered version.

The music changed to the rasping jangle of the Andrews Sisters and Elizabeth Bennet, otherwise in conversation with another, glanced in my direction. Recognition flickered across her face, and I recalled that she had had a good look at me from behind her torch. Her face tightened and tilted back, as if taking aim. There was nothing friendly in that look, nothing as I should like to see.

"Anyway, they're far too old to be here now. That Lydia must be fifteen! Girls like that should be sent back to the cities. Think of the war work they could be doing. It's ridiculous to keep them in the countryside like toddlers. My word, if there were no war, they would probably be mothers. They make them differently in the East End. So I'm told. Right." She put her glass aside and turned to face me, clearly signalling the end of the discussion. "I'm ready for a dance. How about it?"

Her thin body jolted forward and her hand, which had been playing about my arm for some time, took my wrist in a vice-like grip. There was nothing for it, it would be impolite not to. I moved onto the impromptu dance floor, snaking between moving bodies. As I walked through the crowd, the face of Elizabeth Bennet turned to me and fixed me with a stare of her hazel eyes fit to chill the blood. My throat tightened, realising what she had heard, and what she was now seeing. In the heart of the crowd, Caroline turned and we began to dance.

Sometime later, *Friday night is music night* was in full swing. Music blared over our heads and the brassy, jazzy exuberance of it had lit a flame in everyone, even me. My dance with Caroline had been mercifully short, although rather too close for comfort as she squashed her rake-thin body against me at every opportunity and linked her spindly fingers at the nape of my neck. Presently, she found another partner in the shape of a pilot named Monroe. Bingley had brought Jane Bennet to meet me briefly and had then taken her back to the floor for one of several dances. I had tried to catch the eye of Elizabeth Bennet a number of times, without success. I looked at her, and she looked away. It must have been deliberate. My eyebrow twitched and I felt my hands tightening into fists. I watched her hand grasp the shoulder of another woman as they greeted one another and my determination hardened.

The band struck up a Benny Goodman number and it took my mind to another place. They were a poor imitation of the original, but it didn't matter. This was music you could move to. In fact, it gave you no choice, and for a moment I was fearless. Through the crowd of bodies, I advanced towards her. A peel of laughter died on her lips as I arrived, and her friend also turned to face me. There was a silence which, logic tells me, was shorter than it felt, before Elizabeth's face softened into a polite smile and she spoke, straining to be heard above the din.

"Group Captain Darcy, this is my friend Charlotte. Charlotte, this is Group Captain Darcy. I found him in the dark a few weeks ago, walking between Longbourn and Oakham Mount, and it would appear that he was not shot by poachers, for here he is."

After this cheeky introduction, she was silent.

"It's a pleasure to meet you, Charlotte." I shook her hand and she appeared a pleasant woman, albeit the sort that I would not otherwise have noticed. "You haven't actually introduced yourself to me, but I'm told that you are called Elizabeth."

"That's right. My mother will tell you I was named after the Queen, or Duchess of York, as she then was, because I was born on her wedding day. But then Mummy does have rather high ideas!" The girls' eyes met and they laughed. She looked back to me. "That's the only link, I assure you."

"Good. Well. I don't know how the Queen is at the jitterbug, but may I?"

With only the briefest of sideways glances to her friend, she placed down her drink and took my hand as I led her onto the floor with the other couples already going like wheels. Her hand in mine was warm and soft. The music roared up around us and our bodies fell into its slip stream, moving at speed and with purpose, somehow avoiding collision, pounding to the beat. Her figure was small and lithe and had no difficulty finding the rhythm. I watched the expression of slight surprise creep across her face. This was a common reaction and I had foreseen it. Nobody ever expected a man like me to be the master of this fast, fashionable dance. I had learned it attending socials with USAF men shortly after their entry into the war, and so found myself on the right side of the trend as it became increasingly popular with the British. Its frenetic nature did not allow for conversation. One was too busy to talk, trying to keep up with the swing and keep one's partner from certain injury. Silence between dancing partners was the socially accepted norm and it suited me perfectly.

This wordless frenzy, however, was over too soon. As the band blended into a new dance with a new tempo, we stopped, and began to retreat. My hand hovered at the small of her back as we moved through the crowd, not touching and my eyes fixed on the sight of her delicate shoulders. When she reached the bar, she turned and opened her mouth to speak, but nothing came out, like a gramophone that hadn't been wound up. Was it breathlessness, or some other incapacity? The tiniest bead of sweat had formed at her hairline and the swell of her bust rose and fell rapidly, teasingly. A glimpse of a white bra strap was visible where her dress had moved in the dance and her thick hair was in some disarray. For an unguarded moment, I imagined it even more so. It felt wicked to look at her in this way, but I did. I could not tear my eyes away. Coming to my senses, it was in my mind to get her a drink to replace the one she had abandoned and to make a concerted attempt at conversation when Caroline appeared.

"Good grief, Darcy, what a show. Hello Elizabeth, nice to see you. I had no idea you two knew each other. Darcy is a great friend of our family and we to his. He's absolutely always at Netherfield, aren't you? Every moment he gets. He and my brother are thick as thieves."

"Are they? How nice."

"From before the war, of course. And how nice to see so many of your household here this evening. The ladies of Longbourn never miss a party, do they? And why not? Now, *entre nous*, I feel I ought to warn you about something . . ."

"Oh yes. And what is that?"

"Well, Elizabeth dear, I'm afraid it is the youngest Miss Potter." She turned, and there, framed in a mass of dancing airmen and spinning skirts, was Lydia shrieking with laughter as she stole an airman's cap and ran off in the direction of the lavatory. I focused on the airman and realised with a start that it was Smithers.

"The thing is that I know your dear family has only the best of intentions. Both of your parents have lived in Meryton all their lives and they have reputations here. The fact is that people are *talking* Elizabeth. Young Lydia is out at night, keeping company with boys and so on. The whole thing is, well it would be concerning in an older girl, if you know what I mean. It is getting worse. I know that the rector himself is worried."

"That, I doubt." Elizabeth straightened herself and I noted that the excitement of the dance had quite worn off her. She had her breath back. "There are many greater worries in this world. I have all sorts of worries. But they do not include the private business of my neighbours. They do not include who in the village is 'out at night' and who is not. Even the comings and goings at Netherfield"—she flashed a glance at me—"do not bother me. And if others are inclined to worry about these things, maybe they could find something useful to do. Under occupation is a terrible thing."

It was no more than the truth, but the speaking of it was unexpected. Caroline began to fidget with her beads and coloured slightly.

"Well, excuse my interference. It was kindly meant. What a marvellous party this is."

Elizabeth looked at me in an accusing manner and then returned her glare to Caroline before relaxing slightly and leaning back against the bar like a cat who had caught her mouse.

"Isn't it? I'm having a lovely time. And learning a lot about my neighbours, too."

She stopped as a rather sweaty man, not in uniform, appeared with his arm draped around the shoulder of the much-discussed Lydia and another man, slightly older, lingering behind.

"I say Lizzie, they're playing reels next. Will you make up a four with us?"

She smiled at him and looked fleetingly at Caroline and me, before replying, "Love to."

She moved away, and the moment was lost. Watching her form vanishing into the crowd of dancing bodies, I wondered what had become of me, and why? Her words had caught the bull's eye when it came to Caroline. She was a malicious woman with nothing to do. How much more wisdom was there, lurking in the mind of Elizabeth Bennet? I felt a hollow emptiness opening within me. In the time that remained, I drained my drink, observed her dancing with another man and left the building in favour of the cold, lonely walk back to the base.

BEHIND ENEMY LINES

The muddy wheels of the standard issue Jeep rumbled jerkily over the track, and I knew from the sight of my breath and the leafless trees that winter had set in. The utilitarian nature of the vehicle only added to my uncharitable mood. I had been awake since before dawn dealing with various matters that could not be postponed: a mechanical failure that necessitated expensive supplies from London and a fight between two junior officers, to say nothing of my weekly briefing with Arbuthnot. Now, as I returned to the base, along the track where I first saw Elizabeth, my head ached and my body cried out for sleep. Nevertheless, the morning, for morning it still was, was bright and clear. I had dropped Bingley off outside the George Hotel in Meryton, as per his request, and had been driving alone for no more than a few minutes when I saw her.

The rickety door of a barn on the edge of an empty field opened, and there she was, framed by the oak, set in the cold, country morning like a diamond in the rough. Trousers, Wellington boots and that hat again. Her bright white bicycle was flung against the side of the barn like a rag doll. What had she heard that night? And what must she have thought? I recalled the sight of her disappearing back into the dance without me and how I had wanted to pull her back. Only extreme busyness and, frankly, exhaustion, had saved me from reliving that moment interminably between then and now. How ridiculous, that I should be so hounded by thoughts of an ordinary woman of whom I knew so little. I slowed the Jeep and the engine moaned from the effort. A turn appeared and without thinking, I pulled in and got out. The click of the door closing got her attention and she turned to observe me as I walked through the field towards her.

"Group Captain." She nodded and removed her hat, revealing a squashed mass of chestnut curls beneath, lighter than they had appeared at the dance.

"Elizabeth. You are well?"

"Yes, thank you."

It suddenly occurred to me that I had no strategy for conversation, no script. No airman in wartime ever took to the skies without a plan.

"It's a beautiful morning, if cold."

Pathetic, I know. A smile teased across her face and laughter danced in her eyes. I was not reassured but continued regardless. I glanced at her get-up, trying not to stare, not to show too much interest.

"It's nice to see you in the light." She didn't laugh or even smile. "I take it you are in the Land Army? It is important work. Back at home, in Derbyshire, many of the local women have become Land Girls. It isn't harvest time though. Are you particularly busy?"

"There is always work to do on a farm."

"Yes. I know. My family have farmed the same land for many generations."

"Have they? But they must be gentlemen farmers, surely? Grand men in well-cut suits with people to run things for them. You don't do the work yourself, do you? I can't imagine the great Group Captain Darcy ploughing his own field or milking his own cows."

I could not contradict her. I was not used to defending my wealth and status as though they were undesirable. In a deft movement, she closed the barn door and picked up her bicycle.

"But now, I'm all done. I have to go home."

"May I walk with you?"

"You may." She smiled warily.

And so, we progressed out of the field, past the Jeep, and along the track to the north for a few hundred yards. Her manner with me was coldly polite but I was unwilling to just get back in my car and go. Interest in her, combined with embarrassment at Caroline's conduct the other evening, kept my feet treading along beside her turning bicycle wheels, hoping for a peace of sorts.

"I hope your family is well. All of your sisters, and so on."

"Thank you. They are. Did you meet my elder sister Jane? She was at the dance."

"I believe I did, yes. And she is well?"

"Yes. Very. Thank you. I believe that one of your Squadron Leaders is taking her to tea in Meryton this morning, at the George Hotel. You look surprised. Anyway, she is in good health, as is all of my family. You may report back to Caroline that all are present and correct. No clergymen apoplectic with rage, no unmentionable scandals, no bankruptcies, no unwanted babies."

"Elizabeth, I didn't suggest anything of the—"

"You didn't need to. I know very well what people like you and Caroline Bingley think. And what you say."

"You know nothing of what I think."

It was no more than the truth. Despite the extraordinary pull I felt towards her, the fact remained that we had only met twice before and had spoken little.

"Don't I? I think I do, Group Captain. I saw the way you looked at my family last week. I heard you talking with Caroline and saw you turning your nose up at Kitty and Lydia. They may not be polished society darlings, but they are real people, with feelings. Their only crime is to be poor and away from their family."

Her words stung me, immediately, sharply. I thought of my sister. Wealthy and away from her family, and equally blameless. She remained in the United States, where I had sent her to a cousin the moment war had broken out. I imagined her pacing the floor of an apartment in New York, a woman, no longer the child who left, nursing a broken heart. Had I put her in the way of harm myself? The very idea made me wretched. The thought that a stranger would think or speak ill of her lit a spark of rage inside me. As I pondered this, Elizabeth continued her defence of the Potter girls.

"They visit their parents regularly actually, but no doubt it suits certain people to think that they are runaways with no sense of responsibility."

"I didn't say or suggest anything of the sort about them. I don't know either girl, and I doubt I ever will."

I had not intended to sound so harsh, but it spooled out. An aspect of her attack was fair enough, and the truth of that unbalanced me.

"You are probably right. But know this; Caroline Bingley gossips about others to give her something to do and doesn't think about how it might hurt them. You tolerate her rudeness and unkindness, because she's out of the top drawer, just like you. You're no better than her."

With this, we arrived at the top of an unkempt driveway. At the end, there was a mustard-yellow manor house with a blue front door, slightly ajar, and a cat sitting on a wheelbarrow looking at us inquisitively. I thought of my own home, the home of my childhood, given up entirely to the army for the duration of the war, save for a few rooms reserved for family and the remaining servants.

"You know nothing about me."

"Everyone knows about you. And what we don't know we can guess. You're rich and think you're above everyone. Your men might take orders from you, Group Captain, but I don't. The world is changing, you know. Time's up for people like you. The war has turned over a new leaf and there'll be no turning it back when it's over."

With that, she turned on her heel and stomped down the gravel drive, swinging her hat, leaving me standing at the top like a fool.

PAX

Smithers had been looking down in the mouth all morning and had already had a tongue-lashing from Arbuthnot for forgetting to sugar his tea. Sometime after this, I found the boy in my chambers, sorting clothing and looking not at all himself.

"Everything alright, Smithers?"

"Thank you, sir. Fine. Sorry about the Air Commodore's tea. I don't know what came over me."

"Never mind his tea. Let him remember his own sugar."

I knew that would catch his attention, and so indeed it did. His eyes flashed up at me, and he couldn't resist a small laugh.

"Now. You've had a face like a wet weekend all morning. Out with it."

He paused, looking at his own hands. I could tell he was weighing speaking honestly with me.

"Just thinking about the bombing sir, that's all."

"They were certainly going at it last night."

Raids on London were commonplace, as were reprisals on Berlin and any number of other targets. During the war, there had been weeks when it was every single night. There are parts of London that have taken such a bashing, I little know how they carry on. Recently, there had been rather a lull, but for the last two nights, in the distance, the rumble of destruction had sounded. Smithers was a young man, far from home, and it was perfectly natural that it should get him down.

"Let's hope for a let-up tonight, eh?" A look of consternation crossed his face. "Smithers, what is it? Your people don't live in London."

"No, sir. Thing is, sir, there's a girl, here, like. I mean, she lives here, but she's a Londoner."

"What's her name?"

I had no idea that Smithers had found himself a girlfriend.

"Kitty Potter. She's one of the two evacuee girls who live at the big house on the road to Meryton. They're sisters. The other one's—"

"Yes, yes. I know who they are. What about them? They live here."

"I know, sir, but they caught the bus home the day before yesterday, for a visit like. And they haven't come back. Could be fine, but what if it's not?"

I didn't lose any time after he spoke but strode past the mess, out of the base, jumped into the Derby and straight on the road to Longbourn. Jane answered the door, and it was from her I learned that nobody knew where Kitty and Lydia were. Elizabeth had already left, apparently intending to catch a bus to London. I thanked her, gave my best wishes to her family, and headed straight for the centre of Meryton, where I had seen people queuing up for the bus before. Sure enough, there she was, alone and standing beside a rickety sign saying "Bus Stop", muffled up against the wind but shivering still. Relief crept over me at the mere sight of her. I slowed, came to a stop by the pavement, and got out, hardly aware of what I would say.

"I've come from Longbourn. I've heard about it. I'm sorry."

"It's not your fault." Her voice was so much softer than the last time we had spoken, but I couldn't be happy about it. It sounded as though it would break any moment.

"I came to say that you can use my telephone. Or I can call and ask for news, if you're not up to it. Come back to the base with me and we'll do that. Then I'll take you home to your parents with some news."

"That's kind. But I've already tried calling. The vicar's wife let me use the vicarage telephone. I've got a number. I rang and rang but nobody answered."

"I see." It didn't surprise me, unfortunately. The chaos and the workload of war was such that communication was poor at the best of times. Trying to find out the fate of two otherwise unimportant people to whom one was not related was likely to be lengthy and difficult.

"But, we have to know one way or another. Mummy is on the edge. So, I'm just going to go there."

"Go where?"

"To their address, in Stepney." She fiddled in her handbag and produced a small scrap of paper. "I've got it here."

"Is that wise? Have you ever been there before?"

"No, but I'll find it. I have a good sense of direction."

"I don't doubt that you'll find it, Elizabeth. But the bus will take hours. Look at this timetable. It stops at every other lamp post. Then you will have to find the street, speak to somebody. You will be coming home in the dark, if you're lucky, and you may learn nothing. It's freezing cold. Don't give your parents even more to worry about."

"Those are just details. I'll work them out. Mummy needs to know about Kitty and Lydia. She's . . . well, it is hard to explain. She's very tangled up in her mind."

"That's the other thing that worries me about you going to London on your own. You don't know what you are going to find there. Atrocities are hard to look at, Elizabeth. Don't risk looking at them on your own."

My mind spun with the reasons why she should remain here, and suddenly, an idea occurred to me. "Let me drive you there. If you are determined to go, as I think you are. At least you will be there and back in the shortest time."

Her eyes flicked up. "But you're on duty."

"I'm not. I don't need to be back at the base until the morning."

"But it's so much petrol. I can never pay you back the petrol coupons."

"Don't worry about that. I have enough petrol to get us to London and back. Get in." I opened the door of the Derby and it made its familiar soothing click. "We'll go via Longbourn so that your parents know where you are and who you are with. I will get you back for supper time. I promise."

She moved towards the car and her face softened.

"Yes, Group Captain."

"And Elizabeth?"

"Yes?"

"Stop calling me that. If I am going to spend the day with you, then you must call me William."

I opened the door and she got in, gingerly, looking straight ahead as I started the engine and moved away. As promised, our first stop was Longbourn, where I explained the plan to her father and left my card before departing. This duty done, the Derby purred into action and we were away, first on country roads then wider ones. Elizabeth wore a headscarf and twisted her hands together in her lap as we made for the main road to London. Slowly, when I had almost given up hope, she began to relax. The fingers unlaced, the arms uncrossed, the trousered legs stretched out in the passenger footwell. The greens and browns of the fields and the snatches of town and village on the way to London whipped past the window like pictures falling out of an album. After some time, she removed her headscarf and straightened it in her lap before speaking.

"I'm not sure that I've driven to London before. We usually go on the train from Hitchin when we have visited my aunt and uncle in Kilburn. Of course, that was before the war. Mummy is so afraid of the bombs that she won't go as far as Watford now."

I smiled at this, and thought of Mrs. Reynolds sitting in the kitchen at Pemberley, tutting loudly and drawing the two sides of her cardigan together as she listened to the wireless. Maybe they were not so dissimilar as I had thought.

"I don't blame her. I did some training in Watford, with Bingley actually. Very suspicious sort of place." It occurred to me that a bit of light relief might be good for her, and it was a great delight to observe her laughing in return.

"I'll tell her that. She'll be thrilled." She smiled cheekily and glanced out of the window. We were still surrounded on all sides by fields, and I began to mentally plan my route into the East End.

"Do you need me to map read?"

Elizabeth pulled the fold-out map out of the glove compartment without waiting for an answer.

"There's no need. But if you want to, then do."

"I like to keep busy. It helps to cope. I think that is how we have all coped—we've just kept on working at things. In an odd way, that is why Kitty and Lydia are in our house. They are a way of keeping busy. The pair of them are a complete handful. That's the awful thing. Some of what Caroline said is true. They are unruly. They are naughty, really. That night you met me, out on the track, I was looking for Lydia. That's why I had the torch. She'd gone out to meet Edward Lucas, without telling Mummy and Daddy, and not come home. Of course, we all knew but would never tell. But then it got late and I began to worry. So, I went out looking for her."

I kept my focus on the road, but I could feel her eyes on me.

"That was decent of you. It was a cold night."

"Well. It isn't all about one's own comfort, is it? They are worth it, you know. When they aren't giving us the runaround, they are enormous fun. It has been four years, but it feels like forever. My parents had volunteered to take in two pregnant women, but there was some sort of mix-up on the day and they all went to another town. Mummy was most put out. So actually, we didn't go down to the Town Hall when the evacuee children's bus came in. It was later. Sir William drove over and spoke to Daddy. Said there were two sisters, and they wouldn't be separated. You see, there were plenty of people in Meryton with room for one. But nobody had reckoned on taking on a pair. Several people had offered to take one of them but not the other. I suspect Kitty would have plumped for it, but Lydia flat refused. Said they had promised their mum and that was that."

"But your parents did take them?"

The admiration I felt was unexpected but not unwelcome.

"They did. Daddy explained and Mummy put on her hat and coat and off they went. Twenty minutes later they were back with two hungry little girls and our lives have never been the same since."

"That is very good of them, Elizabeth. There are many who wouldn't."

"There are. I don't believe that there is any charity given at Netherfield."

"I know there isn't."

I have seen generosity and meanness in the most surprising places, but Elizabeth certainly had the measure of Bingley's sisters.

"Elizabeth, there isn't anything between me and Caroline Bingley, you know. She is just my friend's sister. I'm not—connected to her in any other way. I would not want you to think that I was. The other night—at the dance—I cursed when she came and spoke to you after our dance."

"It's alright. I understand. Leave it behind. It's nothing compared to how rude I was to you that Sunday."

At this, I did look at her for a moment. The noonday sun bounced off the dashboard and lit up the pearly surface of her face.

"Maybe I deserved it. Leave that behind, too."

"Thank you. You didn't have to do this. It is very generous. Especially after the things I said to you that day."

"Forget it. It doesn't matter, compared to this. That's one thing I've learnt in the war. All the things you thought were important, most of them are nonsense."

"But not all of them?"

"No. Not all of them. I loved my home and family before the war, and I love them still. I miss my sister and my cousin. Some mornings I wake and think I am at home and that is a privilege. Because when it stops, that will mean that the agony has got me. I am closer to people around me than ever I was in peacetime. I listen to men speaking of ordinary things and think 'that is a life.' I trust that, assuming I survive, I shall always remember that."

"So, what's the nonsense then?"

"All the decoration around the edges. You know, money and houses and well-cut suits."

"Cars?" she asked with a smile, looking around her.

"Touché. I love this car like a first-born child. I mean other things. I mean worrying about where a person comes from or who their parents were. I mean even thinking about where a man went to school, or his accent, or the way he stands. It gets in the way of things."

It was true, but that was the first time I had said it. The components of that thought had been swimming around my mind unconnected for some time. Had she brought them together?

"I am surprised to hear you say that. Surprised, and rather ashamed. Because when I met you, I thought that was all you were about."

"Don't be ashamed. That sounds too much like regret."

She turned to me and her full lips curved into a gentle smile. While we were speaking, the landscape around us had changed. Gone were the fields and the sporadic villages. The Derby had slowed and begun to peel along the wide arteries of outer London, lined by shops and imposing houses and nameless parks and gardens. Before long, these scenes gave way to narrower streets, to row upon row of back-to-back houses, giving onto yards, boys pedalling bicycles, women no older than my sister with infants on their hips. They turned to look at the car as we drove by, and Elizabeth shifted in her seat. She began to tense, crossing her legs and wringing her hands. If I reached out my hand, would she welcome it? We passed a large church and the entrance to an underground station from which a stream of people were emerging. Every now and then, Elizabeth glanced at the map and issued an instruction, but the truth was I knew where I was going. I knew how to reach Stepney and the road that the Potters lived on was very easily identified. I had very little time with her before we arrived.

"Elizabeth?"

"Yes?"

"Can we make a deal?"

"Depends what it is."

"Well. How about we agree that whatever happens today, whatever transpires, when the war is over, or before if you are willing, we come to London again? Go to a dance and do the jitterbug? And don't invite anyone else. How would that be?"

To my enormous relief, she laughed lightly before replying. "Yes, is all I have to say to that."

Silence sat between us, quite comfortably, as we advanced further. Before long, the busy everyday scenes of the East End altered to a different view. The change was announced by the sight of a half-blasted brick wall, which I assumed to have been the end of a terrace. Slate tiles lay on the road with winter coats and old chair legs and all sorts of flotsam and jetsam, under a layer of dust that clogged the air. A dog, wearing a lead with no one to hold it, ran about sniffing in the gutter, and I began to regret having brought her here at all. The road, which I had checked carefully on the map before departing Hertfordshire, was here. This *was* it. It was utterly gone, replaced by masonry and misery. An ambulance, driven by a lady in a Russian hat, made its way carefully along the road strewn with debris. A number of fire officers and policemen bustled around the place. If nothing else, I knew who to speak to. The map had flopped like an old lettuce on Elizabeth's lap and she was silent. I parked the car and turned to her.

"You can stay here if you like. I'll just go and speak to that policeman."

"No, I'm coming with you."

I came around to her side to help her out. The place was caked in dust and the pavement had been badly damaged by falling stonework. Her feet looked awfully small against it as she stepped out of the car, but her face was blank with determination. She closed the car door behind her, straightened her winter coat and looked at the unforgiving scene with a steady eye. Quite unexpectedly, as we advanced towards the policeman, she slipped her hand into mine, and there it remained as we picked our way across the chaos.

"Excuse me, Officer, is this Rosemary Avenue?"

"It was, sir."

"I know you must be busy, but I wonder if you can help. I am looking to find out about some friends of mine. Name of Potter. I believe that their flat was in number 4?"

"Well sir, I see you're a servin' gentleman. I'm sure you know 'ow things are. Jerry took out the 'ole street and the next one. There ain't nothing left of number 4 nor any other number. I can't tell you 'bout names—you'll 'ave to speak to Bill down there"—he indicated his colleague who was dealing with a queue of enquiries.

We spoke to Bill after waiting in the bitter cold for some time. It took us hardly any further, as the dead had been counted but not named, and the emergency services were still hard at work. The hour was late, but Elizabeth refused my offer of food. She had cried once, silently, almost secretly, following which we had asked in the local church but again found no new information. It was plain to me that there was no hope. At length, and after some protest, she accepted my argument that her parents would be frantic with worry and we should return.

It was as we approached the car in the indistinct light of dusk that I heard it. A thud of feet against concrete and a breathless cry of "Lizzy! Lizzy, it's you!" The figure of Lydia Potter, dressed in a party gown and high heels, too old for her years, clattered along the destroyed street and into the arms of Elizabeth.

"I thought you were dead!"

"I thought you would never come!"—they both spoke, tears streaming.

It transpired that Kitty and Lydia had escaped the raid by chance. They had gone out for the evening with some old friends at a music hall a mile or so away and heard the blast, from a safe distance. Kitty had broken her ankle in a pothole returning to this scene of devastation in the early hours, and they had remained here, hopeless and desperate, until we arrived. Their parents, with whom they had had a cup of tea before going out, had perished. Understandably, they didn't seem to question or even notice my role in proceedings. While the ladies comforted one another, I spoke to the police and obtained a number to telephone in order to arrange matters. I carried Kitty to the Derby and Elizabeth tucked a blanket from the boot around her legs. Lydia sat beside her on the backseat and held her hand in the darkness while I drove all three ladies home. At Longbourn, amid many shrieks of relief and tears of lament, I helped them out of the car and then made immediately to leave them to themselves. As I did so, Elizabeth caught up with me.

"William?"

I had been expecting a friendly thank you, but she touched her hand to my arm, stood on her tiptoes, and kissed my cheek. We agreed that I would visit the evening after next, at six o'clock. As I drove down the gravel drive, I watched her waving form shrink in the rearview mirror and concluded that there was indeed, reason to hope.

JENETTA JAMES is a mother, lawyer, writer, and taker-on of too much. She grew up in Cambridge and read history at Oxford University where she was a scholar and president of the Oxford University History Society. After graduating, she took to the law and now practises full-time as a barrister. Over the years, she has lived in France, Hungary, and Trinidad. Jenetta currently lives in London with her husband and children where she enjoys reading, laughing, and playing with Lego. She is the author of Suddenly Mrs. Darcy and The Elizabeth Papers.

"The distance is nothing when one has a motive."
—Miss Elizabeth to Mr. Bennet, Chapter VII.

PEMBERLEY BY STAGE

NATALIE RICHARDS

CALIFORNIA, 1860

The stagecoach rocked hypnotically as it jostled down the road. Leather straps swayed back and forth, hanging from the ceiling like pendulums. The creak of leather and wood made a sort of soothing music, lulling a body into a state of catatonia, at least until a wheel hit a rock or rut. It had been a long, difficult journey, one I was ready to have come to an end. Thankfully, we were on the last leg between San Jose and San Francisco.

"You will love San Francisco, Darcy. It is the most exciting place, full of opportunity, fascinating people. I am certain we shall do well there." Bingley had not stopped repeating variations of this theme ever since we left St. Louis nearly a month previously.

His enthusiasm made me smile. "If I did not believe you the first time you said it, I would not have come." In truth, these words belied a confidence I did not feel. Leaving my familiar, orderly life in Boston for the unknown of the West was not a decision I had made lightly. I glanced at my sister, who somehow managed to fall asleep despite the rough road. Was I mad to be taking a young girl to such a wild place? She is completely innocent of the world's dangers. Bingley's sister I worried about less; Louisa always landed on her feet. Why, she spent most of the trip thus far flirting with Mr. Hurst, a railway investor with the Central Pacific Railroad. Caroline, the other Bingley sister, flatly refused to leave and remained in Boston with her aunt.

Despite my misgivings, there was something about the wide open spaces of the West that called to me. Seeing the alien landscape rush past filled me with a sense of excitement and wonder.

"Hold on!"

The stage picked up speed as the driver cracked a whip—and a gunshot split the air.

Georgiana jolted awake. "What was that?"

"A gunshot. It seems we have run into trouble." I wrapped one arm around her and gripped one of the pendulous leather straps with the other. I looked across the aisle and met Bingley's eyes. My friend was white as a ghost, Louisa clinging to him in terror. The other passengers, a widow traveling with her elderly father-in-law and young son, ducked down low.

More gunshots followed. It sounded as though several men were shooting at us, and the man riding shotgun with the driver fired back. I heard indistinct shouts, followed by a cry and a thump as the body of the conductor hit the side of the stage on its way to the ground. Louisa screamed and Georgie flinched against me.

Bingley stuck his head out the window then pulled back quickly as a bullet whistled past his head.

"What do you see?"

Bingley's voice was uncharacteristically grim. "Bandits, at least two on this side. I doubt we can outrun them." He looked at me with a question in his eyes.

I held Georgiana in a close embrace for a brief instant, as if she was still a child small enough to sit on my lap, before trading places with her on the bench. Her whole body shook, but thank God, she was not screaming or in hysterics.

We *could* fight but at what risk? As businessmen from Boston, our skill in a gunfight had been untested. "If we cannot outrun them, we will give them what they want. Save the bullets in case they threaten the ladies." I made sure to meet Bingley and Hurst's eyes to verify we were in agreement.

Louisa was babbling hysterically. "We are going to die! We will be robbed and ravished and left to the wolves and Indians! I want to go home. Charles, we need to turn around and go home!"

"Miss Bingley, be silent! You are not helping." Mr. Hurst commanded. "You have my word I will keep you safe." This, surprisingly, brought an effective end to her cries.

I lifted a corner of the curtain and peered out. "Three on this side." They were close, close enough I could see the lead man's green eyes above his blue-and-white-checkered bandana.

A rifle shot rang out from the other side of the stage, and the vehicle careened sideways.

"Damn," Bingley swore. "I think they got the driver."

The stage left the road as the horses ran wild, spurred on by gunshots.

In an instant, the violence of a collision lifted one side of the stagecoach into the air, slamming the passengers into one another, before crashing down onto its side. The last thing I heard before everything faded into darkness was the screaming of horses.

I woke to the sound of laughter. My eyes opened slowly, blinking away the blackness as the world slowly came into focus. I lay in a heap of limbs at the bottom of a hole. No, not a hole, that was not right. I was lying on a door—the stage's door—I realized as I pushed myself up on one elbow. I heard gasping, pain-filled breaths and looked up to meet Bingley's eyes. My heart stuttered at the ashen cast to my friend's skin. Louisa knelt beside him, feverishly trying to stop the bleeding from a bullet hole in his leg.

"I am sorry," Bingley whispered. "I am so sorry. I tried to stop them."

"Stop—" I startled at a loud thud from outside, followed by a raucous yell.

"Look at these 'ere fancy underthings. They look about the size to fit that little princess ye got there, boss."

My blood ran cold. Georgie! Where was Georgie? Searching desperately about the upended stage, I saw the widow and her child huddled together with the old man, whose neck was bent at an unnatural angle. The boy was hiccupping, his face red from screaming. The woman seemed to be in shock.

"You were out, and she was trying to wake you, shaking you, when the door opened . . ."

I realized I was practically sitting on Mr. Hurst, who was bleeding heavily from a gash on his head, but he seemed to be coming around. The only person I could not see was—

An unmistakably feminine scream split the air.

"Georgie!" I gasped.

"He made her gather anything of value we carried in here, threatened to shoot you where you lay if she refused. She took our coins, watches, and guns, then handed them all over. He took them, and Georgie too, as a hostage." Bingley drew in a sharp breath as Louisa pushed down on the wound harder. "He shot me when I tried to stop him. Said he'd be in touch about a ransom."

I stood and pulled myself out of the opposite door, ignoring the dizziness threatening to send me to my knees. I had no weapon, no plan but to get to my sister. Peeking over the front wheel, I took in the scene.

Most of the horses looked dead, their bodies broken in the crash. The survivors were roped and tethered to the bandits' horses. I could see the still form of the driver a few feet away. Our trunks from the roof were unstrapped and opened. The treasures that we had so prudently selected to bring with us to California were strewn about in the dust or looted. Not far from the wheels was a boulder, the likeliest culprit behind our overturning.

Three of the robbers were stuffing sacks while two others remained in the saddle, including the man with the blue-and-white-checkered bandana. Georgiana was seated sideways across the withers. I let out a breath I did not realize I had been holding when I saw her alive and unharmed.

"Ah, little princess, it looks like your brother has decided to join us," the green-eyed man laughed. "I rather hoped he would." He ran a gloved hand down her hair.

I clenched my fists. His voice . . . there was something ominously familiar about his voice. "Release my sister. Whatever it is you want, you will have it. You have my word as a gentleman. Simply let her go."

"The word of Will Darcy is known to be a formidable thing. If I returned her to you, here and now, you would still make good on the ransom? Even if she was no longer in danger?"

"My word is my bond."

He cocked his head. "I believe you."

I felt my fists loosen.

"Ten thousand dollars in cash or gold. I will send word as to when and where. Do not worry. I will wait a few weeks so you have plenty of time to gather the money." His eyes glittered with malicious amusement.

There was no way I intended to leave my sister in this monster's hands for any length of time, much less weeks. "It will not take me nearly that long. The majority of my funds has already been transferred to San Francisco. I can get them in a day if you leave one of the horses."

The bandit threw back his head and laughed. "Always the clever one, an answer on the tip of your tongue. Well, I could leave her and you would fetch my money, but I won't. I like you groveling at my feet."

"You want me to grovel? You want me on my knees?" I climbed down to stand, mere feet from my sister and the bastard who held her. When I moved, the other bandits all swiveled to aim pistols and rifles at me. But I did not care. I dropped to my knees. "Here I am . . . Wickham."

"I wondered how long it would take you to realize who I was." George Wickham pulled down his bandana and grinned. "But . . . I think it will be much more fun to make you suffer, as you made me suffer when you stole my livelihood and good name. Do not worry, so long as you pay the ransom, dear Georgiana will come to no harm, but until then, she shall remain with me."

"No!"

"Quit fooling around. Let's take the girl and go!" One of the bandits grumbled. Wickham ignored him, all his attention upon me.

I stared at the man I had long ago called friend. I scarcely recognized the dapper, charming gentleman of six years ago in the hardened criminal before me now. "Your own choices cost you your name and livelihood, not me—and certainly not Georgiana." Once upon a time, Wickham treated Georgie like a little sister, tugging on her braids and bribing her with treats. Now, he held a gun to her head. "Look at yourself, George. Is this what you are now? Is there nothing left of the boy I grew up with?"

Something like regret flickered in Wickham's eyes, but it vanished so quickly I thought I must have imagined it. "I am what necessity has made me. We cannot all begin life with the world already in our grasp. Some of us have to bite and claw for what you have always taken for granted." He began to wheel his horse around. "You will await my instructions."

"I will not let you take her!" I lunged to my feet, then froze as Wickham pulled back the hammer on his revolver. The horse side-stepped and pranced as Georgiana held perfectly still with the gun's muzzle pressed into the tender skin of her throat.

"Yes, you will. You have no choice. I have taken it away from you, as you took away mine—when you threw me in prison to rot—amongst the filth of humanity." Wickham's eyes were colder and harder than any I had ever seen. "You took my life from me. I will have this in return." He set off, riding west, picking up speed as the other bandits fell in behind him.

"Georgie!" I cried, chasing after them on foot. One of the bandits fired into the ground near my feet, bringing me to an abrupt halt.

"Will!" Georgiana's scream echoed as they galloped away, leaving naught but dust in their wake.

With the remaining daylight, we scavenged for firewood and a water source to set up camp. Louisa managed to snap the widowed Mrs. Reynolds out of her shock and occupy her with caring for Bingley, as well as gently draw the tearful young Pete away from the body of his grandfather, while Hurst and I dug shallow graves for our dead.

I ached to pursue Wickham but without a weapon or a horse . . . Come morning, I would head out on foot in the hopes of reaching a town or the next outpost.

"How is he?" I knelt by Mrs. Reynolds's side where she sat holding Bingley's hand.

"Not good," she said softly. Sarah Reynolds was a handsome woman, or had been once, before the pain and grief of too many losses made her an old woman at twenty-nine. I had learned that her husband died of typhoid only five months ago, along with her two older children, and I had thought to hire her as a housekeeper once we settled in San Francisco. "The bullet is still in his leg. I've managed to stop the bleeding, but I know nothing of doctoring." There was a hint of bitterness to her tone.

Bingley slipped into a restless sleep, his skin clammy. He murmured over and over, apologizing for Georgiana's abduction.

But I knew the fault lay solely with me. I had brought Georgie to this godforsaken land. And for what?

When Bingley returned home from his first trip west, he carried tales of wondrous adventures and a city of extraordinary freedom . . . stories that made me think perhaps I could start over, escape from the whispers, and begin anew. Now I could lose my sister forever out of my own selfish dreams.

"Hello to the camp!" called a friendly voice. I leapt to my feet, placing myself between the others and this new threat.

"Who goes there?"

"Simply two weary travelers who spotted your fire. Might we stop and warm ourselves?" Into the light cast by the flame stepped two people, a man and a woman, leading a pair of mustangs. They both wore rifles on their backs, and the man carried revolvers holstered on either side of his belt. The woman wore a faded calico gown; a straw bonnet hung from its strings down her back, leaving her light hair to gleam in the fire's glow. The young man was slender, his clothes ill-fitting, falling off his body as if they were made for a man twice his size, his flannel shirt buttoned up to his chin. He wore a Stetson pulled low over his brow, leaving his face in shadow.

"Who are you?"

"I'm Elias Bennet, and this is my sister, Jane. We ain't here to cause trouble. It looks as though you folks have seen enough already." he said with a husky, Southern accent. "We've come a long way, though, and my sister is feelin' poorly."

The woman coughed, swaying slightly on her feet. She looked tired and thin and, despite my wariness, I could not turn them away. Besides, we had no weapons, and these two were well armed; if they decided to take whatever they wanted, I was in no position to stop them. "We have no food, but you are welcome to our fire, and there is a stream down there, around the bend."

Bennet tipped his hat. "Much obliged. As for food, we have some and are willin' to share. It's nothin' fancy, I'm afraid." He dug through his saddlebags while everyone introduced themselves and emerged with a cast iron pot, cans of beans, salted pork, and half a loaf of brown bread. "Was it an accident?" he asked, nodding to the overturned stage as he helped his sister sit down. He started popping open the cans, looking as comfortable as any Boston gentleman relaxing in his library.

Hurst snorted. "Not hardly. We were targeted by a band of cutthroats run by a man called Wickham."

Bennet and his sister exchanged a quick, meaningful look.

Yet, I caught it. "You know him."

After a moment, Bennet said, "Aye, though most know him nowadays as *Smilin' George*. He's been workin' his way through the country, makin' a mess and movin' on like locusts in a cornfield. They say he's a real educated feller from back East but rough, too." He looked around our pitiful group. "I'm sorry you and yours crossed his path."

"We did not simply cross his path. He came after us," I said. "He came after me."

Bennet cocked his head and looked at him curiously. "Now why would he do such a thing?"

Everyone looked at me for the answer to the question hovering in their eyes ever since the attack. The Bingleys knew the story—or some semblance of it. It all happened before we had met but was much spoken of amongst society. While I would have preferred to keep the details private, my fellow travelers deserved to know why they were attacked.

"George Wickham was the son of my father's man of affairs. The elder Mr. Wickham was his most trusted employee, as well as a friend. I looked on him as sort of an uncle. When he died suddenly of pneumonia one winter, my parents took George, who was twelve years old at the time, into our home. We were raised almost as brothers." I paused, remembering, and the only sounds were the crack of the fire and the chirp of crickets.

"What happened?" Bennet asked softly.

"He was always a little jealous of me because my father lived while his did not—and of the fortune I was to inherit. I thought that it was simply youthful discontent, but it only grew worse as time went by. I did not realize how depraved he was until it was too late. We went to Harvard together and both studied law. My father established a firm with my mother's father and her sister's husband. Fitzwilliam, Darcy, and DeBourgh. He hired us both as soon as we passed the bar." I studied my hands, my fingers twisting together. "I am glad sometimes my father did not live to see what happened after."

I flinched when Mrs. Reynolds patted me on the shoulder. I did not deserve her sympathy. Her father-in-law was dead because of the enmity between Wickham and me. "Six weeks after my father's death, I discovered him bribing a witness to lie on the stand. I had him arrested. Investigations revealed he did the same on at least seven previous occasions. He was disbarred and imprisoned; his cases overturned. I thought this would be the end of it, but it was just the beginning."

"Your firm was scrutinized. Every case you ever took was questioned," said Louisa. "I remember the newspapers." There was surprisingly little judgment in her tone, merely weariness.

"Yes. Formerly loyal clients no longer required our services. Our reputation for integrity was shattered. The only people who still wanted to hire us were those who hoped the rumors were true. For years, I attempted to salvage something of my family's legacy, but in the end, I could only take solace in knowing when people spoke of them, it was to say the firm would never have sunk to such depths under their command. Eventually, Wickham was released from prison and quietly disappeared . . . I thought for good. When Bingley told me of his plan to move to California, I realized it could be a chance to begin anew, without the specter of Wickham's perfidy hanging over me." He laughed bitterly. "It seems, however, there is no escape. In taking my sister and bringing harm to my friends, he has exacted the perfect revenge."

Jane Bennet drew in a sharp breath, which led to a bout of wracking coughs. Elias's brow furrowed. "Your sister?"

"Georgiana. He holds her for ransom but also to torment me. I fear no matter what ransom I pay, he will keep her. As soon as I reach San Francisco, I will send help back here, but I am going after him. Mr. Hurst, if you could arrange the ransom in case I cannot rescue her, I would be most grateful." I would leave nothing to chance when it came to Georgiana.

"We may be able to help you with that," Bennet offered.

I swiveled my gaze to the younger man, meeting a pair of earnest, brown eyes. "How?" At this point, I would take all the help I could get.

"We're headin' for an outpost called Velvet, just a few miles from here. On horseback, I can be there in no time, I reckon. They don't have a doc, but there's a gal there who's good with medicines and wagons you could hire to get the rest of the way to Frisco. Plus, I hear Smilin' George's gang goes there for supplies sometimes. It's kind of a wild place, if you know what I mean. If I leave at first light, I can be back with help before noon."

I stared at him until the youngster looked away, seemingly embarrassed. Hope swelled in my breast. I did not know why I felt I could trust this complete stranger to keep his word, but my instincts told me I could. "I would be forever in your debt, Mr. Bennet."

Bennet blushed, making me think he couldn't be more than seventeen. "I have my own reasons to dislike Wickham. If I can help you best him, I will."

I eyed him curiously, but neither he nor his sister seemed open to sharing information.

"Grub's ready," Bennet announced, stirring the pot one last time. "We only have two bowls so everyone's gonna have to take turns."

The next day dawned clear, with birds singing, a gentle breeze ruffling through the manzanitas, and Bingley burning up with fever. I shook Bennet awake when the sun's rays were no more than a hint of gold in the east. "Bingley's taken a turn for the worse," I told the lad.

Bennet nodded, wide awake in an instant. "I'll rouse Jane." He sat up and nudged his sister. "Time to get up."

Jane moaned and coughed wetly before opening bleary eyes.

Bennet and I exchanged a concerned look.

"She's not used to such rough travel and has been coughing for days, ever since we got caught out in a rainstorm," Bennet murmured.

I noticed his voice became lighter, his accent lessened when he was worried. A sudden idea occurred to me. "Let her stay here and get some rest. I will ride with you, and she can ride in the wagon we send back for Bingley and the others."

Bennet bit his lower lip. "There's no denying she could use the rest, but I don't like leaving her behind."

"No one in this group will harm her; I would bet my life upon it." I had not known Hurst long, but already the idea of him hurting a woman was ridiculous.

After a hushed, heated discussion between the Bennet siblings, it was decided. Jane would remain behind with one of the rifles in her possession; Hurst would have the other. Bennet and I would take only the revolvers with us. Bennet would have left all his weapons with the group so Jane would be more secure, but his sister won that argument.

I started to saddle Jane's horse, but Bennet snorted and offered his own mount. "You're far too tall for little Lottie, there. Your feet will drag trenches all down the road. Ride Collie instead."

"Collie?" I studied the beautiful, barely tamed appaloosa mustang before me. "You named this glorious creature *Collie*?" I was horrified. As a man with a healthy appreciation for good horseflesh, it seemed a crime that this horse, who stood nearly fifteen hands tall and weighed at least eight hundred— possibly closer to nine hundred pounds—should be called something so plain and homely as "Collie."

Bennet grinned, his whole face lighting up and pushing his fine-boned features past handsome and into too pretty for his own good. "It seemed to suit him well enough at the time. He followed me about like a puppy when I found him. He might give you a bit of trouble at first, but if you're firm with him from the start, he'll know you won't fall for his tricks, and calm down."

He was right. Collie began to dance the moment he felt an unfamiliar rider on his back. I allowed it for a moment, letting him work out the surge of energy, then gently reined him in. I stroked Collie's glossy brown neck, murmuring praise. Collie fought me a minute longer, then stopped, his ears flared as if he was listening. I looked up to see Bennet watching me with bemusement.

"I think he likes you. He doesn't calm so quick for most, and if he really disliked you, he would've bucked you off."

I arched a brow. "Thank you for the warning."

Bennet laughed. "I wasn't too worried about it. Collie's usually a real good judge of character." With that, Bennet waved a farewell to his sister and set off on Lottie, leaving me to follow, wondering if I had just been complimented—and if so, by Bennet or his horse.

We rode hard and silent down the road for nearly an hour before Bennet slowed and turned off onto a rougher, less-traveled path. "From here on, we'll have to take it easier or risk the horses."

I nodded, though I was frustrated by the slower pace. "Have you been this way before?"

"To San Francisco? Yes. To Velvet? No. I just got good directions from a man back in San Jose."

"What is your business there?" I was curious to learn more about my mysterious, young traveling companion.

Bennet cast me a sidelong glance. "You'll find out quick most don't like it when folks ask too many questions out here."

"Simply making conversation." My curiosity was well and truly roused now. What was Elias Bennet hiding?

Bennet seemed to debate whether to respond. Finally, he said, "My reason is very like yours. Jane and I have been trailing George Wickham all the way from Texas."

I jolted in surprise, making Collie sidestep beneath me. I settled the stallion and stared at Bennet. "Why did you not say something before?"

He shrugged, but I could tell he was tense by the way his knuckles whitened around the reins. "I am saying it now." His accent was near nonexistent.

"What do you want with him?"

Bennet sighed. "I was raised on a ranch with my sisters, Jane and Lydia. Jane's the oldest and Lydia's the youngest, being only fifteen now. Our mother's been gone awhile and our father died of apoplexy last year. He was well-to-do, or so we thought. When he died, though, we lost our spread to debt collectors. Seems things hadn't been going as well as he let on. Jane became a schoolteacher, I worked as a cook, and Lydia took in laundry. We worked to the bone just to scrape by, and Lydia hated every second of it."

I began to see where this story was headed and empathized with the poor boy who had tried his best to keep his family together.

"We managed, at least until Wickham came into town. He styled himself as an army man, recently mustered out and in possession of a small inheritance. He said he was looking to start a ranch further west. In short order, he charmed the whole town, including, I'm sorry to say, me and my sisters. I didn't realize he was spending so much time with Lydia until I came back to our rooms one evening and found Jane crying over the note she left. It said she was going west with Wickham to be his wife."

"So, you went after her."

"Not right away. We weren't real happy she left without talking to us or marrying him in town, but it was her choice, and we didn't know which way she went. But then a couple of weeks later, word spread there was a new wanted poster at the jail with George Wickham's face on it. The money he threw around town, buying trinkets and *drinks on him*, was stolen from a bank in Oklahoma. There's a bounty on his head, his and the others he's running with." His voice turned bitter. "I'll never forgive myself for not seeing through his smooth ways to the snake beneath."

He looked so forlorn; I could not help but offer comfort. I know what it is like to have a sister to protect and to fail to do so. "You are not the blame. Wickham has an appearance of goodness about him which has fooled many people, including all of Boston for a time. You and Miss Bennet have uprooted your lives for your sister to save her from a mistake of her own making. No one could do more, and most would do far less."

"I tried to convince Jane to stay behind. She had good work and suitors, but she insisted on coming with me. Even if we succeed in reclaiming Lydia, there will be no returning to Texas, not when she's known as either an outlaw's wife or . . . or his woman. We'll go to San Francisco to find our aunt and uncle. We'll begin again, the same as you."

We rode in silence before Bennet suddenly said, "You are not the blame, either, you know. Not for your sister being taken, nor in making an enemy of Wickham."

I shook my head. "When I first caught Wickham, he offered to disappear, to travel far away. If I only agreed, my father's firm would still be one of the most prestigious in Boston, and my sister would be safe and sound in her own home." My voice cracked, and I cleared my throat to hide it.

"That may be so, but what of the innocents Wickham sent to prison? Would you be able to live with yourself if you left them there, knowing he interfered in their trials? Or the guilty he allowed free? Would your father wish for you to preserve his legacy at such a cost? It seems to me that you—your honesty and sacrifice—are a far greater legacy to his goodness as a man and as a father than a law firm." He fell silent, blushing as if embarrassed to have said so much.

I could only stare, speechless, as I turned over Bennet's words in my mind. "And what of Georgiana's safety? Was that not worth my silence?"

"If she is anything like you, she would not have stood for the lies, either"—was Bennet's simple reply. "Besides, you couldn't have predicted the man would be so loco as to become an outlaw. If he'd come out west and just started over, it's likely no one would've known he was a crook. Look, we're nearly there." He pointed ahead to a ramshackle collection of buildings nestled between two hills.

"Did you know your speech becomes much crisper and more educated when you speak passionately, then gets deeper and thicker when you catch yourself?" The question burst from me before I considered the consequences of my forthrightness. "It is the opposite of most people's tendencies."

Bennet started and paled. "I don't know what you mean." His Texas drawl had never been thicker.

"Just an observation."

Only the extravagantly generous would refer to Velvet as a town. It did have a firm grasp of necessities, though. I spied a smithy that appeared to be equipped to handle rudimentary repairs and horseshoeing, a dilapidated saloon with one of its swinging doors hanging half off its hinges, what might be a dry goods store, and a wide, two-story structure which dwarfed the rest of the buildings, at the end of the street. I was about to inquire as to its purpose when the door opened and a burly, bearded man strutted out. Behind him stood a half-dressed woman who blew him a kiss before slipping back inside. "Where is the healer woman?" I asked, wanting to complete our business and get out of this place as quickly as humanly possible.

Bennet arched a brow. "You're not gonna like it." He pointed to the brothel dead ahead. "I hear she charges the same by the hour whether it's for healing or for . . . you know." The lad might pretend worldliness, but I could see the tips of his ears turning red. Then again, I suspected mine were doing the same.

Bennet was correct, as he was so often. I did not like it. However, beggars could not be choosers. "How did you even come to hear of this woman?"

"Wickham brings his gang here for her to patch up, or so I was told."

We dismounted, tied our mounts to the waiting hitching post, and with great trepidation, knocked on the door. It swung open readily, revealing a curvaceous woman with buoyant blonde curls and a sensuous, crimson smile. She wore so much paint it was difficult to tell her age, but I guessed her to be on the older side of thirty. She looked us up and down, dismissing Bennet to focus on me, much to my dismay. "Madam," I addressed her with a slight nod.

"Why, a real gentleman!" She dipped into a wobbly curtsey, giving us both an eyeful of her navel down the front of her gown. Bennet choked, sounding like he was swallowing his tongue. The woman straightened, her eyes never moving from me. "A bit dusty from the road, perhaps, but you look good enough to eat." She licked her lips and hugged herself, plumping her breasts up for my view. "Come inside and I'll be more than happy to take the first bite." Opening the door wide, she beckoned us in.

We entered, feeling like we were stepping into a lion's den. Our senses were immediately assaulted by the sights and smells of a whorehouse. A fog of sweat, cigar smoke, and cheap perfume was thick in the air. There was a man staggering down the stairs, pulling up his trousers as he went, guffawing at some private joke. I suspected he was still drunk from the previous night's revelries. Women in varying degrees of undress wandered through the room, chattering and yawning as they bid adieu to their customers.

I glanced at Bennet; my lips quirked up at the sight of my friend's flabbergasted face. His eyes were huge but he was trying desperately not to look at anyone. How old was Elias, anyway? Surely a young man his age would have seen a naked woman before. I remember visiting a few courtesans when I was around Elias's age, but I quickly tired of it in favor of a more meaningful friendship with a worldly widow with no desire to remarry. We got along quite well, remaining friends even when the physical aspect of our relationship came to an end. It was never love—more of a contented, mutual companionship.

"It was a busy night," our guide explained with a wave at the chaos. "Most of the girls will be tired, but any one of them will perk up right quick at the sight of you. We'll even find one for the boy. I have a girl who specializes in breaking in virgins."

I did not think it possible for anyone to turn any redder than Bennet was before, but somehow, he managed it. Looking around, I was discomfited to see that many of the prostitutes, upon noticing my presence, began primping their hair and batting their eyes. "We are here looking for a particular woman." I glanced at Bennet, realizing I did not know her name.

"Mrs. Sabrina Young," Bennet supplied quickly. "We hear she has some healing skills. His friend has been shot, and my sister is ill."

"You've found her," the woman said, then sighed. "And I was so looking forward to my breakfast." She gave me a pointed look. "Ah, well, if it is Sabrina the nurse, you need, I had best get my bag. Have you payment on you? I don't go nowhere unless I get paid up front."

I opened his mouth to explain the robbery when Bennet pulled a gold pocket watch from his coat and held it up. "Will this do?"

Mrs. Young snatched it and held it to the light of a kerosene lamp. "This is decent quality . . . worth a few hours, I suppose. Who is G.T.B.?"

"My father," Bennet answered, his face no longer red.

I swore under my breath. I could tell just from looking at it, the watch was far more valuable than a few hours . . . from the gold alone. The fact it was an heirloom . . . "Bennet—"

"It is not worth a man's life. My father would be the first to agree." He turned and stomped out the door, his over-large duster swishing around his heels.

I watched him go and made a promise to myself to get that watch back, even though it would only be a drop in the bucket towards a debt I could never repay to the lad.

The watch's gold chain secured the services of two wagons, horses, and drivers for the trip to our camp and back. Bennet's last few coins were barely enough to arrange for a night's lodgings. Velvet's boarding house did not have rooms, merely beds with straw ticks laid out like army barracks, but it was better than the hard ground.

I rode alongside the wagon so I could speak to Mrs. Young. I explained Bingley's injury and fever, as well as Miss Bennet's cough, in as much detail as I could.

She listened patiently, then when I was through she said, "Now you've got necessities out of the way, why don't you say whatever you've really been wanting to. I can see a question in your eyes every time you look at me."

"I hear you know Smilin' George Wickham."

She blinked. "That wasn't a question."

"Where can I find him?"

She looked me over warily, with none of the carnal appreciation she displayed before. I was grateful. "What do you intend to do when you find him?"

"What I do depends on what he has done to my sister."

She laughed, "Oh, he does have a way with the ladies, that one does. Convince her to run off with him?"

Bennet flinched. "No, that's *my* sister. He kidnapped Mr. Darcy's sister."

"Two of them? He's got both of your sisters?" She could scarcely contain her mirth. "Well, I haven't known him for long, but I've never seen him to do anything to a woman she didn't ask for—and enjoy! He thinks of himself as a charmer, you see. Hurting a girl would ruin his picture of himself."

"I have never known him to harm a woman, either, but then again, I had not known him to attack a stage, kill three men, wound another, and kidnap a young girl until yesterday. Georgiana is not a woman to be charmed by him; she is the tool of his revenge against me."

Mrs. Young let out a decidedly unladylike whistle. "My, he has been busy! I'm surprised no one came to my door last night with wounds needing licking." She cackled at her own joke.

"Where is he?" I gritted my teeth to keep from shouting at the woman.

She cast me a sidelong glance, a sly look in her eyes. "What's in it for me? He's been a good customer, and I have a feeling I won't be seeing him around any longer if I tell you where he hangs his hat."

"One thousand dollars, in cash or gold, delivered to you or a bank of your choice."

Her mouth gaped open. "With that much coin I could buy my own brothel! Or something more respectable," she added as an afterthought. Her gaze turned suspicious. "How am I to know you'll keep up your end of the bargain?"

I was utterly sick of having my integrity questioned by thieves, murderers, and whores. "Has anyone a piece of paper?"

Bennet, bless his marvelous soul, produced a leather-bound journal and a stubby pencil from one of his saddlebags and handed them over,

"Do you mind if I remove a page?" I asked.

"No."

"Excellent. Thank you." I added 'purchase a new journal' to my mental list of things I owed Elias Bennet as I tore out a page and scribbled down a simple contract. My handwriting was terrible on account of being on a moving horse with only a journal to use as a writing desk, but it was legible. Barely. I passed it to Bennet. "Would you please sign this as a witness to my bargain with Mrs. Young?" Bennet did so, signing simply as "E. Bennet" before passing it back. I handed it in turn to Mrs. Young. "I am an attorney, and this contract is legally binding if you choose to sign it. I have included a note to the effect you will receive an additional fifty dollars in return for Mr. Bennet's watch upon receiving payment."

Bennet's eyes widened. "You did not need to do that."

"Yes, I did."

Mrs. Young gave the document a quick go-over, though from the way her eyes wandered I suspected she could not actually read. This was confirmed when she signed it with a laborious "X" rather than her name. "Done!" she cried as she stuffed the contract down her bodice. "Smilin' George has himself a place up the hill over there"—she pointed at a distant, densely wooded mound back the way they came. "It's an abandoned mining town. The vein up there played out and everyone packed up and left about four or five years ago. I don't think it ever even had a name. The whole hill is riddled with mines, and all their houses are still up there. Just go through Velvet and you'll find the old trail where they used to haul wagons full of ore. Tracks that deep last for years, can't miss 'em. Last I saw him, he'd taken over the biggest house as his own."

Bennet and I exchanged a look of perfect understanding. As soon as our friends were safely in the wagon, we were going after Wickham. I vowed Georgiana would not spend one more night in the bastard's hands.

Upon reaching the camp, I dismounted and crouched down by Bingley's side. "How is he?" I asked Mrs. Reynolds and Louisa.

"I am lying right here," Bingley mumbled hoarsely. "I do not know why you are all so worried about a trifling hole in my leg. It is not as though it is in my head. Though it would not make much of a difference there, according to some . . ." He smiled at Jane Bennet when he said this.

She shook her head. "He keeps making jokes as though any part of this situation is humorous when he's hot as boiled crawdad and has a bullet in him." She coughed, then glared. "He is not comical." Listening to her speak, I realized she sounded much like her brother did when he forgot he was supposed to be an uneducated cowboy. There was something niggling at the corner of my mind, but I could not quite put my finger on it.

Mrs. Young laughed uproariously. "These're my patients? We're going to have a hell of a time!"

Jane and Bingley looked at her, then looked at Bennet and me. Jane's "look" was more of a death glare while Bingley's was frankly curious. "This is the healer?"

"Not just any healer. Wickham's healer of choice," I answered, and understanding dawned on their faces.

It took some time to get everyone and what little remained of our belongings into the wagon. Jane would not leave Bingley alone with Mrs. Young for even a moment, guarding him like a mother bear. Or a jealous wife, depending on how you looked at it. It was nearly noon when our bedraggled caravan set off for Velvet and past two thirty when we arrived. Our responsibilities met, Bennet and I prepared to go after Wickham.

"Where are you going?" Jane asked her brother when she saw us readying to leave once more.

"After Lydia and Georgiana," he replied. "We know where Wickham is."

Jane paled. "You cannot go! Not just the two of you! You should contact the law, gather a posse. You will both be killed! It is too dangerous."

"Jane," Bennet said. "This is why we came here; you know this. We have done too much—traveled too far—to turn back now."

"But that was before Wickham murdered three men! He had not killed anyone until now. A thief is dangerous enough—but a killer?" Jane was adamant.

I had not realized Wickham had never killed before. Did revenge push him over the edge, or was he working up to it anyway? A new wave of guilt threatened to drown me.

The others were gathered close, listening shamelessly. Mrs. Young's head moved back and forth between the Bennet siblings, clearly enjoying the drama.

"All the more reason for us to go!" Bennet replied, heatedly. "Who knows if he will turn on Lydia or Mr. Darcy's sister? There is no one else for miles around who can or will go after him. You have seen this place. Do you think a single one of the men here would lift a finger to help us with no money? Hell, half of them are probably outlaws too!"

"Then take Mr. Hurst with you at least! Surely three guns are better than two."

"I cannot and will not leave you here unprotected. Mr. Hurst stays."

I agreed completely with this statement, though Hurst looked disgruntled to have his role chosen for him.

"I will not allow this," Jane said, her expression set. "I will not sacrifice one sister in a suicidal attempt to save another."

A gasp went through the room, followed by a shocked hush.

Bennet's eyes closed and *she* whispered, "Jane."

Jane was unapologetic. "He needs to know. You think you are as strong and able as any man, but I will not let you kill yourself trying to prove it."

"Is that what you think I am doing? Is that why you think I am here?" The hurt in Bennet's voice was unmistakable.

All of the strange, mismatched puzzle pieces making up Elias Bennet fell into place with a bang. This is why he—she!—wore oversized clothes. This is why her voice lightened and her accent diminished, though did not disappear entirely, when she was upset. This is why, despite the dirt smudges on her face, which I now suspected were strategically placed to disguise a total lack of facial hair, she was uncommonly beautiful for a boy.

I looked up to see Bennet staring at me with dread in his, no her, eyes. It would take time for me to become accustomed to thinking of her as such. "What is your name? Your real name?"

"Elizabeth, though most call me Lizzy." Her chin lifted in defiance. "I can shoot and ride as well as any man, so you have no call to leave me behind."

"The two of you are going up against a gang of murderers by yourselves! And, no offense, Mr. Darcy is from the city, born and raised. How will he be of help when he knows nothing of how to survive out here? You are both wonderfully brave, but you are not thinking practically." Jane was becoming increasingly desperate, terrified to lose what remained of her family.

I blinked at her argument, not expecting her to see me as less capable than Lizzy, but I was forced to admit I would have readily agreed to the charge before knowing she was a she. I was still stuck on that point, trying to wrap my head around Elias being a woman. "Why?" I asked, my eyes fixed on Elizabeth.

She did not pretend to misunderstand me. "My father and I were close. He treated me more as a son than a daughter, something Mama hated. I wonder sometimes if it is what made her spoil Lydia so. After they died, the banks would not give us a loan, believing three women alone could not possibly make a ranch profitable, so we lost our home. We discovered then precisely how difficult it is for women to find work, how differently we are treated due to our *frailty*. No one would hire me as a ranch hand or horse trainer." She paused and took a deep breath.

I found myself hating the thought of her laboring as a ranch hand, surrounded by rough men. Even if they were honorable and offered no insult to the unconventional woman in their midst, it was backbreaking work.

"We moved into town and found work there, the jobs I mentioned before. When Lydia ran away, we knew it would be too dangerous for two women traveling alone to seek her out, but a woman and her brother . . . I was always skinny and only became more so in recent months, so binding my form and wearing my father's old clothes, my collar buttoned to my chin to hide a lack of an Adam's apple, was all it took to disguise me. That, and Jane cutting my hair."

My eyes were drawn to her short, curly mop of mahogany hair, and I wondered what she looked like with it long and loose down her back.

"The rest you know." Elizabeth shrugged, clearly uncomfortable but trying to hide it.

Hurt and anger surged through me. It was unreasonable, perhaps, but I could not help it. I trusted Elias—Elizabeth—with my secrets, with the lives of my sister and friends. I felt a kinship I had never felt with anyone before, not even Bingley, who was like a brother. Realizing she did not feel the same, did not trust me with even the basic fact of her sex, pained me.

I knew it was not logical. After all, we only met yesterday. Did she see me as the same as those men from her home—as a threat—or as someone who would think less of her because she was female? Would she have ever come to trust me enough to tell me on her own? I would likely never know the answer to the latter question.

Good God, Elias Bennet was a woman! My mind just kept circling back to the confounding thought. The girl led me into a brothel, for goodness sake! But she was red as a cherry the entire time we were there, I remembered. My first instinct was to make her stay, to ensure she did not get into more trouble than she already had, but . . . I was forced to admit I would not have made it this far without her. I would still be walking to San Francisco, and Bingley would still be lying out in the elements instead of tucked away in bed with a healer preparing to remove the bullet from his leg. I would have no idea where to start looking for Georgiana.

Georgiana. I could not save her alone.

Elizabeth seemed to read my mind. "It is not your decision whether I stay or go. You are not my brother, my father, or my husband. I am not yours to protect."

But it felt like she was. I felt protective even when I thought she was a man. Despite her claim of it not being my decision, everyone was looking to me as though it was . . . Jane, begging with her eyes; Hurst, bemused but ready to back me up; Louisa, horrified and confused; and Mrs. Young . . . well, Mrs. Young's opinion did not matter.

A large part of me wanted to leave her behind; however . . . I did not feel this need when I thought she was a man. It was not as if she changed, merely my perception of her. She was completely unlike any other woman I knew. In Boston, if a woman behaved as she did, she would be ruined, but I could not bring myself to condemn her. Her loyalty to her family was humbling; her courage, staggering.

"Does your knowing I am a woman make me somehow less capable than I was before?" She clearly took my hesitation to mean I was searching for the right words to turn her away. "Say something, goddamn you!"

"Lizzy!" Jane gasped.

"Daylight is wasting. We need to go now or we will not make it before dark."

The room exploded in uproar, but I paid no attention . . . my eyes fixed on Elizabeth, and hers on mine. I watched them brighten with relief, then darken in confusion. She was not expecting my answer. Well, that made two of us.

"You have not said a word since we left Velvet."

I briefly closed my eyes. "What is there to say?"

"You are angry with me."

"No." It was true, I was no longer angry. I simply preferred to think things over in silence. Usually, I am a methodical person, never prone to rash decisions, choosing careful planning over spontaneous action. The

West wreaked havoc on all my plans, though, demanding quick reactions and changes to my life and view of the world I was not sure I was ready to make. With every step we took up the hill, I wondered if I should have made her stay behind.

"I do not believe you."

Reining in Collie, I stopped in front of her, forcing her to halt and look me in the eye. "I am not angry at you. Surprised by you? Yes. Confused? Certainly. Awed by your bravery? Absolutely. Disappointed you did not trust me? Most assuredly. Angry? No. Today has been entirely out of the realm of my experience, so forgive me if I need a little time to adjust."

Relief and regret warred in her fine, brown eyes. "I am sorry I did not tell you."

"Disguise of every sort is my abhorrence." It always had been, from when I was a young boy. Lies make my skin prickle with discomfort, and on the rare occasions when I told an untruth, I was compelled to admit it almost immediately. My abhorrence only grew when I studied law and became an attorney. Every day I waded through lie after lie from witnesses, clients, even the police at times. I took great satisfaction in picking them apart and revealing the truth. Elizabeth's lie was huge, yet I was completely blind to it. Oh, I knew she was hiding something, but I never suspected the truth because I trusted Bennet from nearly the first moment we met.

Her face fell.

"I abhor lies, but yours did not harm anyone and was never intended to. It was your shield, and I am glad you used it because otherwise you might not have made it here, and we would never have met." I leaned forward, holding out my hand. "Will Darcy, pleased to make your acquaintance."

She stared at my hand, and a slow smile spread across her face like a sunrise lighting up the dark. She reached out and took it, her small hand rough and calloused and *right* in mine. "Lizzy Bennet, at your service."

We left the horses tied up in the woods a short distance from the ghost town. We would walk the rest of the way on foot. Lizzy looked around until she found two short, stout sticks.

"What are those for?" I asked.

"He will have set a watch. We will need to knock him out quietly." She raised an eyebrow. "Unless you would prefer to use my knife, but that seems more bloodthirsty than necessary."

I took one of the sticks without further comment.

We avoided the road as we traveled the rest of the way up the hill. Nearing the buildings, we heard voices in the distance. It sounded like the outlaws were preparing for dinner.

"This is probably a good time to find your sister," Lizzy whispered. "I do not think Wickham would allow her out with the men."

"What about Lydia?" I asked.

"She is probably the one cooking," Lizzy answered with a frown.

Creeping through the trees, we got our first glimpse of the buildings. Stark, weathered plank houses lined a dirt street. Most were in terrible disrepair. Any glass windows were gone, likely removed by the miners before they left. I could see overgrown herb gardens and rosebushes, left untended for years, their sprawling vines dotted with late blooms. A couple of buildings were recently patched up, with fresh boards over the windows and any holes in the roof.

Two men, talking and gesticulating with their hands, entered the smallest of the repaired buildings. I recognized one of them as the man who shot at my feet when I tried to chase them. They were close enough now I could scent the aromas of cooking and freshly baked bread through the open door. I remembered what Mrs. Young said about Wickham taking over the largest house. He would keep Georgie close, so she was probably there.

The biggest house I could see was a few buildings down. It seemed more professionally made than the others, with a railed porch and faded blue shutters on the windows. It probably belonged to the mine's foreman. "I think Georgie is likely in there," I murmured, pointing it out to Lizzy. My belief was supported by the presence of a short, red-headed man sitting on the porch smoking a cigar, with a rifle across his lap. He seemed to be the only guard. "There may be a back entrance."

Moving as silently as we could, we followed the tree line until we stood directly behind the house. There was a door, but it was boarded up, just like the windows. We exchanged a quick glance.

"We will have to get past the guard," Lizzy whispered.

"We cannot get behind him while he is on the porch, and if he spots us he will sound the alarm."

Lizzy grinned. "Then we had best get him off the porch."

This was a terrible, terrible idea. I waited, pressed against the wall, my heart pounding so loudly I was sure the guard would hear it, a stick clutched tightly in my sweaty hands.

"Ready?" Lizzy mouthed.

I nodded, ready as I would ever be.

"Help!" Lizzy cried softly, her voice pitched higher than usual to imitate her sister. I prayed no one but our intended target would hear. "Oh glory, it's a rattlesnake! I can't move! Please, somebody help me!"

I heard a low curse and the creaking of wood as the guard stood. His spurs clinked as he stomped across the porch.

"Help! Oh God, it's going to strike!"

The footsteps came closer, the man rounded the corner and—thunk!

The force of the blow vibrated through my arms, and the guard slumped to the ground with a satisfactory thud.

Lizzy beamed. "I told you it would work," she whispered as she knelt and stripped off his coat and hat, and then tied him up with a length of rope fetched from her saddlebags for just this purpose. I was beginning to believe she kept an entire wagon train's worth of supplies in there. She searched his pockets and boots, where she found a large knife and a handgun. She passed them to me. "You may need these."

I pulled on the man's coat and hat and helped Lizzy drag his bound and helpless form into the woods, where hopefully it would not be found for a good, long while. "I need you to do something for me," I said, bracing for her argument.

"Anything."

"When we get Georgie, I need you to take her down to Velvet right away. I will stay and get Lydia."

"No way am I leaving you alone up here!" She glared at me. "We are partners. I am not going to run off to safety and leave you to get in trouble by yourself. Besides, Lydia does not know you. What makes you think she will listen to anything you say?"

"I will convince her. Please, Elizabeth. I swear to you I will not leave this place without your sister, but there is a good chance I will stir up the whole camp doing it, and I need Georgiana to be far away when it happens." I would also prefer Lizzy to be far away, but I was not going to say so out loud. "I trust you to get her away safely. Please trust me to do the same with Lydia."

Lizzy grabbed my hands. "I do trust you, but don't you see? It is not just my sister I wish to see safe. I also care about you! I would not be able to forgive myself if you were hurt because I was not here watching your back. We need to stay together."

I kissed her. I did not plan to. The desire to claim her, to hold her in my arms, to protect her, was one which had been growing since . . . I know not when. My hands cupped her face, fingers tipping her hat off and tangling in her curls.

She responded eagerly, exploring without hesitation. She tasted of molasses and cinnamon bark, innocence and enthusiasm. Her arms wrapped around me, pulling me closer as if we could meld into a single person. Feeling her lithe form, every delicate, barely concealed curve of it, I wondered how I ever thought such a breathtaking creature could be a man.

We broke apart slowly, reluctantly, our breath mingling in the twilight air. I felt cold at the loss of her warmth.

"If that was an attempt to convince me to leave, you chose entirely the wrong argument." A smile played on her rosy, well-kissed lips.

"No, I kissed you because you are the most extraordinary person I have ever met, and if I did not, I would regret it for the rest of my days. Take Georgie to Velvet, then come back. I will watch the camp, but I will not make a move until you return unless I think your sister is in danger."

Lizzy eyed me with suspicion, but nodded. "Very well."

"Good, then we are agreed," I said, my skin prickling at the lie, just as it did when I was a boy.

With the guard's hat tugged low, I approached the house once again, this time aiming for the front door. I did not see anyone about, so hopefully they were all still eating, but I tried to walk as if I belonged. Climbing the porch, I checked the street one last time before unbarring the front door and stepping inside. "Hello?" I called softly into the dimly lit room.

"Who is there?" It was Georgiana's voice, high and frightened. Thank God she was alive! She probably thought I was Wickham.

"It is me, Georgie. It is Will! I have come to get you out of here!"

"Will!" She shrieked and leapt out of her hiding place and into my arms. "I was so scared."

"So was I, Georgie. So was I. Hush, love," I whispered, squeezing her in a fierce embrace. She was here and whole in my arms. "Are you hurt? Did any of them touch you?"

"No, George kept them away from me. He told me no one would hurt me, but Henry . . . Henry looked like he wanted to. I was so scared, Will." She was shaking like a leaf.

"Which one is Henry?"

"The one who shot at you . . . the one who shot Charles. He has cruel eyes. He and George fought after they brought me here. He thought they should have left you a horse. George said you walking would be fast enough and give them more time to arrange the exchange."

I frowned, puzzled. I thought Wickham shot Bingley, but I suppose there was no way for Bingley to tell while their faces were still covered in bandanas. Had I misjudged Wickham? Had he not fallen quite as far as I thought? I pushed the question aside for later. "You must do precisely as I tell you. We must be absolutely silent if we are to escape without sounding the alarm. Come with me." Holding her hand, I led her to the door. I stepped out first, making sure no one was in sight. "To the woods, hurry!" I sent her ahead as I closed the door and reset the bar. With any luck, no one would think to check if they thought it was still secure. I followed quickly after Georgie, keeping my body between her and the town.

We made it into the woods, where Lizzy waited anxiously. "Thank the Lord! My hair has gone gray waiting for you to return."

"Georgiana, meet Elizabeth Bennet. Lizzy, meet Georgie." I ignored Georgiana's consternation at being faced with what appeared to be a man with a woman's name. "Georgie, I need you to go with Lizzy. She will take you to a safe place."

"What about you? Why are you not coming with us?" Georgie was on the verge of panic, clinging to my arm.

"Lizzy will tell you on the way." I gently disentangled her. "There is someone else here we need to find, and I cannot do it unless I know you are safe." My eyes met Lizzy's. "Keep her safe."

"You have my word," Lizzie vowed. "Come, we do not have much time." She pulled Georgie away, looking back at me to say, "If you get yourself hurt, whatever they do to you will be nothing compared to what *I* will do." With those parting words, the two women who now meant the most to me disappeared into the deepening shadows.

When had Lizzy Bennet become so important to me? How? There was no sudden realization; it was simply there, as if it always had been. My feelings would not be repressed. My mind mocked the absurdity as I had learned she was a woman merely hours ago, for goodness sake! Yet I could not deny it . . . had no wish to deny it.

Which is why I sent her away.

It was inevitable Wickham would discover his hostage missing before dawn, and he would know the only place near enough for her to go was Velvet. The gang would descend upon the outpost, and we would be in even worse trouble.

Getting a clear picture of the crumbling buildings was my first step. I circled it, sticking to the trees. I noted where the horses were stabled, where the well was located, and the outhouse. I slipped out of hiding once, to filch more rope.

Soon enough, the gang finished with dinner and came out onto the street, scattering. No one seemed to notice the missing guard, which told me this was not an organized outfit. My guess was Wickham, being a survivor by nature, managed to surround himself with stronger men with limited enough intellect for him to manipulate. A precarious situation, but one Wickham was cocky enough to think he could handle.

Finally, the man himself stepped out, leaned against the doorway, and lit up a cigar. He puffed at it, staring out at nothing, doubtless contemplating how he would spend his share of the ransom money. Or perhaps, a part of me who remembered laughter and long games of hide and seek wondered, he felt a small sense of regret for his crimes.

A young woman emerged, a pail in her hand. She looked close in age to Georgie; her hair was the same as Lizzy's. This must be Lydia. She headed for the well, so I headed to intercept her. I waited, crouched by a wheelbarrow, as she drew near. Once she was close enough, I could see how tired she looked, how patched and stained her once-white apron was. I could also see the gentle curve of her rounded belly. Lizzy was not going to be pleased by this development.

"Do not turn around. Your sisters sent me to find you," I called to her, pitching my voice low so it would not carry. "My name is Will Darcy." This was a risk. She could shout an alarm and have the whole gang on me in seconds if she so chose.

She did not, though; she just went dead still. Living with outlaws in the woods, frequently on the run, doing their cooking and cleaning for them—this life likely held little resemblance to the one she imagined for herself when she left with Wickham.

"Do you wish to leave here? Return to your sisters? They want to take you with them to San Francisco." From what little I knew of her, I thought the city would probably hold appeal.

"They want me to leave my husband?" Her murmur was barely audible.

So, he married her after all. "I think you have learned by now he is not who you thought he was. He lied to you, as he has lied to many others. Your sisters are not angry with you for leaving, they just want you safe. You know you—and your baby—are not safe here."

She hesitated, a hand to her belly, then nodded. "I want to go home." She sounded so damn young; I wanted to kill Wickham for doing this to a girl barely more than a child.

"Okay, I need you to listen closely, Lydia. Do you know where Velvet is?"

She nodded again.

"Good. Stay in the woods until you are clear of the buildings, then follow the trail until you reach a large, pointed rock. You will find Collie tied to a tree behind the rock. Do you remember Collie?"

Another nod.

"Wonderful. Take him and ride to the boarding house in Velvet. Your sisters are there. Understand?"

"Yes."

A shout went up. They knew Georgiana was gone!

"Go! Go now!" She dropped the pail and ran, not once looking back.

"Spread out! Search everywhere!" I heard Wickham shout. Dusk was fully upon us now, allowing me greater freedom of movement, but I did not have much time. Already, they were lighting lamps and torches for their search. I made my way to the stables, where I surprised another bandit with a sharp knock of my stick. Acting quickly, I confiscated his weapon and bound him, hoping the hasty knots would hold. Then I began to free the horses, slapping them on the rump to send them fleeing into the woods.

"The horses! Someone's stealing the horses!"

A bullet screamed past my ear, aiding me by terrifying the animals even more, scattering them further into the night. If I accomplished nothing else, I gained my loved ones the time it would take the gang to walk down the hill on foot. I thought about taking one of the horses and escaping myself, but I feared Lydia would not be far enough away yet.

Using the stables as cover, I slipped back into the woods.

"Where did he go?"

"Where's Zeke and John?"

"Darcy!" Ah, it seemed Wickham at least knew who was to blame.

"I know you are listening! Come out and face me!"

"This does not need to end badly," I yelled, knowing bargaining was a long shot but trying anyway. "If you swear to take the ransom and go far away, I will give it to you."

"He's lying!" One of the bandits fired blindly in my direction, missing by thirty feet.

"With ten thousand dollars, you can start a new life . . . all of you!" I continued, and then moved rapidly to a new tree. Staying in one place would only allow them to narrow down my location. Another bullet whizzed past, splintering wood.

"Wait! Stop shooting!" Wickham cried.

"Are you crazy? He's seen our camp. He has to die! Forget about the ransom. No man is mad enough to pay up without a hostage!" More shots.

"I know this man. He keeps his word," Wickham argued. "He is the most idiotically honorable man I know."

I dashed through the trees. While they argued, a plan began to take shape.

"I'm done listening to you, George. If we'd done what I said, this guy would be in Frisco by now, collecting our money. Now, even if he did get the goods, he'll deliver it with a full posse at his side to round us up before we can spend it!"

I knelt beside the bound guard. He was awake now and glaring over the gag in his mouth.

Wickham and Henry were still arguing, but where was the third?

"Hey, I caught 'im! Found 'im at the well!"

I stilled. The third man?

Wickham exclaimed. "Who the hell are you?" No, no, no. It was not her. It could not be her.

"Darcy, we have your little friend! What is your name, boy?" Henry's voice, followed by a thud. "I said, what's your name, boy?"

"Elias." Her voice was hoarse, pained. He had struck her. That bastard struck my Lizzy. How did she come back so fast? What had she done with Georgiana?

"We have Elias, Darcy, whoever the hell he is. How much is his life worth to you?"

Everything.

"Do not . . ." Lizzy stopped short with a groan. My fists clenched with rage. I pulled out the knife Lizzy gave me and cut the rope binding the man's feet, then pulled him up. I put the blade away and drew the revolver, pushing it against my prisoner's back. "Zeke or John or whatever your name is, do what I say or you die," I whispered.

The outlaw nodded vigorously.

"Come out, Darcy! Here is a new trade. You for Elias. He can get Georgiana out from wherever you have stashed her, and they can ransom you!" Wickham laughed, triumphant now things were swinging his way again.

"No!" Lizzy yelled, then cried out in pain.

"Stop hurting him! I am coming out!" Shoving the guard in front of me, I stepped into the street which was now aglow with moonlight.

Wickham stood fifty feet away, rubbing his hands together in satisfaction. Beside him stood Henry, holding Lizzy by the throat. Behind them stood a skinny, nervous man . . . the one who went through Georgie's underthings, I realized.

"Here I am, Wickham. It seems we are at an impasse. I have your man; you have mine. What are we to do?" I kept my voice steady, feigning calm I could not feel when I could see blood on Lizzy's lip, a bruise swelling up her eye.

"'E's got my brother!" cried the skinny bandit.

"Yes, I can see that, Frank," said Wickham, gritting his teeth.

Lizzy glared at me. "You were supposed to wait for me, not go and get yourself shot at. I thought for a moment they killed you."

Here she was, held prisoner by a man twice her size, and she had the audacity to scold me! I almost smiled. "I did not want you hurt. You see, I have decided you are mine to protect." He looked at Wickham. "Here is the deal. You let Elias go. I will remain in his stead. In two days' time, my friends will return with the ransom. Do we have a bargain?"

Wickham opened his mouth but Henry cut him off. "He'll bring an army of lawmen down on us! He's seen our place, seen our faces. We can't deal with him—neither of them!" Henry turned his pistol toward me. "I'm sorry, John. I'll try my best not to hit you, but I can't let him go."

"No!" Wickham objected. "We need the money!"

Henry sneered at him. "You came to our group with your fancy plans and clever words, but what have they brought us? Our horses are scattered to the four winds, folks know our hiding place, and nothing but a few dollars and trinkets to show for it! And all the while, you get the nicest house, the pretty little wife you won't share, and the pretty little hostage we can't touch. Well, I'm sick of it!"

"Now, Henry, I am telling you, with this money you can—"

Henry shot Wickham, straight in the gut. The sudden sound echoed through the camp like rolling thunder. Wickham looked down, an expression of surprise turning to resignation as he fell backwards.

"Henry, ye can't . . . " Frank sputtered. "Ye just . . . Why did ye . . . ?"

"Because I never liked the bastard. Always lording it over us like he was better, like he was so special. He was an outlaw, same as us. I'm in charge now, and I say we kill these two, dump them in the mine, track down the little ladies, and sell them to the highest bidder. Guaran-damn-teed money, and no lawmen on our trail." He pointed the pistol at me once more.

"No!" Lizzy, who was frozen in shock after the gunshot, went wild in his arms, kicking and biting, slamming her head back against his chest.

His shot went wild, and with a vicious curse, he slammed the smoking barrel against her head. She crumpled to the ground in a limp heap. "Damn, little devil," he muttered, then realized too late he just dropped his shield. His pistol came up, but I was already firing.

I fired once, twice, three times. The first missed by several feet, the second winged Henry's shoulder, throwing off his shot, and the third struck his throat. It was a hideous death but quick.

I turned to Frank. "Drop your weapon." He did. "Now tie your brother's feet." He complied, despite John's angry grumbles. As soon as he finished, I knocked Frank out with one swift blow, binding him hastily, my hands shaking. I rushed to Lizzy's side, wincing at the dark mark on her temple, a combination of bruise and burn. "Lizzy!"

A long, breathless moment later, her eyelids fluttered and opened wide. "Will! Did we make it?" She frowned, touching her head carefully. "I do not think my head would hurt so much if I was dead, so I think we made it."

"Yes, love, we made it." I laughed and pulled her close. "I do not know how it happened, how any of this happened, but you have become quite dear to me. I do not know what I would have done had you been seriously harmed."

Smiling, she traced my lips with her finger. "Careful, you might really convince me I have truly gone to Heaven."

"Lizzy? Lizzy Bennet, is it you?" Wickham's pained whisper interrupted us.

Much to my disappointment, Lizzy scrambled out of my lap. "Wickham? I thought you were dead."

"I think I am . . . or almost, at least. It is you, isn't it? I did not recognize you in that getup. And your hair!" He paused. "On second thought, I like the hair." His voice was paper thin, his blood pumping into the dirt with every beat of his heart, and still he was an incorrigible flirt.

I looked down at my former friend and felt nothing but pity. "You did not kill the driver or the shotgun rider, did you?" When it came down to it, I did not think Wickham would have been able to kill me. It simply was not in him.

"No. Only wanted the money . . . and to make you sweat a little." He coughed. "I just wanted what you owed me."

Lizzy looked up from examining his wound and shook her head.

"I owed you nothing, George. Your choices were your own."

Wickham laughed, gasping for breath. "Perhaps it was good you came when you did. I did not like the way Henry was looking at Georgie. I never would have hurt her; you have to tell her. Please . . ."

It was the closest Wickham would come to an apology, and I would take it for what it was. "I will tell her."

"You and Lizzy Bennet, hmm? Never in a thousand years—"

"Did you really marry Lydia? Legally?" Lizzy asked.

"Yes, for the babe. I wanted my kid to have my name. Put it down to an unexpected remnant of conscience."

"Damn it, George, why? Why did you do this?"

"What else was there? I had nothing. You had everything."

We stayed with him until he took his last breath, then carried his body and Henry's into Wickham's house. "We can return and bury them in the morning," Lizzy murmured.

I nodded, wondering if everything would sink in by then. I killed a man—and did not regret it. I watched a man die and only regretted the waste of potential, only grieved the man Wickham could have been. None of it felt real. Then Lizzy took my hand in a grip so tight my bones ground together. That was real. She was real, which meant the rest of it was too.

We locked the gang in a shed, grumbling behind their gags. No doubt someone in Velvet would be willing to take them to San Jose and collect the bounty on their heads.

I was surprised to see Collie waiting for us in the trees. "I sent Lydia with Collie."

"I met her on the way back up after I found your sister a hiding place. When I explained to Georgiana what was going on, she threatened to leap right off the horse! To be perfectly honest, I did not need much persuading. When I saw Lydia, I knew you had done something foolish, so we switched horses and I sent her to Georgiana. Then I came the rest of the way at a dead run."

"You could have been killed!" I pulled myself up behind her, relishing the sensation of her in my arms, the knowledge she was alive despite the terrible risks she took.

"You could have gotten yourself shot!" she retorted.

"I suppose we are well-suited, then."

She melted against me. "I guess we are."

SAN FRANCISCO, 1861

"Your young man is here to take you riding," Mrs. Gardiner announced when Lizzy entered her aunt's parlor. I smiled, drinking in the sight of her as if I had not seen her in months rather than a mere two days.

It turned out the Gardiners did quite well for themselves since Lizzy's last visit. They owned a fine, new house in a respectable area, if not a fashionable one, and were delighted to take in their nieces. If they were also delighted one of them planned to marry and leave after only a few short months, they did not say as much. Bingley was not on his feet a full day before he came to call on Jane, and they planned to marry on the first of February.

Lydia was also doing quite well. She reinvented her past, portraying her late husband as a heroic army officer who perished in performance of his duties. The story grew more tragic and dramatic with every telling, making her a great favorite amongst the other young ladies her age. Her child was due in seven weeks, and already she crooned and murmured to the babe with surprising sweetness. She may not turn out to be the most conventional of mothers, but she would be an undeniably loving one.

I led Lizzy outside where Collie and my new horse, a black gelding named Augustine—because someone needed to appear dignified—waited, already saddled.

"Where are we going?" Lizzy asked as she arranged her split skirts. The irritation she displayed as she dealt with the heavy fabric made me smile. My lady had become accustomed to the freedom of men's clothing and was not happy returning to female fashions.

"If I told you, it would not be a surprise."

We rode out of the city, heading south until cobblestones gave way to dirt roads, then dirt roads gave way to green, rolling hills. We continued for nearly an hour, not following any path but the one in my mind. "Here we are," I said at last, dismounting and assisting her down.

Lizzy looked about, curious. "And where is here?" We stood in a wide valley between gentle slopes dotted with trees. The scent of the ocean filled the air, but it was just out of sight, the valley sheltered from the fierce Pacific winds.

"Imagine a house, right there"—I pointed—"with stables, just over there."

She stared at me, eyes wide. "This is yours?"

"I was thinking perhaps it could be ours—convenient to the city for my work, yet far enough away for you to keep horses—if you like it." I took her hand. It was not as rough as when I first met her but still strong and capable.

Her breath hitched as I caressed the top of her hand with my thumb. "What are you saying, Will?"

I knelt. "I am saying I love you, Elizabeth Bennet. From the first moment of my acquaintance with you, I was impressed by your courage, your wit, and your selfless concern for the safety of others, even when it placed you in considerable peril. Since then, my feelings for you have only grown, from admiration to the most ardent affection. I had not known you a month before I felt that you were the only woman in the world whom I could ever marry. I would be honored if you would consent to being my wife."

I nearly fell backwards when she threw herself into my arms. "Yes," she whispered into my ear. "I love you, Will, so much I can scarcely bear it. I never dreamed anyone could be as happy as I am now." Her breath was warm against my neck as we sat on the damp earth, simply holding each other close. I could have stayed there forever, but after a time she pulled back, smiling at me through tears.

I produced a handkerchief and gently wiped them away. "You have not yet told me what you think of this valley."

Looking it over, her brow furrowed in thought. She studied every detail until I convinced myself she hated it. "I think a place this beautiful ought to have a name," she said at last.

I laughed, relieved, as I drew her to her feet. "So long as you do not name it something so ignoble as *Collie.*"

I kissed her, a pleasure I felt compelled to enjoy with the greatest frequency possible.

Laughing, she looked up at me, and the sight of her took my breath away. "I cannot imagine a place more beautifully situated. No matter what it is called, it will be home." I will always remember her in that moment . . . her curls peeking out under her new hat, ruffled by the wind . . . the cinnamon freckles on her sun-kissed face . . . an expression of heartfelt delight shining from eyes I could gaze into forever. Never had I felt like I had come home.

"Pemberley," I said. The name felt right.

"Pemberley? What is Pemberley?"

"It is the place my family came from, before they sailed to America."

"Why do you think it is a good name for our valley?"

I tried to think of a way to put my thoughts into words without sounding like a besotted fool, and failed. "They traveled a fair distance—just as we have—to unfamiliar lands. They could do this because they knew home was not a place but people . . . the people you love. This"—I waved a hand at the valley—"is just a place. We could travel anywhere, live any place, and so long as you are by my side, I am home."

NATALIE RICHARDS is a writer, blogger, and singer. She started her book review blog, Songs & Stories, in late 2010 after falling in love with Jane Austen fanfiction. Her writing can also be found on Figment, the Darcy & Lizzy Forum, TeenInk Magazine, and in the Austenesque anthologies *Sun-kissed: Effusions of Summer* and *Then Comes Winter*. She resides with her family in the Oregon countryside and currently works as a waitress and babysitter.

"By you, I was properly humbled. I came to you without a doubt of my reception. You showed me how insufficient were all my pretensions to please a woman worthy of being pleased."

—Mr. Darcy to Miss Elizabeth, Chapter LVIII.

DARCY STRIKES OUT

SOPHIA ROSE

And it's one, two, three strikes you're out at the old ball game."

The organist played the final fanfare, and the dreaded song was over. Seattle fans, probably feeling all kinds of goodwill, were busy assuming their seats. Darcy loved the song as a youngster. It was part of baseball tradition. Lately, it left a sour taste in his mouth and drew his thoughts back to an evening in July when a beautiful woman scornfully ticked off her long, graceful fingers—the same fingers he had dreamt of holding in his own—the three strikes she held against him. Her words dug deep—especially since one of those strikes might have some merit. However, the others were particularly harsh because they were false. Hearing the woman who he thought far outshone all others, who he thought bright and witty, and who he thought understood him, mistake his character . . . yeah, that still hurt. People got him wrong all the time, but Darcy imagined the exceptional and lovely Liz Bennet to be different. Nearly three months later and he was still not over her spectacular rejection.

Several thrilling minutes after the seventh inning stretch, the game was now tied 3-3 in the ninth, as Darcy took his place in the warm-up circle. His best friend, Richie Fitzwilliam, current batter and most powerful hitter on the New York Lancers ball club readied for his first pitch. Darcy stretched, pulling his arms up and back behind him, as he analyzed the pitcher he was to face; that is, if Fitzwilliam got on base safely. Cummins was a decent relief pitcher and had a hundred-mile-an-hour-fastball in his arsenal. Darcy had batted against the young rookie before during the regular season, but this was October, and the Lancers were in the play-offs.

Fitzwilliam got a piece of the ball and it fouled back toward Darcy, causing him to duck away. Fitzwilliam smirked at Darcy's ungainly movements trying to avoid the ball. Darcy drilled him with a "glad I could amuse you" glare and Fitzwilliam grinned even wider as his eyes took in the dirt and grass stains on Darcy's jersey and pants.

Earlier in the game, a routine fly ball was hit in his direction. *Usually* Darcy could be counted on to catch it. Instead, he was distracted and was forced to dive to make the catch. With the exception of his rookie year, he had never been this unfocused. For the first time, Darcy had struck out with a woman—and reminders still creeped in at the most inconvenient moments. Involuntarily, his thoughts drifted again to that evening three months ago.

The luxurious hotel restaurant was bustling with people enjoying some downtime after the final events of the Major League Baseball All-Star game in San Diego and before they needed to get on planes to head home.

Darcy smoothed down his tie and checked the wall mirror nearby. He knew his tall, athletic frame looked good in his tailored suit, and he ran his hand through his dark, wavy hair. A serious face and piercing blue eyes met his gaze. Darcy tried to temper his expression. He had heard often enough from others that he could be intimidating. And that was not what he wanted tonight. Friendly. Confident. Desirable. A guy with good game. He wanted to impress this gorgeous, talented woman—a dream woman worth pleasing.

Deep breath. Stepping inside the restaurant, he looked for a certain familiar figure. Ah! There she was—near the bar at a tall table by herself. She had shed her professional look for something softer, sexier. Her curly brown hair was released from her usual messy bun, and she was dressed in a blue summer dress. Her long, graceful neck was bent over her tablet, as she seemed to ignore the room around her.

Darcy had little doubt of his success with Liz Bennet. Over several encounters, she had teased and debated with him, resulting in a flattering profile piece for the sports page of the NYC Courier. During their most recent interview, he had even flirted, making her blush from her ears to the rise of her chest.

Unlike some, Liz respected the game and was a professional. She accurately analyzed teams and players while bringing an interesting story to her readers. No wild speculation for shock value, just good journalism. He respected and liked her, and it seemed from the moment he met her, she was all he thought about off the field.

She noticed his approach and raised a questioning brow to him.

"May I join you?"

Liz swept her hand in silent invitation to the open chair at her table.

A cocktail waitress arrived with a menu. He ordered a glass of wine and looked to her.

"No, I'm good. Thanks." She stared at him, waiting.

"Uh, this is nice"—he gestured at the room around them. "You look nice, too. I don't think I've ever seen you out of a suit."

Liz sipped her wine. "Thanks."

He had discomfited her and thought that was cute—and he told her so. Before he could ask her out on a real date, a middle-aged couple stopped by the table and asked for an autograph. "Sure," he had said automatically, as the woman scrambled for a pen and anything to write on. With no little impatience, he scribbled his initials on the napkin and handed it back to the woman. Once again alone, he leaned back, studying the beautiful woman before him.

She was sophisticated and likely accustomed to controlling the conversation in her interviews. Darcy speculated she would welcome the chance to know him off the field. After all, during an earlier interview, when he had remarked that some of her questions were too private, she said, "I'm merely trying to make out who you are, Darcy. I hear such contradictions about you." Yet that had made him nervous enough not to have a witty reply.

But on this occasion, she crossed her arms over her bosom and sat back, listening to him explain his reservations about dating a sports reporter, followed by his efforts to determine that she was more than the usual grubbing type out for a sensational story. Then, he jokingly added, "You know we would be good together."

She huffed out a breath that moved the loose wisps of hair on her forehead and mouthed, "Wow."

Her fine eyes never wavered from his nor did she raise her voice, and yet Liz shredded his heart, leaving his ego on the floor in tatters. She made it abundantly clear: one, she could not stand him for supposedly ruining ex-fellow teammate Wickham's ball career; two, breaking up her sister and his old college roommate; and three, being a pretentious prat who had a disgusting way of managing his celebrity. Those in the industry described her as articulate, sharp, and one of this generation's most promising journalistic wordsmiths. Her words rang through his mind. "Your arrogance and conceit are monumentally egotistical. You are the last guy on the planet with whom I would ever—ever—go out with." Darcy couldn't argue that assessment. He was too dumbstruck with rising fury and a stab of disappointment to do more than watch her stand up and walk away.

The crack of bat made him snap out of his memories and back to the game. Fitzwilliam had a full count as he fouled off yet another one. The Seattle fans were getting loud. The stadium gasped as one when the big guy wearing #17 launched the ball out to right field. Fitzwilliam jogged down to first—but the fly ball hooked foul. The home team crowd sighed with relief, and then cheered madly. Fitzwilliam shrugged, unruffled by his near miss, and trotted back to the plate grinning.

They had played together for four years now and Darcy was grateful for their friendship. Fitzwilliam had been the one to give Darcy the boot up the butt after his cataclysmic fail with Liz. "Stick to baseball, bud." And Darcy had stood by Fitzwilliam when he lost his mother to cancer, and later when he lost his cheating girlfriend, who traded him for a billion-dollar software company owner. Fitz had been there through the whole nightmare involving Wickham and Darcy's little sister, Georgie too.

He also knew Darcy's reasons for the fracture between Liz's sister and Charley Bingley. For that bit of stupidity, Fitz sided with Liz. "Since when is that your business, Darce? Bingley should have told you to kiss off. Not your job to screen the guy's women. That's what lawyers and pre-nups are for."

Fitzwilliam settled back in the batter's box and narrowed his eyes on Cummins, the lazy movement of his bat looking like the twitching of a tiger's tail. Sure enough, there was a solid crack of bat on ball, and a beautiful line drive sizzled toward the gap between the center and right fielders. The ball was retrieved as Fitzwilliam rounded first base and dug for second. Darcy and his whole Lancers' team were on their feet as Fitzwilliam slid into second base.

"Safe." The umpire swept his hands out dramatically and Fitzwilliam fist pumped toward the bench, bringing the Lancers' dugout to a fever pitch.

Darcy took one more swing in the practice circle before for his turn at the plate. He heard, "Now batting, number five, left fielder, Will Darcy," and the dull roar of the stands as they booed him while the stadium screens all flashed, "Make some noise."

"Make some noise, indeed," he muttered.

His jaw tight set and his shoulders back, he strode to the plate. He lived for moments like this—everything on the line and the chance to be the game changer. Adrenaline coursed through him—he was cool and ready. This was not conceit. This was his love of the game and these intense moments.

He gripped his bat as he dug his cleat into the dirt, getting comfortable in the box. Williams, the catcher, made a snide remark. "Offend any more journalists, Dandy?"

Bite me!

The catcher brayed as if reading Darcy's mind.

Darcy was resigned to the nickname acquired in his rookie year. He had shared a Sports Illustrated photo shoot with his dad, wearing a top hat and tails, standing back to back while holding their bats down like canes. Truthfully, Darcy loved the article, featuring his dad, a retired Hall of Famer. Darcy knew he had made his father proud by following in his footsteps. When his dad died later that same year, the photo became especially poignant. His teammates loved to razz him about his good looks, fastidiousness over his uniform and equipment, and his regimented workouts—the picture had only fueled their imagination and generated the nickname. It was good-natured teasing for the most part because he was known for being a team player and putting in a hundred and ten percent effort.

After the death of his father, he had withdrawn from all but the game for a while. He had been shy and struggled with the media side of his career, further building on his cocky, unapproachable status. His little sister, Georgie, now in his care, took over his social media accounts and helped dispel his aloof reputation—at least with the home crowd.

"You're not stuffy, but everyone thinks you are. I need to take you by the hand, I can tell." She had been dead serious, which made him smile.

He should have taken her seriously. Georgie had used the picture from the SI photo shoot as the header and a top hat as his avatar for his social media accounts. He was shocked when the top hats started appearing in the stands as the fans embraced his nickname, even tweeting and messaging in Old English speech with hashtag *DandyDarcy*. When a bunch of fans lined up in left field dressed like the Planter's Peanut mascot calling themselves "Darcy's Dandies," he posed for a picture with them that trended on social media for some time.

Twenty minutes later, Darcy was reveling in hitting a triple for the win before jogging toward the clubhouse. A TV sideline reporter called him over. He kept the grimace off his face and tried to show polite interest. One of Liz's accusations was how he behaved selfishly toward others, particularly those in the media. Of course, she could not know why he was reserved with the newshounds and media people, but it was no excuse. He had not liked the way she painted his character.

I'm trying to be a better man, Liz. Are you watching?

The club house buzzed with energy. Graham Foster earned the game MVP for his powerful pitching performance, but plenty of guys were declaring him, Carreaga, and Fitzwilliam heroes too. Coaches were happy, which was always good, since DeBourgh on a terror could get ugly. He showered and checked his phone. Georgie had texted her congratulations as did Charley, and—*gah!*—Charley's sister. Caro sent him hearts, hugs, and kiss emojis.

Would that woman give up already?

Talk about stalker fans. She *actually* wore a top hat and tuxedo jacket with a black mini skirt to Darcy's birthday party. Darcy had told her. Charley had told her. Heck, Georgie had told her: "My brother isn't interested." But Caro continued to believe what she wanted. Even Liz had thought he was seeing that woman when she asserted his "girlfriend might object" to him asking another woman out. He had quickly set Liz straight.

He called Georgie—one of his regular post-game rituals. "Hey kid! How's it going?"

"Physical therapy went well today. I was like jelly afterward."

"A pool of slime then?"

"You're disgusting. Jelly is not slime."

"Right. So, the new PT is working out better?"

"Yes, I really like Annsley. Thanks for finding her. She's quite the drill sergeant, but she's fun and very kind. She doesn't like baseball though. She doesn't get it." Georgie's horrified whisper made him chuckle.

"That's fine, George. She just has to 'get' physical therapy." He'd called her "George" since she was old enough to get annoyed about it, but now it was merely an affectionate nickname—like "Wills" was for him.

"But she prefers rugby."

"It's a British thing, George. They like their tea, their Royals, and their rugby. Go with it."

His sister giggled and he thought it was the best sound in the world. "Funny you should say that. Annsley has a crush on Prince Harry."

He put Georgie on speaker phone while he did his cool down stretches and she recapped his whole game, dissecting his plays.

"The series is tied, and now you're headed home for the next two games, right? I can't wait to see you. I've made a new friend, and I'm geeked for you to meet her."

"Oh?"

"I met her through Margaret. I got to sit in while she interviewed Margaret about competing in the Paralympics. It was a blast. Margaret showed her the footage her mom did of the Games and her scrapbook and her gold medal. Afterwards, we *shamelessly* begged her to come back and hang out again. Margaret convinced her that her interview story would be even better if she learned what it was like to live with a disability—and she did. That is, she came back and spent the day in a borrowed wheelchair that nurse Jillian brought us. Now she comes just to visit. She likes music. She plays the piano, and she does wheelchair yoga with me and Margaret, though she uses a regular chair for it."

"Your friend—without a name—sounds nice. I'll be happy to meet her."

Georgie snickered. "Good. And don't frown at her and scare her off. She's very nice. And pretty. And really smart." Her voice became sharp with warning. "Oh, and don't wear one of your stodgy suits. Smile and play nice."

He laughed. "Fine, George! I promise to not scare off your friend and to not embarrass you with my clothes."

"You'll be here tomorrow, though, right?"

"I'll come straight from the airport." This satisfied her, and he could sense how eager she was about her new friend.

"Oh! Tell Fitz, his clutch hit was totally fly!"

"His head is big enough already."

Fitzwilliam's timing was right on. He sat down on the weight bench wearing only gym shorts and grabbed Darcy's phone, turning off the speaker. "Darling! Did you catch my action?"

Darcy rolled his eyes and let Fitz flirt with his little sister.

There was a travel day between games so Darcy flew into JFK the next morning. For her last two years of high school, his sister had been home schooled, and her only regular social contact was a live-in nurse and a physical therapist. When she finished high school, she had announced that she wanted her own place and to go to college. Her doctor had cleared it, and Darcy found her a place downtown not far from Fordham.

The outside façade of the Pemberley's Hope high-rise apartments was a pristine wonder of revitalized art deco, though someone looking closely would see the accommodations for people with disabilities. Georgie's one bedroom apartment, like the rest of the Pemberley's Hope interior, continued the architecture in pastels, steel, and glass. After the extensive tour conducted by the building manager, Darcy had wanted to live there himself: gym, spa, pool, art studio, music rooms, and a dining room with meals prepped by a registered dietitian. What sold him was the around-the-clock medical care and that the staff was young, bright, and friendly.

Georgie loved Pemberley's Hope, and Darcy could see that moving there had given her the confidence and liveliness she had lacked when living at his place that was not wheelchair friendly. She had her own life with a modicum of independence now. And probably the biggest relief to him—she had made friends here.

Her next-door neighbor and fellow college student, Margaret Carlstrom, was a Paralympics gold medalist in wheelchair racing. Margaret was teaching Georgie to compete, too. His sister wanted a racing wheel chair, and he put one on special order when he realized she was in earnest. Darcy had met Margaret several times and enjoyed her brash attitude. He was happy to see his sister beating the depression that followed after her accident.

Upon arrival, Jillian, a pretty, red-haired nurse approached him. "Mr. Darcy, I'm glad you came today. We have a guy turning twenty this week, and his parents are in Europe. They don't call much and usually just want to check in with the doctor. They're struggling with the changes in his life." She then whispered, "Can you drop by with some birthday wishes?"

His heart chafed for this young guy who had been left to the care of others. Darcy understood a bit of the parents' side too, as watching Georgie struggle had sent him to his knees in grief and guilt. But that was no excuse. Their son needed them. "Sure. What's his name?"

"John."

"Know what his interests are?"

"Baseball," she drawled. "But you're not his favorite. His favorite player is Carreaga."

He smiled, taking her ribbing good-naturedly. After all, Jose Carreaga was the fan favorite on and off the field. "Happy to do it."

Georgie's door was open and he called out, "Lucy, I'm home!" in his best Ricky Ricardo voice. He froze in embarrassment when he glimpsed she was not alone. A group yoga session was in process.

Margaret cackled. "You've got some 'splainin' to do."

Georgie spun her wheel chair around to him with a grin on her face. The others returned to their yoga positions.

"Will, you're earlier than I expected." She took his coat and tossed it over a chair as he slipped his carry-on behind it.

"Shh!" He grinned. "I'll return in a few. You finish with your friends."

She pulled him down for a quick hug then zipped back over to the contortionists in her living room.

He headed back downstairs for a coffee and to contact Carreaga about helping with a memorable gift for John.

Twenty minutes later, returning to Georgie's room in a rush, he plowed into a woman standing just inside the doorway.

"Oh, sorry!"

He gently gripped her toned arms to steady her and looked straight into the stunned, golden eyes of Liz Bennet.

"Will! This is my friend, Lizzy. She's the journalist I was telling you about. I'm so glad you made it in time to meet her. I told her that you would just be a minute, but she said you were here to see me and didn't want to foist her presence on you. I told her that you enjoyed meeting all my friends. Margaret tried to tell her, too."

"Sorry." He repeated himself and released her arms. Darcy had no idea what to say to Georgie's new friend "Lizzy."

Georgie was beaming up at him. Liz stepped back while rubbing her arms where he'd touched her. *Is she disgusted by my touch?*

Her gaze slowly wandered up his body before her eyes met his. *Is she checking me out?*

"Say hi, Wills!" Georgie giggled.

"Hi, um . . . do you prefer to be called Lizzy?" She turned bright red and fidgeted with the strap on her gym bag.

Georgie said, "Well, that's her name."

"Uh, I really should be going."

Darcy saw this as an opportunity to make a better impression and he wasn't going to let her slip away so easily. "Actually, please stay. I'd like to get to know you. I hear you enjoy music and sports."

He was blocking the doorway and he grinned devilishly when she saw that he was not allowing her to just sneak off. She relented with a huff and made her way back to the living room. He admired the sway of her hips in her yoga workout clothes.

He noted she chose a chair which assured her a little distance from him as she crossed her legs and offered her familiar professional expression: polite, attentive, neutral. Darcy thought the set of her shoulders and her chin betrayed her pretense of ease. He liked the way her eyes tracked his movements to the couch as he took a seat and casually draped his arm over the back. Georgie wheeled her chair to settle at an angle. He quickly sat forward to give her a hug and a kiss.

"Missed you," he whispered before he shifted back on the couch. He could feel Liz's observant eyes on him.

"Lizzy enjoys baseball. Sometimes she stays and watches the game with me. She knows a lot."

"Yes, I know. She's a sports reporter," he murmured as he studied Liz's face.

She had to have known that Georgie was his sister, and yet she was spending time as Georgie's friend. This made him pause.

Had I been wrong about her? Was she one of those snooping types who wanted to pry into my personal life to get a story to further her career, like that Collins guy?

"You know her?"

Liz squirmed under his gaze before twisting to speak to his sister. "Georgie, I have a confession to make." Will was alarmed, dreading what Liz might confess. "I led you to believe I didn't know your brother."

"Why would you do that?" Now Georgie's voice trembled with uncertainty. "Were you using me to get to Will?"

"No, no, quite the opposite really."

True. I'm the last man on the planet she wants to date, right?

Liz's discomfort was evident when she wrung her hands and her eyes darted between him and his sister. She settled on Georgie.

"I came here to interview Margaret for the human-interest sports story. I didn't know until after we got to be friendly that you were Dar—Will Darcy's sister. Um, we—that is—I . . . I kept the fact that I knew Will to myself because he and I aren't the best of friends. I hope you can forgive the deception, Georgie. I didn't mean you any harm."

Liz turned to him and her voice hardened, losing the gentle hesitancy she used with Georgie. "You must think that I came here under false pretenses to dig into your private life. I know how you feel about reporters and journalists. I overheard what you said during the 'Meet the Press' night—that we were all crawling slimes, no better than garbage pickers."

She heard that?

No wonder her "selfish disdain for others" comment. He should have never made that remark in such a setting where anyone could hear. Truthfully, at the time he hadn't cared who heard him, which made her accusation about his character true, but maybe now he could lessen some of the damage.

"I sincerely apologize for those words. I know not everyone is like that hack Collins, and he was the cause of my remarks. He kissed up to me then delved into my private life because he wanted dirt. He was convinced that I was hiding some deep, dark secret that he could expose and make a name for himself."

Georgie cut in. "Will really only has one secret. Me. He doesn't want reporters digging into my life. Not because he is ashamed of me but to protect me. A few years back, there was a lot in the press about my accident and the underage drinking at a party while away at boarding school. However, any journalist worth their salt can get the rest of the story." Darcy tried to interrupt, but Georgie shook her head and Liz frowned. "Thank you for telling me, Lizzy. So, you already know each other?"

And there it was. The sisterly interrogation.

"I met Liz months ago, because of interviews for the *Courier*. Unfortunately, as we just learned, she overheard me make a snide remark about reporters. I also assumed she would welcome a date with me. And I hadn't realized that it was her sister who I mistakenly thought was only into Charley for his money."

Georgie sucked in a breath. "That was Lizzy's sister with the obnoxious mom going on about her daughter snagging a rich guy at Charley's party?" Georgie's eyes darted to Liz, who was blushing fiercely and biting her lip. "Sorry, I guess that makes her your mom, too." Georgie grimaced. "Charley does have a tendency to pick some real lulus, but I'm sure your sister is nice. Not like the others that Will has had to help peel off Charley since college."

Liz sat tall in the chair as she stared down at the Athleta catalog on the coffee table. His sister's chair rocked back and forth with the nervous movements of her hands on the wheels. Silence held for the length of several breaths.

Liz's gaze rose to meet his, and she spoke with deliberation. "I do get that you were just being protective of your friend. I had no idea you encountered my mother at Charley's party. I was away on a writing assignment so was unable to attend. My mom can be—well, she wants to see us all well settled and can let that single-mindedness cause her to come on too strong."

Darcy was floored by her gentle voice and agreeable words. She had been so angry at him back in San Diego. And after Fitz had reamed him out, he was angry at himself.

"No, I interfered without all the facts."

Liz nodded and looked aside. The corner of her lip started to curl. "Did you know they're seeing each other again? Charley asked for a do-over and Jane said they could take it slow and see what happens. Jane's *not* a gold-digger. She's not. She's the sweetest, gentlest, and kindest person you could ever meet, and I do not say that because she is my sister."

Darcy smiled at her smugness. He didn't blame her for wanting to rub his face in it after he hurt her sister.

Liz's throaty laugh tumbled out. "You interfered again? Did you tell Charley to try again with Jane?"

"I learned my lesson the first time. So, no, I didn't tell him to do anything. I asked him if he still had feelings for Jane and then let him know that she was still single. Charley acted on his own."

Liz's cell phone beeped, and it broke the moment. She glanced at the clock. "I really do need to be going."

"See you tomorrow night then?" Georgie asked.

Liz looked over at Darcy before responding. "If you'd like."

"What's tomorrow night?" He rose and walked her to the door.

"Lizzy is coming over and we're watching the game. I invited this whole end of the floor."

"Great! The team needs all the support we can get. It's a tough match up."

"Who's pitching tomorrow?" Georgie asked.

"Denny's going up against Easton."

"Denny is a hottie." Georgie looked at him impishly through her long eye lashes.

Liz laughed when Darcy shook his finger in warning.

"I'll walk you down. I'll be right back, George. Behave!"

His sister muttered, "Bossy" to his back as he left with Liz.

They said nothing until they were in the elevator. Darcy leaned against the side of the elevator and enjoyed watching Liz sneak looks at him. He didn't bother hiding his interest.

"I'm sorry," she said quietly.

He stood up straight at that. "For what? You've been a great friend to my sister. I'm glad and should be thanking you."

"She and Margaret are my heroes. They are amazing women, just like so many others who've adjusted to life with a disability. I love spending time with them." Liz's smile dimmed. "But that wasn't what I meant. I'm sorry for losing my temper and for the way I treated you back in July. I am so ashamed because I never go off like that on people. I pride myself on being collected even when I'm angry. But with you, I just lost it. I can see I misjudged you. I guess if the roles were reversed, I might have questioned Jane about seeing Charley, too. You must despise me."

"No, you gave me a wake-up call. I was sure that I merely had to smile and crook my finger for you to go out with me. That was arrogant, just as you said."

She shrugged, not verbalizing her agreement. "But Gabe Wickham . . . "

Darcy felt her eyes bore into him. He heard her unspoken question. The elevator door opened and they stepped out. *Dare I trust her with the whole truth? Is it my place to explain?*

He could set her straight about his role in Wickham's career. He longed for her to know the other part—Georgie's story. Darcy guided her away from the main flow of people in the lobby. "What are your plans in the morning?" He grimaced at his abruptness. "That is, I would like to share a story with you, though it's not really mine to tell. I'll have to ask if I can reveal the truth."

Her big, golden eyes narrowed but she said, "Okay, I can understand that. I am free in the morning."

Darcy swallowed nervously. "Would you like to meet me for breakfast then? Say eight o'clock?"

Liz pulled out her phone. "Sounds good. Where?"

"Daily Bread at the corner of A Street and Watchtower."

Her eyes lit up. "I love that place. They have the best French toast." Darcy grinned, delighted she too loved the place.

Liz stared at his lips, then she shook her head.

"Right! Daily Bread. Eight o'clock. Better give me your number in case something comes up." He held his breath thinking she would refuse, until she gently took his phone and typed in her information. She sent herself a message from his phone and hers chimed.

"There. Now I need to scoot. I have dinner with Jane. Then I need to work a little on my story for tomorrow before I can get my beauty sleep. And this girl needs her beauty sleep."

"No, you don't." But she was already turning toward the doors. "I'll Uber you a car."

"That's really not necessary. A cab's right here," she said as she stepped out into the chill autumn breeze and raised her arm to an approaching taxi. Liz tucked some hair back over her shoulder and looked up with a smile. "Georgie is excited to spend time with you. In fact, it was her love of you and all the childhood pictures she showed me—okay and the way everyone on the floor speaks of you—that made me realize that I had you all wrong."

Darcy waved the remarks off before shoving his hands down in his jeans' pockets. "You didn't have me *all* wrong."

"But I did. I never guessed how reticent you are. I thought you were a snob. And I never considered that you might have other reasons for being less than forthcoming. I just assumed Bill Collins was right, and you had some sordid scandal that would muddy your Dandy image."

Darcy winced.

And Liz caught it. "Own it, Dandy. Every top hat seller and costume shop in New York loves you for it. And the franchise must absolutely go ape over the merchandise sales from those top hats and bow ties with the team logo on them. And the Dandy Darcy bobblehead giveaway night was a vast success."

He struggled not to roll his eyes as he watched her slip into the taxi. Liz didn't need to know that he had taken great delight in accepting his very own Dandy bobblehead.

Darcy held the door for Liz and leaned in to say goodbye. Her warm smile kept him standing on the curb until long after her taxi pulled out of sight. A horn made him startle and remember where he was.

During dinner, Darcy broached the subject with Georgie about telling Liz more about Wickham.

"I don't want to tell her, Wills."

"Okay, then we won't."

"No, you misunderstand. I don't want to be the one to tell her, but I would like her to know. I don't want to see her reaction to how stupid I was, okay? She knows I was injured in a car accident, but I want her to know it all. No secrets from my friend—if she still wants to be my friend."

"You weren't stupid. You were sixteen. You made a sixteen-year-old girl mistake. Everyone screws up, and you didn't expect a sexual predator at a teen party. Who would have suspected a professional athlete? And you have nothing to fear. Liz will still be your friend. I know she will place the blame precisely where it belongs."

Georgie toyed with the drawstring on the hood of her sweatshirt. "Will, you like Lizzy, don't you? And I don't mean as my friend. I can tell that you're into her."

"Yes. I really like your Lizzy."

"I rather think she's *your* Lizzy. She's into you, too, you know. I've caught her staring at our portrait on the wall over there and my photos on the shelf. I asked her if she thought you were good-looking and she blushed and nodded. I thought she would be a nice girl for you so I got out my photo albums and scrapbooks and—"

"George!" She giggled. "You were planning to set me up?"

"Well, obviously, you needed some help with that. You struck out the first time."

Yep, I'd definitely struck out.

"Telling her about Gabe Wickham will help, and today I thought you made a good impression. But we can't rest on our laurels. Now, what are you going to wear to your breakfast date? And for heaven's sake, get some coffee in you before you go so you don't grunt and snarl like you usually do in the mornings."

"Yes, George."

"Don't be like that." She grinned at his sour expression.

Wearing the blue-gray cashmere pullover Georgie insisted he wear, Darcy looked across the table at Liz. She looked lush in a smart charcoal gray suit and pink blouse—the top two buttons opened to her beguiling cleavage. He wondered what it would be like to loosen her hair from its bun and let it fall down around her shoulders. An eyebrow raised up at him from behind her black framed glasses. He smiled at the thought of Liz as the naughty teacher.

"Darcy? Will?" Her sharp voice cut away, and she looked at him and then the waitress. "What are you having?"

He straightened and cleared his throat. "The special, please. And a large water with lemon."

Liz, resting her chin in her palm and leaning comfortably towards him, grinned. "Georgie warned me that you were not a morning person. I was expecting cranky, not spacey."

"And I suppose, you're little miss *rise with the sun,* full of smiles and song?"

"Not if I can help it, but I do get up to feed Jane's cat. The beast waits until after Jane's left at zero dark thirty for her bakery to bug me for food. We were relieved to discover that Murphy likes Charley. He tolerates me but hates my dad, mom, and Lydia."

"I presume Murphy is the cat. Who's Lydia?"

"My younger sister. She's a loud, obnoxious seventeen-year-old going on thirty, so I don't blame Murph. They don't come over often, since our tiny, fourth floor walk-up makes mom claustrophobic—which sets off her nerves. So, Jane and I go to them."

A young boy approached their booth. He looked partly nervous and partly excited, based on the way he was biting his lip and looking back at his dad.

"May I—um, may I get a picture of you, Mr. Darcy? Uh, please?" The boy stumbled over his rushed words as he held up a phone.

Darcy smiled. "Sure, but let's get one together, okay?"

The boy's eyes grew large, and he nodded vigorously before turning to give his dad a thumbs-up.

Darcy said to Liz, "Would you mind?"

"Of course not. Why don't the pair of you stay right there. Yes, like that. Say 'Dandy!'"

The boy giggled, and Darcy grinned at Lizzy's smirking lips. The picture taken, Darcy grabbed a paper napkin and borrowed a pen from Liz. Asking the boy's name, he signed a quick "For Justin," who then thanked him and ran back to his dad. Liz murmured something about being "so sweet," and he felt a spark zing through him as she reached across the table to squeeze his hand. She removed it when the waitress delivered their breakfast. He still felt her brief touch and glowed in her approval.

Darcy appreciated that Liz had an appetite. She ordered the French toast, and based on how rapidly it all vanished, it must have been delicious. He hated when girls simpered and moved food around on their plate, rarely taking a bite. Closing her eyes as she swallowed her last bite, she licked her lips and exhaled her satisfaction. Darcy licked his lips, too, thinking he had never been so turned on by French toast.

He cleared his throat and leaned back in the booth. "I—I have decided to tell you about Wickham, not just his involvement with me, but with someone very dear to me. I trust that I can depend on your discretion?"

Without hesitation, Liz said, "Yes, of course."

Darcy started by explaining how years ago, he was asked by the coach to mentor Wickham when he was brought up from the minors.

Liz listened in silence, but her lips pressed into a tight line as she was likely hearing quite a different presentation of facts than what Wickham would have strung together in half-truths and implications.

"A few months later, I got a call that Georgie had been in a terrible car accident and she was in surgery. After a red-eye flight across country, I still didn't know if she would survive or not. I was decimating an empty Styrofoam coffee cup when the surgeon sat down with me in the waiting room and explained that she wouldn't walk again. I'll never forget Dr. Gardiner as he said, 'She's a miracle girl and a fighter.'

"After Dr. Gardiner left me, a detective and her partner sat down. The police had investigated, initially believing Georgie had been driving while intoxicated. Her blood tests revealed some alcohol in her system. Further analysis showed a strong dose of GHB. They had a suspect in for questioning. Witnesses from the party placed a guy at the scene, who supposedly had latched on to Georgie. Maria, Georgie's boarding school friend, said that the guy had overheard some other girls at the party mention that Georgie was my sister, and that's when she thought the guy started hitting on her. Even cast about he was a ball player who was friends with me. She said Georgie seemed to like him at first but then was uncomfortable with some of his forward behavior and said she had to go home. The guy didn't take the hint, so Maria and some others distracted him while Georgie slipped away in another friend's car. The other girls were used to protecting Georgie from people trying to get in good with her because I'm a pro baseball player. Unfortunately, none of them suspected at the time that this guy must have slipped something into Georgie's drink."

Darcy gulped down some water. "Detective Forrester showed me a picture of the suspect. Through dawning horror, I recognized Wickham. I asked if he was the one—the one who gave her the drug. But they couldn't confirm anything. That red haze people describe when they are so furious they can't speak or think, it's real. Finally, I pulled myself together enough to explain about our history with the man in the picture.

"Turned out Wickham had a good lawyer who got him off because no one could prove he put in the GHB. So, he was free to go on stalking underage girls.

"The detective was disgusted and promised she would nail that scumwad to the wall. The team traded him but I still had him watched. But as time went on, I stopped the surveillance. I had to focus on Georgie.

"Georgie told me she took full blame and said that this was on her. She admitted she had snuck out to go to the party, she chose to drink, and she chose to be flattered by a handsome, successful guy, and accepted a drink from a stranger. I wanted to kill him, but rants of revenge and murder weren't helpful. She needed to heal and move on, so we didn't really talk about it again for three years." Darcy's hands shook, but his voice had been nearly clinical as he told the story. *Does she believe me?*

"And that's my dealings with Gabe Wickham."

Liz shook her head, tossing down a shredded napkin, and her eyes brimmed with tears. "How can you ever forgive me? I attacked you and trusted a man who could have raped your sister. A guy indirectly or directly responsible, it doesn't matter which, for her injuries and situation. I'm a journalist, and I never once stopped to verify facts. You bruised my ego when you insulted journalists. And that had me ripe to believe anything about you." Her head went down, and she covered her face. Darcy hated seeing any woman cry, particularly Liz. He moved around the table so he could hold her. Her body shook and she whimpered, "I'm sorry," over and over.

"Don't." His voice was like a caress as he cradled her body against him. "Georgie is constantly reminding me that I'm not to blame. You aren't either. Wickham's very convincing. I believed him the first time he gave me some sob story, and I handed over two thousand dollars that I never saw again. I wouldn't be surprised that when he left the team, he owed several thousand dollars between us all."

"You're trying to make me feel better." She rifled through her bag.

"And is it working?"

"A little," she said with a wobbly smile as she dabbed her eyes with a tissue. "I need to get going, but I want you to know that I will never reveal this to a soul. Georgie is the bravest, sweetest girl, and I'm glad we are friends. Will you see her before your game?"

"Yes, I'm going there next. She wants to know about breakfast together."

"Tell her not to worry and that I will be along tonight." She squeezed his hand that was around her shoulder. "Thank you. I know that wasn't easy, and I've given you no reason to think I would treat Georgie's story with care, but I'm glad you told me. I had to know the extent of my own folly." Liz spotted the gift bag he had knocked over in his scramble to sit beside her. "It's not Georgie's birthday . . . ?"

"No. A guy on her floor, John, has a birthday. Georgie and I are taking him cake and ice cream. He likes baseball, and Carreaga is his favorite player, so I got him to autograph a few things last night. He loves to do things for kids. Great guy."

"That is so kind. I know John. He is quiet. You're a great guy too, you know."

The way her eyelids lowered when she said that last part left him with the strongest desire to pull her closer and explore those delectable lips. It didn't help his self-control that she was already staring at his lips. A busboy dropped a plate, and it shattered the moment.

"I really should get going."

Darcy stood and let her rise. "Here, let me help."

He took her coat and helped her into it. Impulsively, he kissed her. He stepped back and looked hesitantly into her eyes for a sign. Almost as quickly, she pulled him to her and kissed his mouth with a fervor he had not expected.

Liz's eyes were wide and her chest rose with rapid breaths. He adjusted her glasses that had gone askew and smoothed the collar on her suit jacket. "I want to see you after the game tonight. I know it will be late, but please?"

"I'll be at Georgie's party." She licked her lips again. "I'll look forward to seeing you. And good luck tonight, Dandy."

With that parting wish and a peck on his cheek, she offered him one sultry smile from the door. He noticed he wasn't the only male in the place to be riveted by her long legs striding away in heels made to do them justice.

Darcy hot-footed it back to Georgie's place after his game. It was later than he planned. Hitting a three-run homer, and later climbing the wall to reach out and take away a home run, caused him to get swarmed by the press afterward. The security guy at the door grinned as Darcy sailed past with a wave. Hopefully, Liz was still at Georgie's.

"Darce! Jeez, wait up," Fitz called behind him. A few residents in the lobby looked up, and Darcy nodded his head in acknowledgement. His best friend was giving him an amused look as they approached the elevator. Inside the elevator, Fitz cracked a big grin as he punched the number for Georgie's floor. "Georgie told me a secret," the idiot sing-songed at him. "And by the way you're acting, I'd say it's true."

Darcy stared straight ahead as the elevator went up.

"So, she gave you a second chance? How'd you pull that off?"

"I apologized for being an ass. And I told her the truth."

"Even about Wickham?"

"Yeah. Georgie wanted me to tell her."

This brought a smile from Fitz. "That's a good thing."

"Yes, she is sunnier. You should have seen her and her friends at the birthday party for a guy on her floor. They were sitting around the table and sounded like what you hear from a bunch of college kids at a café over coffee and bagels. I was so worried when she moved out, but this place is good for her."

"From what I can tell, Liz has been good for her, too."

"Yes, it was a shot in the arm for Georgie to make a new friend beyond the residents here. Lizzy is amazing."

"Lizzy is it, now?"

"That's what she asked Georgie to call her. It's growing on me now that I've spent more time with her away from work."

Fitz winked and led the charge out of the elevator. "This will be fun."

"I don't know why Georgie invited you."

"She thinks I'm cute."

The others had left but Liz stayed behind, helping Georgie clean up. Georgie and Fitz guffawed loudly in the living area while Darcy helped Liz put things away.

"Saw you were interviewed by Bill Collins." Liz looked amused.

"Yeah, tell me again how he got that job? We had to do it three times, and he had a teleprompter."

She patted his back. "Poor baby."

There were two text on her cell phone on the counter. She glanced down and frowned. "Both from Jane. Why didn't she just call? Oh, she did. My phone was on silent for the game."

Darcy waited as she read.

"No." Her voice broke. "No, no, no . . . "

"What's wrong?"

She shook her head at him as she tapped on her phone.

"Lydia's missing—Jane!"

There was silence while Jane talked, then Liz gushed out questions, barely waiting for Jane's responses. "Lydia texted you from a party that she was with a cute guy? . . . She never came home last night? . . . Did you try calling her? Of course you did . . . I'm sorry."

Darcy steered Liz to the chair at the table as she talked to her sister. Georgie and Fitz were now watching in silence, understanding something big was going down.

"What did Mom and Dad say?" She dropped her forehead to the table. "That sounds like Mom. What about the police? Did you call them? . . . They won't? What about that picture she texted you? . . . Even Lydia wouldn't stay out so long. She needs to be found. . . . Jane, send me the picture. Maybe I can figure out where she's at. . . . Yes, I know she might have moved on from that club, but we have to start somewhere. . . . Okay, yes, I'm coming home. . . . I love you, too."

She sniffled and clutched her phone until it pinged. Darcy had been pacing and stopped when her phone hit the floor and a wounded sound left her throat.

"Lizzy!" He moved to catch her before she crumbled out of the chair.

"He has her. I know he does. He took my sister. You said he likes them young. I didn't warn her. Why would I? Where would she ever meet up with him? I knew he would be in town when he brought up the possibility of me doing a feature on you and how you ruined his life. I—oh, months ago, when his team was in town, I introduced him to my parents and Lydia. Last night, I told my mother, without details, what he is really like. Jane says my mother doesn't want to involve the cops. She thinks it's all some kind of misunderstanding. That we are blowing this up."

Darcy scrambled for the phone with one hand while holding Liz against him with the other. His fears were confirmed when he saw a pretty, dark-haired teenage girl tucked against Wickham's side.

"I have to go. I have to figure out how to find her." Liz stirred in his arms.

"I'll help." Darcy's mind was already working and ignoring her protest. "Wait!" he said firmly.

She sagged back on the chair and stared up through red-rimmed eyes as he stood with his own phone out. Darcy leaned down to kiss her forehead. "Trust me," he whispered. She gripped his hand tightly and nodded.

He scrolled through his contacts and found a number. He hit "call" and waited. His thumb rubbed in a circle on Liz's shoulder, and she leaned into him.

"Mr. Darcy," came a gravelly voice.

"Jack, I need your help, again. Wickham took a teen girl. We need to find him. Do you still have the details from when you had him under surveillance for me?" Georgie gasped and Fitz knelt beside her chair, taking her hand.

Jack cursed, and Darcy could hear computer keys clacking. "Yeah, I brought the file up."

"Jack, I'm going to send you a picture of him with the girl from last night." Liz shoved her phone at him and sat up with dawning hope. Darcy traced his finger down her tear-dampened cheek before taking her phone and forwarding the picture. "And the parents don't want the cops involved. They don't understand what a monster he is."

"Okay, I'll start working on this. Tell me what you know." Jack's voice was firm and professional.

"I have her sister here. Liz knows more than I do." He squatted down, their faces inches apart. "This is Jack Austen. He's the detective I used last time when Wickham hurt Georgie."

She nodded and reached for his phone with trembling fingers.

Darcy settled into the chair next to hers and was grateful when Liz reached for his hand. She gave Jack Lydia's movements from the day before, her circle of friends, family, routines, and her social media accounts.

When Liz ended the call, she held out the phone to Darcy. "He sounds thorough. I need to talk to my parents. And Jane."

She stood and went to the door.

Darcy followed. "I'm going with Lizzy."

"Help them," Georgiana warbled.

"I will do everything I can. Fitz, can you stay here a little while?"

"Go. I'll be here. Let us know when you hear something."

"Will do."

He ran down the hall and caught her at the elevator. They were soon at the curb, and he summoned a passing cab. Liz made no objections when he slid in beside her. She gave her address and stared off blankly. Darcy put his arm around her and pulled her back against him. Even now, he made note of how comfortable and right she felt against his side.

The cab pulled up in front of an older brick building in a decent though tired-looking Brooklyn neighborhood still awaiting its trendy makeover like the streets around it. Darcy handed over the fare, and he climbed out. He recognized the blonde who rushed out of the house at the same time Liz sprinted out of the cab. Over Jane's head, he noticed Charley frowning from the door and Darcy said, "I was there when Liz heard from Jane."

A loud female voice came from behind Charley, and he answered, "It's Lizzy, Mrs. Bennet. She's come home with Will." Charley recovered from his surprise at seeing Darcy with Lizzy and whispered, "Lydia's, um, she's a little impulsive and can get caught up in the moment, Jane says. Her mom seems to spoil her, and their dad thinks Lydia is probably just staying with a friend and forgot to call. They don't believe that Wickham is capable of this. Her mom is happy that Lydia is out with a *famous baseball player.*"

As Liz and Jane joined them, Jane smiled at Darcy. "Thank you. We didn't know what to do. Lizzy says you have a private detective." Jane was wringing her hands. "I know Lydia can be irresponsible—"

"Wild and heedless—" Liz cut across Jane's words.

"But she has never stayed out this long before. Mom was supposed to take her shopping at the mall today, and she would never miss that. Now Mom is drinking."

"Let's take this all inside," Liz said, saving him from figuring out what to say to that.

Darcy followed Charley into the building and through the doorway of the first apartment, where a loud TV and a woman's voice were competing. Their mother bore some resemblance to Jane and was going off about her nervous disorder, while their dad was kicked back in a recliner, absorbed by an action movie and ignoring his wife.

"Mom, this is Will. Will, this is my mom." Mrs. Bennet opened her mouth to speak, but Liz tugged him into the kitchen area. "Tea? Coffee? Beer—"

"Stay out of my beer, Lizzy Bennet," warned a male voice from the living room.

"And that's my dad. So, tea, coffee, wine—"

"Nothing, thanks."

"Charley?"

"I have coffee already. Thanks."

They all sat down around a kitchen table while Mrs. Bennet paced, nursing a glass of wine that had a bold shade of pink lipstick stained on it. "He would never hurt Lydia. She adores him. *You* used to adore him and were angry that he was maligned by that arrogant jerk who lost him his career. Remember? He said he wished you could make everyone know what that Dandy Darcy fellow really is like."

Liz was pale, and her eyes were huge as she stared at him and mouthed the words, "I'm sorry." The woman had a head of steam and kept talking about how cherubic Wickham was and how Darcy was the evil villain who ruined him. "Mom." Liz started and then cleared her throat, speaking louder. "Mom!"

"What?"

"*This* is Will Darcy." She offered him a half-smile. "Gabe Wickham lied. He lied to us. He's not the victim. He was the one who ruined his own career, and he is the one who hurt Darcy. I had it all wrong, and I was stupid to believe him. I let one little thing prejudice me against a man who didn't deserve it."

Mrs. Bennet sniffed as she poured herself another glass of wine. "Oh, knock it off, Lizzy. You do go on. I just wonder why doesn't she call me? We are missing the fifty percent off shoe sale."

Darcy was pleased Liz defended him but even more that her mother was too drunk to make a fuss over him.

An hour later, Darcy was feeling less generous. Even Charley's eternal optimism was getting to him. He had been texting Fitz. Fitz was outraged about Wickham, but of course, he thought Liz's mother sounded like a hilarious and entertaining woman. Now, Darcy was trapped listening to a loud TV gun battle competing with a querulous woman arguing to nobody in particular about her baby not being "that sort of girl."

Thankfully, his phone rang. Darcy rushed through the apartment into the hall so he could hear above the volume of the TV. Liz pushed out after him and closed the door.

"Jack?"

He nodded to Liz.

"Jack, I'm going to put you on speaker phone with Liz."

They sat down on the stairs and listened.

Liz interrupted. "He found her! I'm going to call the police."

"Well, it seems the young lady isn't exactly there against her will so she might not come easily. Simpler if someone could persuade her away from him before the police get here."

"We're on our way. Text me the address of the motel. Thanks, Jack."

Then Darcy called Fitz.

"How's Georgie holding up?"

"Georgie is made of sterner stuff than you think." He chuckled as he continued. "And is using very strong language to preface her desire that you 'kick his ass.'"

"Yes, well, I might have to wait in line behind Lizzy. I need to go."

"Where's he?"

"Morningstar Motel on Broadmire."

"Sounds cheap and by the hour. Right. Be careful."

Liz walked inside the apartment to inform the rest. Darcy Ubered a car while Liz convinced Charley and Jane to stay with her parents. They left Jane to sort out their mother, who wailed that there must be some mistake.

Liz slammed the door and leaned on it with her eyes closed. "I'm so sorry. You must think we're all crazy."

"Not all of you."

Her lips twitched over his joke, but then she tilted her head. "Why have you stayed?"

"I want to help your family."

"Yes, but why? My dad refuses to stir off his recliner, my mom blames you and everyone but the culprits, and I played right into Wickham's hand."

She looked full of remorse, and Darcy didn't like seeing this lovely, spirited woman doubting herself.

"Liz, I was too late for Georgie, but I won't stand by and let it happen to another girl if it is in my power to help her." Playfully, he added, "And because I want to ask you out again, and I want you to say yes this time. But first, let's get your sister safely away from that disgusting douchebag."

They rode to a part of town that made Darcy wish he was armed. The driver gave them a long look when he pulled up at the raunchy motel. He was still staring when he pulled away.

"I think he is convinced that you brought me here for less than honorable reasons," Liz said weakly.

"So now I'm a rake who would ravish fair maidens?"

"Whatever would your fans think, Dandy?"

He bit back a grin too, but then they both remembered why they were there and sobered. The motel door swung open, and they were met by Jack and Fitz.

"Georgie sent me. I'm the cavalry, I guess. You had to come across the bridge. And I was closer." Fitz responded to Darcy's astonished expression.

"Thanks, Jack. I guess we'll take it from here. Send me the bill."

"I'll hang out here a bit longer, Mr. Darcy, while you do what you need to do." He showed Darcy the weapon inside his coat and Darcy nodded. "And the cops should be here any minute."

"Okay, let's head to their room. It's on the back side and opens right onto the parking lot."

Liz appeared hesitant, taking in the questionable neighborhood, about confronting Wickham, about Austen's gun. Darcy knocked to no answer, so he knocked again, louder.

A teenage girl wearing a man's t-shirt and nothing else threw the door open. "You're not the Chinese delivery guy."

Liz grabbed Lydia by the arm and dragged her outside. "Just what do you think you're doing?"

Lydia snickered. "Do you really need me to answer that?"

"He's a pedophile. He slips drugs into the drinks of young girls and rapes them."

"Who? Not Gabby!"

Darcy looked inside the room. It was cluttered with clothes flung about, leftover food, and booze bottles, but he still recognized the jerk passed out in his underwear, lying across the bed.

Fitz pushed through behind Darcy. Darcy grabbed him.

"Wait."

Darcy was doing it right this time. There was no lack of evidence for Wickham to get off with a piddling fine and a slap on the wrist. Fitz watched as Darcy held up his phone and slowly videoed the whole room with Liz and Lydia's voices in the background.

"Oh, for God's sake, Lydia!" Wickham had finally roused enough to yell: "Shut up! Would you just shut up?"

Fitzwilliam lounged in the doorway and drawled. "Well if you would stop going for little girls, you wouldn't have to put up with their chatter. Did you get pictures of all those bags of white powder on the table, Darce?"

Wickham was tangled in the sheets and trying to get free while his eyes darted. Once on his feet, he struggled to put his jeans on and then attempted to escape past them. Fitzwilliam punched him in the gut, and he fell back, retching and gasping for air. "That's for Georgie. Been wanting to do that for years." Fitz smirked. "Please, try that again, jackass."

Liz's voice penetrated the din. Lydia was going on about her "bad boy" lover and how no one ever understood.

Wickham took notice when Liz entered his field of vision. He stood up and spread his arms in welcome. "Lizzy."

"Don't talk to me," she warned.

Darcy slammed his fist into Wickham's face. Wickham fell to his knees, nose dripping in blood. Austen secured Wickham's hands behind his back with zip ties. Fitzwilliam had already stepped outside to wait for the cops.

"You hit him." Lydia shrieked.

"Leave him be." Liz jerked her sister back and nodded to Darcy.

When the cops showed up a few minutes later, Lydia was sobbing and threatening to castrate Wickham. Darcy had shown her the pictures on his phone of his sweet, wheelchair-bound sister while he quickly disclosed Georgie's story.

Lydia was primed and ready to tell the cops her age and that she had woken up in that hotel room not remembering how she got there. This might be true. She had gone along with Wickham because she was scared for her life—which was patently not true. Yet, Darcy was in awe of her performance.

With supreme satisfaction, Darcy watched Wickham being put in the back of a patrol car. Elizabeth called Jane, and then they all met down at the police station to give their statements. There, they were met by a grinning Lieutenant Forrester who was once the detective on Georgie's case. She'd heard the news that Wickham was being brought in. "I knew we'd nail him."

It was the wee hours of the morning and the temperature quite bracing. Liz stood outside the police station with Darcy while waiting for her father to come around with his car. "I can't thank you enough on behalf of my family."

"I'm happy it's over and your sister's unharmed. I'm more than happy that Wickham won't be assaulting any more girls. One of my main motivations was you. I don't like seeing you upset and scared." Darcy moved closer, gently placed his hands on her shoulders, and slid them up to her cheeks. He leaned in, observing as her eyes softened and her lips smiled. He whispered, "I like you, Lizzy Bennet, more than ever."

He was pleased when she wrapped her arms around his neck and brushed his lips with a light kiss.

"Okay," she said, and nodded as she rocked on her heels.

"Okay?"

"Okay, I'll go out with you. You might have struck out in the first inning, but you got the go-ahead homer in your last at bat."

She laughed. Darcy pulled her to him slowly, enjoying the heat in her eyes that probably reflected his own. His hands roved low and fitted into her back pockets, pulling their bodies flush together.

"Eh hem!" Darcy heard a familiar voice. "The Bennets are here, and our car has arrived, Darce. By the way, you've got an audience from the windows of the police precinct and the street. I don't think you want your private life to show up on social media. Or Entertainment Tonight."

He didn't, but there was also a part of him that thought it would be worth it.

"Good luck today, Dandy," Liz said as she patted his chest.

"I'll call you after the game," he said with determination.

"You do that. I want the exclusive."

Lydia was being hugged and scolded at the same time by her mother. Liz slid into the backseat of the car with Jane and Lydia. Mr. Bennet drove off without a word and even before his wife had closed her door.

Darcy turned to Fitzwilliam and said, "She said I homered on this one."

"Guess we'd better make sure you get the win in the books."

SIX MONTHS LATER

"Here? You're proposing here?" Her voice was shrill with excitement.

Darcy took in the quiet Florida beach, the sound of the surf, Charley's private cottage, their picnic blanket, and then his lovely Lizzy in her pretty, turquoise bikini. His knee was solidly in the sand, and he held an open box with a diamond ring.

"Well, yes."

She gestured around. "This *is* romantic."

"Yes." He agreed cautiously. "Is romantic bad?"

She brushed his hair back out of his face. "I was so worried. Fitz hinted to me the other day that you were going to propose on Opening Day in front of a packed stadium. This is much better. It's beautiful here, and there is no one watching us like we're the entertainment. I couldn't figure out why you wanted to get engaged in that manner. It seemed so unlike you, and it definitely didn't suit me."

Fitz? He would definitely kill Fitz when he saw him.

"Are you sure, though? I mean, I'm not sweet like Cathy, Hank Denny's wife, and I'm not smooth and polished like Esme Carreaga. I have a full-time, demanding career—like your own—and you know my mother drives you insane—"

He stopped her by reaching to put his finger on her lips. "I don't want a woman like Denny's or Carreaga's. I want my sassy, award-winning journalist who challenges me to be more—who knows *me* and likes me for me. I want you."

She opened her mouth, but he cut her off.

"And yes, your mom and I don't quite see eye to eye on all things, but we share one thing in common. We both love her second daughter." He shifted his position uncomfortably. "Lizzy, I just told you that I love you and want to spend the rest of my life with you. I'm down on one knee offering you a ring—and all of me. I'm waiting for you to give me the signs for our next play. Will you marry me?"

She threw back her head and laughed. "I am the happiest person in the world. Happier than Jane, maybe." Then she cried out, "Yes, Will, I love you and will marry you."

Darcy jumped up and spun her around as she continued to laugh with tears running down her face. She grabbed the box, but he snagged it back to take out the ring and put it on her finger. It fit perfectly—*thank you, Jane.* They crashed to the sand, kissing.

Later, while sharing the lounge chair on the deck and looking out toward the water shimmering under the moon's rays, he watched her turn her ring to catch the light. The diamond's fire winked on her hand, and he held her tightly, marveling that this beautiful woman had said she would be his wife.

"Will, when did you fall in love with me?"

"I can't give you an exact moment. I was attracted to you from the beginning, and I admired you then. You were the first woman I considered having a serious relationship with." Nuzzling her ear, he laughed softly as he said, "And then I wanted to hate you after the scene at the restaurant, but I never could." She stroked his cheek, and he turned his head to kiss her palm. "It's no excuse, but I changed after losing my dad and then Georgie's accident. I thought I was doing alright. I needed a wake-up call like you gave me to see how I had changed, and I didn't like it. Meeting you again at Georgie's apartment gave me hope again that I might have another chance with you. I don't know, Lizzy. I was in the middle before I knew I had begun."

"Did I sneak in and steal second base on Dandy Darcy?"

"Second? No way! You completely stole home." He squeezed her bottom, and she surged forward laughing. "And you? When did you fall for me?"

"Hmm, it might have been the day I first saw your spacious and luxurious condo. Or maybe the day you got me a World Series jersey with your name on it—" He jabbed her side and she giggled.

Sobering, she said, "I think it began during that first breakfast we shared at Daily Bread after you told me about Gabe Wickham, and I learned that you were the real deal—a guy who took responsibility for others, whether it was a younger sister or a ratfink sleaze. You let me flay the skin off you with my words but still treated me with kindness and took my words to heart. I didn't deserve your forgiveness. How could I not fall in love with you?"

"What did we say about forgetting the past?" he warned. "I forgave you and you forgave me. We've moved forward. It's spring. A whole new ballgame."

Lizzy's reply was lush and low. "Put me in, Coach, I'm ready to play."

It was corny, and he knew it. Laughter bubbled up between them, but he gasped as he said, "Play ball" because Lizzy had already started the game. His last coherent thought was that they would both win this one and every game after.

SOPHIA ROSE is a native Californian currently residing in Michigan. A long-time Jane Austen fan, she is a contributing author to *Sun-kissed: Effusions of Summer* and *Then Comes Winter* anthologies. Sophia's love for writing began as a teen writing humorous stories for creative writing class and high school writing club. Writing was set aside for many years while Sophia pursued degrees and certificates in education, special education, family history, and social work, leading to a rewarding career working with children and families. Health issues led to an opportunity to read and review books, beta read, and return to writing stories that lean toward the humorous side and always end with a happily ever after.

"Heaven forbid! That would be the greatest misfortune of all! To find a man agreeable whom one is determined to hate!"
—Elizabeth Bennet to Charlotte Lucas, Chapter XVIII.

THE RIDE HOME

RUTH PHILLIPS OAKLAND

The knock on his door was loud and insistent, tugging him from an uneasy sleep. When the knock sounded again, Fitzwilliam Darcy rolled over, rubbed his hand across the scratch of stubble on his chin and groaned in irritation, "Sod off!"

His eyes were assaulted by the bright light from the hall as Charles Bingley opened the bedroom door. "Good, you're still awake," Bingley slurred as he walked into his guest bedroom. "Can you drive into the city for me?"

"It's nearly—" Darcy turned to look at the clock "—one o'clock!"

"I'm afraid I'm a bit tight." Bingley held up an open bottle of wine and turned it upside down, showing it was empty.

"Shite, Bingley, can't whatever it is wait until morning?"

"I need to you pick up Lizzy. Something's happened with her date, and she needs a ride home."

Darcy sat up and stared into the darkness. Lizzy. Elizabeth.

Even though he'd been rude when they'd first met and later accused her sister of being a gold digger, who would have guessed such a pleasant person would carry such a huge grudge for so long? Their argument the week before when he'd dared to tell her he'd fallen for her was scorching enough. He had no wish to get close enough to Elizabeth Bennet to be burned a second time. "Trust me, I'm the last bloke she's going to want to see tonight. What about Jane?"

"We're engaged!" A stupid smile broke out on Bingley's face as he gripped the door for support. "So, we've both been celebrating"—and he held up the wine bottle again.

"Congratulations," Darcy deadpanned. "What about her family? She's got a house full of sisters not three miles from here."

"What's the point in waking up their whole house when you weren't even asleep yet?"

"Cab? Uber?"

Bingley shook his head. "Look, I know you and Lizzy don't get along, but Jane's worried. Lizzy said something about her date harassing her . . ."

Darcy's panic at his friend's last words pushed him out of bed in a flash. "Where is she?" As he snatched his jeans from the end of the bed, Bingley gave him the name of a coffee shop in the city. In less than five minutes, Darcy had programed the GPS in Bingley's bright red Porsche then sped through the iron gates of Netherfield, focused on driving on the right side of the road.

It wasn't until he was half way to his destination that the adrenaline had dissipated enough for Darcy to realize he had just placed himself in a difficult position. One more week and he would have had Bingley firmly established as head of the American office at Pemberley Media. Then Darcy would have headed back to England without ever seeing Elizabeth Bennet again. Now he could imagine the hour-long drive back to Meryton: the stony silence, the palpable animosity, the dagger-like looks. It would be sixty minutes of hell, but it would be worth it to know Elizabeth was safe.

He was lucky enough to find an open parking space in front of the coffee shop she was waiting in. He steeled his resolve and opened the large, wooden door.

The shop was nearly empty, but he saw Elizabeth sitting in a corner booth staring into a cup of coffee. Her hair was loose and flowed in shining waves down her back; her dress was blue, short, showing off her long legs.

His first thought was to quip about some old Jewel lyrics he'd once heard her sing: "Consoled a cup of coffee, but it didn't want to talk." However, he now knew she interpreted his flirting banter as not-so-subtle criticism. So, he cleared his throat and said the only thing he considered safe, "Hiya."

He prepared for the inevitable cold stare, the narrowing of her fine eyes, and the suspicious wrinkle of her adorable brow. There would probably be an oh-so-obvious insult thrown in for good measure. Elizabeth did nothing half-arsed.

When her eyes rested on his face, her entire expression brightened. "Hi," she called out as she stood. "What a surprise!"

He was confused as he took a quick glance about the coffee shop. There was no one behind him, and the woman before him was without a doubt Elizabeth Bennet.

"I'm here to take you home." He was amazed the words came out of his mouth, because he was still gobsmacked by her unexpected reaction to seeing him.

"Aren't I the lucky lady?" It was a flirty, playful statement—the kind he'd only dreamed about her giving him. Her voice was sultry and low, and he found her American accent endearing, even though most Yanks slurred around their consonants so much he'd develop a headache trying to figure out what they were trying to say.

She then took two shaky steps forward and stumbled, but he caught her before her lovely arse hit the floor. Her arms linked around his neck as he lifted her to her feet. He smelled gin.

"You're drunk?" That would explain a great deal, but it concerned him as well. He'd never noticed Elizabeth drink more than a glass of wine with dinner.

Her head flopped back from his chest and she squinted to keep his face in focus. "Thank you, Captain Obvious," she said before her face fell forward, causing her forehead to strike his collar bone.

"Did your date do to this to you?"

"No, no, no, no, no, no, no, no, no . . ." Elizabeth continued to mumble that one syllable into his shirt until her voice became so soft, he thought she might have drifted to sleep.

He did his best to support her against his body as he moved her toward the door. "Let's get you home." Thankfully her legs appeared to have once again engaged and her impossibly high stilettos propelled her forward.

When they reached the door, she abruptly stopped. "You're taking me back to Chuck's, right? Not my parent's house. Do you have any idea what my mom will do when she finds out what I did tonight?"

"You're over the legal drinking age, and you were smart enough to call someone to come and get you. Your mother should be happy that you're safe."

"You think . . ." Elizabeth shook her head as if attempting to clear it. "You think Frannie Bennet is going to be upset because I got drunk?" She then laughed. Soon she was all but doubled over in hysterics. It was clear Elizabeth wasn't just drunk. She was blooming pissed!

She then straightened up and pointed a finger at him. "You may be gorgeous and smart, but when it comes to my mother, you don't know *squat*!"

Her upbraiding was almost comforting because it was familiar territory for them, but somewhere in that insult she'd called him "gorgeous." Gorgeous! As he led Elizabeth to the car, he reasoned that gorgeous was far superior to either *cute*, *handsome*, or the term American girls most often applied to his cousin, Richard, a *slayer*. Gorgeous had a certain quality of uncontrolled adoration about it—an "I'd lick you from head to toe if I got the opportunity" connotation—yet without sounding cheap. Given that just a second ago he thought Elizabeth hated his guts, it could not help but give him the smallest glimmer of hope as his body twitched like a pubescent schoolboy's.

He discreetly adjusted his errant appendage while inhaling gin fumes and wondered if perhaps he was suffering a contact high. Elizabeth made her feelings about him quite clear the week before. Alright, he had inadvertently insulted her, but he was simply trying to explain that he'd realized that he'd be dating *her*, not her embarrassing family. *Egotistical*, she'd called him. *Condemnatory, contemptuous, supercilious.* Oh, Elizabeth Bennet was quite good at coming up with words of four or more syllables when she was angry.

Darcy carefully leaned Elizabeth back against the side of the Porsche while he reached for the door handle. He felt her legs give out and abandoned the search to wrap his arms about her in support.

"God, you smell good!" she said, inhaling deeply. "Charlotte asked me how you smelled, and when I said I didn't know, she practically screamed at me that it was impossible to slow dance with someone as delicious as you and not breathe him in.'"

His stomach plummeted remembering their dance at the Annual Meryton Charity Ball. It was just one in a long line of examples of how he'd misinterpreted her feelings. "But, you don't find me delicious."

"Oh, you're beyond delicious, Slick, but I'll never admit it to *you*!"—poking him rather sharply in the chest—"Not after you said I wasn't hot enough to waste your time on. Who is hot enough for you? Behati Prinsloo? Gisele Bündchen? Or are you still nursing some teenage crush on Heidi Stupid Klum?"

"Heidi doesn't have a middle name, and she's not stupid."

Elizabeth's laugh rang loudly through the deserted street.

He pretended not to hear her as he reached for the handle to the door, but Darcy grimaced at the memory. Yes, he'd been madly in lust with Heidi Klum when he was thirteen. Okay, so she was still smoking hot years later, but he'd long ago outgrown leggy, blonde, German women who would never be more than a fantasy. He now preferred leggy American brunettes who, when standing right in front of him, appeared to be equally unobtainable.

He pressed Elizabeth against the car to keep her from slipping down while he leaned to the side and opened the car door. When he straightened, Elizabeth was looking at him with a wide-eyed expression. "Why, Mr. Darcy! You are very"—she shifted her pelvis against him—"impressive!"

He wanted to kiss her. She was so maddeningly close and apparently willing, but she was drunk. His parents taught him that women were not objects. He twitched again. *Damn, sometimes being honorable sucks.*

"Get into the car." He hadn't intended for his voice to sound so demanding and he cringed at her snort of derision as she slid into the passenger seat. However, his mood lightened considerably when he found it necessary to lift her silky-smooth legs inside the vehicle. Her skin was so soft, and he decided not to be too hard on himself when he realized his fingers lingered on her calves a second longer than necessary.

He was leaning across her to buckle the seatbelt when he felt her arms wrap around his back and her face snuggle into his neck. "You're so warm!"

This was becoming more difficult by the minute. Apparently, a drunken Elizabeth was an affectionate Elizabeth. For a moment, he considered the possibilities: one brief snog. It wouldn't be like he was groping her breasts or shagging her rotten. It would be just a kiss, probably the only kiss he'd get from her—ever—*she already hates me!* How much worse could it get than that?

He couldn't do it. "I'll turn the heat on," he replied as he slowly pulled away, savoring every retreating inch of contact and silently cursing the fact that he was a gentleman. *Sometimes being a gentleman is the pits.*

"Spoil sport," she muttered as he gently closed the car door.

He stood outside the car for a moment, allowing the cool air and the momentary distance from Elizabeth to clear his mind. By the time he climbed behind the steering wheel, Elizabeth's eyes were closed and she appeared to be asleep.

Grateful for the reprieve, he started the trip back. Everything was quiet but for the hum of the engine. Darcy had convinced himself that the remainder of the drive would be easy, when Elizabeth's voice cut through the silence. "Not that I'm complaining, because it was really, really, really . . ." She seemed to fumble for the right word.

"Good?" he offered.

"No."

"Kind?"

"No, no, no."

"Ridiculous?"

She laughed again. "Yes, it is ridiculous, but that's not it either. It was *really* nice of you to pick me up. But why didn't Chuck or Jane come?"

"They drank too much celebrating. They're engaged."

"Oh, yeah. Chuck said something about that when I called. Then he apologized about six times for not calling me right away to let me know. He and Jane are so much alike, never wanting to upset anyone."

Darcy agreed. "They are always apologizing to each other. Yesterday she was chopping onions and Bingley's eyes began to water. Jane was horrified that she'd poisoned him while Bingley was doing his best to beg forgiveness for having eyes in the first place."

Elizabeth laughed. "God, I can't imagine those two having sex. 'Jane, darling, I'm sorry. Did I squeeze your nipple too hard?' 'Oh, Charles, sweetheart, do forgive me! It appears that in all the excitement, I've left dainty, little teeth marks on your bicep.'"

Now they were both laughing, and every time it would begin to quiet down, Elizabeth would do another impression. "'Dearest, I fear I have drooled into your navel.' 'My love, I suspect I've pierced your eardrum while screaming your name in ecstasy.'"

Then, to his surprise, Darcy joined in. "Oh, babe, allow me to make it up to you for staining the sheets."

To his great satisfaction, Elizabeth found his contribution exceptionally funny. He loved her laugh. It was no giddy, girlish giggle, but a deep, full laugh.

"We are awful," she said when she'd calmed down, "but I suppose for me, it's because I'm a little jealous."

"You fancy Bingley?"

"No, no, no! All that apologizing would drive me crazy. When a man makes love, I don't want him to be sorry. I want him to mean every single thing he does with a ferocity that takes my breath away."

There was no more laughter, and the temperature inside the car felt like it increased twenty degrees. Darcy knew he would do just that. He'd mark her skin, drown in her body, and rock the entire bed with each thrust until she came. Then he'd shout his orgasm to the rooftops and not care who heard. When they were finally sated, he'd leave her sweaty, body quivering, only to do it all again. And he'd never apologize for it. *Never!*

His entire body hummed, and his blood pounded in his ears. God, he needed to change the subject before he humiliated himself.

"So, if you're not jealous over our friend Charles, what are you jealous of?"

"Jane has found the one thing every red-blooded woman wants: someone who makes her feel—every day—like she is the most beautiful, most sexy, most cherished and most appreciated person on the face of the planet. It's not difficult for Chuck, of course, because Jane is the most beautiful—"

"She is not," he said.

"Why do you have to be such a cantankerous, contemptible shit? What did Jane ever do to you?"

"She's not the most beautiful woman in the world."

"Really! Name one, just one, who's more beautiful, and don't you dare say Heidi Klum!"

"Screw Heidi Klum. It's you, damn it! You!"

"Now you're joking."

"You look in the mirror every day. You *know* how beautiful you are."

"Ha! You said I wasn't hot enough to waste your time."

"I was an arse that night. I didn't take the time to even look at you, but later, when I did . . . And your mind is so bloody quick—even now when you're drunk."

"But everyone says Jane . . ."

He recognized that he was too distracted to drive, so he pulled over to the side of the road. Once the car stopped, he faced Elizabeth. "For months, I've listened to you, your mother, your aunt, and half of Meryton talk about her 'boundless beauty.' Yes, Jane's a great girl, but they're wrong. I know you don't want to hear this from me, but, Elizabeth Bennet, you walk into a room and I am so blown away, I can't breathe."

Her eyes were huge, and he suspected he scared her, but he refused to apologize. Instead he faced forward and stared out the window. There, he'd said it. Quite frankly, he was surprised he'd held out that long.

"Well, well, well, well, well!" Elizabeth sounded quite surprised. "Imagine that. You think I'm hot."

"Of course."

"Really hot."

"Obviously."

"You finally went and did it."

"Did what?"

"Made me like you."

He hesitated a moment before responding. "That's the gin talking." He then pulled back into traffic.

She had been silent for about five miles; consequently, Darcy was startled when she said, "I don't believe alcohol makes you say things you don't feel. It just makes you voice thoughts that a rational mind would tell you are best kept silent." She was quiet another moment before she laughed. "I'm being ridiculous—telling you that it's not rational to admit I like you. I sound like you did last week." In an amusing imitation of his accent, she said, "I've tried for months to forget about you. I've reminded myself daily of how my family will react to your mother, your youngest sister—"

"I was wrong to say that. I thought to be open and honest—to lay all my cards on the table."

"Why is it so important for you to point out other people's shortcomings? I know my mother can be a nightmare. I know Lydia was a disaster waiting to happen long before she spilled company secrets to George Wickham. I know you could have Heidi Klum if you really wanted to. I don't need you to remind me!"

"Heidi Klum? Now you really are being ridiculous."

"There! See what I mean? I know I'm being ridiculous. How would you like it if I ticked off everything about you that's wrong?"

"I thought your list was fairly comprehensive last week. You mean to say there's more?"

"You bet your excellent ass there is. For one"—she turned in her seat to look at him—"you have the best lips ever born on a man's face. I can't look at you without wanting to reach out and trace their outline. I bet they're soft too. Soft and strong."

Whoa! Where the hell had that come from?

"And your hair is so shiny." Elizabeth reached up, apparently to brush a few strands back from his forehead, but instead her fingers first went in his ear, then brushed his cheek before hitting his nose.

"Elizabeth," he warned. It would be a shame to wreck the car and die a fiery death just when things were becoming interesting, so he took her hand and held it on the console between them.

"And don't get me started on your voice. How is a woman supposed to think when everything that comes out of your mouth sounds so . . . sexy?"

"And these are my faults?"

"Damn straight. It ought to be illegal for any man to be as blessed by Mother Nature as you are. Why couldn't you have a gimpy leg or big wart on your nose? Your nasty disposition was your only saving grace until you showed up tonight and proved you're a nice guy after all. You are too perfect. It's intimidating."

"Wow." He was speechless.

"So, I suggest you dispense with the honest criticism and get back to the sincere flattery if you want me to have my wicked way with you tonight."

Dear Lord, if only! If only he didn't have principles, he'd take her up on her offer at the next rest stop. *Sometimes having principles is bloody inconvenient.*

Her hand slipped out from his, found its way to his thigh, and squeezed.

"Holy hell! Do you live at the gym?"

The past six months he'd been attempting to burn off his feelings for Elizabeth with a punishing exercise regimen. He was flattered that she noticed the only success from the effort. "I try to take care of myself."

"I'd like to take care of you." Her fingers drew little circles on his thigh. "Every amazing inch of you."

Good Lord, he was tempted. He could just imagine all the naughty things her fingers could take care of for him. But she was drunk, and he was a decent human being. *Sometimes being a decent human being is torture.*

He took her hand back to the console. "So, tell me about your date tonight. Anyone I know?"

"Bill Collins."

"The new reverend?" A picture of the man came to mind. He looked a great deal like Colin Farrell with thinning hair and a paunch. Darcy's aunt, who lived in a neighboring town, had headed the committee who hired him, and it was clear the man was just her type of minister—far more sheep than shepherd.

"The very same. My mom was so excited when he asked me out that she interrupted our conversation and accepted on my behalf. I didn't want to go—knew it was a *huge* mistake." Elizabeth stretched her hands far apart to demonstrate how huge, nearly blinding Darcy in the process. "But what could I do? I'm a lady. Sometimes being a lady bites ass."

On this of all nights he could sympathize. "So, did he hit on you?"

"You're jumping ahead, handsome. Let me tell the story. The man was taking me to dinner so the least I could do was look nice and attempt to get to know him better. Perhaps there was more to him than meets the eye, and I was willing to make the best of the situation. So, I made an effort. If I have to say so myself, I look pretty damn good."

"You look phenomenal."

"I'm glad someone else thinks so."

"I think we've already covered my thoughts on how you look—all the time."

She glanced over at him with those big eyes and smiled. He loved her smile. Even through the alcohol haze, she was stunning. "Thank you. You know, when you want to be, you're quite the charmer."

Her hand was wandering again, and Darcy had to swerve to avoid sideswiping an exit sign. "So, your date?"

"When Bill picked me up, he was so worried we would be late for our reservation. I don't think he noticed how I looked at all. He didn't open my car door, and when we got to the restaurant he walked in before me and didn't even bother to hold the door open until I could catch it behind him. It shut in my face. He didn't pull out my chair, he didn't offer me something to drink, he didn't ask what I wanted to eat. I know this is the modern age of equality of the sexes but traditions need to be upheld."

"He's a wanker."

"You're a quick study, Ace. Now, it took all of five minutes for me to realize that a single glass of cabernet was not going to get me through that dinner without my inflicting bodily injury on the man sitting across from me. So, I ordered a gin & tonic. When Bill began a lecture on the evils of alcohol, I changed it to a martini."

"Sounds perfectly logical to me."

"Bill talked for three hours straight. I heard all about where he went to school, how your aunt got him the job at the church, and his future plans. I swear, I should have dropped my napkin so I could take a quick peek under the table and see if he had a year's supply of oxygen being piped directly into his lungs, because I swear, he never took a breath. The man must be a freak of nature."

Darcy couldn't help but chuckle. "He would make one hell of a swimmer."

"Doesn't swim. He walks. Not regular walking, but that stuff they do in the Olympics that looks like ducks waddling."

"Racewalking?"

"That's it." She gave him a critical once-over. "You don't racewalk, do you? Because I don't care how difficult it is—and believe me, after this evening I know exactly how difficult it is—that is not sexy."

"No!" he defended immediately. "I run. At least five miles a day." When he saw her look of appreciation, he felt compelled to add, "Usually more."

"What else?"

"Else?"

"You don't get guns like these"—she squeezed his bicep—"from just running. Wow! Have these gotten bigger in the last two minutes?"

"I lift a bit—free weights." Her hand moved up and down his arm, using just enough pressure to make his blood boil. He took her hand to the console once more. "Back to your date?"

"Yeah. Where was I?"

"Racewalking."

"So not sexy."

"Agreed. So, what happened next?"

She sucked in a big breath and blew it out in a gin-saturated huff. "I was only permitted to order broiled chicken or fish with steamed broccoli. No butter. No sour cream. No sauce. No salt. No carbs. Nothing."

He laughed. "Sounds awful."

"You should have seen the waiter. He made a face that reminded me of Caroline Bingley the night she saw the Target bag in my parent's hallway."

"That bad?"

"Oh, yeah. Bill repeated your aunt's strictures on why he should eat a salt-, fat-, and sugar-free diet, and therefore, I must do the same. He also insisted that each bite be chewed thirty times. So, I ate a three-hour dinner more appropriate for a ninety-year old suffering from diverticulitis, but halfway through the second martini, it didn't taste too bad."

"Nothing would."

"Still, I figured things could be worse. Eventually the guy would want to take me home, and the date would end. But about the third, or was it the fourth martini, he started talking about *our* future. He told me to speak to my mom about the level of sodium in her cooking. He wanted to make sure she fed him properly on Christmas Day."

"But Christmas isn't for months. And why would he be eating at your parents' house?"

"Because we'd be married."

He wasn't sure he'd heard her right. "Married?"

"Now you get the picture, Sherlock. Good ole Bill made a lot of assumptions tonight. Like the one where he knew my hormones were raging out of control, but that I needed to rein in my impulses until our wedding night. I must admit, I've never before seen a man his age wear a purity ring. Which is no problem, really. If abstinence is his thing, more power to him. But to assume I couldn't control myself with him, now that was crazy talk. Then"—she paused dramatically—"he informed me that because my martinis were fifteen dollars a pop, I'd be paying my own tab. That was the only thing he'd said all night that made perfect sense to me."

Darcy couldn't believe any man would treat a woman in the manner she described. Darcy would hold the door for Elizabeth. He'd place his hand on the small of her back as she walked in front of him to their table. He'd pull out her chair, and while gently easing her to the table, he'd lean close to her ear and ask if she'd like champagne. He'd pay attention to every word she spoke, encourage her to eat whatever she liked, and never assume she'd pick up the check. He'd drive her home. He'd walk her to her door. He'd ask if he could come in, and if he was damn lucky, he'd get to undress her slowly, make her body tremble with desire, and he'd make damn sure she came not only first, but second too. After all, he was a gentleman with principles. *Sometimes, being a gentleman with principles rocked.*

Speaking of being a gentleman . . . "Why didn't Collins take you home?"

"Oh, he planned to, but I'm afraid this is the point in the story where alcohol overrode reason. As we were leaving the restaurant, he described to me the appropriate amount of tongue to be used during our—as yet—unscheduled first-date kiss. I told him to take his tongue and shove it up his ass. I'm afraid that by then I'd forgotten all about being a lady, and apparently, the limits of human anatomy. I stormed off and was six or seven blocks away before I realized that he was my ride home."

Darcy couldn't believe anyone could be so socially inept. "He's a complete shite."

"Thank you. On an evening when I was doubting my ability to judge people, it's nice to know I had at least one person pegged from the get-go."

"Only one person?"

"Yeah." She hesitated before continuing, and he could tell the alcohol was finally making her drowsy. "I learned . . . I really screwed up. I mean, you can be a first-class jerk, but you're not—you're not malevolent, heavy-handed, insufferable, unbearable, domineering, or any of those other words I threw at you last week. Well, maybe just a little. So, yeah, anyone who can convince your aunt not to prosecute Lydia over the Wickham debacle deserves Heidi Klum."

He frowned and stared straight ahead for several minutes until he could no longer keep his disappointment quiet. "What I did, I did in confidence. I don't want to insult your sister further, but I had hoped that Lydia had learned to keep her mouth shut."

"Oh, don't blame Lydia. It was Bill who told me. He'd heard about it from your aunt Cathy."

"Catherine," he corrected.

"Oh, yes." Elizabeth changed her voice to a close imitation of his aunt. "Lady Catherine de Bourgh." Then she laughed again. "Someone should remind that woman that she lives in America now. We don't give a crap about her fancy title."

Then she became serious, at least as serious as one can be after three *or four* martinis. "I can't tell you how much it means to my family that she wasn't arrested, but why in hell would you go out on a limb for Lydia?"

"I did it for you." She was obviously stunned silent but he wanted to make sure his confession made it through the gin. "Only for you."

Darcy spent the remainder of the drive to Meryton waiting for Elizabeth to respond. He thought several times that she might have fallen asleep, but she only stared ahead saying nothing. He would have paid anything to know what was going on inside her head. Did she now feel some misguided sense of obligation to him? Did she think he was some kind of sick stalker, sticking his nose into her family's business as a way to control her? And how could he defend himself if she remained silent?

When the Porsche finally pulled back into Bingley's garage, Darcy looked again to see if Elizabeth had fallen asleep, but she was wide awake. He opened her car door and helped her to stand.

As he helped her into the house, she finally turned to him and said, "You did it for me? After I insulted you and said I'd rather slit my wrists than ever to speak to you again, you still saved Lydia for me?"

"I'd do anything for you."

"Still?"

"Still."

That was when she grabbed the lapels of his jacket, tugged hard, and kissed him. Her mouth was warm, wet, perfect. The hands that plunged into his hair were rough and insistent. Her body molded against his was soft and yielding—and drunk. *Bloody hell, she is still drunk.*

He picked her up, carried her through the house and up the massive staircase. Lizzy spent the trip nuzzling his throat, driving him mad with small kisses and little nips of her teeth. Knowing there'd be no guest room ready for her, Darcy laid Lizzy gently in his bed, slipped off her shoes and tucked her in. When he came back from the bathroom with a glass of water and some Ibuprofen, he found both the blue dress and a matching bra lying on the carpet next to the bed. He drank in the sight of her exposed skin and wondered just how much of this torture he must endure before going completely starkers. He was only human after all.

He whispered an oath then tried to gently wake her. With a groan of protest, Lizzy sat up, which allowed the blankets to slip over her breasts to her waist. Then she fumbled, trying to cover herself while taking the pills. When she finished the water, she lay back and sighed.

He tucked the blankets over her shoulders and said, "We'll talk about this when you're sober if you want to."

"You scare me to death," she mumbled as she turned to her side.

"And why is that?"

"Because I could really fall for you. Really, *really* hard. And when you eventually leave me for Heidi Klum, it would hurt. It would hurt more than I could ever bear."

"My lovely, lovely, Elizabeth,"—he bent over and placed a soft kiss on her forehead. "Heidi Klum can bugger off."

Darcy woke up to the heavenly scents of bacon and coffee. He rolled over and fell hard onto the floor, having forgotten that he'd spent a restless night on the couch in Bingley's game room.

He groaned and opened his eyes to find Elizabeth standing over him with a tray in her hands.

"What time is it?" he grumbled while crawling to sit on the couch.

"It's nearly noon." Elizabeth placed the tray in front of him containing a spread of scrambled eggs, bacon, toast, fresh pineapple, and coffee. "I remembered that you liked your eggs scrambled and your coffee black. I took a guess at the toast and bacon—and who doesn't like pineapple?"

"I love pineapple," he admitted as he grabbed the mug. "This is great. Thanks. How's your head?"

"I had a rough night, but it's amazing what a lot of water and a full breakfast can do. So . . ." She seemed to be having a difficult time finding the words, and he feared what she might say next. At last she said, "Thank you for last night."

His heart sank. He did not want her thanks, and this sounded like the beginning of the big brush off, but then what more could he have expected? "You're welcome." He just wanted the conversation over with so he could nurse his wounds in private. "Thanks again for breakfast."

She got up to leave but hesitated again before sitting back down. Then her words gushed out. "Look, I'm really sorry about my behavior last night. I was all over you like some drunken prom date, which is an appropriate analogy as I was drunk, even though we're both too old for prom. You were such a gentleman, and I was touching you like some strumpet in heat and, well . . . I'm totally humiliated. You deserved to be treated as respectfully as you treated me. So, I apologize. Again. And again."

Her apology was sweet, but it was not what he wanted to hear. Well, if she was going to blow him off, he might as well push all his chips in. "Thanks, but I have to be honest. I wasn't offended."

"I know. You were so *nice*"—she smiled that smile he loved—"and I was *ridiculous*."

A glimmer of hope began to grow. "How much of last night do you remember?"

"All of it. From 'Hiya' to 'Heidi Klum can bugger off.' Every single, beautiful word."

"You said some beautiful words yourself."

They sat there smiling stupidly at one another for a full minute as the glimmer warmed into a steady flame.

It was Elizabeth who broke the silence when she reached for the fork and loaded it with eggs. She held the fork before his mouth.

Suddenly ravenous, he leaned forward and closed his mouth over the eggs. As he chewed, she said, "Twenty-four hours ago, I thought I'd never have the chance to tell you how sorry I was for what I said to you last week. Now here we are. Life can be so strange."

She held out another bite, and before taking it he said, "I'll never forget when you said there was nothing I could say that would convince you to go out with me."

"Oh, please! Don't remind me. I was such a jerk."

"Elizabeth, I was rude. I deserved every word."

"And I had jumped to the all the wrong conclusions. If anyone deserved to be put in their place, it was me."

"Let's not argue over who was the biggest fool. I don't think that discussion would make either of us look very good." He held up a slice of toast for her to bite.

She accepted his offering and fed him more eggs. "Well then, let's remember only the things that make us happy."

"Like this, now?"

She gave him that smile again and in that instant, he swore he could feel his heart pass from his chest into her hands. Somehow it didn't scare him at all. "Yes. Like this, now."

He pulled her into his lap, and they kissed—long, slow, and impossibly sweet. *Yes, being a gentleman certainly has its rewards.*

He let her take the lead and felt her body press closer, her breath come quicker, and her kiss turn deeper—and she was perfectly sober. *Yes, being a gentleman with principles rocks!*

Long after what remained of his breakfast had turned cold, she said, "Jane and Chuck have invited me to spend the weekend, and I need to get a few things. So, what do you say, Ace? Can you give me a ride home?"

"Sure thing, Sherlock."

Mild-mannered business woman by day, hopeless romantic by night, RUTH PHILLIPS OAKLAND was always a fan of the fictional gentleman from Derbyshire, but it was her discovery of Jane Austen fanfiction in 2006 that inspired Ruth to become a writer. Ruth has written dozens of short stories posted online and the published novel entitled, *My BFF*. Ruth lives in New England with her favorite husband of over thirty years and is thrilled to be included in this anthology with so many of her favorite authors and friends.

"In essentials, I believe, he is very much what he ever was."
—Miss Elizabeth to Mr. Wickham, Chapter XLI.

I, DARCY

KAREN M COX

AUTUMN

"Mr. Darcy is a putz."

"Pardon?"

"Mr. Darcy." I rolled my eyes at Corbin's characteristic blank look. "*Pride and Prejudice*? Ms. Smith's senior English class? Remember?"

"Hell, no, I don't remember. That was more than ten years ago."

"And I could never forget. You probably never read the book anyway."

"You're probably right." He laughed—that self-effacing, "aw-shucks" chuckle that, for some reason, women found adorable. "So, remind me. I guess the main character was Darcy. Hey, just like . . ."

"I'm ashamed to share his last name. Mr. Darcy is the 'hero'"—I air-quoted the word with my fingers—"of *Pride and Prejudice*, and I'm not surprised it didn't stick with you, because it's forgettable—a two-hundred-year-old book by an English spinster who most likely never spent any time with a real man in her whole, lonely, miserable life. A book where everybody gets married, as if that's the be-all, end-all objective of existence. In the words of the kid from *The Princess Bride*, it's a 'kissing book.' The illustrious Mr. Darcy is the main schmuck in a book full of schmucks. He starts out somewhat reasonable, but then he gets led around by his gonads just like every other dude in the story."

"You seem to know a lot about this book."

"You would too if your last name was Darcy." I mimicked an affected tone. "So, *you're* Mr. Darcy. Ha-ha-ha-ha. I've been looking for you all my life." With a grim shake of my head, I took a sip of my bourbon and branch. "His first name was even Fitzwilliam."

"That sounds a lot like William."

"Yep. My mother's little joke—English lit major that she was. Bought me a lifetime of misery with that name."

"So, that's why you go by Liam?"

"Exactly."

"I guess you're not a fan."

"I'm not *not* a fan, Corbin. I just think Mr. Darcy is a romanticized, overblown, emotional outlet for every woman who refuses to be satisfied with a real-world, flesh-and-blood man. He's also the reason all these women, and some men, are infecting this hotel on the very week I'm negotiating the most important business deal of the year. Just look at them." I cast a surreptitious glance around the hotel lobby.

Corbin's gaze followed mine, but he wasn't nearly as sly. "Oh, I don't know. I think they're sort of cute in their dresses and bonnets. It's no different than dressing up for 'Rocky Horror' or wearing Peyton Manning's jersey to a football game—both of which I've seen you do in the past."

"Not the same."

Corbin's eyes twinkled with mischief. "It looks pretty much the same to me."

My only response was a bland stare.

A light chuckle floated over the air. "Actually, Jane Austen knew a lot about men."

I turned and startled. Her voice had the same effect on me as the first bites of my grandmother's homemade cinnamon rolls—comforting and sweet and just a little spicy.

My cheeks grew hot with embarrassment. A young woman sat across from me—shocked, big blue eyes staring out of a beautiful face, corn silk blonde curls covered in an old-fashioned bonnet. The woman seated right behind me was wearing street clothes—and an amused grin—as she looked down into her glass of chardonnay. She didn't even grace me with a look as she continued.

"Miss Austen was close to her father. He was a minister of the Church of England and supervised much of her education. He also ran a boarding school for boys from their home. And she had several brothers. So yes, I'm sure she spent plenty of time with real men, and given her keen powers of observation, she probably knew men better than they knew themselves."

I sat, silently mortified that I had been caught discussing women—and literature—in public.

"Maybe," the young woman with the velvet voice continued, "that's why she never married."

"Lynley," Blue Bonnet Girl replied, obvious affection in her voice, "you're such a cynic."

Constitutionally incapable of rudeness, especially where pretty women were concerned, Corbin scooted his chair around between this Lynley and the blue-eyed one.

"Don't mind him. Sometimes, he gets a little grumpy. I'm Corbin, and you are . . . ?" He held out a hand, which the blonde took.

"Jane."

"This is Liam, and I promise . . . his bark is worse than his bite." He turned expectantly to the other woman, who still hadn't looked at me.

"I'm Lynley."

"Can we buy you ladies a drink?"

"Well . . ." Lynley glanced at Jane, who shrugged a delicate shoulder.

"To make up for general grumpiness. My friend here had a tough week." Corbin held up a finger to signal the waitress.

"Of—of course. If that's okay. No offense intended."

"None taken," Lynley answered. "Everyone has a right to express his opinion, even if it's an erroneous one."

The waitress approached, and Corbin gestured around the table. "Another round here. What'll you have, Jane?"

"Club soda."

He pointed at Lynley. "Chardonnay?"

"Sure, I guess."

When the waitress left, Corbin smoothly filled the awkward silence, addressing his question to the blonde. Typical. "So, do you live in the DC area, or are you traveling?"

"We're both from a small town in central Virginia."

"Oh, do you work together? Just friends?"

"Actually, we're stepsisters. My dad married Lynley's mom when we were little." Jane smiled warmly at Lynley. "But we're great friends, too."

"That's nice." Corbin leaned back as the waitress set drinks down on the table. "And you're Jane. At a Jane Austen conference. Clever."

Her smile brightened. It was like a perpetual beacon that she just turned up and down to fit the conversation. "Like your friend Liam's, my mother was an English lit major, too."

"Are you enjoying the conference?"

"Oh yes! We come to this meeting every year."

"But you're not dressed up." I frowned at the woman next to me.

"Dressing in period costume is optional, but Jane here is giving a talk about men's undergarments worn during the British Regency and thought costuming would add to the presentation." Her eyes flickered toward me. "First impressions often make a significant difference in how well you're received."

Jane blushed while Corbin gave her a speculative glance. "Men's undergarments . . . interesting," he murmured.

"And I'm combining business with pleasure on this trip. Jane's going back home after the conference ends, but I have a meeting day after tomorrow." Lynley turned to face me for the first time. "I'm curious, Mr. Darcy . . ." She faltered. "Um . . ."

"It's Liam."

"Yes, of course." She stared at me. "Um…what?"

"You're curious. . . ?" I asked.

"Oh." She closed those big, brown eyes for a second and shook her head, as if to clear the cobwebs out. I recognized the gesture, given that I often did that myself, but on her it looked infinitely more charming.

"Curious, yes." Her eyes opened, her equilibrium apparently restored. "Why do you despise the fictional Mr. Darcy so much?"

I back-pedaled, anxious to soften my previous hyperbole. "Despise is a strong word. It would be absurd to say I despise a literary figure, a man made of make-believe."

"You don't think that literature can be a reflection of real life?"

"Sure it can. But, like I said, Mr. Darcy isn't a reflection of real life. I think he's been put on a pedestal. It's irrational."

"Irrational? How so?"

"To start with, he's stand-offish and rude, and insulting to Elizabeth Bennet for most of the book, but that's all overlooked once she sees the big estate and talks to the housekeeper."

"My, my, you do know the story."

"Mother, English lit major, remember?"

Lynley smiled. "I think I'd like your mother."

"You probably would." I leaned back in my chair, considering her. "And what's more, Mr. Darcy isn't any kind of hero I'd aspire to be. He's actually kind of stupid."

"Really?"

"First off, he's got the hots for a gold digger."

"Well, most would say her mother was the gold digger."

"In my experience, the apple doesn't fall far from the tree." I was on a roll now. "Two, he's a complete social klutz. If Darcy really had a thing for Elizabeth, and yet he still made all those blunders up to and including the time when he proposed, she wouldn't give him the time of day after that, no matter what the revered Jane Austen would have you believe. Any time a real woman encounters a real man who actually acts like Mr. Darcy, she brushes him off like a piece of lint."

"You think so, do you?"

"I do."

"And is this assertion based on personal experience?"

I glared at her and ignored that little dig. "The idea that Elizabeth and Darcy would live happily ever after is a complete fairy tale."

"A fantasy."

"Yep. A fantasy that's been perpetuated by women for two hundred years. The *perfect* Mr. Darcy."

"I wouldn't say Mr. Darcy is perfect"—Lynley tilted her head, a mischievous grin on her lips, her eyes sparkling with humor—"he's just forgiven."

I smiled despite myself and conceded the point with a nod. "Perhaps."

Corbin picked up his glass and held it up. "To forgiveness." He clinked his glass to mine, then Lynley's, then held it up to Jane's. "And to new friends."

The next morning, I sat, absently drumming my fingers on the table in the hotel's conference room while the board of directors blew up around me.

"What kind of asinine, hippy-trippy idea are you suggesting?"

"That's the stupidest thing I ever heard."

"It's a recipe for a money pit."

I let them all spout off, and slowly the sound retreated until they were all staring at me, some with shock, some with puzzlement, some with condescension. These were men and women I had known most of my life, my father's contemporaries, people he had worked with and trusted, and now they eyed me, the young chairman trying to prove himself, with varying degrees of suspicion. Corbin and I exchanged glances.

"We're not talking about giving up on the principles that got us here. Castleton is synonymous with quality in the restaurant business," Corbin began. "We've got the pizza parlor chain, the low country seafood restaurants along the coast, the steak houses throughout the Southeast and spreading into the Midwest. This is just a different avenue, an expansion into a new area that will draw a new generation."

"It's not a step away from tradition," I cut in. "It's really a return to tradition: restaurants using locally sourced produce and livestock."

"It's too labor intensive to be profitable," George Whitman Sr. piped up.

"Not really, sir, not if we're willing to develop seasonal menus and be flexible when there are supply issues. There would be a learning curve, of course, and we're planning to start small to be fiscally responsible. In fact, Corbin has a spot handpicked for a test run."

Corbin took his cue and ran with it. "We're looking at Charlottesville. It's a university town, large enough to support a new restaurant, yet small enough to have that cozy atmosphere.

"In addition, central Virginia has varied agriculture already in place. We'll have sources for apples, grapes, berries, poultry, dairy, beef . . ."

"And," I added, "it's close enough to our headquarters in Alexandria to manage efficiently."

"A farm-to-table eatery." Mr. Whitman shook his head. "I never thought I'd see the day we went in for a fad."

"We won't be calling it farm-to-table. The term has been overused and used incorrectly to the point it has no meaning anymore. What we'll offer is simply good, local eats."

"Maybe that should be the slogan," Corbin joked.

"If we end up opening additional restaurants, we'll use the readily available sources in those new locations. This won't be a chain serving the same food everywhere. The restaurant will build a brand on adapting the food to the locale, so it will both support and reflect the community it serves. It's a great idea with minimal financial risk for a conglomerate like Castleton."

There was a murmur of ascension spreading around the table now. It was almost too easy.

"Do you know what you're going to call it? And who's going to head up the first location?" asked Whitman Sr.

"Corbin here is going to be the guinea pig." I put my hand on his shoulder. "So, I let him pick the name."

Corbin beamed from ear to ear, his enthusiasm contagious. "It will be my pleasure to welcome you all next summer to . . . Seasons."

WINTER

I wound my way down the curvy two-lane highway, light snow swirling around my windshield. Why Corbin rented a house in this God-forsaken nowhere was beyond me. We could afford a nice place in Charlottesville. So how did he end up in some little Podunk called Alton?

It had snowed a couple of inches in the night. Usually, the mountain protected this area of the state from bad storms, but this late winter squall had burst through, leaving a light, pristine covering over the ground. It looked like a Christmas card.

I was about five miles from town when I hit a patch of ice hidden under the snow. It took ahold of my Lexus SUV, slung me around in a one-eighty, and landed me in a ditch across the road, facing the opposite way.

After a couple of deep breaths to get my heart rate back down, I put the vehicle in low gear and tried to ease my way out of the grass and back on the road. The wheels only spun, digging into the soft ground. Swearing a blue streak, I wrenched open the door and got out to look. I was good and stuck, and my left rear tire was flat as a pancake. I'd just pulled out my phone to call Corbin and look for a towing place that might be open on a Saturday morning when a pick-up truck pulled up beside me.

"Hey, mister, you okay?"

I whipped my head around at the voice, eerily familiar, and stared straight into lovely brown eyes. "Yeah. Yeah, I'm fine."

She recognized me too, I could tell, but her smile grew chilly.

"I remember you. Lynley, right? We met in DC last fall. You were at that convention with the dresses and . . ." I gestured with my hands, toward my head, where a bonnet would go.

"Yes, that's me. And you're Mr. Darcy."

She remembered! I'd certainly not forgotten her, with her silky voice and her eyes sparkling as she championed Jane Austen over a glass of chardonnay. I smiled at the memory. "Guilty. You live around here?"

"You've got your wheels dug in my property."

I just stared at her.

"My farm borders the highway all along here."

"Your farm?" I glanced around, but being winter, there were no livestock or crops to be seen. An orchard of trees dotted the background landscape, and a greenhouse stood over to the right.

"My stepfather's farm, originally, but Jane and I are part owners now."

"Ah." I leaned my arms on the open passenger window and gave the woman in the truck cab a second look. She was pretty—surrounded by the outdoors—in a way that didn't show up in a hotel lobby bar. Her cheeks were pink from the cold, and the sweater and toboggan suited her better than the prim business wear she wore the first time I saw her. I waited for her to look back at me, and then I tried my most charming smile on her. "Interesting coincidence, running into you again."

"Isn't it just?" She sat back, arms folded, a little frown on her face. Fairly adorable. How come I hadn't noticed this when we met?

"Don't suppose you know someone who could pull me out of here, do you?"

She leaned forward, her left hand resting on the wheel and looked beyond me at the Lexus, considering. Finally, she shrugged. "Yeah, hop in."

"I can just call if you're busy." I lifted the phone in my hand. "What's the number?"

"Hop in. It's just down the road a piece. And, he may not answer the office phone on a Saturday."

"But he'll give me a tow on a Saturday?"

She sighed, resigned. "If I go with you and ask him, he will."

We drove about two miles and pulled off the highway to the right. Lynley parked in front of a shabby, white, cement block building with a big, glass garage door. An old Sunoco gas sign leaned up against the front of the building, and various bits of vehicle carnage were scattered over what passed for a parking lot. A tall, heavyset man in coveralls and sporting a red and black watch cap with ear flaps was polishing the door's glass with a squeegee. He dropped it in a bucket and jogged over to the driver's side as Lynley rolled down her window.

"Hey, Lynley. What are you doing here?" He spoke fast and his voice was a little breathless, like he'd just run a lot farther than the twenty feet from the garage to the truck. Or maybe he was just excited to see her. His eyes were all bright and glassy.

"Need a tow, Tommy. Can you help me out?"

"Sure, but your truck looks fine to me. I mean, for as old as it is. I wish you'd let me talk to my uncle over in Kent about a new one, like mine. It's . . ."

"I'm not the one who needs the tow."

"Oh. Who is it, then?"

Lynley jerked her head toward me, and the man ducked and squinted into the truck cab. He gave her a woeful look. "Didn't know you had company, Lynley."

"Not that it's your business, Tommy Collins, but he's not my company. I found him a couple miles back on the side of the road. Can you help him or not?"

"You picked up a stranger? I don't think that's a very good idea. Don't you watch the news? Just the other week, I saw on Facebook where some gal—"

"Tom!" Her voice rose and sharpened. "He's not a stranger. I met him in DC last fall. Liam Darcy, this is Tom Collins."

I nodded curtly. I couldn't help but notice this Tom talked more to Lynley's chest than her face. Not that she was on display in her black turtle neck, but that didn't seem to deter him. "I think it will need a new tire as well. If you could just tow it to the local Lexus dealer?"

"Ain't no Lexus dealer in Alton, buddy." He laughed, a guffaw worthy of ten Appalachian mountain men. "I could probably repair it for ya, though." He glanced around at the vehicle parts strewn about the property. "Or find something that would get you on your way."

"Um, a repair would be great, thanks. Just need to get it to a dealer."

"Yeah, so you said."

There was an awkward silence that Lynley filled. "Well. Ok, Tom, just follow us back, and I'll let the two of you sort it out. I've got to get to the bank before it closes." She rolled up the window, just barely missing the poor fellow's nose, and did a U-turn into the road.

"Is that guy's name really Tom Collins?" I asked.

"Yep. Well actually, no, not really. It's a nickname. His real name is Elwood Wayne, but his mama thought he was tiny when he was born. So, she called him Tom Thumb, and the 'Tom' stuck."

"And no one thought to tell her she'd named her son after a mixed drink?"

"Apparently not." Her lips twitched.

"Tell me about your farm."

She glanced over, that little frown returning. "What?"

"Farming is my business, indirectly."

"But you . . ."

"There's my car." I pointed as she drove past it. She made another U-turn and pulled onto the shoulder.

"Here you go." She stopped the truck and looked straight ahead. I tried in vain to think of some conversation that would keep her there—or an opening so I could get her phone number.

"Thank you for your help. Maybe I could call you. Take you out to dinner or something. To thank you."

"You already said thank you. Don't worry about it." She looked at her watch.

"Sure, okay." What was wrong with this woman? *Mr. Darcy* was trying to find a way to ask her out, and she looked at her watch like she had a million places to be instead. "Here's my number, in case you change your mind." I pulled a pen out of my jacket pocket and wrote my cell on the back of one of my cards. She just looked at it, stunned. Well, she ought to have been stunned; I never give women my cell phone number. I got out of the truck and started toward my vehicle. Tom Collins had just pulled up and was looking at the tire and shaking his head. On impulse, I turned back toward Lynley, but the truck was pulling onto the road.

I didn't even know her last name.

When I finally got to Corbin's, I was exhausted. Not physically—all I did was wait around an hour and a half for Tom Collins to repair my tire. But mentally, the constant dribble of inanity that came from his mouth just about did me in. I decided his name, although ridiculous, was nothing compared to the man himself. First, he boasted about his truck for at least twenty minutes. Who cares about a truck? I have three of them. A truck is a tool, a utensil, like . . . a fork or a hammer. Hey, I like a sweet ride as much as the next man, but I've never understood the fascination with transportation that occupies some people's attention.

But the worst part was listening to him talk about Lynley. She was smart. She was hot. Every guy in town wanted to date her. He himself had asked her out and was convinced that the third time would do the trick, now that it was winter and she wasn't so busy. She'd be foolish not to date him, he said. He was a successful businessman, with a brand-new truck, after all, which he threatened to show me after he fixed my tire. He went on to tell me how Lynley's biological clock was ticking; he'd heard all about it during that lady psychologist's show on satellite radio. His new truck had XM radio, free for the first three months. His uncle really set him up right.

Yeah. Exhausting.

Plus, the tire and Tom Collins debacle put me so far behind that I had to stay through the weekend until Monday, when I could get to Charlottesville's Lexus service department. Instead of a Saturday jaunt to check in with Corbin on the restaurant, I ended up spending the weekend in Podunk Alton.

Not that seeing Corbin was a chore. He made his own fun wherever he went, which was one of the reasons we'd become friends in the first place.

He opened the door of his rental house on Broadway with a great big grin.

"You made it!"

"Finally."

"Come on in. I was just on my way out the door to pick up pizza and beer."

"I might go with you. I need to pick up a razor and a toothbrush, too. Looks like I'll be around until Monday. I can't find a decent hotel anywhere in this town. Can I bunk here?"

"Absolutely. Lost weekend in Alton! Take a load off—I'll get your stuff while I'm out."

"That would be much appreciated." I sat on his couch with a sigh, thankful to finally have some quiet.

"Be right back."

Which, for Corbin, meant a couple of hours at least.

"Make yourself at home," he called as the door slammed behind him.

"Don't mind if I do," I muttered, swinging my legs around and propping my head on a couch pillow.

I breathed deep and closed my eyes.

But sleep wouldn't come. The insides of my eyelids were painted with brown eyes and curls under a toboggan—and a light and pleasing figure. The soundtrack of my solitude was Tom Collins's voice repeating, "She's really smart. She's hot."

I sat up, found the TV remote, flipped through a few channels, and stopped at some random ball game. I went to the kitchen, found a Diet Coke (blah, when had Corbin started drinking that swill?) and some Fritos and nacho dip, and plopped back down on the sofa.

I glanced around for a coaster, because my mama raised me right, but all I found was a Sports Illustrated magazine to set my drink on. I moved it over, and the book resting underneath caught my eye.

Pride and Prejudice.

"What the hell?" The weird coincidences kept piling up. Why was Corbin reading the story of Mr. Darcy?

"What the hell . . ." I repeated and opened the book to the first page.

"It is a truth, universally acknowledged, that a single man in possession of a good fortune, must be in want of a wife."

I snorted, thinking that was exactly the sort of sentiment I expected from the vaunted Jane Austen, and exactly what I'd remembered from high school English. I kept reading. And muted the ball game.

". . . Mr. Bingley might like you best of the party." I grinned. So, Mr. Bennet was a snarky bastard; I hadn't remembered that. I appreciated snark, although I wasn't particularly gifted with it myself. I kept reading.

"You mistake me, my dear. I have a high respect for your nerves. They are my old friends. I have heard you mention them with consideration these twenty years at least."

A bark of laughter escaped me; the sound of mirth echoing into the quiet.

By the time Corbin returned, the Diet Coke was warm, the chips were almost gone, and I was at Mr. Bingley's house. In the middle of Chapter 10, I silently confessed I'd been entertained, and was now half in love with Elizabeth Bennet myself, damn it.

"Got pizza, got beer. Got toothbrush and razor."

"Corbin," I asked, holding up the book, "I'm curious—why the sudden interest in Jane?"

"Jane? Well, I…uh." He squinted at the book in my hand. "Oh, right. Jane. Austen."

"What other Jane would I be talking about?"

"I don't know." He shuffled past me into the kitchen and put his bags on the counter.

I followed him. "Maybe a blue-eyed blonde Jane who wears Regency bonnets and gives conference presentations about men's underwear?"

"Funny you should mention her." A stupid grin swept over his face. "I ran into that Jane recently."

"She lives here."

"She does. How did you know that?"

"The brown-eyed, possibly wicked, stepsister happened to drive by right after I blew out my tire."

"You saw Lynley today?"

"She got me the tow truck, right after she informed me my Lexus was digging a muddy rut in her field."

"That's Lynley for you, spicy on the outside but sweet underneath."

"Maybe. Besides, I thought Jane was more your type."

"She is."

"So, you have a thing?"

"I do. Except I don't think it's just a thing."

"Corbin…" I sighed, shaking my head. "How many times have we been through this? Remember when we opened the restaurant in Savannah?"

"Yeah."

"What was her name?"

"Melanie."

"And then in Jacksonville, there was…"

"Rhiannon."

I crossed my arms and gave him my best censure-provoking look.

"I know. I happen to like Southern girls. Nothing wrong with that."

"No."

"But this one is different." He squirmed a little under my paternal glare. "I would like to talk to you about her farm and . . ." His phone rang, and he fished it out of his pocket, checked the number. "Go get cleaned up," he said over his shoulder, "'cause we've got company coming." He answered the call and walked away. "Hey there." His voice softened into this annoying, gooey coo.

I grabbed my razor and toothbrush and stalked off to the guest room.

They arrived just as the sun was setting over the mountain to the west—the angelic Jane and the fascinating Lynley. In a scoop neck sweater thingy and short skirt and boots, she managed to look sexy yet classy at the same time. She drank craft beer with more ladylike sophistication than some women had drinking the finest champagne. I kept expecting low rent opinions or boring conversation from this farm girl, yet she surprised me at every turn. A double major at Virginia Tech in ag and computer science, she had returned to her stepfather's farm after graduation and tried to bring the operation into the twenty-first century. Along with Jane, who did the bookkeeping—in addition to running her own CPA firm—the sisters had first expanded the farm by remodeling the aging greenhouse and selling cut flowers to regional florists.

In between conversations about movies, UVA basketball, and local gossip, I learned that Fairlight Farm raised poultry; grew cole crops such as cabbage, kohlrabi, and broccoli to extend the growing season March to December; and were adding pear and cherry trees to the old apple orchard, which had been their father's staple crop for many years. I grew more interested as Corbin asked Lynley about her plans for the future—had she considered wine grapes, berries, cattle? His questions made perfect sense to me; this was just the kind of local supplier Seasons was after, but I was confused by the awkward glances she threw my way each time the topic came up.

Finally, I'd heard enough to comment. "We should sit down. Discuss some of the particulars of your operation. My company, Castleton, needs local supply chains for the restaurant Corbin is spearheading for us in Charlottesville, and it sounds like Fairlight Farm could be a good fit for us. We could discuss it, m-maybe over dinner?"

Lynley looked back at me, stunned. "Are you seriously asking me this, after . . ."

"Ah, yeah. Um, I thought perhaps—"

Lynley threw her napkin down. "I don't know what kind of game you're playing, but I think it's completely inappropriate, given the circumstances. Excuse me." She got up and headed for the hall closet to retrieve her coat.

Jane muttered an apology and followed her sister out of the room.

Corbin and I sat and stared at each other.

"What just happened here?" I finally stammered.

Our chairs scraped the floor simultaneously as we stormed the front door. They'd made it as far as the porch.

"I knew they were friends, but I didn't realize Corbin worked for him." Lynley shook her head. "And you knew, Jane! How could you put me in this situation?"

"I know you were upset before, honey, but I think maybe we should talk to them again. I can't believe they would be so unfair."

"No way, in any Circle of Hell. I'm not putting myself through that again."

I caught up with the two just as they reached the sidewalk. "Wait." I took Lynley's elbow, but she shook me off and whirled around.

"Back off, Mr. Darcy."

I stepped back, hands raised. "Okay."

"Come back inside," Corbin pleaded. "We'll talk about it."

"Go ahead if you want, Jane," Lynley answered, her voice as frosty as the night, "but I'm leaving."

Corbin looked between Jane's down-turned face and her sister's fiery expression. Finally, Jane turned toward the house with Corbin following behind.

"What is your problem?" I hissed at Lynley. "Fairlight Farm is your business, isn't it? You should treat it as such and realize what Castleton could do for you. This is an opportunity that doesn't come along every day, especially for an operation like yours."

"What do you mean, an operation like mine?"

"A small-time operation. You need a buyer for all that expansion you're planning. Unless you want to keep selling flowers and apples to the locals."

"What's wrong with selling to the locals?"

"Nothing." I pinched the bridge of my nose to ward off the headache I felt coming on. "I don't understand why you're being so difficult and . . . spiteful."

"I'm spiteful? Maybe you better look in the mirror, pal. I've already been down this road with you. Don't play dumb with me."

My mind whirled as I tried to understand the fury and indignation pouring off her. It was made even more difficult by the strangely appealing spark of anger in her eyes and the patches of flame burning in her cheeks. "I'm sensing subtext here," I murmured to myself.

She paced out and back, ignoring or perhaps not even hearing me. "I'm sure you're too important to remember a penny-ante sales pitch like mine."

"What?"

"I met with Castleton's vice-president last fall, about supplying some of your restaurants with produce."

"You did?"

"You don't remember then. I figured as much."

"So, enlighten me. What were you told?"

"I was told that your chief supply chain officer axed my proposal, due to expansion into other markets that required more established and 'stable' suppliers. The vice president who met with me was very sympathetic but said his hands were tied. That was before he offered to soothe my sorrow with a night on the town, ending in his hotel room."

"What?" I repeated. "Who was this?"

"The vice president of acquisitions, George Whitman."

"This has to be some kind of mix-up. Mr. Whitman would never do that! He's been one of our most loyal board members for thirty-five years."

She looked momentarily confused. "That can't be. This guy was young."

"Unless . . ." I paused, dreading her answer. "Was it Whitman Jr. who said this to you?"

"Perhaps. Does this younger Whitman work for you?"

"Yes, but . . ."

"So, whether he was senior or junior is irrelevant—except for the sexual harassment angle. *You're* the one who squashed a substantial opportunity for a *small-time* operator like me."

"But . . ."

"You personify big business at its very worst, and I've got no use for Castleton or for you."

She yanked open her car door, and while I stood there agape, she threw the car in reverse and backed recklessly down the driveway. I watched the tail lights disappear down the street, and then, shivering, I went back into the house.

I found Corbin and Jane sitting at the kitchen table.

"I'm sorry about Lynley storming off," Jane said quietly. "She was angry when Castleton shut her down without what she thought was a fair chance."

"I think I know who she talked to, and maybe what happened there. Trust me, he's *not* a vice president at Castleton. It's not the first time he's exaggerated his own importance to people outside the company, but it is the first I've heard about this level of inappropriate conduct. You can bet I'll deal with it."

"She looked him up on your website before the meeting. George Whitman *is* a vice president at Castleton."

"George Whitman Sr. is, but my guess is she talked to Whitman's son. He works for us, for now, anyway. Still, I don't get her foolish outburst with me. A businesswoman ought to have better control of herself."

Jane sighed. There was no trace of her perennial smile now. "Lynley *does* have self-control. She's as professional as they come, and that made the sleazy proposition hurt even more. The encounter with Castleton really shook her confidence.

"She went to the company headquarters last fall, surprised that she actually got to talk to Mr. Whitman in person, but the name was the same so . . ."

"Whitman took advantage of her unfamiliarity with the board and officers." I turned to Corbin. "This is one reason why we need to get photos up on the website."

"Lynley was on cloud nine after the initial lunch meeting. You remember, she had a business appointment the day after we met you all."

I didn't remember that. All I could recall was my ineptitude and Lynley's voice, her eyes, her smile . . .

"It was a last-ditch effort," Jane went on.

That brought my attention back to the present with a jolt. "What do you mean?"

"I do the books, so I know that things have been precarious for a couple of years now. Last fall Lynley and I put our heads together with Dad because the farm isn't doing well. The things Lynley has tried—a website, new crops, making connections with other farms in the region—they've helped, but it just isn't enough. We're on the verge of having to let people go, or sell off land to meet mortgages, pay off equipment—stuff like that. Lynley has been doing some IT consulting on the side, but she might have to break down and take a full-time job if things don't change, which means even less time and resources for the farm."

"So, you needed a bigger buyer like Castleton to keep growing."

"Just to keep up, really. That's why she contacted your company."

"Jane, I know Lynley is upset about what happened with Whitman, and rightfully so. In fact, I'm downright furious and embarrassed about him mispresenting my company. But I wasn't blowing smoke when I said I was interested in working with you.

"I may be able to make amends for how Whitman treated her. If that had been a legitimate interview for a new supplier, Lynley *would* have had a fair chance. From what I've heard here tonight, Fairlight Farm is a perfect fit for what we are trying to do for the Charlottesville place. Won't you let me try to fix this?"

"It isn't entirely up to me."

"I know, but I want to make a start, and perhaps you're a softer sell." I tried to lighten the mood with a joke, but she just tilted her head and looked at me thoughtfully.

"I suppose I'm softer than Lynley, at any rate. How?"

"First, I'd like to meet your father, see the operation."

"I don't want to go behind Lynley's back."

"Me neither. No pressure, I promise, but unless I can see the farm and talk to someone, there's no way I can make this right. And I don't think Lynley will listen to me right now."

"She'll cool off. She'll listen . . . eventually." Jane's smile returned. "But you're right. She probably won't listen right now."

SPRING

The March wind blew my car all over the road. Sharp, crisp sunlight broke through billowing purple and gray clouds outlined in white. Why was the weather always tempestuous when I drove into Alton? Much like the woman I was driving in to see.

I'd toured Fairlight Farm now and talked to Mr. Barrister. I'd laid eyes on the greenhouse, seen the chickens, perused the business plan Lynley, Jane, and their dad had drawn up. Their ideas were good ones: careful, incremental expansion, a balance of familiar and new concepts, sound farming principles. I wished all our potential suppliers were this organized. It was going to work out well for them to supply Seasons with quality ingredients for the chef's recipes. Now I just had to convince the last third of the ownership that I wouldn't screw her . . . over. Treat her badly. You know what I mean.

Her stepfather told me I'd find her in the greenhouse. I walked down the charming flagstone path and carefully opened the door. The warm, humid and perfumed air stole my breath for a second. I smelled the hyacinth, let my gaze run over the colorful sea of gerbera daisies that I knew would find themselves on restaurant tables and in sweetheart bouquets all over Hertford County. I saw a flash of white behind a potted lilac and approached the aisle with, I had to admit, a certain amount of trepidation. I'd repeatedly faced a boardroom of powerful, opinionated men and women with equanimity. Why did this slip of a young woman unnerve me so?

I stopped at the end of the aisle and waited. She was so engrossed in her work she hadn't seen me approach. Humming to herself, she smiled ever so slightly while inspecting little beds of herb plants and intermittently wiping damp soil from her fingers on her gardening apron. I wondered what she was thinking.

"Lynley?"

She startled and stood there, staring at me, wild-eyed. I had a vision of striding over and yanking her into my arms before I captured that rosebud mouth with mine. I could almost feel her fingers tangled in my hair and hear my own blood roaring in my ears.

She closed her eyes, in that endearing gesture of gathering her wits, and when she opened them, the cool professional demeanor enveloped her like a regal robe. Under it, though, I saw a glimmer of uncertainty.

"Hello, Mr. Darcy."

"Liam, please."

"Liam, then. What are you doing here?"

"I came to talk to you. You've seen my offer?"

"I have."

"Well, I'm here to answer any questions you might have as you consider it."

"You didn't have to make a special trip, just for me. You could have called. You could have sent someone else."

"I could have. I thought this situation deserved some personal attention, given—well, given everything."

"You needn't apologize again. I did read your letter." Her voice dropped to a whisper. "Many times."

I grinned and took a step closer to her. "You did?"

"I'm glad you fired the horse's ass."

"Even his father agreed there had to be consequences. What George Jr. did to you, well . . ."

"It's bad for business?"

"It is. It's also embarrassing for Castleton."

She looked down at her feet. "I'm sure."

"And most importantly, it was wrong."

"Yes."

"So, will you?"

"Will I what?"

I let the moment hang, suspended with possibilities. "Will you consider my offer?"

"Your offer?" She took a step toward me, then stepped back. "Oh, right. Castleton's offer. Yes. The offer is more than fair. Generous, in fact."

"Thank you."

"It is, as you said last winter, a good opportunity for us."

"About that . . ."

"My stepsister Mary is an attorney over in Richmond. She's going to look over the contract, and if she okays it, Jane and Dad and I have decided we'll take Castleton's offer."

She stepped forward again and extended her hand. I shook it and held it, until she almost wrestled it away from me. Such a little hand. Such a capable hand. She put down her trowel and untied her apron, laying it gently on the table beside the plants.

"I traded a floral arrangement for a twelve-pack from that new microbrewery over in Sussex County. You wanna come up to the house and try one? I've heard they're pretty good."

"Sure." My tongue had gone all thick and stupid and felt too big for my mouth.

We ambled, side by side, up the path toward the house, both of us perhaps knowing that once we went in, this fragile thread connecting us could break.

I cleared my throat. "I re-read *Pride and Prejudice.*"

She laughed. "You did?"

"I did. And then I had a long talk with my mother about why she named me after Mr. Darcy."

"Really?"

"I'd always assumed it was a joke, but after I talked to her, I realized it wasn't."

"What did she say?"

"She said she gave me that name because she wanted me to grow up to be the kind of man Mr. Darcy was—down deep inside. She wanted me to be a man who would stand up for the people he loved and truly help them, even if it was behind the scenes. She wanted me to see people for who they are, not what they have."

"All good aspirations."

"And she wanted me to be a man who could learn from my mistakes."

"That's actually a lovely sentiment. Did you forgive her?"

"After hearing her explanation, it seemed like there was nothing to forgive."

"So, you revisited the fictional Mr. Darcy. Any new revelations to share?"

"I still think Mr. Darcy is a putz."

"He has his moments."

"But not for the reasons I remembered."

"Oh?"

"No. He's a putz because he sees something genuinely appealing in Elizabeth, and he rationalizes first off that he doesn't see it, and later on, that he shouldn't want it. And that's stupid, because attraction hovering over real substance, that's what every man wants in a woman."

"It is?"

"Then he inadvertently insults her at a time when her feelings should have been paramount. A bitterly rejected proposal shouldn't be necessary to make a man honest with himself. So. Putz."

She stopped. I did too, and we faced each other.

"But to his credit, after he gets over being angry, he considers her point of view and changes his manners."

"True."

"Then he proceeds to save her future."

"I think that's a bit extreme, don't you?"

"You wouldn't think so if you were female and living in Regency England. Trust me, saving her family's reputation by finding the wayward sister was a big deal."

"I guess."

"Empathy, followed by action. It's the one-two punch of the romantic hero."

When we reached the back door, I tried again to say what was in my heart. "Lynley, I . . ."

"Yes?" She stopped, her fingers on the door handle. Her eyes were bright and shiny, and wary. I thought about how Whitman had wronged her, how it might look if I pursued her now, after all that had happened. Perhaps if we'd been just two people discussing Jane Austen over a drink in a hotel bar, and none of this other had occurred, there wouldn't be all this baggage, this awkwardness. Friends, that's what we should be now. Friends, with a good business relationship, because that seemed to be all she wanted.

"You think this craft beer would work for Seasons?"

"I wouldn't ask you to try it if I didn't think so." She smiled, beautifully—and opened the door.

SUMMER

I sat in the lounge at Seasons on opening weekend, listening to the happy sound of glasses clinking and the murmur of multiple conversations around me. Corbin had outdone himself. From the warm cherry wood trim to the rich, gold walls decorated with local art, the dining area radiated comfort and upscale chic. And here in the bar was a more casual feel—red leather seats in the booths and on the barstools. The warmth of cherry wood trim and furniture carried over from the dining room. Poster-sized black and white photos of local farms and the farmers who ran them were scattered on walls painted in muted earth tones. I picked up my drink and wandered around, admiring the photography—and nearly choked on my bourbon and branch when I rounded the end of the bar and saw Lynley's face over a corner booth. Her amused little smile reminded me of that time when she'd overheard me dissing my literary namesake in a hotel bar—wow, almost a year ago.

A waiter barely avoided bumping into me as he rushed from the kitchen.

"Oh, excuse me, sir." He glanced up. "She's a looker, isn't she? We're calling this table the Bachelors' Booth. A group of guys will always choose to sit here if it's open. If there'd been a hot farm girl like that running around my hometown, I might not have left."

"Hmmph."

"People say the woman pictured on the other side of the bar is more beautiful, but there's just something about this one . . ." He trailed off and we stood, side by side, gazing up at the photograph. He shrugged and walked around me while I sipped and continued to stare. I couldn't tear my eyes away.

"It's embarrassing, isn't it?"

I turned, and there she stood, the object of my affection, lovely in a red dress that was just clingy enough to be sexy. Yet, she also exuded a prim demeanor—a little purse clutched in front of her.

She stepped up beside me and looked at her own portrait. "I had no idea what Corbin was planning when he sent that photographer down to Alton. He said the pictures were for publicity, and I thought, you know, pamphlets or something. Never dreamed he'd . . ." She held her hand up, indicating the photo. "There's one of Jane on the other side."

"You make farming look very appealing."

"I'm sure," she answered, her voice dripping with sarcasm.

"How are you, Lynley?"

"I'm good, Mr. Darcy." She grinned. "I know, I know you're Liam, but it tickles me to call you Mr. Darcy."

"You look just as at home in that lovely dress as you do in jeans and boots, or a gardening apron."

"Well, aren't you the smooth one?"

"No, I'm really not, as you are quite aware."

"Actually, I believe you are—except for rare instances of literary faux pas."

"Why are you here?"

"I came up to see how things were going on opening weekend."

"See if there are any glitches?"

"Yeah." She fidgeted. "No."

"No?"

"Corbin said you'd be here tonight. Look, can I buy you a drink? Oh. Never mind. You've already got one."

"Let me get you one, and we'll find a table. Chardonnay's your favorite, isn't it?"

She nodded. "Yes, thanks."

I stepped over and got the bartender's attention. "Chardonnay for the lady, please." I waited with my back to the room—and her—while I tried to figure out what to say. *"Lynley, I know we didn't get off on the right foot."* No, that was an understatement. *"We've known each other a while now."* Blech, too trite. Crap.

I turned back and she was gone. Glancing around, I saw her sitting at a high top by the window. A guy in a suit had approached the table—geez, they moved fast around here—but Lynley just smiled and pointed my way as she thanked him.

"Friend of yours?" I asked, not liking the tension in my voice.

"No, just a knight in shining armor seeing a lone damsel in perceived distress."

"I don't think there's much distress you can't handle."

"See that, right there"—she pointed at me—"exactly the right thing to say. Yep, you're a smooth one." She took a sip. "But I am, in fact, a little distressed."

"Why?" I reached out a hand, drew it back.

She was focused on her drink, not on me, so she missed the gesture. "And regardless of how awkward I feel, I had to come here tonight—to thank you, on behalf of the families who depend on Fairlight Farm, since they don't know specifically who to thank." She looked up at me then, that wild-eyed intensity in her eyes that made my blood simmer. "We're on track for a record year, and I am—we all are—indebted to Castleton, to you." She closed her eyes briefly and sighed. "I know your generosity is because of what happened with Whitman, and I'm not sure how I feel about that. But the end result is, I'm grateful to you, for helping me save Fairlight Farm."

I sighed too. Gratitude. Not what I was hoping for. "I'm sorry, very sorry, if you, in any way, feel uneasy about the partnership Castleton has with Fairlight Farm. It was a good fit, based on sound business judgment, one I would have wanted for my company regardless of those other circumstances. The debacle with George Jr. was an unfortunate detour, but the outcome was the right one. Besides, Castleton is my company, and it was my responsibility to set things right." I did put my hand over hers this time and wondered if she felt the connection too. "So, don't be distressed."

"A happy ending for all?"

"Of course." I sat back, gazing at her, then sat forward again. "Nope. No, not yet."

"What?"

"Lynley, almost from the first minute I saw you and heard your voice, I've been . . . attracted, no, drawn. . . no—I tried to tell you in the spring, but I just couldn't. But now we've cleared the air, and I have to be honest." I put my hand back over hers, to ground me. "I want to see you."

"You are seeing me." She waved her hand, as if in greeting. "I'm right here."

"See you. Socially. Hell, I'm screwing this up. Can I take you out to dinner some time?"

She blinked, and I worried I'd overstepped.

"Out to dinner? Like, out, out. On a date, out?"

"If you're not interested, just say so. It won't change our business relationship, and I'll never mention it again, but being around you makes me settled and it makes me happy, and . . ." I shrugged. "Well, I had to take a chance."

A shy smile crept across her features, warm and soft, like a winter's dawn. "I'd like to go to dinner with you. I'd like that . . . very much."

"You would?"

Her lips twitched in a mischievous grin. "Well, maybe. It depends."

"On what?"

"Where would we go?"

My heart gave a joyful leap. "Where would you like to go?"

"I've heard about this great little restaurant that's new in town. It's one of those local joints, with the farm-inspired menus and the uptown atmosphere. Do you know the place?"

"I do." I stood and took her elbow as I led her to the hostess stand. "And I bet I can get a table."

AUTUMN, AGAIN

We walked hand in hand along a fence row at Derby Farms, my family's place in the Shenandoah Valley. Derby is a sprawling one-hundred-acre farm that has been in the family since before the Civil War. I brought Lynley here to meet my parents and visit the place most dear to me in all the world. The day we arrived, she made me very happy by gasping, "Stop the car!" as we crested the hill and the house came into view. She rolled down the window, leaned out, and turning back to me with a big smile, she announced, "It's wonderful! I've never seen a house fit its setting so well. It just belongs here, doesn't it?"

I had to agree, and then I thought to myself how much she belonged here too.

Now, we strolled around the cherry tree orchard and into the woods, the cool crisp autumn air rustling the orange and brown leaves. The sun was bright and the sky clear. It would be cold tonight; it might even frost. It would be a good night for a bottle of wine and a fire in our room—among other entertainments.

I brought our joined hands up to kiss her fingers, making her new engagement ring wink in the sunlight. We'd come to Derby so I could give her that token as well, and ask her, surrounded by the land I loved and the history I sprang from, to share my life. Some people might think it was too fast, but really, I'd known her for a year, and when you know, you know. She's the one. And I'm a man of action.

"Mr. Darcy," she began, and somehow the appellation didn't annoy me coming from her. "When did you fall in love with me? I know you carried a torch for a while before I knew, but how did that spark ever ignite in the first place?"

"It must have started from that first moment, that first lively banter."

"You mean your snarky comment about the literary Mr. Darcy. Perhaps it was my snarky comment in return that intrigued you. Like your fictional predecessor, you enjoyed having someone not ingratiating and servile, and my impertinence roused your interest and made you take a second look. You actually knew almost nothing good about me, really."

"I saw your compassion when you stopped to help me with my car last winter. For me, an almost stranger, you risked encouraging Tom Collins to ask you out again."

"Now, now, Tom isn't *so* bad. Like Jane says, there's someone out there for everyone."

"Is that what Jane says?"

"So, there's someone out there for Tom. It just isn't me."

"No, it isn't you." I stopped and took her in my arms. "You're mine now, I'm afraid."

"I'm not afraid. Not at all." She leaned up and kissed me. "My Mr. Darcy: he's good, he's honest, he's honorable. He's handsome as sin."

"Well, I do have to live up to my namesake."

She laughed.

"Honestly, though, I think most any man could be the perfect Mr. Darcy, if he chose." I leaned back against an ancient oak tree, keeping my arms around her.

"Choosing to is the important phrase, I think."

We stood there in momentary silence, enjoying the breeze, enjoying each other's company. Finally, my Lynley spoke:

"You have it wrong, you know."

"What do I have wrong?"

"You men, you think everything is about you. But you're not the only one to miss the point. A lot of people think *Pride and Prejudice* is about Mr. Darcy."

"Isn't it?"

"He definitely plays a role. He makes mistakes: he's a snot, he's haughty, and he has to eat crow. But his errors are mostly about delivery and image. Elizabeth herself says he changes very little in essentials.

"No," Lynley continued. "The person who grows the most in *Pride and Prejudice* is Elizabeth Bennet. She learns to see Darcy for what he truly is, despite his faults and despite hers. She's the one we watch as she dumps the chip off her shoulder, so she can clearly see the past and forge into the future."

"Say what you will. I'm still indebted to Mr. Darcy's example. He isn't perfect . . ."

"Just forgiven." She finished my sentence with a grin. "There are a million ways a man can become a Mr. Darcy."

"True."

"But it takes an Elizabeth Bennet to see them."

KAREN M COX is an award-winning author of four novels accented with romance and history: *1932, Find Wonder in All Things, At the Edge of the Sea,* and *Undeceived.* She also wrote "Northanger Revisited 2015," which appeared in the anthology *Sun-Kissed: Effusions of Summer.* Originally from Everett, Washington, Karen now lives in Central Kentucky with her husband, works as a pediatric speech pathologist, encourages her children, and spoils her granddaughter. Like Austen's Emma, Karen has many hobbies and projects she doesn't quite finish, but like Elizabeth Bennet, she aspires to be a great reader and an excellent walker.

ACKNOWLEDGEMENTS

"I must learn to be content with being happier than I deserve."
—Jane Austen

I have been blessed to be surrounded by extraordinarily talented and generous people. My thanks to my Dream Team of authors who wrote smart, original stories under a slim deadline, did not quibble over the hard edits, made time for "final look" and then "final look AGAIN", offered great insight how best to get this book to the world—and all with remarkable verve and great affection for Fitzwilliam Darcy and his creator, Jane Austen. I have been a fan of each of these authors for such a long time that I must frequently pinch myself to comprehend my good fortune. I am lucky to have been on this journey with them—maybe we will all get to meet in "real life" one day.

The idea of this Darcy point-of view anthology has been a long time in coming, and I have had strong opinions of how I wanted it all to look from the onset. Multi-talented author Beau North created the gorgeous announcement banners. It was the first visual branding for this endeavor—and she was totally on point (and patient) with designing exactly what I wanted. Then she created the promo art for each story for social media. If you haven't seen them, check out the hashtag #TheDarcyMonologues—the spectrum of the collective is clever and fresh.

The amazing cover art is the genius of Shari Ryan of MadHat Books. She took the cover concept and created exactly as I envisioned. Shari professionally, quickly, and concisely handled my countless questions, suggestions, and "just one more tweak" in the demanding format of the print interior—even had a special script code written to make it happen. And then when the original concept had to be scrapped because of the print-on-demand company's limitations that were beyond our control (long, convoluted story only to be shared over strong cocktails), Shari AGAIN created the present cover and interior for both print and e-book. I could not recommend her expertise more!

With a project of fifteen authors from around the globe, word and style challenges will occur. Katie Shapcott from the UK and Lisa Brown from the US (Looking Glass Revisions) split the task of proofing the stories, making sure that British vs. American spellings and phrasing were correct as per each of the authors' prose—and, of course, citing back to me the

Chicago Manual of Style when I would bleat, "Are you sure? That punctuation looks odd." Too bad it would totally take the reader out of the story if I were to footnote all their wonky findings. I learned a lot; I look forward to working with both on future projects.

A special thank you to Judy-Lynne for graciously bestowing upon us the title *The Darcy Monologues*. We had learned she had used it first for a short story written years past at the Republic of Pemberley. Once we had the name with her blessing, everything began to click in place.

Many bloggers and reviewers have encouraged us from even the faintest whispers of this project. The Jane Austen community of readers and writers has rallied behind the collection, and the resulting momentum has been hopeful as we endeavor to create something worthy to honor Jane Austen. Thank you for sharing in our fervor of Darcy too.

Claudine at Just Jane 1813 is really the unsung hero in all of this. She has tirelessly coordinated multi-blog events for the announcement, cover reveal, blog tour—and all that that entails. She has beta'd stories, set up the playlist on Spotify, massaged my words in the Introduction (even an editor needs an editor), made key marketing suggestions, and talked me off a few ledges when the anthology faced the occasional glitch. A great part of the success of this book is due to Claudine's good sense and calm (think: Elinor Dashwood)—I am forever in her debt.

I must thank my excessively tolerant family and friends who always support my hare-brained schemes. Nothing seems irregular to them and if it does, they seem to like me just the way I am.

Lastly, and I beg your indulgence as I purloin Cassandra Austen's eternal words for my own Mr. B and our ever-growing children: Never forget you are *"the sun of my life, the gilder of every pleasure, the soother of every sorrow..."*

—Christina Boyd

CHRISTINA BOYD wears many hats as she is an editor under her own banner, The Quill Ink, a contributor to Austenprose, and a ceramicist and proprietor of Stir Crazy Mama's Artworks. A life member of the Jane Austen Society of North America, Christina lives in the wilds of the Pacific Northwest with her dear Mr. B, two busy teenagers, and a retriever named BiBi. Visiting Jane Austen's England was made possible by her book boyfriend and star crush Henry Cavill when she won a trip to meet him on the London Eye in the spring of 2017. True story.

www.ingramcontent.com/pod-product-compliance
Lightning Source LLC
Chambersburg PA
CBHW060543310726
48982CB00009B/1354/J

* 9 7 8 0 9 9 8 6 5 4 0 2 7 *